Lilly stared into the darkness.

Her awareness of Cross McCree beside her was a living thing, crawling over her, heating her. She thought back to when the rain had kept them confined in the shallow cave. She thought of how his eyes had looked in the campfire light. She thought of how he had called her pretty. She had believed he thought her plain, which she was.

Yet she knew well there was a pull between them.

The knowledge whispered through her blood. She listened to Cross's breathing and wondered if he was asleep.

Slowly, instinctively, she turned her head to look at him. She could not see him, but she heard his head turning…and felt his breath upon her face.

Anticipation…fear…longing for what she didn't know shimmered over her body….

Dear Reader,

Though best known as a contemporary writer, Curtiss Ann Matlock published her first historical, *The Forever Rose*, with Harlequin in January 1990 to much success. This month we are very pleased to have her back with her historical Western, *White Gold*, the unforgettable story of unlikely partners who must face countless dangers and their own growing attraction on the sheep trail west.

Also returning this month is Suzanne Barclay, the author of the Knight Trilogy whose January title, *Lion's Heart*, is the beginning of a new medieval saga featuring the Sutherlands, a clan of Scottish Highlanders.

Our other titles this month include well-known Harlequin American Romance and Superromance author Muriel Jensen's *A Bride for Adam*, the story of a mail-order bride who is forced to keep the secret of her own sons from her new family, and *For Love Alone*, a tale set in the time of Henry VIII, from Barbara Leigh, the author best known for her medieval, *To Touch the Sun*.

We hope you will keep an eye out for all four titles, wherever Harlequin Historical novels are sold.

Sincerely,

Tracy Farrell
Senior Editor

Please address questions and book requests to:
Harlequin Reader Service
U.S.: 3010 Walden Ave., P.O. Box 1325, Buffalo, NY 14269
Canadian: P.O. Box 609, Fort Erie, Ont. L2A 5X3

CURTISS ANN MATLOCK

WHITE GOLD

Harlequin Books

TORONTO • NEW YORK • LONDON
AMSTERDAM • PARIS • SYDNEY • HAMBURG
STOCKHOLM • ATHENS • TOKYO • MILAN
MADRID • WARSAW • BUDAPEST • AUCKLAND

ISBN 0-373-28851-4

WHITE GOLD

Copyright © 1995 by Curtiss Ann Matlock.

Books by Curtiss Ann Matlock

Harlequin Historicals

The Forever Rose #37

CURTISS ANN MATLOCK

is the author of sixteen novels and three novellas. Her books regularly appear on the Waldenbooks Romance Bestseller lists, and her work has won a number of awards, among them the 1989 Oklahoma Writer of the Year Award from the University of Oklahoma. Originally from North Carolina, she has lived for the past fifteen years in Oklahoma, where she enjoys raising horses and researching the Old West.

This book is for Bob Hooker, Mark Whitman
and Gordy Whitman, who helped me with
information on sheep and mules and horses.
I've tried to write you guys a Western.

This book is for the best editors a writer
could want—Leslie Wainger, Don D'Auria
and Tracy Farrell, who have given unfailing
encouragement and support.

This book is most of all for my father-in-law,
James Matlock,
who loved Western movies as much as I,
and who loved anything I ever cooked.
He taught me about living and loving.
I miss you, Pa.

"Life is what we make it,
always has been, always will be."
—Grandma Moses

Chapter One

New Mexico Territory, 1853

The words on the sign of the crumbling adobe shop were printed in both Spanish and English: *Platero—Joyero,* and below that, Silversmith—Jeweler. The weathered plank door wobbled as Lilly opened it. A small man with thinning white hair and bent shoulders looked up from a cluttered table. "Ah... *Buenos días, señora.*" Though at least sixty, his eyes lit with the appreciation of a woman, and he gave a gentlemanly bow.

With shaking fingers Lilly removed the earrings she wore and held them out in her open palm.

They were drop pearls hung from gold filigree, made in Paris, a gift from her father to her mother on their grand European honeymoon tour. Over the past five years, when she had given up everything else, Lilly had clung to the earrings, this final connection to her family and heritage. Even that time down in Mississippi, when she and Tyler had been so strapped as to have to live on spoonbread for three days, Lilly had refused to sell them. She had almost sold them that time in New Orleans when Tyler had gotten the pneumonia, but the hotel manager had given her a job cleaning, and that had seen them through.

Now, however, the time had come to let them go. Timing was everything; Tyler had taught her that. She was playing her hand, and the earrings were her stake. The earrings would enable them to start again.

The little man lifted his eyes and gazed at her a moment. Then gently he took the earrings, walked to the window to examine them. Lilly watched his eyes closely, saw the keen interest in them.

"One thousand American dollars," she said.

The man's eyes widened, and he shook his head. She gripped the handle of her small shopping basket, fearing he would dismiss her and the earrings. But the little gentleman continued to examine the pearls and gold. Lilly had been often with Tyler when he had pawned their things, and she knew how the game was played. She and the old gentleman dickered, Lilly in English and the jeweler in Spanish.

When Lilly emerged from the small dim shop, eight hundred dollars—a hundred less than she'd wished—weighed the drawstring bag that swung from the waistband of her petticoat beneath the folds of her skirt.

She stood for a moment and lifted her face to the bright sun. Though it was May, the breeze caused her to shiver. She felt the chill all the way through her shawl, gown and chemise. Tyler said it was because Santa Fe was in the mountains and because Lilly had thin, Southern coastal blood. She couldn't argue with him about the truth of that, and she just figured it went to show that God had intended her to remain where she'd been born and not go traipsing halfway around the world.

Tyler never responded to that reasoning. Tyler was glib, and sometimes his best glibness was in knowing when to keep silent.

Lilly opened her eyes and gazed at the sky. It stretched forever blue, without a tree to crowd it out. Back home pines and cypress would crowd against the sky blue. And back home was where she wanted to go, more than anything in the world.

Swinging her basket onto her arm, she lifted her skirts and started off down the street, neatly sidestepping manure piles. There were no sidewalks here, no paving of any kind. This was a coarse, crude land, dry as a desert, though Tyler and everyone else assured her that this was no desert. It was to her, a girl brought up at the edge of the swamps.

There came the jingle of harness and the squeal of the cumbersome two-wheel carts, and always the jabber of the strange language. Here there were creole Spanish, Mexicans, Indians and a few Anglos, as the New Mexicans called all light-skinned people, all mingling together, trading their goods. Lilly was the only American woman in sight—easily identifiable by her hooped skirt and wide silk hat adorned with lace flowers. She felt as much of a curiosity as a single white egg in a basket of brown ones.

She headed for Montoya's Mercantile, which was nearly in the middle of the street, a large, squat adobe building with a pole-and-thatch veranda. It was at Montoya's that she and Tyler had arrived by coach last fall. In the weeks following they had come here to make their purchases, for Mr. Montoya dealt in everything from eggs to top hats to shovels. He was also the only true gentleman Lilly had met, the only person who could speak fluent English with her, and the only trader who got regular shipments of St. Louis newspapers.

"Good day, *señora.*" Mr. Montoya greeted her warmly and with his proper half bow. "I am so pleased to see you. I have been saving you something…wait." His silver goatee trembled as he smiled, and his hazel eyes twinkled behind his round spectacles. He held up a finger, slipped behind his counter and then, with a flourish, he smacked a bundle of papers on the scarred wooden counter.

Why, it was Godey's Ladies' Books!

"Especially for you, *señora,*" Mr. Montoya said, beaming. "Three of them, and only two months old."

"Oh . . ." She reached out, touched them, a link with the life she had left behind. "Thank you, *señor.* It is very kind of you." She pulled the drawstring bag from the slit in her skirt.

Mr. Montoya held up his palm. "No, *señora.* These I give to you." He smiled, his eyes gentle and warm.

"Thank you, *señor,* but I really do have money to pay you today. In fact, I've come to sign up for passage on the next wagon train leavin' for St. Louis and to buy treats for a small celebration. We are goin' home."

The man's eyes widened and he smiled at her, sharing her pleasure. "Then of course you will take the magazines as my gift," he said.

He told her the next group of freighting wagons would be leaving the following week and that now there would be a fine coach for the passengers. She paid him the down payment required for booking passage, and he handed her a voucher. Clutching it, she thought: five more days, and they would be going home. Her mind took her past the long, dreaded trip out over the prairies and clear back to Pasquotank County, back to the pines and the river and white clapboard houses, all calling to her with promise.

She stuffed the voucher quickly and securely into her bag and eagerly went about choosing tea, rare honey and lemon drop candy, too, Tyler's favorite things. To these she added cheese, a roasted chicken, fine wheat flour and a dash of lard for making true biscuits. Oh, and wine, though not expensive. Lastly she purchased six Cuban cigars that Tyler adored. These she had Mr. Montoya tie with a ribbon.

With her basket full of goodies and her breast full of hope, Lilly bid Mr. Montoya goodbye.

She swept quickly out the door and right into a man's chest. She bumped him so hard that she lost her balance and would have fallen if the man hadn't caught her.

"Oh!" Things toppled from her basket before she got it righted. "Excuse me." Her gaze came up, and she found herself looking into eyes as pale blue as the sky at noon.

The eyes, so startling in a dark, scruffy-bearded face, held her.

"Pardon me, *señora,*" he said in a low tone. Very slowly he released her and touched the brim of his battered hat. Then he bent to retrieve the things spilled from her basket.

"No...it was my fault. I was hurryin' and not lookin'," she said, now speaking to the top of the man's sweat-stained hat. The hair hanging out beneath was brown and sun bleached.

Suddenly a dog was there, and the man murmured to it, laid a hand on its head. "I'm afraid some of the candy spilled, and my dog got it," he said as he straightened. His hands were darkly tanned, callused and chapped. He wore the brown canvas trousers of an American, but the serape of a Mexican. And there was the hint of an accent to his speech, though it sounded neither Spanish nor English.

He reached out and placed the things, Tyler's cigars and the bag of tea, into her basket. His face came up and there they were again, the clearest, most iridescent blue eyes she had ever seen. He held out the bag of lemon drops.

"Thank you," she said, taking the bag.

His eyes...they were cool, and intent with sharp interest of a man for a woman.

It was as if he touched her.

Lilly returned the interest before she realized, which brought heat sweeping over her from head to toe.

"Cross, *mi amigo.*" Mr. Montoya's voice jarred Lilly. The older gentleman appeared in the opened doorway, smiling, and his eyes shifted curiously to Lilly. "May I present the Señora Blackwell. *Señora,* please meet Cross McCree."

The man's blue eyes remained boldly intent upon her as he slipped the battered hat from his head. "Señora Blackwell," he said. His voice was almost a whisper, yet easily heard.

"Mr. McCree," Lilly said and gave a proper nod, averting her eyes as a proper lady should—and to hide her confusion. Her cheeks burned. With a flash of a smile she once again bid Mr. Montoya goodbye and turned away.

She felt the blue eyes following her, and, before she could stop herself, she looked back over her shoulder. He stood there, watching her, the little black-and-white dog sitting at his feet, doing the same. Her cheeks again burning, Lilly faced forward and headed for the boarding house...and Tyler.

While he'd long become accustomed to seeing Americano men all around the Territory, Cross had seen very few Americano women in his entire life. And certainly of the few he had seen, none had been a woman such as this—a lady with skin as pale as a freshly scraped doe hide, eyes the color of high mountain grass and hair of dark honey.

Her dress was a curiosity in itself, covering her from neck to toe and spreading out from her waist in a wide bell shape that seemed a ridiculously cumbersome contraption. The woman had to hold it up to walk. Still, she seemed to float along, back straight, head high.

But she paused once and turned to look back at him, before floating off down the street again.

Cross's eyes followed her, followed the sweep of her spine and grace of her walk. Then he turned to see a knowing smile upon Pablo Montoya's thin lips.

"A striking woman," the older man said, his smile widening as he turned back into the shop.

"Yes," Cross agreed. He didn't think he'd call her a beauty—not like a few of the dark-haired *señoritas* he knew—but she sure drew a man's eye. "A *señora*, you said?"

Montoya nodded as he walked back behind the long counter. Cross followed, moving deeper into the dim interior of the big room that smelled of warming adobe, coffee beans and hides. His boots made a soft thud on the packed earth floor, and his spurs jingled lightly. His dog, Pan, padded silently and obediently at his heels.

"She is the wife of Tyler Blackwell," Montoya said, his careful English reflecting his noble Spanish heritage, "a gambler who has been working out of Calderon's this past winter. They are from the southern American states." He adjusted his spectacles upon his face as he spoke, then peered over them. He smiled and winked. "Surely there is no harm in enjoying gazing at a woman, even though she is married."

"I would say that depends on the disposition of the woman's husband," Cross observed.

Montoya chuckled. "True, my wise amigo! Very true. Still... it would be hard not to gaze at such a lady, eh?"

"Oh, I would have to agree with that," Cross said. "Especially after eighteen months out on the Llano, when I've had enough of lookin' at the backside of sheep."

"I have not been out on the Llano, and I enjoy looking at a lady," Don Pablo said with a chuckle.

Poking his head behind a curtain, he called for coffee, and quickly a young woman came from the back room carrying two steaming cups on a wooden tray. She gave Cross a seductive look and smile, and he returned with his own as he lifted the cup to his lips. Don Pablo gestured firmly, sending the girl back behind the curtain.

Then the older man retrieved a piece of paper from beneath the counter. He fell into Spanish. "I have the figures here for your pelts...one hundred twenty-eight coyote, five black bear, forty-two buffalo, twenty-three wolf, ten goat and twenty-five sheep. Is this not correct?''

Cross leaned lazily against the counter and nodded. ''That's correct.'' He, too, spoke in Spanish, as fluently as speaking English.

Don Pablo scribbled some more on the paper, then slid it across the counter. ''Prices are not what they once were, but there is still profit to be made. This is an approximate total for the pelts, minus what you will owe me for your list of supplies and the leather saddlebags you wish made. Is this acceptable?''

Cross studied the figures a moment and again nodded. ''You are fair as always, *señor.*'' He raised an eyebrow. ''There's no problem with having the bags ready in five days?''

''They will be ready.'' The courteous gentleman nodded and bent to open the safe beneath his counter. He brought up a metal box and began counting out gold coins. Cross scraped them up and split them between two leather pokes.

As he closed the money box, Don Montoya smiled. ''You are a man of means now, amigo.'' He gestured to Cross's poke. ''You have cold cash and a great herd of sheep. Are you still set on trailing them to California?''

''That's the plan.''

Don Pablo ran a hand over his goatee. ''Several men have made fortunes doing such, it is true. I have heard Kit Carson himself left Rayado early this spring with a sizable flock.'' His dark eyes sharpened. ''But John Gallantin took a flock south along the Gila this past winter. The Yuma got him.''

''John Gallantin should have known better. A man who lives by takin' scalps is goin' to lose his sooner or later.''

Don Pablo nodded. "True. But the Yuma massacred all twenty-five sheep drivers with him, their dogs, the oxen standing in their traces and the innocent sheep, as well."

The man's gentle eyes rested on Cross and reflected the graphic reality he left unsaid: that the drivers and animals would have been butchered, leaving little to tell one from the other.

"Nothin' worthwhile in life is ever gained without risk, I guess," Cross said quietly, returning to English. "Besides, I'm travelin' with the Big Duff and headin' up through Ute country. Maybe they'll treat us kinder."

The older man's eyes crinkled, and he gave an amused chuckle. "So much like your father you are, Cross Mc-Cree," he said, in English now, too. The respect in his voice caused a small swelling in Cross's heart.

"A high compliment, my friend." Grinning, Cross stepped back and gestured at himself, again falling into Spanish. "Now, I need to purchase new duds...from the skin out. I'll be headin' for the bathhouse, and I sure don't want to be putting these things back on. But first—" he gestured at the shelf "—give me a big box of those puros up there, those long ones."

"Ah...and I shall join you," Don Pablo said with pleasure.

From the box he handed Cross one of the thin cigars, then struck a match for each of them.

Chapter Two

As Lilly came down the dusty alley, a stream of chickens came cackling out of the entrance to the courtyard of the boardinghouse, with Mr. Gallegos right after them. A fat man, he moved with surprising swiftness. He reached down and caught a hen, jerked it up and wrung its neck in one swift, hard swing. The hen flopped limp.

His black eyes swung to Lilly. He nodded and gave a grunt in greeting.

"Hello, Señor Gallegos." Lilly stared at the limp chicken hanging from the man's sweaty, fat hand.

He gazed at her for a moment, his florid face without expression, yet seeming to leer at the same time. He reminded Lilly of a fuzzy black caterpillar on the hottest day of the year, and whenever he looked at her, she felt as if he were crawling all over her.

"Eggs," he said and gestured at the clucking hens with the dead one. "From so many...*gallinas*...I should find more eggs." His black eyes accused. "You rent only a room. Eggs from my chickens I keep."

Lilly said, "Perhaps you should build a coop for the chickens. Then their eggs—and their mess—would be all in one place."

He frowned in thought. Mr. Gallegos had learned his English when he'd been a mule skinner on the freight wagons to St. Louis, and he knew curses more fluently than any other English. "A *gallinero*," he said at last and shrugged. "And what would eat the bugs around my casa, eh?"

He had a point, Lilly supposed, though chickens in his courtyard didn't help the bugs she found in her room. And if she found an egg or two beneath the scraggly bushes beside her door, she believed she could consider them as much hers sent from heaven as belonging to Mr. Gallegos's chickens.

With another grunt, he hefted his loose gallus strap up over his dirty shirt and shooed a few of the chickens back into the courtyard. Lilly followed, slowly, lifting her gown over chicken feathers and other things that she'd rather not identify.

Mr. Gallegos was disappearing into his kitchen when she stepped into the courtyard, her thoughts racing ahead. Tyler hadn't come in until dawn and most probably would still be asleep, in which case she would have time to spread her treats on the table, all displayed when he awoke. She would present the treats first, before telling of booking their passage east.

Then she saw Tyler lounging in the doorway of Delores Trujillo's room.

Lilly stopped still as the air.

The afternoon sun washed over the doorway. Tyler was still tousled from sleep, wearing the rumpled shirt and trousers he'd worn the night before. Even so, Tyler Blackwell was an extremely handsome man, with golden curls and golden eyes and a smile that could make women glad to have their hearts broken and men glad to lose their money.

That was the smile he was bestowing on the Mexican black-haired beauty who gazed up at him with bold, come-hither eyes. Back home Delores Trujillo would have been considered a common woman. No better than she needed to be, Mammy Ethnee would have said. Lilly watched Delores put her fingers to the ruffles of Tyler's shirt. A flaming scream played at the back of Lilly's throat, but she choked it back, knotting her hands into her skirt.

Tyler's head came up, and his eyes lit on Lilly. Immediately he straightened and took a casual step back from the black-haired woman. He cast Lilly the same easy, winning smile he had a second ago been giving Delores.

"Well, honey, I was wonderin' when you were gonna get back."

Lilly forced her stiff legs to move. She strolled toward them, slowly, with a pleasant smile and every bit of elegance she possessed.

"I woke up and couldn't find a scrap of coffee," Tyler said, "so Sēn-or-ita Delores here was good enough to lend us a bit—sugar, too." He held out a cup and tilted it to show the ground coffee and sugar.

Delores tossed back her long black hair, showing her bare shoulders to good advantage, and cast Lilly a lazy smile. *"Buenos días, señora."*

"Buenas tarde," Lilly said, pointedly saying afternoon. "It was kind of you to be so generous to my husband, but we won't be needin' to borrow. I've just come from the market." She shifted the basket forward.

Delores shrugged. "Another time, perhaps," she said with a suggestive smile.

"Perhaps." Lilly took the cup from Tyler and returned it to the woman. Hers and Delores's gazes met, and in that instant Lilly conveyed the truth: Tyler might dally with the woman, but it was Lilly he called his wife. Then she slipped her arm intimately through Tyler's and politely bid the woman good-day.

Sauntering beside her, Tyler put his hand over Lilly's and leaned close, speaking as eagerly as a boy. "You have a mighty full basket, honey."

"Yes." She went inside, set the basket on the table as she passed. She tossed her shawl on the chair back, unpinned her hat and laid it upon the bed. She felt Tyler's eyes upon her.

She couldn't meet his gaze, not until she had settled her jealousy. Her pride wouldn't let her express it, and screaming and yelling was an action beneath her. Besides, it would do no good...memories of other places and other colorful women flickered through her mind. Screaming and yelling would never change Tyler.

She pressed her hand to her belly as she stepped to the washstand. Five years she had been Tyler's wife, yet she had never been woman enough to satisfy him.

The knowledge cut deeper than she could ever speak of.

Forcing her eyes to look at her reflection in the cracked, smoky mirror, she slowly unpinned her hair.

The crack in the mirror ran from the top of her head down to her breasts, and it seemed a reflection of her life. The room behind her was reflected dully. It was little more than a hovel, with a dirt floor, straw mattress bed, a chipped water pitcher and cracked basin, a rickety table and two rough board chairs. Quite a comedown for two people who hailed from the best families of Pasquotank County in North Carolina.

Lilly was a Treece, Tyler a Blackwell, and the Treeces and Blackwells could trace their ancestors back to the first to ever come to settle permanently in America. This was quite a point of honor among people back home in Pasquotank County.

Somehow, over the years and experiences she'd had since marrying Tyler, pride in such a thing had begun to seem foolish to Lilly—though she wouldn't have admitted such heresy aloud. Still, when a person has had to sell everything of value in order to eat and have a roof over her head, she tended to put little stock in what blood ran through her veins and more in the common sense that ran through her head.

Oh, it was common sense she had, not great beauty. She knew this very well, and in a way it brought comfort, for common sense was what had kept them fed and going these past years.

Suddenly the memory of the blue-eyed man came full into her mind—Cross McCree. She leaned toward the mirror and gazed into her own eyes, as if sharing a secret with herself. Cross McCree's look had made her feel very thoroughly a woman.

She put down the hairbrush and turned quickly from the mirror.

Tyler was delicately investigating the shopping basket. Occupying himself until the tightness between them passed. How young he looked, like a little boy finding treasures.

"Good grief, Lilly—lemon drops and Cuban cigars! They must have cost a mint." Tyler held the sack of candy in one hand and the ribbon of cigars in the other, as if uncertain of which he wanted to partake first. "Did you rob someone while you were out?"

His golden eyes came up to hers. They held the familiar boyishness that had first captivated her all those years ago when they both were still children. Tyler had never outgrown his boyishness, nor a boy's weaknesses. Yet, even knowing this, Lilly found he could still captivate her.

She shook her head, and for the first time felt the absence of the pearl earrings. For the past three years she had worn them constantly bobbing at her ears; the safest place for them had been attached to her.

Tyler's gaze lit on her ears, then returned to her eyes.

"Where are your pearl earrings?" he asked, his drawl low and long.

"I sold them."

The silence held them. They stared at one another. A chicken cackled on the other side of the door, a burro brayed in the alley, Mrs. Gallegos's laugh, which resembled the chicken's cackling, floated through the glassless window.

Lilly searched Tyler's face, even as he searched hers. She was about to lay out her hand, and she was so afraid of losing.

Tyler broke the silence with, "You sold them?" He was incredulous.

Nodding, Lilly took two steps toward him, her words pouring forth like a fountain. "All our put-by money was gone, and, well...I know I've been stubborn about the earrings, honey, but I suddenly saw—" she pulled the drawstring bag from her skirts as she spoke and fumbled to open it "—that we've been talkin' about goin' home whenever we could get the money, and here I had it all along hangin' on my ears."

She held the voucher for the passage out to him.

He stared at the coarse paper slip, glanced at her and then back at the voucher again. "You already booked the passage to St. Louis?" Slowly he set the cigars and candy on the table.

Lilly nodded. "At Mr. Montoya's. We're on the next company goin' over the trail—next week. Only five days."

Again he stared at the voucher, but he didn't reach for it. Lilly held tight to it.

Raking a hand through his curls, Tyler went to the window. "Why didn't you ask me first, Lilly?" His voice was uncharacteristically low.

"We've been talkin' about it since we got here," she answered, feeling as if she were near a door that was about to slam in her face. "As soon as we got enough money together we were goin' back. So...now we have the money. I meant it as a surprise."

He turned and arched an eyebrow. "Did you?"

She breathed deeply, clutched the voucher. "I thought it best to go ahead and book passage with the money from the earrings, before it could slip from our hands." Which was as kind a way as she could think of to say that she had feared Tyler would gamble the money away before they could purchase the passage. "I know the money from the earrings won't get us all the way back to Pasquotank County, but now that Keane Randall is dead we can at least go back to St. Louis. Once there or maybe down in Memphis we can save for goin' all the way home."

Tyler shook his head. "That trader said he'd heard Randall had died of a heart attack. We don't know for certain that he's dead."

"Even if he's alive, he isn't goin' to be lookin' around every corner for you. We'll get through the city and head downriver."

Her tone was more of a command, and she surprised herself. Tyler stared at her. She stared back.

Ever since they had left Pasquotank County four years before, Lilly had dreamed of returning, and Tyler had promised they would, yet they always seemed to keep going west, always to places Tyler heard were grand for gambling. They'd left St. Louis and come to Santa Fe because he'd heard the Mexicans were avid gamblers, and because he was deeply in debt to Keane Randall, a powerful man who was willing to take the debt out of Tyler's hide.

Tyler had won a goodly amount of money on the trail, because there'd been little else for the drivers to do but play cards. Tyler was quite proficient at cards, which was as much a game of skill as it was luck. It was all the other forms of gambling—horse racing, cockfighting, dice—games that were little more than pure chance, or dependent upon someone else's skill, where he kept losing his shirt. And such games abounded in New Mexico Territory. Here gambling was perfectly respectable for both men and women and was enjoyed to the hilt. Tyler simply couldn't keep out of it.

Lilly looked into his soft golden eyes. "Tyler, I want to go home."

She bared it before him, all her longing and desire. Her eyes, her voice and every fiber of her body coaxed and begged him. She glanced to the table, where her extravagant offerings lay, echoing all the things they had left behind and could have again, if only he would turn for home. They were her bribe. That was the truth of it. He knew it, she knew it, and none of it needed to be said.

A crooked smile came across his lips...but it did not touch his eyes. His eyes were the barren color of prairie grass at the end of summer.

Fear surged through Lilly. She couldn't recall ever seeing him look quite this way. She grasped for something to say to make it all right.

"I know it's a long trip back." She stepped toward him. "But it won't be as hard as when we came. The weather is warm now, and Mr. Montoya said that they are now usin' a big coach for the passengers. And you can build our poke in games all the way to St. Louis."

Tyler looked down at the floor and began shaking his head.

"But why not? We've been plannin'—"

"No. *You've* been plannin', Lil." His eyes were prairie fire now.

She saw his anger, and it was fuel for her own. "It hasn't been me alone. You've talked of it."

He had talked of it. He'd talked grandly of how he would buy back her precious Cypress Crossing and how they would build it up again as it was when the Treeces had commanded the land. Sometimes when they talked Tyler would speak of running the lumber business, or sometimes he spoke of building a shipping line to rival his father's. It was more to rival his father than as a gift to her that he would buy Cypress Crossing, Lilly knew, for Marsh Blackwell had coveted Cypress Crossing for many a year, had been furious that he'd never been able to have it.

Lilly had had her doubts about Tyler's grand dreams, but that hadn't prevented her from believing that somehow, some way, she and Tyler would eventually return home and somehow she would have Cypress Crossing again.

Tyler gazed out the glassless window. Lilly sank to the edge of the bed. She felt suddenly so tired.

After a long minute she said, "It's been a long time now, Tyler. Your daddy would forgive...probably already has forgiven. You were young and reckless then and made a mistake. That's all. We can go back, and—"

"Stop it, Lilly!" Tyler broke in harshly. His hands knotted into fists, relaxed and knotted again. In a very quiet, sad voice he said, "Stop foolin' yourself about that, Lil. It doesn't matter that it was my family's company. I took money—embezzled. My father isn't one to forgive and forget. Not even his own son."

She gazed at his tense, set shoulders and knew what he said was true. She could still see the look on Marsh Blackwell's face as he'd thrown his son out of the house and out of the family. "It is only for your mother that I don't cut off your hand," he had said, and Lilly knew he had meant it. She had once seen one of his slaves who'd had a hand cut off by the man, for nothing more than stealing bread. She'd seen the marks upon Tyler's back, inflicted by his own father for infractions of childhood. Marsh Blackwell was as hard and cold a man as could be found.

"We don't have to go back to Pasquotank County," she said in a small voice, with her dreams breaking and shattering in front of her mind's eye. She had to reach for what she could get. She couldn't let go. "We could go to Rocky Mount, at least, where we could be near Portia and Grant."

He cast her a withering look over his shoulder. "And do what? How would we live? Are you thinkin' that my brother would take me into the cotton brokerin' business? I've tried business, and all of it is dry as the boll in August." His gaze met hers evenly. "I'm no cotton broker, Lil . . . I'm a gambler." It was flatly said, a statement, his voice carrying no pride, yet no apology, either.

She stared at him. Her heart pounded painfully in her chest.

He breathed deeply, seemed to look for answers in the rough adobe wall before his golden eyes came back to hers. They were hard.

"I don't want to go back there, Lilly. Not now. Maybe someday, but not now."

Each word fell heavy as stone upon her. She felt as if she were closed in a box and couldn't breathe. The sounds came to her again: chickens and burros and the voices in the strange language. She smelled the scents of garlic and onions and dry, sun-warmed dirt. The rough cedar-trunk bedpost swam before her eyes, and for a moment she saw the fine, sweeping cherrywood post of her bed back home. That bed had come down from Richmond.

Would she never hear the gentle drawl of her own dear people? Would she never again smell the dusky odor of the swamp? Would she and Tyler never again sit hand in hand on the porch of a white clapboard house and listen to the wind in the pines?

Oh, God, she could not bear it. Her home. She could not live cut away from her home, no more than a tree could live with its roots chopped off. Every part of her fought the prospect, for to lose the hope of going home was to lose hope of living. At home she and Tyler would have a chance . . . together. Out here, Tyler and all life as she knew it was slipping away...away to the fever of gambling, and women, and want...away to the wind that sucked all from a human being and left only dust.

Suddenly Tyler crouched in front of her and took her hands between his own. "Our best bet lies out west, Lilly. I met a fella last night, honey—Joe Darcy. He's on his way to San Francisco. He owns a saloon out there—just a small place, but with plenty of room and plans for building bigger. Only he needs a partner for doin' that. Someone who knows how to run the gaming. We got to talkin' and workin' out a deal for us to build a real fancy gaming house. A real gentleman's club with style."

"San Francisco?" Lilly said in a bare whisper, her mind foggy with pain and disappointment.

"There's a boom goin' on out there not only in the goldfields but all around. People spend their gold by the handful—why, Darcy says gold dust is so plentiful, people make their livin' by just scraping up what falls between floorboards of saloons and eatin' houses. It's a new and growin' place, Lilly, and now's the time to get in on it all."

She stared into his golden eyes, so hopeful and eager and certain he was on to finding his pot of gold. California...San Francisco, Sacramento. California was a paradise, it was said, a land where gold lay waiting to be picked up from the ground. A land Tyler could believe in.

"What kind of deal?" she asked, thinking that she had heard the same thing a hundred times in the past four years.

"He'll let me in for half for only six thousand...and I was wantin' to raise that before I told you anything about it." His eyes flickered, sinking. "My luck's been thinner than weak chicory lately, so I kinda figured once I got hold of about a thousand, we'd head out for California. It'd be less than half of that to buy passage, the rest for supplies." His eyes came back to hers. "I'm sure I could win enough on the trip to stake us once we got there, just like I did comin' out from St. Louie. I might even win all we need to buy in with Darcy... or maybe I won't want to buy in with him. Maybe I'll just start our own place.''

Lilly looked from his eager eyes to his curly hair. Tears blurred her vision. What could she say? How could she tell him that she had no faith in any of it, that he'd said the same things for the past four years, and that here they were in a dilapidated hut of a boarding house in a foreign land, sneaking eggs from the landlord's chickens?

What could she do? Leave him? He was her husband, whom she had married until death do them part.

His boyish eyes pleaded. ''Honey, out in California I'll build you a house, one bigger than any back home. I'll give you Paris gowns and jewels and the finest carriage pulled by a pair of perfectly matched grays. I'll give you the world, Lilly.''

She lifted her hand and pressed it to his cheek. ''Oh, Tyler, I don't need the fancies of the world. I need us and a solid home. *Us*, Tyler... together in a home of our own.''

Her heart ran full and painful. She thought of a child, but only for a moment. She would give up even that dream, yes, give up thought of a child and Cypress Crossing and any bit of home, if only she and Tyler could be settled somewhere in a home of their own.

If only Tyler would want her, as she did him.

He blinked, and pain flashed darkly in his eyes. He straightened, slowly and stiffly, and gazed down at her for a long second. The look in his eyes made her flinch.

''Maybe you don't need things like that, but I do,'' he said at last. ''I never was cut out for run-of-the-mill, Lilly, and you know that.''

And that was probably the most honest that Tyler Blackwell had ever been with her, or with himself.

The silence was great between them, and Lilly knew he

wanted her to go to him, ease his hurt, just as she always had. But she couldn't seem to move.

Tyler said, "I'll give you so much in California, Lil, that you won't ever miss back home. I'll build you a clapboard house just like Cypress Crossing. We'll plant honeysuckle to grow up on the porch and magnolias in the yard, and a fig tree, too, just like there. I'll give you a kitchen and servants, and we'll have ham on Sundays and buttermilk biscuits every breakfast, just like we used to. Remember—you always liked so much mint jelly on yours that it fell off.'' He smiled an achingly beautiful, coaxing smile.

Lilly looked at him. She recognized the winning smile for what it was . . . and yet it touched her. For she had nothing else.

Rising, she crossed to him, wrapped him in her arms.

She could never leave him, for she knew that Tyler needed her. If she left him, she might find life, but Tyler would be forever lost. She couldn't do that to him. She had to stay, and she had to hold to hope that they could get through. Even if she couldn't see how.

He clasped her to him, held to her as if for dear life. And she held to him.

She wondered what they would do when the earring money was gone.

Chapter Three

Duffy was already ensconced in a steaming tub when Cross entered the bathhouse room. "Draw up a tub and join me in paradise, laddie." Duffy soaped his sparkling blond-white beard as he spoke, caressing it lovingly.

Cross grinned at the sight. "How did a raunchy old mountain man like you come to like bathin' so damn much?" He dumped his saddlebags and bundles on the crude wooden bench. Pointing for Pan to lie down, he flicked his hat to a peg on the wall.

"An acquired taste, laddie," the Scotsman replied with a wink. "An acquired taste." He reached for an amber bottle sitting on a nearby stool and held it high. "This be the true and excellent brew—whiskey from Kentucky and God himself," he said reverently as he lifted the bottle to his lips.

Duffy Campbell had come from Scotland in his twenties and was nearing fifty now. He remained a handsome man, with sparkling blue eyes and a shock of blond-white hair and beard that gave him the air of a regal patriarch. Because of his size, he was known far and wide as the Big Duff. He was an expert on both sheep and every gambling game known to man. He'd lost most of his brogue now, though he enjoyed resurrecting it on occasion, especially for the ladies. "As good at warmin' up a lassie as runnin' a soft hand up her thigh," he always said of his accent.

A young boy, with black hair hanging in his eyes, baggy clothes and bare feet, stumbled through the curtained doorway under weight of two large, steaming kettles.

"Henri." Cross relieved the boy of one kettle. *"¿Cómo está?"*

"Bien, gracias." The boy beamed at him. "I have a good job now," he said in Spanish. "I grow."

Cross poured the kettle into one of the half-filled tubs and said in the boy's language, "You sure do. How old are you now?"

"Padre Domingo figures eight," the boy said, "but I think I am nine."

"I'm sure you must be right," Cross said seriously, then pointed to the other tub. "How about bathin' the dog?" He flipped the boy a coin.

Henri looked uncertainly at Pan but grinned when the small collie slowly wagged his tail. *"Sí, señor."* And he began to wrestle the dog up into the tub.

"Keep them fleas over there with you, laddie," Duffy admonished, chuckling at the sight of eager boy and reluctant dog.

Cross sat and dug into the saddlebags. "Here's your share from the hides," he said, tossing a poke bag to the Duff. "Could be a bit more after Don Pablo gets a final tally for the supplies we ordered."

Duffy jingled the bag and grinned happily. "Ah…I hear the pleasures of this world a-callin' out to me."

Cross's gaze rested on his friend. "We'll need money on the trail and when we hit California, too."

"But it's here we are today, lad." Duffy laughed and took a long, savoring drink from the bottle. Duffy had the amazing capacity to drink and never be drunk.

A faint uneasiness echoed within Cross. He'd traveled beside Duffy Campbell for a long time; he liked the big man, respected him for his ability with stock and keen prowess at following sign and trapping. But Cross also knew that the Big Duff had a great weakness for pleasures of the flesh, namely liquor, womanizing and gambling. The Duff lived for each day and asked nothing of tomorrow. While last fall he had eagerly embraced the idea of joining Cross in taking sheep to California, his enthusiasm for the endeavor was waning.

Cross carefully removed his knives—a small one tucked in its sheath beneath his shirt at the back of his neck and a big bowie knife worn at his belt. He laid both knives, a cigar and some coins within reach of his tub, then stripped out of the rest of his clothes and pulled two panetelas from one of the bundles. He tossed one cigar to Duffy and clamped the other between his teeth, stood there buck naked to light it, then lowered himself into the warm water.

"Almost as good as enterin' a woman, be it not, laddie?" Duffy said around the cigar in his mouth.

"At this moment, better."

Cross closed his eyes and puffed on the sweet cigar. He'd been wantin' one of these for four months. The water felt like a warmed angora blanket wrapped around him. It was damn good after the fourteen months he'd endured on the Llano, where the sun blistered through a man's shirt in the summer and the wind froze him in the winter, and where his only full baths had been in a muddy arroyo during the rainy season.

His sweet water-savoring was interrupted by a bloodcurdling scream from the boy and a bark from Pan.

Cross's eyes popped open, and with one keen glance he saw the boy jump up into the tub with Pan and the object that had put him there—a wrist-fat snake—slithering out from beneath the crude cabinet nearby, hissing angrily at being disturbed by all the commotion in his room.

In a fluid motion, Cross picked up the knife and sent it through the air. The blade hit its mark, plunged dead center through the snake's head and the woven grass mat and into the dirt floor beneath.

"Damn bull," Duffy said.

The boy regarded Cross with round eyes like buckeye seeds. His small, skinny arms clutched Pan around the neck as he struggled to keep the dog in the tub. Both boy and dog were now soaked.

"Pan, lie down!" Cross commanded, and the collie slowly lowered himself in the water.

"Lie down," the boy mimicked slowly as he again went to washing fur.

Duffy tossed a cake of soap into Cross's tub and winked, drawing up one huge foot and scrubbing it thoroughly. "Francisco Calderon has dressed up his place. Ye'd hardly know it. He hired a batch of fancy ladies come up from Mexico City—ladies of quality, they are supposed to be. So Francisco says. I didna' see them—it bein' too early. And mon, ye should see the painting he has behind the bar! A painting all the way from Italy, though it seems a lot of trouble to go so far for a likeness of a naked female."

Cross sniffed the soap. "Where did you get this?"

Duffy grinned. "From a new shop next to Calderon's. Got me a vest bright enough to be puttin' yer eyes out, too. The Americanos are sure bringin' in the world."

"Yeah . . . well, I don't think I want to be smellin' like a woman." Cross tossed the fragrant soap cake back to Duffy and looked around for the plain lye bar provided by the bathhouse.

"It beats smellin' like sheep or those hides we brought in," Duffy declared, took a swig from the whiskey bottle and passed it over to Cross.

Cross tipped the bottle to his lips and savored the rich, burning liquid. It spread warmth over his chest like a woman's silky hair. He grinned at Duffy. "This sure beats that lamp-oil tequila we got from Sanchez."

Duffy laughed hard. "That lamp-oil stuff will give ye hair on yer chest, lad. But this—" he took back the bottle "—this'll put hair on your soul."

Cross stuck his panatela back in his mouth and began to scrub his skin with the strong soap. "What did you hear about our chances of findin' herders?"

Duffy stroked his wet beard, his beloved vanity, into place. "It appears, laddie, that employing help in that direction is gonna be a bit difficult. Carson left Taos about a month ago with a large herd and took the best of the drovers with him. There's plenty of men around, but for our needs, we must be careful in choosing."

Cross nodded and absently scrubbed his foot. He'd heard the same thing from Don Pablo.

Between them, he and Duffy had collected ten thousand head of sheep. They'd been at it for nearly fourteen months, increasing their original herds by watching every ewe, saving lambs from brush, coyotes, bears, cats and stupid mamas. They'd been lucky, too, in finding several small stray herds out on the Llano.

Sheep aren't animals to stray from one another, or their herder, but sometimes during a stampede a small flock would break off from a great one and not get found. Also, shepherds died, naturally or unnaturally, and what sheep weren't rounded up by the Indians were left to wander. Cross and Duffy had claimed as their own any they found, and purchased all they could get their hands on. Duffy had won five hundred head in a monte game. And for these sheep the two of them had endured the cold rains and cutting blizzards and scorching sun out on the grassy Llano, living in crude shelters and getting the few supplies they needed from small missions or rancheros.

The truth, incredible to some, surely, was that Cross and Duffy liked that sort of life—liked the solitude, the enjoyment of the wild land, the reliance upon themselves. In that world they reigned as corulers with God. They did what they liked when they wished in a world they thoroughly understood.

But the endeavor, this time, went further for Cross. He'd been spurred on by growing reports of the profit to be made in the goldfields surrounding Sacramento. Hardworking men there were wanting meat to satisfy their hunger, had stripped the area bare of it long ago. Here in New Mexico Territory top price for a single sheep was a dollar and a half a head. That same sheep could be sold out in Sacramento for six to ten dollars a head. Antonio Luna and a *compadre* had reportedly made seventy thousand dollars from one trip two years ago—they'd taken nearly twenty-five thousand head over. Just last year that wily old mountain man, Dick Wootton, had made nearly fifty thousand.

Sheep were proving to be every bit as valuable as the gold, and to Cross's way of thinking a much surer fortune to be made. It was a trip for men who knew woollies and the land—for men such as himself and Duffy.

"Now, laddie, do na' get bedeviled," Duffy chided, breaking into his thoughts. "Hell, we be sittin' prettier than ever in our lives! We got a little jingle in our pockets, a fortune in woollies and before us some magical nights of pleasure." He winked and the leathery skin around his eyes crinkled. "I see no reason why we cannot bide our time here in this lovely place for a few weeks. The sheep are safe with Don Antonio's men and summer stretches long ahead."

Cross had to smile at his friend, a man who took life as one big lark. Then he said quietly, "There's crossin' the mountains before the snows to think of." He paused, formed his words. "I am taking my sheep to California, Duffy. With or without extra hands."

A soft grin split the Duff's beard. "Aye. Ye be one to clamp the bit and charge when ye get a notion. Ye have yer mama's Indian determination and yer papa's Scot thriftiness."

"What happened to your Scot thriftiness, Duff?" Cross drawled.

Duffy winked and lifted the whiskey bottle high. "I believe there's a maverick Irishman in me background, laddie—and here's to him."

The boy and Pan came to the edge of Cross's tub. Clean but shriveled and thoroughly disgusted, the young collie lay down as if trying not to call further attention to himself. The boy solemnly passed Cross the ivory-handled knife that had killed the snake.

"Ho-kay, Señor Cross?" the boy said expectantly.

"Okay." Cross tossed the kid another coin, then pointed at the snake.

The boy picked up the snake and happily ran out. The reptile would not go to waste; it would make a fine feast.

Cross curled his legs and slipped farther into the seductive, warm water, savoring puffs on his cigar. He laid his head on the hard edge of the tub and closed his eyes and only partially listened to Duffy jabbering about the sights of town. Duffy could talk a scorpion's legs off.

Cool spring air along with the scents of sun-warmed adobe and burning piñon wood wafted through the glassless window and mingled with those of soap and tobacco. Cross's mind drifted to thoughts of his sheep, memories of building fires around groups of ewes, keeping those fires going day and night, trying to keep the newborn lambs warm, because the spring had been a devil of rain and cold wind. The thoughts turned to fantasy pictures of driving the flocks into the Sacramento Valley, of the piles of gold he'd receive for them.

Cross had never had more than a few gold pieces in his hand at one time, never needed more. Whatever he needed he knew how to get from *Chihowa nan atali,* Mother Earth in the Chickasaw tongue of his mother. Fur for warmth in the winter, leather for moccasins to cover his feet, honey to provide for his longing for sweet. The man-woven fabric and boots he wore were a luxury, never a necessity. The only necessities that the earth would not provide for him were his knife and his cigars, and those he could gamble or barter for.

But now...now was coming a time when he wanted more than drifting with the seasons. These days he was beginning to think of building a place to call his own.

His father had said this time would come upon him. A time he would begin to want a woman and a home. His own piece of the earth, as was the right of every man, the tendency of most. He had had enough of the mountains and dreamed of lush grassy meadows. His father would have said it was his mother's blood calling him to settle on flat land, for his father had been a Highlander. Perhaps it was so, for his mother's people had been stockmen, and Cross had an affinity for this, too. He dreamed of his hacienda, shimmering coral in the sun, surrounded by the sea of grass that fed sheep, cattle and horses.

So caught up in his fantasies, Cross heard Duffy's quiet movements too late to save himself from a shaving bowl of water that came cascading over his head.

"Damn you, Duff!" He sputtered, wiped the burning water from his eyes. "You put my cigar out!"

"Quit yer daydreamin' over them sheep and get out o' that tub, or I'll be leavin' ye behind!"

Cross rose and reached for a towel. "You gonna join me in a shave?" he teased.

Duffy preened his soft beard. "Nah. The lassies love to feel this on their breasts, and I wouldn't think of deprivin' them."

With Duffy prodding him every two minutes, Cross quickly shaved his beard away, trimmed his thick mustache and dressed in the new clothes he'd bought at Montoya's. Nothing fancy, just durable as he'd worn before—knee-length johns, brown duck pants, a linsey shirt and new wool serape.

"Here ye are, able to buy some new duds for the first time in almost two years, and what do ye get?" Duffy, dressed in all the finery that he'd purchased—a waistcoat of shiny, blue-striped silk, black frock coat, silk tie at his stiff collar and a fine top hat—gave Cross a disparaging wave.

"Guess I never learned the art of bein' a peacock," Cross commented as he slipped his knife into its worn leather sheath on his belt.

Duffy adjusted the collar at his neck. "These duds impress the ladies, and maybe ye should have thought of that. The Señora Otero may need some impressing, since ye have been gone so long this time. So beautiful and passionate a woman as Marquita Otero surely would not have wanted for suitors to warm her bed, and women generally don't take kindly to men who ignore them. Perhaps she tired of waitin' for ye and has even married by now."

Self-conscious, Cross said, "Perhaps." He focused on adjusting the knife down the back of his shirt.

Duffy chuckled. "I hope ye plan to go with a gift, at any rate. After I've had me fill of the cantinas, I'll be wantin' a quiet place to recuperate—and if Marquita has no place for ye, she'll have no place for me," he added emphatically.

"I don't know about that, Duff," Cross drawled. "Just look at you. How could Marquita not be won over by so fine a gentleman?"

"Ye have a point, lad."

They parted outside in the bright sunlight. Duffy gave a happy wave and headed away down the narrow, hard-packed and dusty street, on his way to Calderon's Saloon. Cross, with Pan once more padding at his heels, headed the opposite way, on his way to the casa of Marquita Otero.

It had been over eighteen months since Cross had visited Santa Fe, and the village had grown considerably. There were many more Americanos here now, bringing not only their big freighting wagons and board-lumber buildings, but also their faster pace of life and eagerness for making money.

Still, Cross found Santa Fe a beautiful and pleasant town. It was as close a home to him as any town would ever be. He tossed a coin into the basket of a crippled beggar and bought a spicy goat cheese chile *relleno* from a stooped Pueblo woman—both things he had done as a boy with his father.

From the age of five until he was nearly eighteen Cross had lived in the mountains with his father. They'd brought their furs here to trade, always getting the best price from Pablo Montoya, though several times they'd dealt with visiting Navaho or Comanche traders. Here in Santa Fe, along with his father, Cross had come to know the vastly different people who lived in and visited the village—the *ricos* and *patróns*, their *caporals*, the *mesteneros*, who captured and trained the wild mustangs, Indian tribes, who derived their lives and spirits from Mother Earth, Anglo traders from the Santa Fe Road, who told of cities like St. Louis and beyond, and the lowly peones, whose faith in God was at times all they had to live on.

Cross remembered those years with his father fondly, years when he'd learned from his father all he could about the world and himself as a boy growing into a man. His father had taught him that he could have anything in life that he wanted, but not everything. He would need to choose, and to learn to choose carefully.

Early in his own life, for reasons he had never fully explained, Rafe McCree had come out of the Carolina mountains. For a time he had made his home with the Chickasaw tribe in northern Mississippi, where he'd taken a wife. But always he longed for the big mountains he had heard of in the West. When his wife's family had moved to the Indian Territory, Rafe McCree had not stopped there but continued on to the Rockies. Here he felt at home. But here his wife had died, of a broken heart that longed for the civilization she had left behind. Rafe McCree had carried the guilt.

Seeing a lovely young woman drying her shiny black hair in a sunny window, Cross paused to enjoy the sight. He watched her run the comb through the long tresses over her bare shoulder and felt no shame in his thoughts, for simply watching would bring no one any harm. As the familiar fire rose in his blood, he recalled the Americano woman he had met that morning at Montoya's. She, too, had brought the sweet fire to his blood, and he thought how he had been out on the Llano an awfully long time.

The young woman glanced up to see him and smiled an alluring smile. Cross returned one of his own. The next instant a matron of considerable size appeared, scowled at Cross and scolded like a wet hen as she reached out her flabby arms and pulled the shutters closed with a bang.

Cross continued on, walking faster now, drawn by a sudden eagerness to see Marquita. He imagined her greeting him as she always did. Then he wondered if, as the Duff said, she would be angry that he'd been so long away. Marquita was a beautiful, passionate woman, as the Duff had pointed out. Perhaps she would have a man with her, or perhaps she had even become respectably married.

Cross's heart dipped with these thoughts. He sincerely hoped she had not taken up with another man, and he was tinged by shame at his selfishness. Marquita was a good woman and deserving of a man's love and devotion. He was a man of two minds, he reflected ruefully. He cared deeply for Marquita and wanted the best for her, yet he wanted the pleasure she always gave him, too.

How good her skin always smelled, how sweet her food
and attentions were to a man. She was a special woman, and
thinking of this, Cross considered that perhaps he should
marry her. It was not a new thought.

Ten minutes later he neared Marquita's small casa. It sat
off by itself on a narrow street where children played, dogs
snoozed, goats wandered and chickens cackled.

His heart beating rapidly, he looked for signs of her. She
might have left . . . and death was a constant shadow in this
land.

Anticipation and apprehension burning in his chest, he
rounded the dwelling and entered through an opened back
gate in the adobe wall. All looked familiar—the packed
garden walk, the rough wood containers of spring flowers,
the dried flowers and peppers hanging near the door, the
lines strung for laundry. A woman was hanging clothes now.

Marquita. He recognized the flow of her thick dark braid
down to her buttocks and the way she stood, sexily, even in
so mundane an act as hanging clothes. Pleasure swelled inside him. He switched his gaze to the line and the clothes
hanging there, and relief flooded him.

Then he slipped up behind her, drew back and smacked
her bottom, saying, "I see no man's shirts on this line."

She let out a squeal and spun around in a fury, her hand
upraised. Cross caught her wrist and laughed down at her.
She froze, and her dark eyes widened. He noticed added
lines around them, and that there were gray hairs at her
temples. Then wondrous pleasure seeped over her features
and overflowed on Cross. She threw herself at him, and he
twirled her off the ground. He was welcome, and powerfully glad of it.

Chapter Four

Tyler sat at the table, wiping his cards. Each day he wiped them free of the grime of strangers who had handled them the night before.

As he wiped, he watched Lilly moving around the room. He knew she didn't feel him watching her. She wasn't there with him. Whenever Lilly was extremely tired over something, she would retreat within herself. She answered whatever was asked her, even looked him full in the face, but her eyes were distant, as if her spirit had gone somewhere far away. He hated it when she did that. It made him feel unsettled, made him want to smack her.

Tyler forced his hands to relax. He had learned long ago that pain was vastly inferior to honey for getting him what he wanted.

Through the haze of one of the cigars Lilly had bought him, he glanced at the voucher for their passage to St. Louis. It remained where Lilly had tossed it on the table, a pale scrap of paper against the dark, scarred planks.

Her back was to him; she was preparing a pot of tea. He slid his hand out, picked up the voucher and stuffed it into the pocket of his vest.

Lilly turned, pouring the hot water into the teapot for the precious tea. His eyes rested upon the delicately painted roses on the china.

Tyler hated that teapot.

It was one of her keepsakes, that relic of her mother's. Wasn't worth much, but once a lady in whose house they'd boarded had taken a shine to it and offered a week's free rent for it. Lilly wouldn't give it over. She had slept out in the open for two days rather than part with the damn thing. When she had caught him trying to slip away with it, she'd had a fit.

She'd cried, acting as if the teapot was something sacred, which was crazy as a quilt, because Lilly hadn't even known her mother. Lillian Treece had died when Lilly was only two. It'd been her Mammy Ethnee who had filled her head with how great a woman the Mistress Treece had been. Tales, that was all Lilly knew. And over this she had said, "If you give that woman my mother's teapot, Tyler, I will leave you."

Now that had set him back on his heels. After all the things he'd done, she would up and leave him over a silly damn teapot. That was Lilly; he often felt he couldn't fathom her.

He'd never quite fathomed why Lilly had married him in the first place. He'd charmed her. Tyler had never met anyone, except perhaps his father, whom he couldn't charm. But sometimes he suspected that Lilly had known who and what he was better than anyone else. Yet she had married him anyway.

He liked that about her, the way she looked at things head-on. And over the years he had come to rely on her. She was his compass, his anchor. A cold chill swept over him as he thought of being without her.

She had stayed with him, he reminded himself, and it wasn't likely she would leave him now.

He watched her bring around the china pot and pour cups of tea. His hand knotted, and the strong urge to reach out and smash that damn pot came over him. Maybe if he could smash it, he could smash her memory and desire of Pasquotank County, too.

He said, "I've been thinkin', honey. We should plan on leavin' for San Francisco by this comin' Wednesday. That's when Joe Darcy's group is goin', and we can travel over with them." He watched her carefully.

Her eyes came to his. She blinked, but he saw no emotion there.

"The sooner we get out there, the sooner I can go about gettin' that house I've promised you." He gave her his best smile.

"You can cash in the voucher for St. Louis for the money for the trip," she said flatly, then lifted her cup of tea and drank deeply.

He'd need more than what the voucher would get him, he thought, thinking of the bag attached to her petticoat.

"It won't be nearly so dusty out there in California," he said. "I've heard San Francisco gets plenty of rain. And it's right on a bay—at the mouth of a river, just like back home."

She didn't say anything, which annoyed him no end. Here he was trying to do his best by her, and she was dragging her feet.

She went to sit on the edge of the bed, brought up her sewing box, opened it and delved inside. Lilly was a heck of a seamstress, and Tyler had often joshed that he should set her up in a shop. But he spoke only in jest; he wasn't having his wife work as a seamstress or anything else. Blackwell women were quality.

Tyler tapped the deck of cards into order, stared at them a moment, then carefully set them down. He stubbed out his cigar in the dish, removed his vest and hung it neatly on the chair back. He flexed his hands, then rose and went to stand in front of Lilly.

She stilled but didn't look at him.

He bent and kissed her softly but firmly. Then he took the needle and spool of thread from her hands, tossed them into the sewing box and pushed the box aside. He pushed her back on the bed and went with her. Her eyes came to him, yet not her spirit. He kissed her hard, willing her back to him.

He had never been a man long on desire. He enjoyed the attentions of women rightly enough, but he didn't care much for the intimate business between them, hadn't ever since he had seen his father go at it with one of the housemaids. The memory of that scene often haunted Tyler and caused him to go weak, so he pushed it aside and watched Lilly's face. Her eyes were closed. She was so pretty, regal, like a queen, and he was proud of her.

She was his, had always been his.

He went at it quickly, pushed her skirts up, shoved her legs apart. He was glad for the fabric of her pantalettes separating her sweat-dampened legs from his. He hated how his trousers stuck to him, hated the rivulets of sweat that inched down his neck.

He fumbled for the strings that tied her pantalettes, and his hand found, too, her heavy purse bag, hidden there beneath her skirts. His hand closed around the bag as he shoved himself between her legs. Her muscles stiffened, and her breath came in a whimper. The sound of it excited him. Then he lifted his mind above the messy business at hand.

After he finished, he dropped atop her, then rolled away because he was so damn sweaty.

Her eyes regarded him, searched his face. He'd brought her back to him, he saw with satisfaction. He'd showed her who she belonged to.

He took her hand and kissed her palm. Then he rose, turning his back to her and adjusting his trousers that he'd pushed down to his knees but hadn't removed. He stripped off the dress shirt and undershirt, both of which were now damp with his sweat, and went to the washbasin.

Watching him, Lilly almost laughed. It was as if he had finished plowing a field and now needed to bathe away the effects of it.

Sadness overwhelmed her amusement. She felt bereft, empty. Her body ached. She felt a longing for something that she knew not.

Always it was like this. Tyler would take her and leave her feeling like a used rag. She wondered what was wrong with her, why she was not content in that she did her duty.

Slowly she sat up and searched for the ties of her pantalettes. Tyler had ripped them, she saw.

Finishing at the basin, Tyler then dressed in a fresh shirt, collar and cuffs. A dapper man was Tyler Blackwell. He came and had her button the collar and cuffs she spent hours whitening and ironing. Then he kissed her cheek and headed for the door, a man eagerly heading toward his passion.

"Tyler," Lilly called.

He turned.

"I want a horse for goin' to California. My own horse and saddle."

His eyebrows rose, then came together in a puzzled frown. "You don't know how to ride."

"I will learn."

He stared at her, trying to read her as he would an opponent's hand. "You would be a lot more comfortable in the wagon and safer, too. Horses can be tricky critters. We'll get our own wagon this time."

"I want a horse," she said, gathering every fiber of determination she possessed. Men rode horses, and men went where they pleased.

"Well, we'll see what we can find," he said at last, with an expression to let her know he wasn't at all happy with the

idea. He shook his head. "You sure do get notions sometimes, Lilly."

"I guess we both do," she said.

If he noticed anything in that comment, he didn't show it.

She stood at the door and watched him go. Delores Trujillo and Mrs. Gallegos were sitting outside in the shade of
the courtyard wall. Delores tossed back her raven hair, bar-
ing her neck and shoulders to the tops of her breasts, and
gaily greeted Tyler. He tipped his hat to the ladies and went
on out of the courtyard.

Feeling very tired and sweaty, Lilly slowly turned back
into the room. It was only then that she noticed the absence
of the weight that had caused her drawstring bag to bump
against her thigh.

Frantically she stuck her hand through the slit in her skirts
and felt for the bag. It was gone.

Tyler had ripped it away when he had taken her.

Cross felt satiated as a fat bear ready for hibernation.
Cool night air sweetened by blooming columbine floated
through the window and teased his bare shoulders, while
coffee and the remnants of Marquita's passion warmed his
insides. He smiled to himself, thinking of how he'd criti-
cized the Big Duff for indulging in the desires of the flesh
and here Cross himself had done just that all evening—enjoyed fragrant soft sheets on his back and Marquita's fragrant soft skin on his front—forgetting that he was
supposed to be hiring drovers and assembling supplies.

He lifted his eyes above his mug and watched Marquita
before her mirror, brushing her lustrous long hair by the
glow of a single candle and golden afterglow of a setting
sun.

Her beauty came more from her lively expressions than
from her features. He wondered about her age. She had
never told him, beyond saying she was older than he, which

he'd already known, because when he'd met her years ago he'd been fourteen and she a married woman for a long time. She seemed to him ageless, yet there were more lines around her eyes than he remembered, and the hair at her temples was turning silver.

Marquita Otero was a widow who washed, cooked and sewed for others to make a living. Cross knew she had men friends, others before him, and perhaps others along with him, though of these he never knew for certain. He knew only that he was always welcomed into her home and her heart, as if he were the only one—or the only one besides her departed husband. There was a part of Marquita, as giving as she was, that remained forever devoted to a dead man.

She looked up into the mirror and caught his eyes and smiled at him. Swinging her hair forward over her shoulder, she began to replait it. Tenderness swept him, bringing him up from the chair and across the small room to lay his hand over hers.

"Wait...leave it down." He took her hair and let it fall, all warm and silky, through his hands. "I have something for you." He pulled a small wrapped bundle from his saddlebags and handed it to her. "I meant to give it to you first thing, but..." And on this he blushed as memories of what had distracted him filled his mind.

Eager as a child, her work-worn hands tore into the paper. "Oh, Cross...you are a man to spoil me." She struggled mildly with the English words. At the sight of the tortoiseshell combs, she exclaimed, *"¡Oh, amor mío!"* Her shining eyes flicked up to his, and then she whirled to the mirror to fit the combs into her hair.

He'd gotten the combs back in the winter, from a trader coming up from Chihuahua, who'd gotten attacked by Apache and in escape had gotten lost on the Llano.

Cross said, "I thought I'd better make it good since I haven't been here in so long." His heart swelled to see her joy, and he felt very much a tall man.

Touching one of the combs in her hair, she turned gentle eyes to him. "You do not need to bring me *things, amor mío.* You are gift enough."

Then, with a saucy smile, she moved to the sideboard and began assembling bread and cheese. "I was be-gin-ning to wonder what had happened to you—if perhaps you had found a woman to marry and had for-gotten your Mar-quita."

Cross shook his head as he again lowered himself comfortably into the chair. "Nope. Not many women out on the Llano," he added dryly. "And you—I thought that by now perhaps you would have married." He watched a sad smile touch her lips. "Why are you not married, *cara mía?* I know you have had chances. You should have a man to keep you warm every night . . . and to be blessed by you."

He watched her carefully as she brought the food to the table, stepping over sleeping Pan as she came. "Are you proposing to be that man, my Cross?"

He went stock-still. He hadn't intended her to take his inquiry like that. Or maybe he had.

"What if I am?" he asked quietly.

She looked thoughtful, though continued to hide her eyes. "Then you would be paying me great honor," she said with a shake of her head, "but I would have to explain that my Juan remains with me. Even you have not made me forget." Her eyes came up at last, and she smiled softly.

Cross nodded, feeling an odd mixture of relief and disappointment. A sense of hanging out in the wind.

The next instant her hand caressed his hair, an action that struck him as one he would use on a son. He looked up to see her gazing down at him with both amusement and understanding. "We both know your heart is not with me, *cara mío,*" she said in Spanish.

He answered in kind, "I care deeply for you." Though he felt love for her, somehow he did not feel honest to say the words *I love you.*

She smiled a mystical smile. "The heart is wide," she said, still in Spanish. "You have been dear to me these years, and I have tried to give what I could, but our day is approaching an end. It is this which makes you think along these lines and try to hold on. My home and arms have been a haven for you since the death of your father. And you have been a comfort to me after losing my Juan. But now, you outgrow me. See... you were gone for so long because you are forming dreams for your life. No...shush." She touched her finger to his lips. "Do not protest or feel badly. We have been good for each other, but it was never to last forever. This I have known... and you have, too, deep inside."

He took her hand and kissed it, wrapped his arm around her waist and laid his head against her. She stroked his hair. He knew she was right, about everything. She had been for him a refuge, a place to come to rest and to rejuvenate, between his random adventures out into the wild world. But the time had come when he would leave her home and her arms and would not come back.

He turned his head and burrowed into her soft belly, savoring the comfort of her for a few more precious seconds. Then he gently pulled from her and rose.

"I need to visit Padre Domingo to see if he can recommend some reliable men for herders. And I had better check on the Duff."

"*Sí,*" she said. "The Duff, that one bears watching."

Cross put on his hat and tapped his thigh for Pan. At the door he turned, glanced at his bundles lying on the floor. "Is it all right if I return?" He couldn't recall ever asking her this.

She smiled. "Of course. You are always welcome to use my home as your own . . . my friend."

Friend, she called him. Her voice weighed heavily on him.

He and Pan walked through the village, and all around them was activity, for the night was a time for visiting and relaxing and enjoying life. Cross barely noted any of this, however. He looked far beyond, to the west, to see the first twinkling of the stars in the wide twilight sky.

He felt the change inside him. Physically he'd been a man for many years, but in his heart he had remained a boy, enjoying all that came to him with scarcely a thought for the morrow. He'd laid his head wherever he happened to be, had taken pleasure as it came, worked when he must. But out there on the Llano something had happened to him. He had taken on responsibility of many lives, he guessed, by having to care for all those sheep and the dogs and at times the Duff, too.

Today he had come to Marquita with the last vestiges of his boyhood, almost as if to leave them with her understanding heart. He knew that now. He'd shifted from flowing where life took him to deciding where he would go in life.

Haze from the smoky lamps and *cigarros* and cigarillos clouded the crowded saloon. The table where Tyler and three other men sat was in the back corner, giving the feeling of being out of the general hubbub.

The game had grown to six men for a while, but the stakes had gotten too high, so two of the men had quit, leaving Tyler playing with Duffy Campbell, a Scot who claimed to be a lowly shepherd but who dressed like a theater dandy, Don Domaso Lopez, a prominent *rico* of the Territory, and a saddle tramp out of Texas who called himself Pool.

It was Pool whom Tyler kept a close eye upon, while careful not to appear to do so. Pool was one of the thousands of saddle tramps who roamed the West from the Gulf to the coast of California, a man with a gun on his hip and a hand quick to use it. Normally a man of his type kept to the penny-ante games, unable to afford a game such as Tyler and Duffy Campbell and Don Domaso Lopez were having. But Pool had joined and had produced gold coin, plenty to keep him in the game.

It was the gold that kept Tyler at the table, when instinct tugged at him to leave. But Lady Luck was sitting on his shoulder and weaving her spell over his hands. Just one more hand, and he would politely leave . . . but right now he had to play one more hand.

He shuffled the deck elaborately but slowly, letting his movements be clearly seen.

"Ye're quite the hand at that, laddie," Duffy Campbell said, with open admiration. The Scot seemed amazingly open about everything, but his blue eyes twinkled as much with sharp intensity as with merriment. He missed nothing.

Tyler returned with a lazy smile. "I trust you find nothin' to complain of?" He had not been so foolish as to try cheating the big Scot. Tyler was smart enough to recognize a man with skill to match his own.

"Not a smidgen . . . and that's what I'm speakin' of. I commend ye." Duffy grinned and tossed back his whiskey.

"Well, I ain't so certain. Not by a long shot," the drifter, Pool, said. "Your luck is so high, could be that it ain't all luck." His small, dark eyes shone hard from beneath his bushy brows.

A coolness touched Tyler's shoulders. He tapped the deck and looked at Pool, casting the man a hint of a grin that refused any offense.

Tyler said smoothly, "I have considerable skill. Wouldn't you say that's so, Don Domaso?"

Don Domaso nodded. "Perhaps Señor Pool would prefer a new deck," he suggested in his soft gentleman's voice.

Tyler had played many a game with Don Domaso and enjoyed the man's skill. Usually Don Domaso was talkative and very much a free spender, but this evening he was quiet and reserved. Tyler figured it was because of the drifter. There wasn't any love lost between *Tejanos* and Mexicans, the war years being not too distant. Though neither man said anything untoward to each other, the animosity between them was thick enough to cut.

"Yeah ... let's try that," Pool said, his dark eyes baiting.

Tyler graciously inclined his head and called for Calderon to bring a new deck. A chill shook his arm as he set his own aside. Any change could change his luck ... but he would see. The gold coins gleamed up at him. "I pass my deal to you," he said amiably and handed Pool the new deck.

"And we're watchin' you now, laddie," Duffy said, chuckling.

Pool gave a sardonic smile and shuffled the deck.

One by one Tyler looked at his cards. His face remained totally impassive, though amiable, while he saw that he had been dealt another possibly winning hand. His gaze met the Scot's, and he saw the amused questioning there. Tyler returned with an amused questioning of his own.

Then he looked back at his cards. His heartbeat picked up tempo.

He had the grand feeling of riding with the power of the universe. He would win enough tonight not only to retrieve Lilly's earrings and bestow them on her, but to set them on the road to California.

He had to get Lilly to California, for once there she would never leave him. And when he got to California, nothing would stop him. He would prove to her he could do all the things he had promised.

* * *

The windows of Calderon's Saloon shone as bright yellow squares in the dark night. As Cross and Padre Domingo entered, with Pan between them, the musky scents, babble of voices and tinkling of a piano assailed them. For a moment one noise cracked above everything else—the Big Duff's booming laughter.

Peering through the smoky haze, Cross saw his friend sitting with three other men at a table in the rear. The Scot's pale hair shone like a beacon.

"It appears the Duff is a big winner this night," Padre Domingo said, his voice gentle and amused.

"The Duff laughs even when he loses," Cross said ruefully as he saw the Duff throw down his cards. Taking the padre's arm in a protective gesture, Cross directed him toward the bar. The commotion of so many people in one place drew Pan's attention, and Cross slapped his leg as a command to stay close.

Cristo, the bartender, greeted them with an eager nod, bobbing excessively to the padre. Cristo was a young, handsome man, who could not talk. As a boy his tongue had been cut out by the Apache.

"Cristo, you have not been to mass in a month," Padre Domingo scolded mildly. "You will come this Sunday?"

The young man shrugged and with motions asked what they would have. The padre had wine, and Cross whiskey. Cristo was just filling their glasses when the proprietor, Francisco Calderon, hailed them. A man nearly as big around as he was tall, he lumbered across the room and took Cross in an exuberant and back-slapping hug. "Welcome, amigo. I was afraid the Apache had gotten your scalp, but the Duff tells me you return a man rich in sheep." He cast a woeful eye down at Pan. "But you know if I allow you to bring a dog, others will try to bring in their horses. One must draw a line, my friend."

"I can leave," Cross said, and Pan, as if realizing he was being discussed, swished his tail uncertainly.

Calderon's belly shook with laughter. "No! I am the owner. I say who can bring their dogs or their horses—or even their women, no?"

Then his eyes lit on the padre, and a plaintive scowl crossed his features. "I do not wish to be inhospitable, padre, but you will ruin my business."

Padre Domingo smiled tolerantly. "I am looking for Henri. He has not been home this night."

"Sometimes he works in the back." Calderon adopted a noncommittal tone. "He may be there tonight. I do not know."

"This is no place for a boy, Francisco."

"Indeed. I do not allow him in the cantina. But surely there is no harm in him working in the back. He is a good worker, and it is hard to find such these days."

"I have heard he is hawking for the whores," Padre said, his pleasant manner turning stern.

Calderon shifted his eyes and shrugged. "About that I do not know. I have allowed him to help in the kitchen. Whatever else he chooses to do is none of my affair."

With a cool smile, the padre pushed away from the bar. "You allow him to work like a dog for a pittance of what you would have to pay a man, while to an orphan boy it is riches too good to resist. No more, Francisco, or I will be forced to go to my brother."

The padre's eyes twinkled as they flitted to Cross. Padre Domingo knew he had the upper hand; his brother was the alcalde and could make no end of trouble for Calderon. Padre Domingo was protective of the street urchins he took under his wing, and only God could help those who took advantage of the children in his care.

As the padre walked away toward the back rooms, the burly Calderon gave an elaborate sigh. "Padre Domingo enjoys harassing me," he complained to Cross in careful English. "He never liked me marrying his sister." He sighed heavily. "I would give her back, if I could." Then he tossed off his gloom, smiled and puffed out his chest. "So—what do you think of my place?"

"You appear to prosper," Cross answered. His eyes roamed the room. The place was filled with Mexicans in floppy, wide-brimmed hats and baggy coats and shirts. Here and there was a *rico* or a flashy vaquero or an Anglo face— a mountain man or a farmer bound for the goldfields of California, or rough drifters who did just about anything. There were a few women, too, all older and married. This was not a place for young *señoritas*.

"*Sí, mi amigo,*" Calderon said expansively. "Oh, many travelers of the trail stop off in Las Vegas and spend much of their money before they get here—but when they do get here...I am ready!"

Cross lifted his glass. "And then you kill them with this Taos lightning that'll rot holes inside a man."

Calderon took no offense, simply laughed. "Most of my patrons do not wish to spend their money on fancier drinks. They save their money for gambling—like our friend the Big Duff, eh?" He gestured toward the Duff, then pounded the bar to bring Cristo hurrying to serve him.

"How's Duffy doin'?" Cross asked, peering through the smoky haze.

His gaze flickered over the Duff, who had a thick stogie clamped in his teeth, and then to the three other men at the table—an Americano, a dandy gambling man by the look of him, in an expensive fawn-colored top hat set back at a jaunty angle on his curly fair hair and a fancy matching coat. What Don Pablo had said about the Señora Black-well's husband being a gambler for Calderon flashed into his mind.

Sitting next to the gambling man was Don Domaso, a *rico* of an old Spanish family, who sported dark, slick side-burns brushed in a sharp point toward his cheeks and a gold-trimmed coat. The fourth man at the table was a *Tejano*, a rough drifter, Cross pegged him by his clothes—coarse woolen sack coat and worn slouch hat. Though Cross couldn't see it, he would bet the man had a handgun on his hip.

"Oh, the Duff win some, lose some at the monte table earlier," Calderon said as he poured a drink from the bottle Cristo brought. "Then he sit in the game with the Señor Blackwell." He gestured, indicating the dandy-looking one, and the Señora Blackwell came again into Cross's mind. "He's a good gambler and has brought me business. The Duff has been there at that table now for a long time—maybe three, four hours, so he holds his own. Here... *invita la casa.*" He handed Cross a jigger of whiskey from his private bottle.

Cross drank and savored the smooth liquor. "*Gracias, amigo.* I will light candles for you." With a tip of his hat to Calderon, he patted his thigh for Pan and headed in a lazy stride toward the Duff's table.

Duffy called a high-spirited greeting and announced in his booming voice to all and sundry, "This be my good friend, Cross McCree."

As Duffy made short introductions, Cross swept the other men with his gaze. Don Domaso gave him a polite nod of recognition, and Blackwell cast an easy grin and hello. The *Tejano*, Pool, focused a cold, snake-eyed stare at him.

"This place 'pears to be goin' to the dogs," the man said contemptuously, looking downward at Pan.

Tense silence followed. Those at the closest tables had heard and turned their heads. Cross simply met the man's gaze calmly. It took more than a little goading to get him riled.

"And a good thing it is, too," Duffy commented, smiling brightly as he cast a keen, speculative glance from Cross to the drifter. "Perhaps the presence of a few dogs like Pan here would bring a bit of culture to the place. Now, I believe ye are up to deal, mon."

The man shifted his dark eyes to the big Scot. Cross moved back several steps, an acceptable distance from which to watch the game.

The *Tejano* dealt the hand, his eyes snake sharp. Don Domaso folded, slid his chair back and leisurely stretched his thin frame—yet Cross noted it as no idle move, but one calculated to be ready to get out of the way.

It was between the Duff, the gambling man and the *Tejano*. The gambling man won with a full house, and his hands moved swiftly to gather his winnings. Duffy laughed as usual and vowed to get even. The *Tejano*'s eyes were focused on the gambling man's nimble hands gathering the cards.

Instinct told Cross that he had stepped into a situation that was growing hotter by the minute. Duffy confirmed his suspicions with a quick, very clear look of caution. His long rifle was propped against the wall near his elbow, but it was made for the plains and mountains and about the best it could do in quarters like this was serve as a club. Cross knew the Duff generally had a knife on his belt but just might not be wearing it with those fancy clothes. Cross silently cursed. None of this was his fight... but the Duff was his friend.

The *Tejano* lifted the whiskey bottle and drank deeply, took up his cards and tapped them on the table. A muscle in Blackwell's cheek twitched again... and again. His amiable expression took on a strained edge. Duffy became very quiet, his twinkling eyes brightly alert.

Suddenly the *Tejano* reached out and grasped Blackwell's wrist.

"Let's see your cuffs, slick."

The gambling man's amiable expression vanished. "As you wish." Quickly he loosed his cuffs and opened his sleeves. There was nothing. The *Tejano* rose, leaned over and jerked open Blackwell's coat, looking first in one side and then the other. His face twisted with high frustration at finding nothing.

Looking properly righteous, Blackwell shook off the *Tejano*'s hands, sat and buttoned his cuffs. "If you continually think I am cheatin', might I suggest that you fold and leave these other gentlemen and I to enjoy our game."

The snake-eyed man hesitated. He knew he looked like a fool and was searching for a way out.

"Are ye gonna play, mon?" Duffy sat back in his chair, ready to move. It was just like the Duff to force an issue. The Duff liked the excitement of going straight into a tornado rather than around it.

Cross slowly straightened. It was the Duff who worried him, because the Duff would need three seconds to either swing up the rifle or get out his knife, if he had one.

"That man's cheatin'," the *Tejano* said coldly.

Blackwell, white with strain and with sweat shining on his face, looked at the man for a long second and then flashed his eyes at Duffy and Don Domaso.

"I have no complaints, mon," the Duff said, not so jovial now.

Don Domaso nodded in agreement.

"If you wish, sir, I will return your money from the last play," Blackwell said to the *Tejano*.

"The last play?" the snake-eyed man snarled. "I don't want yer money, dixie. I want you to own up to bein' a dirty cheatin' bastard!"

The *Tejano* leaped to his feet, knocking his chair over behind him. Cross saw the Colt Dragoon at his thigh just as the man's hands pulled out the big revolver.

The speed of the blowup took Cross a little by surprise. In the blink of an eye he saw Blackwell's pale eyes widen with terror, his hand reach inside his coat. Cross palmed the knife from the back of his neck as fire leaped from the *Tejano*'s Colt, and an earsplitting shot rang out. The gambling man flew backward with the force of the bullet. The *Tejano* swung the smoking Colt toward Duffy, who was bringing around his rifle.

Cross sent his knife flying unerringly across the table and straight into the *Tejano*'s chest at the same instant that the Colt spit fire again. The *Tejano* crumpled, bounced on the table, slid to the floor.

A motion brought Cross swinging around to see Pan in midair—straight at a man with a pistol drawn. The man went down with a frantic scream, Pan at his throat.

Cross and Calderon reached Pan and the screaming man at the same time. Cross hauled up Pan, and Calderon took hold of the man, who flailed his arms and screamed until Calderon gave him a hard punch to the jaw.

A stunned stillness fell over the room. Cross glanced around, his muscles still poised and ready for defense.

Blackwell lay sprawled on his back beside the broken chair he'd been sitting in, his belly a mass of crimson blood. He groaned.

The snake-eyed man lay crumpled on his side, hair across his face, the ivory handle of Cross's knife in his chest catching the light.

Where the Duff had been was empty. Moving quickly, Cross rounded the table and found Duffy lying on his side.

"Duff?" Cross pushed the table away and knelt beside his friend.

Duffy, a hand pressing his shoulder, gasped, "Get the damn chair out of my legs and give me a hand up, lad."

"Stay there." Cross unwrapped the Duff's legs from the broken chair. Then, grasping Duffy's bloodstained hand, he lifted it to look at the wound.

"Ah, lad, ain't nothin' worse than I've had before."

Cross breathed a sigh of relief when he saw that the bullet had gone straight through. Where it had hit in the shoulder it wasn't likely to have done any lasting damage—providing infection didn't set in. He grabbed the bottle of whiskey off the table.

"Give me a swig of that afore ye go wasting it on my body," Duffy said.

Chapter Five

Lilly awoke and sat right up in bed. She fumbled with the lamp, lit it and checked Tyler's watch. He rarely carried it with him to the saloon, for he had no need to check time there. It read just past midnight.

She felt as if a storm was coming, but when she opened the door and looked up it was into a starry sky with a bright full moon. A devil's moon, Mammy Ethnee used to call it. Lilly used to ask her why it couldn't be called a God's moon, because it was so pretty. Mammy Ethnee had said it could be but it wasn't.

Light shone in Delores Trujillo's room, and Lilly plainly saw the shadow of a man near the window.

She had on other occasions seen a man's shadow at Delores's window, and once she had seen a man sneaking into the woman's room. Since she was often awake at night, Lilly liked to stand in the dark in her doorway and stare at the stars. She had figured Delores was a Jezebel, so she hadn't been surprised about the man. She had actually envied Delores for having the companionship of a man during the lonely hours of the night, and that attitude surprised her and made her worry that she was getting as coarse as this land.

She thought of the blue-eyed man she had met that morning. Cross McCree.

She was instantly ashamed of herself.

Yet...life wasn't as cut-and-dried as she'd once believed, she thought, rubbing her upper arms against the chill.

The light in Delores's room went out. Lilly kept standing there, staring at the woman's room.

Finally she moved her gaze. Mr. and Mrs. Gallegos's rooms were dark. The bright moon shone from the western sky, and it was so light Lilly figured she could have written a letter by it. She heard music from somewhere in the distance and laughter from out in the alley. She wondered how Tyler was doing.

He'd taken all the money she had, and if he lost it, they would have nothing.

She began to shake. Turning back into the room, she shut the door and went to the fireplace and stirred up the embers, placed the few remaining pieces of wood upon them and watched them catch.

A dread hung over her, and her mind drew dark pictures of her and Tyler thrown out into the street in the foreign land, no food or shelter, no one to help them. What would they do? What would she do if Tyler didn't return this night, and she was left all alone without anything at all?

She jerked around, strode to the door, opened it just enough to squeeze through on her knees. In the darkness she stretched her hand beneath the bush there beside the door...feeling...touching a chicken that let out a cackle and fluttered away. Lilly's fingers found the warm, round object. She grasped it and quick as a wink pulled it back into the room and shut the door.

She carried the egg to the rickety sideboard and set it in a bowl. Somehow having the egg made her feel less desperate. She heated enough water to make a cup of tea, then blew out the lamp and sat sipping tea in the dark. She had always liked the dark. Even as a child she had been more comforted than scared by it.

She wished the hard chair was a rocker, because nothing was better at soothing nerves than rocking in a good rocking chair. A noise outside the room in the alley caused her to jump and spill her tea. It was probably a dog. There were many dogs around, just as there were chickens and goats. And snakes, she thought, drawing her feet up into the chair.

Her mind went back, seeking refuge in the dear and familiar, to Pasquotank County and the great white house on the river where she'd been born. Blond angel hair and a sweet voice were all she truly recalled of her mother, and her memory of her father consisted of his silhouette swinging against the orange glow of a rising sun, where he'd hanged himself from a cypress tree after the death of his beloved wife. Mammy Ethnee had tried to catch her before she'd seen, but she'd slipped from the old woman's hands and run into the yard.

Still, Lilly loved the river and the trees that jutted out of it, and she loved the house. She loved sitting there in a rocker on the porch, drinking tea and watching the sun rise over the river. She loved cutting the camellias and bringing them into the house, and making mint jelly with Mammy Ethnee—Mammy Ethnee's and her mint jelly was the best in the county. She loved the scent of the pine oil polish on the oak floors and banisters and the floral wallpaper that had come from France. She loved Sundays, when Shandy would drive them to church in the buggy, Mammy Ethnee going to her church and Lilly to hers—the white-steepled church sitting at the edge of the swamp—and then she and Mammy Ethnee would exchange the latest gossip on the return trip. Sometimes Shandy would have gone fishing during services, and when they came home they'd have a fish dinner with crusty hushpuppies and steamed cabbage. Every Monday Lilly and her friend Mary Kate went on visiting rounds, and at least twice a month there were parties—the

Pritchards had a supper at least once a month—and for each event Lilly got a new gown.

That's where she had met Tyler again when he'd come home from college—at one of June Pritchard's marvelous suppers. He was so handsome, a charmer of women—Lilly had seen that from the first.

She had known he was a rake and wild as a March hare, just as Mammy Ethnee had said. But she had always adored him. She knew he'd married her for money, and she truly never could blame him for all that came after. It had come as a bitter blow when Uncle Raymond had blown his brains out and it'd been discovered that he had bankrupted Cypress Crossing. That he'd lost everything that should have been Lilly's.

From the beginning Lilly had known that Tyler needed her, and she'd needed that—to be needed by someone, have someone of her own. He still needed her, more now than ever before. And she still needed that.

There came a banging—pounding on a door in the courtyard—and anxious voices.

Lilly sprang from the chair. Not bothering to light the lamp, she went to the door and opened it. Two men were at Mr. Gallegos's door.

A great fear knotted her stomach.

A light was lit within the Gallegos's kitchen, and the door opened. Low, urgent Spanish words Lilly couldn't clearly hear or understand were exchanged, and then Mr. Gallegos pointed in her direction.

Carrying a lantern, Mr. Gallegos led the way across the courtyard to her. He didn't have on a shirt and had only one of his galluses pulled up over his pudgy torso. Lilly stood frozen, her gaze on that gallus.

"Your husband has been shot," Mr. Gallegos said bluntly.

Lilly heard him distinctly, but she couldn't seem to understand what he said. She searched the men's faces. They were dark, foreign-looking men.

Mr. Gallegos said, "You must come."

Lilly saw his mouth move beneath his bushy gray mustache. She heard his words but couldn't respond.

And then Delores Trujillo was pushing through the men, jabbering at them in Spanish and pulling a shawl around her bare shoulders. Lilly noticed that the woman's breasts bobbed beneath her thin, skimpy chemise.

Delores grabbed Lilly by the arm and said firmly, "Come... I will go with you."

Once Lilly got moving, her mind began working, too. "How bad is it?" she asked Delores. "Ask them—" she gestured "—ask them if Tyler is still alive."

Delores, huffing from the pace, conversed in quick, brief words with the men. "He's alive," she told Lilly.

Lilly prayed for God to keep Tyler alive until she arrived.

The door of the saloon stood open and light poured forth. The two men hurried ahead, as if to make way, though there was no need, for there were few people inside.

Lilly's steps slowed when she saw Tyler. He lay on the hard-packed dirt floor. An Indian blanket covered him to his chest. He moved and moaned. A priest in a drab brown robe knelt beside him.

Lilly felt herself going light-headed, but she kept her eyes focused on Tyler and kept putting one foot in front of the other until she reached him. She sank down beside him.

"Tyler?" Her voice came out a strange whisper. "Tyler?"

His golden curls spread on a dingy pillow. His face was white and awash with tears. He opened his eyes. The pain

Lilly saw there took her breath. He brought a frantic hand from beneath the blanket and grasped at her.

"Lilly... I prayed to see you."

His hand was covered with warm, sticky blood. She wanted to run screaming from the room, but she clasped his bloody hand in both of hers and looked into his eyes.

"Yes, honey... I'm here."

Tyler squeezed his eyes closed and sucked in a ragged breath. "Can you imagine me prayin', Lil?" he said with a painful chuckle. "I thought God gave up on me a long time ago...but he brought you." He broke off in a painful cough.

Lilly glanced up into the faces surrounding them, frantically looking for someone to tell her what to do. Someone to help them.

Everyone's eyes shifted away from hers, all except the priest's. With pity, he shook his head.

"Help me, Lilly," Tyler managed and gripped her hand, crushing it.

"Of course I will, honey," she crooned, and touched his brow. She glanced up. "Someone bring me a wet cloth," she said. Tyler so hated to be dirty and sweaty. She could at least cool him off, and she could be there. She could do that.

Cristo started to hand her the dirty wet rag he used to wipe the bar, but Cross intercepted him, grabbed the cloth and went back to the bar to get a clean one.

The woman didn't look at him when he extended the cloth. She didn't take her eyes from her husband. "Tyler," she called to him in a soft, melodious voice.

She sat there, her brown hair in a rope down her back and her velvet robe spread out on the filthy dirt floor, and gently she wiped her husband's face, even smiled at him, though tears flowed down her pale cheeks.

Cross moved back from the wide circle the others formed around the two. He leaned against the same post he had earlier before the violence had erupted. Pan lay close at his feet.

Swallowing hard, Cross looked from Blackwell stretched on the ground, dying, to the Duff sitting in a chair. The doctor was bandaging Duffy's shoulder. The doctor had quickly abandoned Blackwell and turned to the Duff, as if relieved to turn away from inevitable death and have something as simple to do as cover a clean wound. Duffy held a bottle of Calderon's tequila by the neck and drew deeply from it.

Cross thought how it could have been the Duff lying beside the gambling man.

He looked at the Señora Blackwell and wished he had thrown his knife five seconds earlier. If he had, the woman's husband would still be alive, or at least there was a chance he would be. Cross suddenly felt vaguely guilty about that. He felt he should have protected Blackwell, for the woman's sake.

Tyler Blackwell was lucky, if such could be said, because he was gut-shot bad. He could have been gut-shot and not so bad and have lingered for days in pain. Cross had seen this happen. But the gambling man was sinking fast. He'd held on only to see his wife, had called for her over and over.

"Lilly, I guess you drew a poor hand with me." He spoke in a breathless whisper. Tears and desperation flowed from his eyes and made Cross's stomach churn.

"Shush..." she said, wiping his face over and over. "Don't you forget...you're gonna take me to California and build me a big house like Cypress Crossing."

The gambling man tried for a smile that came out a grimace. His voice was hoarse and desperate. "I won us a stake tonight, honey. A herd of sheep."

The man's words sent cold shock traveling up Cross's spine. He'd been listening and thinking that he shouldn't be, and now every cell in his body listened intently. He watched the man strain toward the woman.

"I got the paper in my pocket. I won't be leavin' you penniless, Lil. The sheep...they'll...get you home, honey." He sank back on the pillow, closed his eyes.

"It's all right, Tyler. It's gonna be all right. It will." Her voice cracked with hysteria.

Blackwell's eyes popped open, and he stared at her, grinned slightly. "I got a winnin' hand with you, Lil...you have...sure been some kind of woman." His voice faded, his eyes closed and his raspy breathing stopped.

It took Cross a minute to realize that the gambling man had died. He was busy thinking about the sheep. It had to be his and the Duff's sheep.

He looked over at Duffy, but the Duff was looking at the gambling man. Tears streamed down his florid cheeks and disappeared into his white beard. Duffy Campbell was never ashamed of tears, said it took strong men to cry. Cross had felt right teary eyed himself, until Blackwell had said what he had about the sheep. Now one part of Cross's brain absorbed the tragedy, and the other part was thinking about the sheep. He couldn't have said which of his thoughts was stronger.

It didn't have to be his and the Duff's herd, he reasoned, as he watched Padre Domingo offer prayers over the dead man. The *rico*, Don Domaso, owned sheep and trafficked in great herds—and there were two dozen other big ranchers of the Territory and a thousand small ones, and any one of these men could have been in a game with Blackwell this evening.

But Cross knew with a heavy dread that the sheep in question had been the ones he and the Duff had spent the better part of eighteen months gathering.

* * *

Hands were tugging hers from Tyler's, and Lilly, her gaze focused intently on Tyler's face, pushed them away. A second time the hands came, and Lilly, without removing her eyes from Tyler's face, went at them, slapping and beating until they left her alone.

She continued to sit there, holding Tyler's hand and gazing into his face. Tyler had always been uneasy in the dark, and Lilly didn't know if he was in the dark now, but if he was, she didn't want him to be there alone.

She couldn't sit there forever, though. The hands came again to remove hers, and this time she let them. Any strength for fighting had completely deserted her.

It was the priest; he folded Tyler's hands across his chest. Lilly wiped the blood from her hands with the wet cloth. When the priest started to pull the blanket over Tyler's head, Lilly stopped him.

"He has a lovely face," she said. She felt a little silly, but she simply couldn't stand for Tyler's face to be covered. He had never even liked a light sheet over his face.

Slowly Lilly got to her feet. The priest helped her. She looked at the people around her, noting the faces as foreign and the expressions of pity and no more. A vile hate rose within her.

"Where is he—the man who did this?"

Dark eyes stared at her.

"He is dead, *señora*," a big, burly man told her. He gestured, and she followed the line of his hand, seeing the shape of a body beneath a blanket several feet away.

Slowly she walked over to the body and stared down at it.

"Cross McCree killed him," the burly man said.

Lilly barely heard him. The wild urge to pound the killer, even in death, assailed her. She bent and yanked back the blanket.

A face, white with a rough, sparse black beard and opened eyes, black and mad, stared up at her. It was the face of a devil.

Her stomach rose to her throat. Unable to look away, she thought his eyes fastened on her. Her head spun, and she felt herself sinking into blessed darkness.

Someone's arm held her. A cool cloth came to her forehead, and she heard Delores's voice.

"*Señora?* Lilly?"

Lilly opened her eyes. Delores was staring at her with concern. But it was a man who held her and a man's voice that said, "Here, drink this."

She looked at the glass he held and then upward at the man himself. She found herself looking into familiar, intense blue eyes. The face was only vaguely familiar, but the eyes were unforgettable.

It was the blue-eyed man she had met that morning. Only just that morning. Was she dreaming still?

She stared at him, and he stared at her. Cross McCree, she thought.

He pressed the glass to her lips. She sipped the amber liquid that burned her throat. Immediately she choked and coughed violently. Pushing him away, she struggled to her feet. Cross McCree and Delores helped her, but she pulled away from both as soon as she had her balance. She didn't want anyone touching her. She looked at the blue-eyed man again, and he looked at her. Then he turned away.

Lilly slipped into silence, as if in silence she would be safe.

They brought a cart pulled by a burro to take Tyler's body home. Someone brought a bag of coins and pressed it into her hands. Tyler's poke.

When the priest strongly suggested she ride, she shook her head and stood beside the cart. Suddenly Cross McCree appeared out of the deep shadows. His eyes were dark in the dimness, and he stared intensely at her. He reached out, took her by the waist and lifted her up and set her in the back of the cart with Tyler.

"Padre Domingo has a bad back and can't be liftin' you up from the street when you faint," he said.

They gazed at each other, and she realized the difference in him—he had shaved his beard.

Then he moved back into the shadows, fading from her sight.

The priest led the little burro. Lilly rode in the cart, bumping along beside Tyler. The bag of money occasionally jingled in her lap.

The waning moon bathed them in bright silvery light. Tyler looked as if he was simply sleeping. The cart creaked loudly and obnoxiously. Delores walked alongside. She had covered her hair with her shawl and had her head down, as if in prayer.

That reminded Lilly that she should pray. She tried, but the bouncing and creaking of the cart didn't help, and her mind was numb. She figured if God was all He was supposed to be, He could handle the prayer. She wished for Mammy Ethnee. Inside herself she became the little girl who would climb into the old woman's lap for comfort.

When she raised her head she saw a figure, a man, walking behind them at a certain distance and not venturing any closer. He wore a striped serape. When she saw the small dog at his feet, she realized he was the blue-eyed Cross McCree.

Cross always had been an even-tempered man—too even tempered to Duffy's mind—but at this moment the younger man was as mad as Duffy had ever seen him. It was the wrong time as far as Duffy was concerned. Duffy had seen a young man killed for nothing but meanness this night, had almost been killed himself, and his wound burned like fire in his shoulder. He didn't feel like dealing with Cross's righteous notions.

"I didn't lose the entire herd to Blackwell, laddie," Duffy said. "I lost half of it—which was mine, I dare to point out." He straightened a little, pushing away the guilt that tugged at him, and took another draw on the bottle of whiskey Calderon had brought him.

"I had thought we were partners," Cross said tersely. "I guess I was wrong."

The condemnation in his friend's tone provoked Duffy no end. "Aye, likely," he said, "if ye thought being partners meant livin' by yer rules, laddie. I live by no one's rules but those of Duffy Campbell and God as I see Him. And if all ye are interested in is yer sheep after seein' a man killed tonight and killin' one yerself, ye ain't the man I've always judged ye to be."

Cross's eyes took on the sheen of steel. "Men live and men die. I was responsible only for one man's death, and I think more of seekin' to save your life than I do of taking his. And beyond them both—I'm still alive."

"Aye..." Duffy said stiffly, having little to add to that truth. He lifted the bottle to his lips. He'd barely taken a swig when Cross grabbed the bottle from him and drank deeply.

The only ones left in the cantina, Duffy and Cross sat sharing the bottle at the same table where earlier the fateful game had been played out. Their only light was the single candle on the table. From time to time Duffy looked down at the dark floor, where he could see young Tyler Blackwell's blood a darker stain in the dirt near his boot. When asked how he would clean the bloodstains up, Calderon had shrugged and said, "They will mix in with the sweeping and people walking, just as the tobacco spit." He spoke from experience, of course.

The guard had come, but since justice had been meted out, there was nothing for them to do. Law was simple in this land, an eye for an eye. Stealing a horse would have brought much more outrage.

It was a hard land, Duffy thought morosely. The image of the lovely young woman holding her dying husband's hand stayed with him. He drank deeply again, melancholy sweeping him in his memories. Games of chance had been the root cause of his having to flee his home country of Scotland, and in the twenty-five years since he still hadn't learned to stay away from them.

Slowly he raised his eyes and gazed hard at Cross, and Cross stared hard and angry back.

"We have been together for nigh on five years. I would have thought ye knew by now that I don' like to be tethered, lad."

Cross looked away. "Aye ... I guess I know that."

Disappointment lined the younger man's face, and guilt and pity swept over Duffy. He drank again from the bottle, seeking to drown his torment.

"I had planned on winnin' the sheep back," he said. "It would have been an easy thing, if Blackwell hadn't gone and got himself shot. I'm a better card sharp than he is—or was—by a mile." Though knowing his weakness for gambling, Duffy had always found pride in his skill.

Cheerless amusement cracked Cross's dour face. He raised an eyebrow. "Was he cheatin' ... like the *Tejano* said?"

"I don't believe he was at that particular moment. He had been earlier, however, when Pool entered the game, and in Pool's favor, which is the joke of it. After Blackwell saw the gold Pool put down, he decided to hook the fellow into playin'. Poor judgment. Pool's gold came ill-gotten for sure. That young Blackwell was quite good at cards, but he had little judgment." He stood and stretched painfully. "Let us go see if Marquita will put me up with ye." He found his legs unsteady. "Ye may need to get a cart for me."

"The only one I know of took off a dead body and a lady," Cross said. He slid his shoulder underneath Duffy's. "Come on. I'll be your crutch."

Instinctively they paused in the deep darkness of the portico and carefully looked around. The dead *Tejano* had turned out to be Pool Puckett, a known *pistolero,* and the runty man Pan had taken down had been Pool's brother, Rudd. Calderon said the two had been frequenting his place off and on since early spring. They were hardcases, who were sometimes joined by three other men, two of those being known Mexican bandits. It was rumored the group traded in stolen goods with the Indians to the south. Pool Puckett had been quick to use a gun and had shot another man over the affections of a woman out at one of the rougher cantinas closer to the trail. It was safe to say Rudd Puckett had not been at all happy about what had happened to his brother. He'd come to several minutes after Calderon's punch, but by then they had had him tied. The guard had released him, having no true reason for taking him away to jail. The squatty Rudd Puckett's parting words to Cross had been to see him in hell for killing his brother.

"I suppose we will need to step carefully for a while," the Duff said as they started down the street.

Cross silently reflected that Rudd Puckett's threat had been to him alone. Also, he couldn't recall a time when he hadn't stepped carefully. Danger existed always, either in the form of other men or nature. It wasn't something he worried about.

He had been worried about the woman, however, and had followed her home, just in case Rudd Puckett had been cowardly enough to take his ire out on her. Plus he had felt responsible for her somehow, now that her husband was dead.

The moon was far to the west and dawn hinting in the east as the two men and the small black-and-white dog made their way through the narrow streets. Cross noticed that a beautiful morning was coming. It seemed strangely obscene so soon after the savage happenings in the night. Immense thankfulness at being alive swept over him, so much that a lump rose in his throat. He tightened his grip on his friend, glad the Duff was still at his side.

"Gettin' maudlin on me, lad?" Duffy said.

"Killin' can do that to a man, I guess." Cross kept his eyes on the dawning sky.

"Aye...makes us know our lives are no more than tiny sparks that quickly fly upward." He wiped his nose with his sleeve. "Times like this I wish for fruit of my loins."

"You don't like tetherin', remember?"

Duffy nodded sadly. "Been my curse, that."

Marquita was up but still in her light wrapper when they got to her cabana. She fussed over Duffy, and he sopped it up the way dry bread did gravy. She led them to the bed in the back room, paused in her fussing to hug them both, before returning to scolding them for their reckless ways. Duffy kidded with her, telling her that if he had such a good woman as herself he wouldn't be out in saloons. The two had always enjoyed easy banter.

After getting Duffy settled in bed, Cross returned to the main room with Marquita. She was stoking up the fire, preparing to make coffee. He went to her, touched her hair. She turned and touched his cheek, her eyes full of warmth, yet for the first time Cross could see the motherly hint to it. He realized then that she had often looked at him in such a way.

He started to go into her bed and then recalled that things had changed. He went over to the bench formed out of the adobe wall, sat and began removing his boots.

Marquita came over and took his hand, pulling him up. "You go to my bed. I am up for the day."

She gave him a little shove, and Cross went. He was darn tired, and the comfort her feather mattress would provide was too good to resist. A feather mattress was a grand luxury only afforded the rich. Marquita had come by hers from a prosperous and grateful trader.

Marquita followed him and helped him get his boots off, just as she had the Duff, and then she left him.

He stripped to his underwear and stretched out on the clean sheets beneath the blanket. The sheets and blanket smelled of Marquita. Through the opened door he watched Marquita go to the shelf on the wall that served as an altar. She lit the three candles there and bowed her head.

Self-conscious of her intimate moment, he turned his eyes to the window. Dawn came.

He thought of the Señora Blackwell with the grass green eyes. Lilly. The name suited her.

He thought how life certainly played out strangely at times. Cross's life had entwined with Tyler and Lilly Blackwell's like threads of a rope, without him ever having said more than a handful of words to either of them. And now Lilly Blackwell owned half of Cross's herd of sheep.

He wondered if all that had happened had been set in motion the moment the fair Americano woman had bumped into him and he had indulged in thoughts about her.

They buried Tyler that very afternoon in the churchyard cemetery. Lilly told the priest, Padre Domingo, that Tyler hadn't been Catholic, but the priest said that didn't matter. Lilly did notice Tyler's grave was among others that seemed separate from the main cemetery. Perhaps this area was saved for people who weren't Catholic, or Mexican. She didn't ask.

Padre Domingo stood at the head of the grave and re-
cited words in Latin. He was a pudgy man with silver hair
and the kindest, warmest eyes Lilly had ever seen. She had
given him a handful of coins from Tyler's poke, well over a
hundred dollars, though she wasn't certain exactly, because
her mind was so muddled, to cover the burial, headstone
and donation to the church. She had turned the obligation
over to him, and he had kindly taken it on.

She looked at the few mourners. Delores and Mrs. Gallegos had said it was a Mexican tradition that women did not
go to the graveside. Mrs. Gallegos had been a little upset
that Lilly would go, and very upset that Lilly hadn't a black
dress, so she had brought her own black mourning veil for
Lilly to wear. Lilly had worn it out of courtesy to the older
woman. She wore the green silk dress that was Tyler's favorite and told Mrs. Gallegos that was often what Americanos did. Of course, there wasn't a lot of truth in that, but
the idea seemed to appease Mrs. Gallegos.

Mr. Gallegos had put on an almost clean shirt. Next to
him stood Mr. Calderon, in a very flashy Mexican suit, his
hat in his hand. Joe Darcy, the man Tyler had talked of going into partnership with, had come and introduced himself. He seemed a kind man, and Lilly had better thoughts
about Tyler's proposed venture with him, though of course
that was all over now.

Cross McCree had come. He had killed the evil-eyed man
who had killed Tyler—a *pistolero*, Mr. Gallegos had called
him—with his knife.

She didn't think Cross McCree could see her face clearly
through the heavy black veil, but each time she looked in his
direction, he was looking at her. He appeared as he had the
day she had met him, in sturdy clothes and striped serape.
She raised her eyes to him again, and he was looking at her,
without expression but with intensity. She could remember
how she had felt the previous day, when he had spoken to

her, but she felt nothing in this moment. Nothing but aloneness. She couldn't fathom that Tyler had died. Not Tyler, who had been so full of life.

It certainly seemed strange to be staring at his coffin set in the hard, dry ground. It was a far cry from the Blackwell family plot back in Pasquotank County, which was situated at the edge of a swamp. She had an instant where she thought Tyler whispered that he liked it here better, and she felt glad for him.

Padre Domingo finished, and one of the two grave diggers began shoveling dirt atop Tyler's casket. The first plop brought a good jolt to Lilly. She started to cry, for the first time since sitting beside Tyler as he breathed his last. The plopping of the dirt so unnerved her that she turned and started away in long strides.

"You go wash," Delores said, gesturing emphatically. "I will make your coffee."

Lilly looked at her for a moment, but didn't speak. The silence had come over her again. She stepped to the alcove where the bed sat and pulled the curtain. She thought that she might want to scream, but she would be ashamed of herself for that. She took off the green silk dress and put on her wrapper. She hung the dress on its hook and also neatly put away her corset and petticoats. Tyler had always admired her neatness. His clothes hung there beside her own. It hurt her eyes to see them.

Delores not only made Lilly coffee but shared a sparse meal of cheese and bread brought from her own larder. In the Mexican manner, she had boiled the coffee and the sugar together; the coffee was strong, but so was the sugar. The sweetness was a soothing balm to Lilly.

"It will get better," Delores said and lit up one of the thin, dark Mexican cigarettes, blew out a long stream of smoke. "I know. I have buried two."

Lilly looked at the woman, saw the pity pouring from her normally sharp dark eyes.

Delores got up and strode to the bureau. She snatched up something and returned to toss it in Lilly's lap. It was Tyler's poke.

"You will not make it unless you come to your senses," she said caustically. "Hide your money. There are many who know you have it. Luis Gallegos, for one. He has been waiting his chance." She spat to the side. "Do not trust that one more than that. He will try to get between your legs, too."

She poured the last of their coffee, and they sipped in silence. Lilly gazed at the wet spot Delores's spit had made on the earthen floor and thought about how dirty Mr. Gallegos was.

Delores said, "You no longer have the protection of a man. You will have to learn to take care of yourself."

Lilly lifted her gaze to Delores. She thought that many times it had been she who took care of herself and Tyler, more than the other way around. It was simply that she had had Tyler's presence. How odd that the mere presence of a man should make such a difference.

"You must think," Delores said and tapped her temple. "Making plans will keep you from the crazies. What will you do? How will you live?"

Lilly struggled to come out of the empty, silent void. She looked at Delores and then looked down at the bag in her lap.

"Count what is in the bag," Delores ordered.

With clumsy motions, Lilly emptied the contents onto the table. There were silver and gold coins and paper drafts, too. As she counted, her motions became more certain, her mind more clear. All told there was over twenty-five hundred dollars.

Lilly sat back and stared at the pile. "I can go home," she said at last, her voice hoarse.

The fact came clear into her mind for the first time. Her heartbeat picked up tempo as the prospect filled every nook and cranny of her brain.

She could go home, to Pasquotank County.

She could go home to Mammy Ethnee, and the river and the pines and brick-lined streets and white clapboard houses with proper cook stoves and indoor water closets. Back to her friend, Mary Kate, and to cousins Arden and Robert. She pictured all of it, eagerness quickening inside. She could go home!

Delores picked up a folded piece of paper, handed it to her. "There is this, too."

Puzzled, Lilly unfolded the paper and read.

It wasn't Tyler's handwriting, but it was a fine, flowing script, which deeded over five thousand sheep to Tyler Peyton Blackwell. It was signed Duffy G. Campbell, with a flourish.

"It's the sheep Tyler won," Lilly whispered. It didn't seem real, yet the memory came back to her. Tyler, racked with pain, had told her he was leaving her well provided for, that he had won a herd of sheep. He had been so proud. Tears filled her eyes. One streamed down her cheek, fell on the ink and smeared it. With a swift motion, Lilly wiped the tears away.

"It's five thousand sheep," she said to Delores, pointing at the paper. "He won them from Duffy Campbell. Do you know who he is?"

Delores nodded. "He is the big *compañero* to Cross McCree—the man who killed the *pistolero*. The *pistolero* shot Duffy Campbell, too, in the shoulder."

"Where do you suppose they are—the sheep?" Lilly asked. She found the concept of so many sheep in one place hard to understand.

"In a pasture," Delores said dryly and snuffed out her cigarette. "You are a woman of some means now. Five thousand sheep are worth, ah . . . five thousand dollars, at least."

Lilly looked at her. "So much?"

Delores nodded. "That much here, and six, maybe seven times that in California, where they will no doubt go. My cousin went as a herder last year with the Oteros, taking a great herd, biggest yet. He said the sheep, they sold for seven-fifty apiece American."

Lilly gazed at the paper and wondered if it could be true. After all, this was only a small scrap of paper and seemed far removed from a fortune in sheep.

"You are very fortunate, *señora,*" Delores said. "Your bed will be cold, but you will not go hungry." She rose and gazed down at Lilly. "You look like a weak piece of straw, but I think there is the strength and sharpness of a cactus thorn within you."

She walked to the door. "Drop the latch after me."

"Wait," Lilly said. Springing up, she got her silver hairbrush and took it to Delores, holding it toward her. "I thank you for all you have done."

Delores's gaze came up in surprise.

"Please," Lilly said.

Delores smiled her sardonic smile. "I would rather have the green dress—the one you wore today."

Lilly swung around and retrieved the dress from a hook on the wall. She pressed both the brush and the dress into Delores's hands.

"Generosity is for fools," Delores said.

"Give and it shall come back to you," Lilly said.

Delores's sardonic smile deepened. "Drop the latch, and fasten it. You are a woman alone now."

Her gaze lingered meaningfully on Lilly, and Lilly nodded.

She closed the door and dropped the latch, fastened it. She turned and looked around the room. The aloneness seeped upward like rising floodwater. Her eyes fell on Tyler's poke, which she had flung to the table in her haste moments ago. Crossing to the table, she took up the bag.

Without letting go of it, she lit the oil lamp and left it burning on the table. Still clutching the bag, she went to the bed and curled up on it. Her gaze fell upon the dark shadow on the wall that was Tyler's second-best suit, and the tears threatened again. She felt guilty because she was glad to be going home and because, though she missed Tyler, she knew she would get over his loss.

She even felt relief, God forgive her.

"I wish it could have been different, Tyler," she whispered.

She closed her eyes and slipped away from the pain and fear into sleep.

Chapter Six

Lilly slept thirty-four hours. She awoke once for a drink of water and once to pass it and twice upon hearing knocking at her door, but she simply told whoever it was to go away and turned over and went back to sleep, until the dawning of the second morning.

She came wide awake. For a moment she thought she heard Tyler calling her name, and then it hit her like the felling of a giant pine. Tyler was dead, and she was a widow.

She lay still and absorbed this, listening to the beating of her heart and to the muffled sounds from outside: a rooster crowing, hens cackling, a dog barking, someone calling angrily.

She was alone, totally.

With that thought, she wanted to go back to sleep. However, she forced herself to sit up, throw her legs over the side of the bed. The bar remained set across the door. The room was musty, and she was thirsty enough to drink an entire trough of water. She opened the shutter to the small window, and then she remembered the poke and was frantic until she found it tangled in the quilt. For an instant, there on her hands and knees upon the thin, lumpy straw mattress, she seemed to hear Tyler laughing at her. It was both a sweet and irritating sensation.

As she fastened the poke inside her skirt, her mind began making up for lost time. She would need to see to passage to St. Louis, and there were the sheep to deal with. She supposedly owned five thousand sheep but had no idea of where they were or who was keeping them. If she hadn't read the words on the paper, she would have thought she had imagined them entirely. And it could be that there were contingencies; perhaps because she hadn't claimed them immediately they had been taken over by someone else. This was a foreign land with foreign customs.

Well, she sincerely hoped not. She would need the money those sheep could bring. The money in Tyler's poke would enable her to buy back her mother's earrings and get her home, but once she got there, she would need money to keep her until she could somehow find a way to keep herself. This thought jarred her. How in the world would she keep herself?

She could be a seamstress, but suddenly she saw herself entering through the back door of homes she had before entered from the front, saw herself on her knees fixing the hem of Glades Henderson's dress, and she didn't like that picture at all.

Well, it wouldn't do to think that far ahead.

Taking up the pitcher, she went for fresh water. When she opened her door, a bulky bundle rolled inside and landed at her feet. A boy, she realized with amazement.

The little figure scrambled upward. He stared at her, and she stared at him. He was brown as a scorched nut, topped by a thatch of glossy black hair, and dressed in the loose, undyed cotton clothing of a peon.

He turned and started to sprint away, but in two strides Lilly caught him. "Wait... *un momento*... " She grabbed his arm and turned him. He faced her uncertainly, his dark eyes fearful and curious at the same time. "I'm not going to hurt you." She smiled encouragingly. He gazed at her solemnly. "Who are you?"

He rattled back to her in Spanish. Lilly understood one word, the name Cross.

She looked across to see the door to the Gallegos's room standing open. Taking hold of the boy by the arm, she tugged him across the courtyard.

She rapped on the doorjamb and called. Mrs. Gallegos came through the archway at the rear of the room. Upon seeing Lilly, her gaunt, wrinkled face broke into a tender smile. "Ah...*señora,* you are feeling better, yes?"

"Yes...*sí.* Mrs. Gallegos, do you know who this boy is?"

Mrs. Gallegos came forward, peering around the table. She nodded. "Henrique. He is...ah, how you say, guard?"

"A guard?"

Mrs. Gallegos's head bobbed. "Cross McCree, he come...two times." She held up two fingers. "When you no open door, he put the boy to watch for you."

The boy said eagerly, "*Sí*—Cross McCree."

Lilly thought that at least they could all understand the man's name. "Cross McCree came to see me? Why?"

Mrs. Gallegos shook her little birdlike head and shrugged. "I do not know, *señora.*"

Lilly looked down at the boy and opened her mouth, then realized he wouldn't understand. She asked Mrs. Gallegos to ask the boy what he knew. The older woman and the boy exchanged words.

"It is about your sheep," Mrs. Gallegos said curiously. "That's all he knows."

Lilly gazed at the boy a moment, and then said, "Come...*por favor...un momento.*" She pointed at her door. "Thank you, Mrs. Gallegos," she added over her shoulder. The older woman cast her a curious smile and wave.

With the boy in tow, Lilly went back to her room. She set him in a chair, got Tyler's little tin of lemon drop candy and placed two pieces on the table in front of the boy. Then she went to dig paper, pen and ink from the case where she kept them. When she turned around, she saw the boy was watching her every move. The candy lay untouched.

She sat at the table and scribbled quickly upon the paper. Folding it, she handed it to the boy and looked him in the eye. "*Tomar* Cross McCree."

The boy giggled at her poor accent, and quite possibly at her choice of words, but he bobbed his head. He looked at the candy. She took it up, held it out to him upon her opened palm. He snatched it and lit out on a run, his brown bare feet flying.

Lilly closed the door and hurriedly washed and changed into a fresh dress. She wondered if Cross McCree wanted to buy her sheep . . . or if he intended to tell her there had been a mistake and the sheep were not hers after all.

She coiled her hair into a proper chignon, thinking of what Delores had said, that Lilly had to look out for herself now.

She gazed into the mirror and tried for a strong, confident expression. And then she thought that surely Cross McCree would not have come twice to her door just to tell her there had been a mistake with the sheep.

Duffy felt well enough to join Cross in going to see Lilly Blackwell. "I want to give the lady my condolences," he said.

"You just like a feminine face," Cross told him.

"Aye, that, too," the Duff admitted, his grin cutting through his white beard and mustache. With his arm in a sling to protect his shoulder, he walked along slightly bent and stiff. "And I'm damn tired of bed," he muttered.

Cross would rather have seen the woman alone and was mildly annoyed at the Duff for coming, though he didn't scrutinize his feelings.

It didn't matter if the Duff came or not, Cross told himself. He would still have a look at the woman and conclude his business with her. That he wanted to see her did not seem strange to him; Cross enjoyed studying objects of this world—studying a woman was the same as studying a coyote to him. Though perhaps a woman was more pleasurable to look at, he allowed.

Cross had allowed the boy to come, too, and he ran ahead of them now, eager to again see the Americano lady with the skin the color of goat's milk, which was his own description. The boy was enthralled by the Anglo woman, the first he had ever seen up close.

"She speaks gringo Spanish," he said derisively, "but she gave me candy."

Señora Gallegos was washing clothes in two leaky tubs, her loose skin swaying on her skinny arms. She greeted them eagerly and offered in Spanish, "The *señora* is up and about now." Wiping her hands quickly on her apron, she made it her business to escort them to the woman's door and to knock.

Cross remembered to slip off his hat. Almost immediately the door was flung open, and Lilly Blackwell stood there. Her eyes dominated her pale face and were green as mountain grass. Quickly her gaze passed from the boy to the Duff and then settled on Cross.

"There are guests for you, Señora Blackwell," the old woman said.

"Cross McCree," Henri said proudly and pointed with a little flourish.

The Americano woman's eyes flitted to the boy, and she smiled softly at him. She looked at the old woman. "Thank you, Mrs. Gallegos."

And then her big green eyes rose up to Cross.

"Hello, Mr. McCree. I've been told you have wanted to see me." Her voice was the same, soft and of a distinctively feminine tone, with the strong drawl of the Southern states. Yet, she was cool, distant, showing absolutely no memory of their previous meetings.

"Yes, *señora*." He bowed stiffly in the Spanish fashion and gestured to Duffy. "Allow me to introduce my friend, Duffy Campbell."

"How do you do?" she said properly and extended her hand.

Duffy took her hand and did a deep bow over it with all the savoir faire nonchalance of royalty. "My pleasure, madam. Allow me to offer my condolences upon your recent loss."

The amusement that had slipped upon her face vanished. "Thank you," she whispered, and then more forcefully, "I am glad to see you, Mr. Campbell, because I, too, wish words with you. Please come inside."

She led the way. Cross's eyes followed the line of her back down to the edge of her swaying skirts. Her gown was of a striped blue fabric, fine and elegant such as Don Antonio's wife might wear. The Anglo woman stood out in the shabby room like a flower in a dry arroyo, he thought.

She bade them sit in the only two chairs at the table. Cross turned his and straddled it, tossed his hat on the table. Duffy sat properly, and gingerly, because the chair was none too stout and his shoulder pained him. He balanced his hat on his bent knee. The boy faded into the shadows near the hearth.

Cross realized then that she was not a beauty, as had been his impression that first time he had seen her. Her nose was too big and straight, her lips too thin, and her skin too devoid of color for her to be called beautiful. Her hair pulled back so starkly simply emphasized these features. Her eyes came close to lovely, but her movements were what drew a man's attention. She moved with the grace and elegant womanliness that made a man feel all male.

The woman unfolded a piece of paper, placed it on the table and slid it across to the Duff. Cross's gaze lingered on her pale, slender fingers, watched as she withdrew them and gracefully clasped them in front of her.

"Just before his death, my husband spoke of a herd of sheep he had won," she said in her drawling accent. "Your name is on this paper, Mr. Campbell. Did he in fact win these sheep from you?"

"Aye, that he did, madam."

"Was it a fair hand, sir, or do you have cause to believe yourself cheated?"

She threw the question out there, bold and square and honest, with her gaze skewered on Duffy.

The Duff drew himself up and said, "It was a fair hand, Mrs. Blackwell. I assure ye of that. I have, as did your husband, a certain skill with cards, and I know when I'm bein' cheated. I will also tell ye that Pool Puckett's accusation against your husband at the time was false. Ye have no reason to feel ashamed for your husband."

"At the time," the woman murmured, gazing at Duffy for several long seconds. Then she breathed deeply. "Thank you, Mr. Campbell."

"We did not come here to dispute your ownership of the sheep, *señora*," Cross said. "I came to purchase them."

Her gaze came back to him.

"I am prepared to offer you six thousand dollars American money," he said.

She blinked. "That is a goodly sum," she said, speculation in her eyes.

"It is a fair sum, and it is the amount of money at stake in the game your husband won."

She nodded thoughtfully and moved her hands together. Cross found his gaze drawn to them again, and the hair on the back of his neck prickled.

"I owe you a debt of gratitude, Mr. McCree," she said. "You revenged the killin' of my husband."

"I was not so much revenging the killing of your husband, *señora,* as trying to stop a crazed killer," Cross said.

She gazed at him a moment, her eyes wide and green and pained. Then she took a small step backward and seemed to draw inside herself. Silence reigned as they all waited, and Cross wasn't certain for what. He could discern nothing from the woman's expression, beyond the fact that she was considering, and he didn't know why she would consider so deeply. She had to sell her sheep, and he had made her a good offer. He had expected an immediate yes, maybe even a grateful one.

"Perhaps you would like to speak to someone to advise you on the price I am offering, *señora,*" he suggested, a little piqued.

Her gaze came to his. "Your offer is perfectly acceptable, Mr. McCree."

Cross thought it would be settled then, but still she hesitated and did not say she would sell.

After a moment she said, "Where are these sheep? Surely I am incurrin' debt to someone for their keep," and she cast a questioning look from Cross to Duffy.

"The sheep are pastured on the ranch land of Don Antonio Baca," Cross said, bringing her gaze back to his. "The fee will be small, and I will take care of it."

She studied him a moment longer and then said, "I would very much like to see these sheep before I sell them."

Cross McCree came for her in a buggy that was small but showy, a one-seater, gleaming black with red and gold accents and black canvas top decorated with a colorful red fringe.

"This is quite a conveyance," Lilly said.

Cross McCree nodded. "It belongs to Don Antonio."

He held out his hand to help her into the seat. Lilly hesitated, shy about touching him. His blue eyes were steady, and there was a hint of laughter there. Feeling foolish, she took his hand. It was strong and callused and warm. Quickly she slipped her hand from his and sat. She looked down and found him looking up at her, his blue eyes bright in his darkly tanned face. She shifted her attention to settling her skirts. Quite suddenly she felt the heat of the day.

This was pure foolishness, she told herself. A sheer waste of her time going out to see these sheep. She didn't know why in the world she hadn't simply sold them to Cross McCree and gotten herself straight down to Señor Montoya's to redeem her passage to St. Louis.

But somehow she wanted to see them, these sheep Tyler had left to her. It wasn't easy to let the sheep go, because they were in a way a tie with Tyler, his offering to her of which he had been so hopeful and proud.

And they were hers, all hers. Lilly had never in her life owned anything of such substance as five thousand sheep.

Cross McCree knocked his hat against the canvas top as he was getting in, and he plopped heavily onto the seat beside her. Lilly yanked her skirt out of his way just in time, though it fell back against his thigh when she let it go, for the seat was small. She would have to take care in order for their arms not to touch. Cross McCree fumbled with the reins and looked as out of place in the fancy, delicate buggy as Lilly felt riding there beside him.

"I don't imagine you spend a lot of time in a buggy, Mr. McCree." Lilly hid a smile.

"I don't...but I can imagine you have." His voice was low and soft and speculative and his eyes reflected the same.

Lilly turned her eyes forward. "I did once."

Cross McCree snapped the reins and they were off.

The little black-and-white dog, Pan, rode at their feet, leaning against his master's leg. The boy, Henrique, had come along, too, and he rode in the small flat space behind the seat. The path they traveled out of town was so rough Lilly was afraid the boy would bounce out, but Cross McCree assured her the boy was no fool and would hang on. For the first half hour, until she became convinced, Lilly kept checking to make certain the boy did just that.

She felt annoyed at Mr. McCree for paying the child so little regard. He appeared to pay more attention to his dog than to his son. While the boy was clothed in near rags and did not have even sandals, the man was the same as the first time Lilly had laid eyes on him, in the same serape and the same hat and tall, scuffed though fine leather boots. Once, when his serape parted, she saw an elaborate bone-handled knife at his belt.

Lilly turned from it and looked at the wide open land. Above stretched a perfectly clear blue sky. The eye could see for miles over the land that rolled away to the south and jutted up in rocky hills and abutments to the north. A grand land, Tyler had called it when they had first arrived, and Lilly thought how fitting the term. It was grand, awesome in its bigness.

It was also hard and bare of woodland, save the scrubby piñon and sticky brush. The grass grew in tufts, sometimes thick as pasture back home, and sometimes sparse as it was along the ocean beach. The sun bore down mercilessly, and Lilly was glad for the shade of both her satin bonnet and the buggy's top.

For an instant it seemed strange and totally wrong that the sun should still shine and the wind still blow and Lilly ride along in a buggy, while Tyler lay dead back in the cemetery. And for that same instant she had the odd sensation of being in a bad dream and that if only she could awaken, she would find herself home in Pasquotank County.

Cross McCree was a man of few words, though he did not appear sulky or disagreeable, only a quiet man who was comfortable in his silence. After finding his pale blue eyes regarding her intently each time she looked his way, Lilly took care to keep her eyes averted. She was uncomfortable with the feelings he brought to her, and she would not have him get the wrong impression. She was, after all, a lady of good breeding, a woman widowed only days, who most certainly did not have interest in a married man—or a man who simply was living with a woman, as many of the Anglo men did with the Mexican women.

She found herself repeatedly wondering about him, however. She wondered at his medium brown hair and dark skin and his blue eyes and his English, which he spoke with the trace of a Spanish accent. Perhaps he was the misbegotten son of a rich New Mexican—such as this Don Antonio. There were many among the upper classes, the *ricos,* who were direct descendants of creole Spanish who bore the traits of fairer hair and blue eyes.

Cross McCree was not the only one to study her. The boy did, too. Once he leaned so close to her that she bumped her bonnet askew on his chest when she turned her head.

Cross McCree laughed. "He is fascinated by you," he said. His blue eyes swept her from head to toe in a manner that brought heat to her cheeks. "He has never been so close to an Anglo woman."

"Oh."

She jerked her face forward and thought how she must appear to the boy. Lilly, in the only dress she owned that could remotely be considered fitting for a widow—a gray-blue day gown—over three petticoats, her high-topped kid boots and her straw sunbonnet with the flowing ribbons, most definitely was not Mexican.

And then Cross McCree added in a low voice, "Neither have I."

Their eyes met again. Lilly looked away quickly.

She felt Cross McCree's eyes upon her. His interest was of the same sort as the boy's—simply that of seeing something peculiar. The thought was a disappointment and brought annoyance.

The path they took across the rough land was little more than an animal track, and the only other person they came upon was an old man on a tiny burro. For all the talk of this being a country of sheep, Lilly did not see any, though she did see a band of funny looking goats with long hair.

Just when Lilly was wondering if they would have to travel halfway to St. Louis to see her sheep, Cross McCree turned the buggy through a narrow pass between small hills, and they came out into a valley spread with a white, lumpy mass. The dog at their feet gave out an excited yip.

Lilly stared. The mass ebbed and flowed over the land, like a big, billowy cloud before the sun. Closer and she began to see the individual critters—and they did not look like sheep to her. They looked like the goats she had seen earlier, only much more scrawny.

Cross McCree cast a wave to a lone shepherd sitting on a hill far across the immense flock, but he didn't head in the man's direction. He directed the buggy into the edge of the herd, causing the critters to flee. They did a funny scurrying hop and let out frightened bleats. The boy leaned over Mr. McCree's shoulder and spoke excitedly, and Mr. McCree answered fluidly in Spanish. The boy jumped from the slowly moving buggy, and the dog followed.

Cross McCree pulled the horse to a stop and wrapped the reins around the brake.

Lilly peered at the animals. "They look like goats," Lilly said. They milled about, heads down, grazing. They were small and thin, with almost no hair and horns that curved backward.

"These are churros," Mr. McCree said. He alighted, rounded the horse and lifted his hand to Lilly.

Eagerly she took his hand, gathered her skirts and hopped down beside him. Squinting even in the shade of her hat, she gazed out at the animals. "Are these five thousand sheep?"

"This is about fifteen hundred of them," Cross McCree said with a chuckle. "We cannot keep all ten thousand head together. We break them up onto bands spread from here up the valley to near the Taos Pueblos."

"Ten thousand?" Lilly cast him a quizzical glance.

His gaze went out across the herd. "Duffy Campbell and I were partners. Half of the herd—the sheep he lost to your husband—was his. The other half are mine." His eyes came back to hers; they were unreadable.

Lilly said, "I see," and turned her gaze again to the sheep. She felt a tugging of guilt. No doubt he was supremely disappointed to have lost his friend's partnership. Yet, she had gotten the sheep in fair payment that no one disputed.

Out of the corner of her eye she saw him pull a thin long cigar and single match from beneath his serape. He tucked the cigar between his lips and struck the match on his boot heel, touched the flame to the cigar. His movements were slow and deliberate, even his inhaling, as if savoring each minute action.

The boy came from the herd, tugging a sheep by the horns. The dog, tongue lolling, urged the animal from the opposite side, until the two brought it to Lilly. Cross McCree knelt and held the animal fast.

"One of your ewes, *señora*," he said around the cigar clamped in his teeth.

The little animal's eyes were wide with fear. Its tail twitched rapidly, and it tried to lunge away. Cross McCree stroked its neck and spoke softly.

Lilly felt a flood of wonder and tenderness. She dropped to her knees and ran a hand down the ewe's back. "But aren't sheep supposed to have wool?" she asked, perplexed.

He laughed aloud. "These sheep were recently shorn," he said. "In any case, churros are not great wool producers, not like sheep from your American states. Their hair grows thinner and more shaggy. They are mainly meat animals."

Lilly noticed his use of the term "your American States." She rose, and he let the ewe go, and it bounded off to rejoin the herd. The boy and dog ran again into the herd, chasing the bleating animals.

Lilly watched them, and then looked out across the mass. Slowly she began to walk toward them, watching them graze and nuzzle each other. Timid little creatures they were but adorable, with their big blue-brown eyes and soft bodies. Their legs were thin, their feet tiny.

They were hers, she thought, sweeping the mass with her gaze. Tyler had won them fair and square, and now they belonged to her.

Cross McCree strolled up to join her. "Have you seen enough?"

Lilly shook her head. "No," she said and peered up at him beneath the broad brim of her hat. "I would like to see the rest. Please, if it would not be too far and you have the time."

He looked curious, but then he said, "We can see another herd a couple of miles up the valley."

As they traveled, Cross McCree explained how the sheep possessed a strong herding instinct, which compelled them to stay together, and therefore even a band of such a size was easily cared for by a single *pastor* and two or three dogs. By day the sheep were slowly moved along on the grass, fast enough so that they did not destroy it but slowly enough for them to eat leisurely. Each night after they were watered, the sheep were content to bed down; the *pastor*, carrying a torch, would walk around the perimeter of the herd, bunching them together, where they would stay all night, as long as they were not disturbed. In the morning the process would start again.

In this part of the world, the animals had one breeding season—September—and they lambed some five months later. They were shorn in the early spring, as much for their health as for their wool, for their quality of wool did not equal that of the types of sheep grown in the American states, so the export value on it was low. Still, they were a hearty species that thrived in the dry, rocky terrain of the Southwest and provided good meat and adequate wool for the people.

And they were *hers,* Lilly kept thinking.

It was not easy, riding across the tufts of grass and rocky ground in the light buggy. A number of times Cross wished for his horse. He tried to picture Lilly Blackwell upon a horse, she with that gaudy beribboned bonnet and voluminous skirts, balanced up on a saddle. He found the image laughable.

He showed her the second band of sheep, and she asked to see the third. At each stop she walked out among the sheep, for no good reason that Cross could determine. The animals scattered in front of her, of course, and would not let her touch them, but she went anyway, a strange apparition in that soft gray dress and the wide bonnet with the colorful ribbons that fluttered out behind her, flashing in the sun.

At the third band, the boy, with barely a backward glance at Cross, raced out after her, and Pan chased after the boy. Cross drove the buggy around south of the herd and over to Jesus, the *pastor.* He and Jesus sat on the back of the buggy in the shade of its fringed top. Cross shared one of his panatelas with the old shepherd, who was elaborate in his appreciation and caressed the thin cigar lovingly with his bony, leathery fingers before finally tucking it into his mouth. Such fine cigars were a rarity in his poor world.

Cross lit both their smokes and thought how it would behoove him to stock up enough of the panatelas to share with his herders. Jesus would be going. He was of untold years, but he was sturdy and a master herdsman. Using few words, the old man told Cross that the watering holes were already growing dry, and that a panther had killed an old ewe, but the next time the panther had come Jesus had been ready. He tapped his old musket, a relic having belonged to the old man's father.

In companionable silence Cross and the old man sat watching the herd, the dogs, the boy and the woman.

"Madonna," Jesus said, his tone close to reverence.

Cross glanced at the old man, then back at the woman. He said, "Anglo *mujer*," which was woman.

The old man gave a gap-toothed grin, and his dark eyes sparkled in his wrinkled skin. "*Sí—muchísima mujer.*"

Cross gave a reluctant half grin. She was very much a woman, he silently agreed. A woman who had cajoled him into spending the entire afternoon and evening escorting her all over the countryside, all in order for her to see sheep that she had no need of seeing. He didn't know who he was most irritated at—her for cajoling, or himself for allowing it.

Cross's experience with Anglo men was limited, and his experience with Anglo women all but nonexistent. In fact, he thought ruefully, it could be said that his experience with women in general was of a restricted nature.

Cross had grown up with his father and various other mountain men and a goodly number of Indians. Except for his relationship with Marquita, any other contact with women had been brief. He came in contact with the females during visiting and fiestas, but he participated in little of either, for crowds tended to give him a choking feeling. He'd had a number of encounters with whores and had enjoyed the flirtatious and innocent attentions of a couple of Indian maidens. Those Anglo women he had seen at the forts had been from a distance. He had not approached any of them, for to do so might have gotten him shot, or at least in a hell of a fight. A Mexican man, which he was taken for half the time because of his skin and manner of dress, or an Indian man, which he technically was by half, were not to mingle with an Anglo woman. It was an unwritten code that had to do with the nameless centuries-old conflict between the races, and it made as much sense as the unwritten code that accepted, partially at least, an Anglo man taking a Mexican or Indian bride.

Cross did not concern himself with the prejudices of other men; men were men, had been foolish from the beginning of the world and were slow to change. He lived as he pleased and tried to keep peace whenever possible. When it wasn't possible, he defended himself. At those times he had seen Anglo women, he had not considered them interesting enough to break his peace.

Lilly Blackwell, however, was very interesting.

To begin with, she wore more clothes than any female he had ever seen, even those few Anglo women. He wondered at that. So many clothes did not seem practical or comfortable. She was also the first female he had ever seen with skin the color of goat's milk, borrowing the boy's description, which was quite apt. It had been Cross's experience that even the skin of Mexican and Indian females could be shades lighter where it did not see the sun. He held a powerful wondering of what Lilly Blackwell's skin would look like beneath the layers of fabric that covered her from her neck to her toes.

And then there were her eyes—green—the color of the grass that grew high up on the mountains around lakes there.

He had to smile to himself. Those eyes were the one thing she had in common with every other woman he'd ever known. With her eyes, when she chose, she could beguile a man.

She was plenty curious, too, like all women. But unlike the other women with whom he had conversed and who always questioned him about which food he liked and if he found them pretty and if he would be returning soon, this woman asked him numerous questions about the habits of the sheep, how he had gotten so many and what he planned to do with them.

"I've heard there is great profit on sheep in California," she had said, when he'd told her that was where he meant to take the sheep. "How much do you think you will get for them?"

"Maybe seven or eight dollars apiece," he had answered. "Maybe more, or maybe not so much. It will depend on the market conditions when I get there. There are many ahead of me, at least four big herds last year, and another of six thousand head that left only a month ago."

"How far—to California?" she asked.

"Depends on the route taken. It is under a thousand miles straight across, but going north the way I plan and to the goldfields, it'll be over a thousand miles. It won't all be desert that way, though."

His eyes touched hers, then she looked away. This woman did not look at him, as other women did, either with open friendliness or with admiration and wanting. She hid her eyes, and the feelings behind them.

She was a widow of only three days, he thought. And she was a refined Americano.

She was quiet for many minutes, and then she said, "You will buy these five thousand sheep from me for six thousand dollars... and you will sell them for thirty-five thousand in California. That is quite a profit."

This time her green eyes regarded him openly.

"Yes." He nodded slowly. "And it is quite a risky trip, too."

He brought his thoughts back to the present as he watched her coming toward him from the sheep—the woman, the boy and the dog. The sheep parted and gave her wide berth. She paused and looked down, and immediately the boy bent to the edge of her skirts—freeing them from a cactus, no doubt. Her gown was more suited to a fancy Eastern drawing room than to the rough land of the Territory. He wasn't certain what a fancy Eastern drawing room would look like, but he had seen Don Antonio's parlor, and he imagined a drawing room as even more elegant.

Cross stubbed the fire from what remained of his cigar and gave the stub to Jesus, who would finish it later. Pan, his tongue lolling, came up and went directly underneath the shade of the buggy. The boy, sweating but smiling, came and flopped down with the dog. The woman came more slowly.

She was breathing hard, and wisps of hair had loosened and hung around her face that was flushed and damp with sweat. Cross stared at her. She was no longer the plain woman of before, but one vibrant and beautiful.

Jesus hopped from the wagon, and Cross alighted, too. Jesus immediately went to giving the woman little bows. *"Buenos días, señora."*

Politely returning the greeting, she smiled and nodded at the old man and sank down on the buggy where Cross and Jesus had just gotten up. From somewhere she'd gotten a lacy handkerchief and was patting it to her face. Her eyes came around and lit on Cross's, skittered away as they had before.

He watched the flush deepen on her face, and he wondered why she did not unbutton her high collar. He thought she could darn well faint from heat.

Cross introduced her to Jesus, speaking in both Spanish and English, and then he motioned for Jesus to hand over the water bag. He held it out to the woman.

"Perhaps you would like some water, *señora.*"

She looked at the bag uncertainly. Undoubtedly she'd seen few woven wool water bags, and this one was worn, considerably dirty from months of use. She eyed the mouthpiece as she would a dead snake and shook her head. "Thank you, though."

Cross uncorked the end, placed it to his mouth and drank deeply. Deliberately he wiped his mouth with his sleeve. The woman watched him.

The boy raised up from beneath the wagon and asked for water. Cross gave him the bag, and the boy drank eagerly, then squirted water into Pan's mouth. Cross again took the bag and drank. Out of the corner of his eye he saw the woman looking at the bag, and he could almost see her dry swallow.

"I believe I could do with a bit of water, Mr. McCree," she said softly.

Slowly she took the bag, placed it gingerly to her lips and drank. Finished, she patted her lips with her handkerchief.

"We need to be heading back now," Cross said in a manner that meant to tell the woman he wasn't taking her to see any more sheep.

The sun was far to the west, and the temperature dropped with the brisk breeze. Lilly welcomed it, enjoyed the feel of it on her damp face.

She thought of the sheep.

Silly, but she dreaded selling them. And suddenly six thousand dollars looked very small. How long would it last her back in Pasquotank County? She would need to find a place to live, to keep herself. She could perhaps buy a small cottage, one down in Cotter's Mills, where dock laborers and mill hands lived. It would surprise many, but so would have a few of the places she and Tyler had been forced to live in the past years.

She did mental figuring, and with buying a cottage and saving two thousand for emergencies and old age, six thousand dollars was not going to last long.

She would need to get a job, of course, and the specter of the seamstress again came to mind. Funny how she'd often suggested working as a seamstress to Tyler, and she would have done it gladly. She would have swallowed her pride for Tyler's welfare—indeed, she had done so on many an occasion—but when there was only herself to consider, she wasn't as eager. She thought of being a governess, or perhaps a housekeeper, but the results were the same: she would be entering as a servant the homes where once she had been a guest.

A thought whispered across her mind: in California the sheep would be worth thirty-five thousand dollars. Maybe more.

It was Tyler's voice, she thought, and the idea lodged in her mind like a piece of one of his lemon drops gone sticky.

The buggy took a good jolt, and Lilly turned to check the boy. He was dozing, and his hold upon the back of the seat appeared mighty precarious.

"Stop," she ordered Mr. McCree. "Your son's about to fall out."

She tugged on the boy, telling him to come up into the seat. He looked hesitantly at Cross McCree, who was scowling. Then the man took hold of the boy and practically lifted him over into the seat.

Lilly scooted to make room and put her arm around the boy, who slumped against her, exhausted.

When Cross McCree didn't continue on, she looked up at him.

"The boy is not my son," he said. "He is one of Padre Domingo's orphans. He wanted to come with the great Americano lady... and it was best that you did not ride out with me alone."

Lilly felt heat on her cheeks. "I see," she said.

Cross McCree shook the reins, and they again started off. The boy was warm and heavy against Lilly's side. She felt better knowing that Cross McCree was not the poor father she had assumed him. Though she still thought him careless about the boy.

The boy was an orphan, like herself, she thought.

There would be no one for her back in Pasquotank County. Her only living relatives were her cousins, Arden and Robert. And they would be of little help to her when she went back. Robert was just as tight as Uncle Raymond had been. Lilly had never liked Arden and Robert, anyway.

There was Mammy Ethnee, of course, and Lilly longed to see her. But Mammy Ethnee couldn't help Lilly, except with advice. Mammy Ethnee could be long on advice, which was worth a lot but not in a way that could pay for keep.

Surely her best friend, Mary Kate Jennings, would still be her friend, but Mary Kate had her own family and was very prominent in society. A dwindling six thousand dollars would not allow Lilly entrance to that world any longer. She'd come very far from that world, she thought with a deep sigh.

Of course, there was a good chance that she would marry again and to a man who would give her security, if not great wealth, taking care of her troubles. But that prospect held about as much appeal as a dead skunk.

All of her life had been governed by men—first by Uncle Raymond and then by Tyler. Now she was free. Now she did not have to depend upon a man's generosity, or lack of it, but her own strength and cunning.

If she had been a man, she thought, she would do as Cross McCree was doing and take the sheep to California for a big profit. It was only because she was a woman that she would have to settle for six thousand dollars. And that fact brought a burning rebellion into her chest.

Thirty-five thousand dollars would not only see her home to Pasquotank County but it would be an investment to keep her in the style she once knew. For thirty-five thousand dollars she could buy into a profitable business, like Pritchard's Lumber and Pine Tar Mills or Simmons Shipping, and slip back into her place in Pasquotank County.

Thirty-five thousand dollars would also go a long way to buying back Cypress Crossing, which was what she wanted more than anything in the world.

She could have that, if she took the sheep to California.

Chapter Seven

Lilly Blackwell wanted to partner with him in taking the sheep to California. For doing so she would share in all expenses and, because he would be bearing the bigger burden of the work involved, she would give him five percent of whatever her sheep sold for there. Of course, she could hire someone to do it for her, but since the sheep were already under his care, and he had already planned to take them, the practical thing was for them to go together.

Her green eyes were quite satisfied with it all.

And her manner brought irritation crawling all over Cross. She acted as if whatever she chose to do was acceptable.

He had pulled the buggy to a stop at the boarding house. The sun was dipping below the horizon, and the shadows were long in the narrow street. The woman sat looking at him. The boy, still lying against her, started to stir.

Maybe he had expected this ever since she had started questioning him closely about the sheep and the price he would get for them in California. In any case, her proposition came only as a mild surprise. He didn't like it, because he'd been the one to gather these sheep with backbreaking work in the first place, while Tyler Blackwell had come by them with no more than the turn of a card. Besides, Cross stood to make a good profit if Lilly Blackwell would simply sell him the sheep, which made him feel vaguely guilty of greed and further annoyed with the woman because of it.

He didn't doubt her determination. No matter the worry in her eyes or the tremor of her chin, the woman had hold of a rare opportunity, and she wasn't about to let go. He supposed he had to admire her gumption. And he further supposed that if he didn't agree to her proposal, she would find someone else to take her sheep, and he'd be out any profit at all.

His inclination was to leave her to find someone else and be damned. But guilt had him here, too, for she was a woman alone, and men with knowledge enough for taking sheep to California were few, and honest men who wouldn't take every fleece she owned fewer still.

He said suddenly, "I'll do it for ten percent."

Their eyes dueled for a moment, but he held his ground. Green eyes or no, he knew his worth.

He said, "If you would like to look around for someone else . . ."

"No. Of course not. Ten percent, then."

For long seconds the two of them regarded each other. Her green eyes reflected the unnamed and vaguely uncomfortable questions Cross felt swirling within himself. Questions that had nothing to do with sheep.

Cross said, "I've hired the herders, and they will receive half pay at the start of the trip, the balance at the end, after the sale of the sheep. I will give you an accounting for all equipment and stores, and you will reimburse me your share. Is this acceptable?"

"Yes."

He gave a terse nod, alighted and came around to help her down. Her skirts got tangled, and she practically fell from the seat and into his arms. She righted herself, stood squarely, removed her dainty lace gloves and extended her hand.

"We have a bargain, then, Mr. McCree."

After a moment's surprise, Cross took her hand. It was small and soft, but she gripped firmly.

She suggested they go to her room for paper to draw up the deal. He saw no need for a deal on paper, but he didn't say so. He told the boy to stay to watch the dog and the rig. The woman whirled back around, dug into her skirt, pulled out something and handed it to the boy. It was candy, Cross saw.

"*Gracias,*" the boy said with a shy smile.

"You're welcome," the woman said and sailed away, leaving Cross to follow in her wake.

Cross entered the room behind her and left the door wide open. She swept her hat from her head, tossed it atop the table, where it floated like a water lily arrayed with ribbons. Her hair came loose somewhat, falling like silken strands.

"Would you light the lamp?" she asked over her shoulder.

He did so, as she brought paper, ink and pen from a box. She sat to write, without asking Cross if he would prefer to do it. Perhaps she thought he couldn't. He turned the remaining chair and sat straddling it.

She wrote in a fine, flowing hand. The women Cross knew who could write were few, and he watched with fascination. His gaze strayed to the top of her head. Her hair was rich, shiny brown. His hand itched to touch it.

She made one copy for him and one for herself, all proper, then signed each paper and handed the pen to Cross. Her eyes were dark in the lamplight. He read what she had written, dipped the pen and signed. He felt her eyes upon him.

He folded his copy and slowly rose. She stood more quickly.

"Thank you, Mr. McCree. Now, I will need to know when to be ready to leave, and I would appreciate it if you could recommend a livery where I could purchase a wagon and team. I won't need a big wagon—just enough for my trunks and myself.'' She gestured toward the two trunks sitting against the wall.

Cross stared at her. That she intended to go, too, had not entered his mind. Not a woman such as she. He'd assumed she would wait in Santa Fe for his return.

He shook his head. ''I agreed to take your sheep, *señora*—not you.''

She stared at him openmouthed.

''I will take your sheep and bring your money back in a bank note, or I will send it. Much business is conducted in this manner between here and California.''

''Oh, I realize that, Mr. McCree,'' she said quickly, her expression apologetic. ''I was not for one moment castin' aspersions upon your character. I didn't mean to offend you in any way.'' She folded her hands primly in front of her, brought her eyes to his and spoke in that soft drawling way that she had. ''However, sir, the sheep are mine, and it is prudent for me to go along with my investment. That way I am on the scene to receive payment, with which I can book immediate passage on a ship for the East Coast. So, you see, it is more practical all the way around that I go.''

Her use of the words *aspersions* and *investment* echoed in his mind. He wasn't certain he knew what aspersions meant. He regarded her. She appeared soft and melding, even somewhat humble, but like the lowly little burro, there was a great stubbornness in this woman.

''If that is what you prefer, you could book passage with one of the companies of freighters going out and await our arrival. I think you would find that much more comfortable.'' He showed her that he could speak as well as she did.

''Yes,'' she said, ''I could do that, but I prefer not to.''

She *preferred!* She faced him calmly, and he sensed her digging in her heels. *Damn little burro.*

"This trip will not be a buggy ride on a sunny day, *señora,*" Cross said. "And it won't be the same as travelin' on a wagon train with other women and family folk around you. This is driving sheep, and sheep walk slow. We will travel every day, rain or shine, and it could take us as much as six months. We are likely to come upon Indians, who would be most interested in you. And you would be the only woman among thirteen men. I trust you understand what I am saying on both counts. A sheep drive is not a place for a woman."

He let his gaze rest boldly on her, on the swells of her breasts and the tuck of her waist. He'd hate to see what Indians or bandits might do to such a woman as she.

"I traveled under similar circumstances to come here from St. Louis, Mr. McCree," she said softly, her eyes refusing fear. "I came out here through not only rain but through ice and snow, and we were always under the threat of Indians and bandits."

"You had a husband to accompany you then, *señora.*"

"No matter whether I travel with a train or with the herd, I will be alone, Mr. McCree. And I will be traveling through rain, over mountains and across deserts. Many women have done so, alone, and managed quite well."

"And many of them—with or without husbands—have died…or been taken by the Indians. You have heard of these women, haven't you?"

She inclined her head. "I've heard. I don't believe this has stopped the women comin' after them, and I don't see why it should stop me." She gazed at him with the placidness of a burro that had planted her feet and wouldn't be budged.

Cross looked at her, once more thoroughly, purposely and boldly running his gaze from her head to her toes and back again. When his eyes once more looked at her face, he was rewarded by seeing her blushing furiously.

"*Señora,* you are not at all like the women who have made the trek to California," he said bluntly. "My first concern is seein' we get every head of sheep we can to California. I cannot allow you to slow us down, nor can I be bothered with seein' to your safety and comfort a hundred times a day."

Her chin came up, and her eyes blazed. "I am perfectly understandin' of that, Mr. McCree. That is my first concern, as well. I did not hire you to take my sheep—I went in partners with you." She waved the paper. "I realize I know next to nothing about sheep or drivin' them, but I want to do what I can in this endeavor."

At that he smiled grimly. "You do know you may make far less than thirty-five thousand for your sheep?" he said, feeling the need to clarify that point.

In that deceptively soft voice she said, "I was married to a gambler, Mr. McCree. I understand such risks." She lifted her chin. "Now can you please recommend somewhere for me to purchase a team and wagon?"

"Mules," he said, plopping his hat low over his eyes. "A wagon won't be able to make it through some places we will have to go, so we are going on mules. Which means that if you are determined to go, you will be doing so without those trunks." He turned and went to the door, then paused and looked back at her. "You think about everything I have told you. It would be much better for you to simply wait here. But if you're still hell-bent to go the day after tomorrow, be ready at dawn."

He left her stewing on that.

Lilly stood in her doorway and watched him stride away through the courtyard entry. Then she looked downward at the paper still clutched in her hand—the partnership agreement.

Cross McCree's signature was made in a fine hand.

Suddenly she was very tired. With slow movements, she made a fire and set the kettle above it. Her clothes felt scratchy from dried sweat, and she began peeling them off. She had tied Tyler's poke with all of her money, wrapped so it would not jingle, around her waist, and it had been a heavy weight all day. She found that in several places the cord had rubbed her skin raw.

With barely lukewarm water, she stood at the basin to wash. Oh, how she wished for a tub bath. Her last tub bath had been over two months previous, when she and Tyler had been staying at the hotel—before he had lost, on two horse races, the goodly sum of money he had won from the freight drivers, and they had been forced to find cheaper accommodations. Once she had asked Mr. Gallegos for a tub in which to bathe. He had acted as if she had asked for the moon. Tyler had loved tub bathing, too, but he could go to the bathhouse, so he did that and always told Lilly they would get them a tub sometime. Sometime had never come.

The fabric of her wrapper was cool against her skin, and she dabbed rosewater on at her temples and her neck. Her eyes came up and she caught her reflection in the smoky mirror. There would not even be a basin to bathe in on the trail to California, she thought.

Mules, he had said.

Oh, my Lord, how could she manage it—going all the way to California on this drive? She'd never ridden a mule, didn't even know how to ride.

Clutching her wrapper together, with her legs quivering weakly, she slowly backed up and sat on the bed.

Deep in her heart Lilly had always considered the women who traveled out from places east of the Mississippi of heartier stock than herself. She was a woman who had never wanted to come, who adored pretty, clean dresses and pretty, clean shoes and pretty, clean parlors—and pretty, clean tubs. And if she had to go anywhere she would much prefer to do it by train.

For a brief, bittersweet moment, her honeymoon trip to Baltimore fluttered across her mind—she and Tyler, dressed in their best, with servants bringing their cases and the porter pouring them wine.

Then, harshly, the memory of the trip out from St. Louis came to the fore. Tyler had thought having their own wagon and traveling with the freighters would be safer and more comfortable than a stagecoach, where they would have to rub shoulders with all manner of scroungy characters. Lilly had taken several stagecoaches in Texas, and she would just as soon walk any distance as to have to bounce along all day beside a man who sweated whiskey, or eat at the tables set by people who did not know the use of water, either on themselves or their dishes. And she never again wished to share a bed with lice. Also, Tyler had figured the extra money he could pick up in games with the freight drivers would more than make up for the extra time, which it had.

But, however hard and uncomfortable the trip out from St. Louis, Tyler had been with her, his mere presence an effective shield from even more discomforts, such as the big, dirty mule skinner who had kept looking at her as if to drag her off behind a bush any minute. And when Indians had been sighted, there had been the protection of many guns.

The stories she had heard about Indian attacks flashed across her mind, the horrors piling on top of one another while her heartbeat pounded like an Indian tom-tom.

She breathed deeply and turned from those fear-ridden thoughts only to be assailed by a hundred others that crowded and skittered across her mind like the pitiful, frantic sheep she had seen that day.

Her eyes lit upon Tyler's second-best suit still hanging in its place on the wall, and anger came as fierce as a summer storm.

She had never wanted to leave Pasquotank County and the comfortable, genteel life she had known there. She had never wanted to travel from one town to the next, one relative to another, one gambling debt to another, only to end up out here at the end of the world, where bathtubs and stoves were few and paved streets nonexistent. And she darn sure had never wanted to be a widow left alone in a foreign land.

Damn you, Tyler Blackwell.

He had been the cause of her coming out here. And many women who came trekking west probably came for the same reason—because their men led them and needed them, or because their men up and died on them, and they had to do the best by themselves that they could. Which was what Lilly was trying to do.

Those sheep were hers, she thought fiercely. They were her future. She would see to the handling of her own property and governing of her own life. Never, ever again would she willingly turn her life over to the hands of a man.

Her gaze shifted to her trunks. She saw Cross McCree's firm, set jaw as he'd plopped his hat on his head and told her she could not take them.

He thought she didn't fully understand the hardships and dangers of this trip, and she would have to admit that she did not—and she didn't want to, either. If she understood everything, she would not go.

But she was going, she thought, experiencing a sudden rise in conviction. She had to get out of Santa Fe, and any way she went was a long, dangerous journey. The plain truth of it was that she would rather be traveling with Cross McCree—a man she was bone-certain knew the land and how to survive on it—than anyone else.

There, that was the truth of it, which she hadn't been able to tell him. She knew she stood the best chance of survival with Cross McCree, and wasn't that just a pin in the cushion, because here she was dependent once again on a blasted man!

Nevertheless, she would go with *her* sheep to California, see to their sale and catch the first ship bound for back East. By the time winter came, she would be home in Pasquotank County.

Duffy and Cross sat at the table, drinking sweet coffee. Two lanterns atop the sideboard and shelf cast a dull yellow glow around the room. Several moths flapped at the lanterns' glass. Marquita busied herself with cleaning up their meal. Cross munched absently on a rolled tortilla spread with goat cheese. His eyes strayed to Marquita, and he watched her black hair sway down her back. He suddenly wondered what Lilly Blackwell's hair would look like when not caught up in a twist or braid.

"Women are given to changing their minds," Duffy said.

Cross nodded. He had told them what had transpired with Lilly Blackwell, and he'd had enough of talking in the telling. He wanted nothing more but to sit and enjoy the peace of the night. Once he started the sheep up the trail, he would have little of sitting or peace. Especially with the woman coming.

The woman's presence changed certain aspects of the drive. The men would have to take care of where they did their business and the things they said. Maybe not so much what they said, he thought, because most talk would be in Spanish, and Lilly Blackwell didn't understand much Spanish.

The woman should be safe enough from the drovers Cross had hired. Except for one man, all were New Mexican or Navaho breed, men who, no matter their station, were born and bred with a respect for women. That one exception, however, was a man named Uriah Plover, an ex-cavalry man, the only Anglo among them, who knew the country, was handy with a gun and would hold steady in a fight. Because of those reasons and because he'd found his choices of men available for such work to be few, Cross had hired him, not because he liked the man, for he judged Plover a low sort, a man of brute instincts, the sort to take what he wanted to satisfy his appetite. None of that would have affected the company, if the woman had not decided to come.

Damn the woman for complicating things.

"I have found that men change their minds often, as well," Marquita said, bringing a bowl of water to the table.

"I didna' mean to belittle the fair sex, lassie. Now, ye knows I wouldna' do that." He grinned like a fat, happy tomcat. "I only meant that while Señora Blackwell has said she wishes to go on this trek, she may change her mind by tomorrow, after she has thought about it. And if she does not then, I predict she will change her mind and turn around within a week."

Marquita cast him an indulgent smile. "Many women have traveled over the mountains to California. Why should not this woman?"

The Duff stroked his beard. "Ye have a point there, lass. But a woman travelin' with a bunch of men drivin' a herd of stock is ver' different than a woman traveling with men carryin' their families to a new land to make a home. Especially a woman such as Lilly Blackwell."

"Oh? And what such a woman is she?" Marquita said, eyes sparking. "Does she not have two arms and two legs like the rest of us?"

Duffy raised an eyebrow to Cross. Cross chose not to answer.

Marquita told Duffy to take off his shirt so she could change the dressing on his wound. The two of them bantered easily, and their voices crawled over Cross.

"I think I'll go have a smoke," he said, rising.

Pan scrambled to his feet and followed Cross out into the night air. The distant sound of guitar music and voices floated up from a small cantina at the foot of the hill. A baby cried in the house next door. Here and there night birds called.

It was true what Marquita said, he thought, many women had made the journey to California. Although he did not think many women such as Lilly Blackwell had done it.

Marquita's words came back to him: what such a woman was she?

She was an Anglo lady, he thought, unable to come up with anything better. That term meant to him someone of grace and respect but not someone equipped to deal with the raw world. He thought of her hands, pale and slender, soft hands that had seen little of either hard work or the sun. The image of those hands filled his mind, and he felt a rising inside as he imagined those hands touching his chest.

Such indulgences were foolish, he told himself, shutting off the thought.

Maybe he had first had the idea of taking the sheep to California as a grand adventure, but he knew now the seriousness of the task. This trip would mean a great deal to all. To the herders it would mean twice as much as they could hope to earn in six months' time, money with which to purchase extras for their families, and for two of the men at least—Jon and Paco Salazar—it would mean freedom from indenture to Antonio Baca. For Don Antonio's son, Arrio, it meant breaking out on his own, being a man away from his father.

For Cross it would still mean adventure, yes, but it would also mean money for him to start his own hacienda.

Each of them would start on this journey with their hopes and dreams, and along the way they would face grave dangers: swollen rivers, snakes, storms, Indians, desert. Any among them could die before realizing all that they went for.

Lilly Blackwell was no different from the rest of them. She had her reasons for going, too.

He should have instructed her as to her clothing, he thought, cursing himself. He'd been too surprised by her intentions and then too taken up with sparring with her to think of that.

She wouldn't last an entire day. She would discover this to be no easy ride and would turn back for Santa Fe, as well she should.

He found the prospect disappointing, and then realizing this, he straightened himself. The idea of her coming might be intriguing, but that didn't change the foolishness of it.

From where he sat, with Marquita wrapping a fresh cloth around his shoulder, Duffy could just see Cross, a deep black shadow in the thin moonlight. Since Duffy's blunder in gambling away the sheep, things had been strained between him and Cross. Duffy regretted it, but what could not be changed had to be accepted. In any case, his mistake with the sheep was only a part of what separated him from his younger friend. Cross had become a man with a purpose, an ambition that called for determination and diligence. No longer was he content to simply take life as it came, as was Duffy's way.

"This woman, Lilly Blackwell," Marquita said. "Is she pretty?"

"Who is to say what is pretty?" Duffy said. "I myself would have to say that compared to your moonshine, Lilly Blackwell is but a small star." He winked.

She playfully pushed at him. "You are a flatterer," she told him, lapsing into Spanish. Her gaze strayed to Cross. "He is taken with this woman?"

"She is a woman a man would notice," Duffy said, carefully watching her face. "I do not know about anythin' further than that."

He could read nothing in her expression. He thought of the past nights when Cross had bedded down in the back room, on the floor beside Duffy's cot. Duffy hadn't asked him about it; a man's business with a woman was always his own. Still, Duffy wondered. He had long thought Marquita a fair and winsome woman.

Marquita tied the cloth. She had experienced hands. Where they touched his bare skin, he felt tingling. He moved his shoulder, testing. It pained him, more than he thought it should. He did not seem to be healing as fast as he had in years past. He thought how he was nearing fifty.

When Marquita went to turn away, he reached out and grabbed her wrist. She paused but did not immediately turn. He tugged gently.

She slowly faced him, and her eyes told him to keep a certain distance.

"When Cross takes to the trail, will I be welcome to stay?" he asked.

"You may stay…in the back room," she said, pulling her arm away. Yet, her eyes led him to believe there could be more. Then she frowned. "Cross may need you on this trip."

Duffy shook his head and looked down at his cold coffee. "He has little need of me these days, lass."

Things were changing all around Duffy. Cross no longer looked to him for advice and guidance, and there were more and more people streaming into the Territory, into the mountains. And he was growing older. He had the feeling of moving through a narrow, rocky pass, uncertain of what he would find on the other side.

Suddenly Marquita's hand came down upon his shoulder. It was warm. "Cross is a man like any other—he will always need a good friend."

* * *

Cross made coffee by the light of the small fire flickering in the fireplace. He moved quietly, not wanting to awaken Marquita, who still slept in her bed. Pan was not with him—Cross had left him out with Jesus—and Cross was surprised to find he missed the little dog. The few extra supplies Cross would take with him were ready and in a small pile near the door. He would go to the livery, where the horse and mules were stabled, pick up Lilly Blackwell, if she still intended to go, and return here for his things and to make his goodbyes.

There came the breath of a movement, and Duffy appeared. "Why don' ye shut her door?" he whispered and inclined his head toward Marquita's bedroom.

"It squeaks loud enough to wake the dead," Cross whispered in return.

The two of them quietly sat and drank coffee and munched on tortillas and spicy beef left over from the previous night. Leaning their arms on the table, their heads close and speaking in hushed whispers, they discussed the route Cross planned to take following the Rio Grande out of the Taos Pueblos, northward and westward almost to the river's source, where they would head west over the Divide. Cross was very familiar with the country east of the Green River, but had never been beyond. Duffy, on the other hand, had been all the way to the ocean of California, and Cross had been counting on his knowledge of the best routes to take. Now he had to rely on all the Duff could remember to tell him.

Duffy had drawn a map as best he could from memory. He told Cross that the grass should be adequate, providing there had been enough spring rains, until the desert land the other side of the Wasatch Range. Cross was to keep south of the Great Salt Lake to avoid the worst of the desert there, though all the land to the Sierras was dry. The sheep would have to be pushed in order to make certain to cross the Sierras before a possible early snow. "I almost wish I were goin' with ye, lad," the Duff said, shadows in his eyes.

Cross shifted his gaze to the table. He thought about how things had changed between him and the Duff. He wished for an instant to go back to where they had been the past years, to the easy camaraderie of going where the wind and the trap lines took them. He said, "You're welcome, Duff. You know that."

Duffy shook his head. "Aye…and I imagine I'll be along when me arm is in full commission again." Cross looked up to see Duffy's eyes level upon him. "But I find that staying here with Marquita brings me comfort, for now."

The two of them studied each other.

"She is free," Cross said. He felt a tightness in his chest.

"Aye—as she always has been," Duffy said, nodding, and they shared dry, knowing smiles. Indeed Marquita had always had her own mind and done as she pleased. "But what of ye, lad—would I be steppin' in on yer hearth rug?"

Slowly, and a little sadly, Cross shook his head. Then he lifted his gaze to the Duff. "I would not like to see her heartbroken." He meant it as a warning, though he had no idea of how he would back it up.

"It is not my intention to do that," Duffy said very seriously.

They finished their coffee in silence.

When Cross started to rise, Duffy stuck out his big hand. Cross took it, and they shook firmly. Tears glistened in Duffy's eyes. Cross felt a burning in his own.

"I'll go see if the woman is still comin'," he said, "then I'll come back for my things and to tell Marquita goodbye. Fill the water bags for me, okay?"

"Cross McCree has come," Delores said, turning from the opened doorway where she'd been smoking a cigarillo.

She had brought sweet coffee and bread to share. Lilly had packed everything she owned, down to her precious teapot.

Lilly heard the clop of hooves in the alleyway, too, and went to the door beside Delores.

The sound of the hooves stopped, and a moment later Cross McCree appeared through the courtyard entry. He gazed at her and came slowly forward. His expression was devoid of emotion. "*Buenos días,* ladies," he said, mixing the languages.

Delores sent him her normal sensuous smile and bid goodmorning. Lilly said, "I am ready, Mr. McCree."

If she thought to get a reaction, either surprise or admiration, she was disappointed. His gaze raked her from head to toe, and he seemed to find her wanting. Lilly ran a hand over her skirt. She was wearing her wool cloak, for the morning was chilly, and her sturdiest dress, a blue chambray. She had skimmed down to her chemise, pantaloons and one slip underneath. Delores had suggested she do away with all of that, but Lilly wouldn't. She might be going out on a hard trail, but she was a woman and there were proprieties.

She lifted her chin. "I have discarded my trunks, as you said."

His gaze followed her gesture to her things that she had piled on a rug in the middle of the room. She had formed bundles of her clothes and few precious possessions and wrapped them in blankets and tied them with string.

Her trunks and all of Tyler's clothes she had given to Delores. Delores could sell the clothes at the market for a tidy profit, and Lilly was just as glad to see them bring some good to the woman. Delores had proved a great help to her.

Lilly kept Tyler's derringer, thinking that perhaps she might need it, though she knew little how to use it. She also kept his cuff links, because she had bought them for him on their honeymoon and he'd thought enough of them not to pawn them in all these years; they weren't worth very much. And she had kept his favorite deck of cards, too, rescuing them from the discard pile at the last instant. Tyler had taught her to play, and she might need to amuse herself.

Keeping her sturdiest bonnet, she had divided the rest between Delores and Mrs. Gallegos; there was simply no way she could pack them into the bundles. She had also given the two women most of her few dishes, except for her beloved teapot. She could not bear to part with it, especially now that she had lost her mother's earrings. The previous day she'd visited the jeweler to purchase them back, only to be told that he had already sold them and to a gentleman who had taken them south into Mexico. The news had been a sharp blow indeed.

"Let's get loadin'," Cross McCree said.

She followed him out to the alley. There sat three mules and a fine, sturdy-looking line-backed buckskin horse. The buckskin bore a saddle, a very nice saddle, if Lilly was any judge, and elaborate bridle, too. Obviously this was Cross McCree's horse, and just as obviously the mule with the worn black saddle was for Lilly. A second mule was strapped with bundles. The third mule stood patiently waiting with canvas and rope draped across his back.

Cross McCree undid the rope and threw it and the canvas across his shoulder, then stomped back to her room.

Incredulous, Lilly followed, saying, "One mule for all my things?"

"That's right," he replied. With a swift shake he spread the canvas. It was a bag, and he began to stuff her bundles into it. "We'll take what we can."

"I imagine, Mr. McCree, that we will take it *all*," Lilly said. "If it will not fit, I will buy another mule."

"Can't," he said. "We're leavin'."

Lilly looked at Delores, who shrugged at her.

Well, we shall see, Lilly thought and began to sort her bundles and stuff them into another of the canvas bags.

It was amazing how much Cross McCree managed to tie onto the mule. Lilly wondered if the animal would be able to move. When she suggested he put some things on the mule that had but few bundles, he said he couldn't; that mule was his. And in the end Lilly was forced to leave behind two velvet gowns and her crinoline. She insisted Mr. McCree find room for her cherrywood case. It contained not only her sewing notions but her most precious possessions.

"The case must go," she demanded.

"And where do you suppose I put it?" he said, giving a wave of his hand to the heavily laden mule. She had to admit it appeared if she put one more thing on the animal, he would collapse.

"Put it on that other mule," she said.

"That mule will have more loaded on him—my things." His face was set as a rock mountain.

Lilly looked again at the animals. They could remove something of hers, she thought, but as if reading her mind, Cross McCree said, "I'm not unpacking it all for that one case."

Lilly marched over to the mule she would be riding and set it behind the saddle. "There—tie it on."

He did so, with much muttering.

Back in the room, Lilly gazed for one last time into the smoky mirror and adjusted her straw bonnet upon her head, tied the ribbons securely. Her gaze moved to her ears, and she wished fervently for her earrings, for she felt almost naked without them.

Suddenly Delores came behind her. "Here," she said, removing the dangling earrings at her ears. "They are only pewter, but the stone is true turquoise. They light your eyes—and a woman should not be without. They will give you courage.'' She took Lilly's hand and placed the jewelry there.

Lilly slipped the wires through the holes in her ears, then turned her head from side to side and watched the earrings bob gently. They did bring out her eyes—and give her courage, and she whirled with a grateful heart toward the Mexican woman. Delores shrugged away Lilly's appreciation, saying that now she could buy new and finer ones with the money made from all of Lilly's castoffs.

Slipping on leather gloves, Lilly took a last look around the room, resting her eyes for a long moment on the bed where she and Tyler had slept. Then she turned and left, not at all sorry to be doing so.

While Cross McCree made a final check of the animals and their lashing, Lilly made her goodbyes.

Mr. Gallegos stood leaning against the courtyard door frame, one suspender drooping from a pudgy shoulder and a cigarette doing likewise from his lips. Mrs. Gallegos came forward and pressed a bundle into Lilly's hands. Lilly smelled the aromas of tortillas and cheese.

"*¡Válgate Dios!*" the older woman said, wrapping Lilly in a hard, bony hug.

Lilly turned to Delores. Delores, arms folded, simply gave her characteristic sarcastic smile. "*Adiós.*"

"*Adiós, amiga,*" Lilly said. She wished to say more, but sometimes emotions were too deep for words.

Cross McCree held the mule's head for her. After her first unsuccessful attempt at mounting and getting her skirts all tangled on the cherrywood box, he boosted her into the saddle with a firm hand to her bottom. His face held the impatience of a man sorely tried, and that sent starch up Lilly's spine.

He handed her the reins and went to mount his horse, which was in the lead. Without a word he started off. Lilly

was still trying to get her feet into her stirrups and her skirts
tugged down as far as possible over her legs.

Delores stepped over and helped, then smacked the mule
on the hip. "Yaaaa!"

The mule started off at a slow walk. Lilly risked a backward glance, and Delores waved to her. Then the mule broke
into a trot to catch up with his fellows, sending Lilly
bouncing nearly out of the saddle and frantically grasping
for the saddle horn.

They wound their way through the streets, going north.
The sun promised brightness, yet the morning remained
cool. People were awakening and getting about, and a
number of them called in greeting to Cross McCree. Lilly
they stared at.

She rode along on her mule, doing nothing other than
hanging on and letting her mule follow the ones in front of
it. Her direct forward view was the rear of a mule, and if she
lifted her gaze just a might, she could look across the heavily
laden backs of the two mules and see the rear end of Cross
McCree's buff-colored horse with the deep brown tail. She
eyed that tail resentfully. His horse wasn't as tall or regal
looking as the fine horses she'd seen many of back East, but
it was a good-looking animal, obviously well cared for. And
it was a horse. Leave it to the man to ride a horse while he
gave her a mule, she thought.

Once she dropped her reins, and Cross McCree had to
stop and alight to retrieve them for her. He didn't speak, but
the disparaging glance he gave her said it all. Lilly met his
looks with a frank one of her own. She refused to feel re-
morse or shame.

Near the outskirts of the village, Lilly was surprised when
Cross McCree stopped in front of a small, humble house. It
was a house like a hundred others, earth-toned adobe, gap-

ing doorway in the middle, chickens pecking at the dirt in front and a goat chewing on a nearby bush.

Immediately Duffy Campbell, in a white ruffled shirt opened casually at the neck and black trousers, appeared through the open doorway. He was smiling, and Lilly had the feeling this big, robust man smiled a great deal.

He came forward in long, slow strides and gave her his regal bow. His arm remained in a sling and his bow was stiffly made. She thought she had never in her life seen such an abundance of pale hair. "Good day, madam," he said. "I see ye are starting off." He stepped forward, and extended his hand. "Allow me to help ye alight so ye can rest."

But Cross McCree, tying his horse to the rail, said, "There isn't time for her to get down." He disappeared into the house.

Mr. Campbell lifted a bushy eyebrow to her.

"I'm quite fine where I am, thank you, sir." She really didn't want to go through having to get up in the saddle again.

"Ah...and a pretty picture ye are there, madam," he said, his voice thick with amusement. She, too, had to smile.

Cross McCree reappeared, carrying two bags of the sort the old shepherd had carried water in. He went to tie these on to the pack mule, and a woman came from the house, bringing canvas sacks to him.

The woman turned, and Lilly and the woman looked each other over in the covert manner of women who are curious but mannerly enough not to allow it to show. Mr. Campbell drew the woman forward and made the introductions between them in his very aristocratic manner.

"My dear Marquita, allow me to present Madam Lilly Blackwell. Madam, this is Señora Marquita Gonzales de Otero."

The woman lifted her hand to Lilly, and Lilly took it. "Hallo, Señora Blackwell," the woman said. Her shake was firm, her hand the rough one of a woman who worked hard. She was a number of years older than Lilly, but still a beauty, with soft, friendly eyes and hair that was dark and lustrous, finer than Delores's. And she was amply endowed, Lilly thought with a twinge of jealousy.

"Hello, Señora Otero." Lilly returned the greeting. She wondered whether the woman belonged to Mr. Campbell, or Cross McCree. Or perhaps to both.

Then Cross McCree made his goodbyes. Lilly felt an intruder and averted her gaze to the adobe walls, the chickens, the water barrels. Still, she was aware of Mr. McCree hugging Mr. Campbell, and then the woman, and she could not help but feel the closeness between the three and their sorrow at parting. The woman remained within the circle of Cross McCree's embrace as he walked over to his horse. She held him tight, her dark head pressed into the hollow of his shoulder. They murmured something to each other and kissed quickly.

Lilly looked down and adjusted her reins. Tyler came full into her mind. There was no one to bid her goodbye, no one to care for her safety. The deep pit of loneliness opened up to swallow her. Blinking, her gaze strayed to the big Duffy Campbell, and she saw him wiping his eyes. She felt the absurd urge to cry, too.

"You are in good hands, madam," the big man said to her. He stuck out his hand. Slowly, she put hers into his. She took comfort from the compassion she saw in his eyes.

As Cross McCree started them off, Mr. Campbell called, "In a few weeks I may just come after to find ye in the mountains, mon!"

Lilly's mule started off on his own, following the mule in front of him. The hooves echoed, clip-clop, over the hard-packed dirt and sandstone. Within minutes they left the village of Santa Fe behind. Lilly's gaze moved from the mule tail swishing before her upward to the horse's tail and then to the back of the man who led the way.

She was totally dependent on this man, just as she'd always been dependent on Tyler. The thought rankled no end. And then she felt disloyal in thinking that with Cross McCree she felt much more secure.

Chapter Eight

The sun was bright and the air crisp as it can only be in the high country. As long as they walked along slowly, Lilly found the task of staying on the mule quite easy, even relaxing. These times she could look around and almost enjoy the countryside.

She found a certain beauty in the raw vastness. Somehow this Western sky seemed larger than anywhere she'd ever been, and close enough to touch. The land had a majesty about it that made a person feel both small and grand at the same time. It seemed that here, if a body could survive, a body could become one with the universe.

These were fanciful feelings that came to her just as they were leaving Santa Fe, but after that she had little time to enjoy scenery or indulge in poetic thoughts. She was too busy trying to stay in the saddle.

The brisk pace set by Cross McCree caused Lilly to jiggle precariously. And when her mule broke into a trot, such as when going up or down a hill, or when he fell behind and sought to catch up with the others, she was in grave danger of bouncing right off. After futile attempts at trying to stop the mule, or to at least slow him down in order for her to get her breath, she simply gave up and closed her eyes and held on for dear life. There was no need to see where the mule took her, for she had given up any attempt to guide him, indeed none appeared needed. He followed those ahead of him quite readily. She had no doubt that if Cross McCree led them over a cliff, her mule would follow.

They halted once. "You can have time to refresh yourself now, *señora*," Cross McCree told her.

Seeing no stream or pond, Lilly wondered how she was to manage that, and then she got his meaning. She did have to go, so she struggled to get her stiff body off the mule. Again the cherrywood box strapped on behind the saddle proved an obstacle. The next instant Cross McCree was there helping her.

Once on the ground, she found her eyes only inches from his own. His were startling blue against his deeply tanned skin, and the scent of him, of sun and tobacco and man, came to her.

They stared at each other.

"I won't be around the entire trip to help you in and out of the saddle," he said.

"I don't expect you to be," she said and stepped away.

He averted his eyes and tied the mule's reins around a bush, which the mule at once began to eat.

"Keep an eye for snakes," he said as he strode away into the brush.

With some embarrassment and quite a lot of trepidation, Lilly stepped out the opposite way. Her legs wobbled painfully, and her back protested.

Hesitantly, fearful of stepping on a snake at any moment, she entered the brush. She thought of Cross McCree's high-topped, thick leather boots and saw her mistake in not getting sturdier boots for herself. She wore the shoes she had bought for the trip out from St. Louis. They were good, strong shoes, but a snake could easily bite her bare ankle or pierce the thin layer of leather into her foot.

A lizard skittering across a rock scared her, though she bit her tongue on a scream. She told herself she had used the necessary in the open before and knew how to go about it. Returning, her limbs moved more easily, the muscles having relaxed with movement. She held her skirts high and tight; she had come much farther than she had intended.

She reached the horses. Cross McCree was there, propped against a rock. She froze when her eyes met his. Heat flushed her face, and she realized she was still holding up her skirts. She dropped them and focused on smoothing them.

"Would you like some water?" he offered.

He held one of the colorfully woven sacks toward her. This one was cleaner than the one belonging to the shepherd.

She was powerfully thirsty, but she wanted to limit her visits to the bushes, so she shook her head. Seeing him drink deeply, however, she decided to have at least several sips.

"What sort of bag is that?" she asked when she handed it back to him.

"Navaho. Woven wool—from sheep just like yours. It will eventually grow wet, but water can be held all day without leaking. When it does grow wet, the cool is often welcome." He hooked the bag back onto the pack mule.

Lilly returned to her mule, and Cross McCree came to hold the animal's head. Lilly lifted her foot into the stirrup and struggled to pull herself into the saddle. The next instant Cross McCree's hand on her derriere shoved her, and she went flying up into the seat.

Indignant, Lilly looked down at him.

"I could have made it, if you would simply have given me a chance."

"Not in those skirts."

"Mr. McCree, women have been wearing skirts and mountin' horses in them for hundreds of years. If I am awkward, it is simply from lack of practice."

"You will get all the practice you need on this trip, then, *señora.*" He tossed the reins at her and strode away to his horse.

She watched him mount, his body movement strong and lithe, muscles moving as only men can move. She experienced a sharp stab of envy—and of longing, strong and unbidden.

Shocked at herself, she averted her eyes to her mule's charcoal gray neck and quickly grabbed hold of the saddle horn as they again started off at a brisk walk.

As she struggled to stay in the saddle, it occurred to her that Cross McCree could be deliberately making the trip hard on her. The supposition grew to a certainty, bringing determination as strong as the sun above. She would withstand, she thought, for this trip was the beginning of going home and doing so as a woman of means. And she would withstand because she would not give him the satisfaction of seeing her fail.

Tyler had always said she could be one stubborn woman.

The thought, as real as if he were speaking to her, took the edge off her loneliness, and she smiled, imagining Tyler riding a mule beside her, a sight in his buff hat and coat.

They came over a hill. Stretched in a big valley beyond were the first big bands of sheep—clearly two of them stringing out toward the north, separated only by a wide area of grass.

It was a magnificent sight, but Lilly was too sore to appreciate it. It had been nearly three hours since she had gotten on the mule that morning, and it felt like forever. She thought that she would have returned to Santa Fe, but even if she could have found her way, her legs and backside would never have withstood the trip on the mule. She could only thank the Lord that the day remained wonderfully cool. She had slung her cloak back from her shoulders but not taken it off.

Cross McCree headed toward the sheep, trailing the two pack mules, and Lilly's mule trotted after them. A small dog broke away from the edge of the herd and ran to meet them. It was Cross McCree's little Pan. He danced around the feet of the man's horse in eager greeting, so close that Lilly feared he might be trampled.

"Mr. McCree," Lilly called.

He slowed and looked over his shoulder.

"Please stop. I should like to get down and walk awhile." Her voice cracked, and she swallowed, forcing down the urge to cry.

He stopped his horse, the pack mules stopped, and Lilly's mule followed suit, halting as firmly as if his legs had suddenly grown into the ground. Lilly bobbed forward, then settled and gave a great sigh of relief.

Mr. McCree turned his horse and rode back to her. "Any time you want to stop that mule," he said, "all you need to do is pull back on the reins and say so."

Lilly cast him a black look. "How novel an idea, conversin' with a mule. However, apparently the animal doesn't understand English."

"*So* is the Spanish word for *whoa*. *Ho* might be equally effective." His amused grin was annoying.

Not bothering with explaining that several times that morning she had pulled on the reins and said "whoa" and "ho" and even "stop, you damn bugger" to no avail, she drew her leg over the saddle horn and slid to the ground, and with no help. Let the man keep his poor opinion of her; she had to find ease for her aching muscles!

Holding to the saddle, she straightened. Her muscles cried out in both pain and relief. Now that she had finally reached solid ground, she wasn't certain her legs would walk. Mr. McCree told her to just follow the sheep, and with nothing more, he turned his horse, leaving her still hanging on to the saddle, watching him ride away.

Cross left the pack mules with Lorenzo Lopez, one of his two wranglers, and rode up and down the length of the four big bands of sheep. It was a glorious sight that set his heart to pumping—the remuda of horses and mules, the masses of sheep, the men and dogs, all passing over the spring green grasses beneath the bright, promising sun. Excitement gripped Cross, and he was loath to stop now that he'd gotten everything started. Keep them moving, he told the men; they would skip the nooning. This day, and as many as possible in the months to come, the sheep would not be allowed their usual lie-down in the afternoon, as was their innate habit, for the day remained cool, the spirits eager. Possibly the sheep felt the excitement, too, for they gave little resistance.

The men would eat as they walked. And the woman, too, Cross thought, catching sight of her walking along at the rear edge of the herd. She would do a sight more walking than she ever had in her life. He turned his horse; he had more things to think about than the woman.

Large, mottled bellwether goats led each of the four bands. They walked along grand as kings with their subjects following behind. At times one band of sheep would merge into the other ahead of it, but the dogs and herders would leisurely separate them again. They kept the sheep to bands of twenty-five hundred, which were unusually large bands but still easier to guard and graze than one enormous herd.

There were few strays; the churro always kept close to the safety of the herd. The problem came when a number of them took a notion to go look over a hill. Where one sheep went, another was eager to follow, and then another and another, until half the herd was streaming off the wrong way. Normally the dogs righted this situation easily, and whenever Cross got the chance, he helped on his horse. He had always enjoyed herding the sheep on Domino.

Gaspar Perez and his son Chino were shepherding the mixed flock of ewes and lambs. Having been born in February and March, the lambs were only a couple of months old but had had time enough to imprint with their mothers. Still, ewes were notoriously bad mothers and would heedlessly leave the slower lamb behind when seeking safety or running off at the lure of choice grazing. Gaspar and Chino possessed the uncanny ability of being able to recognize which lamb belonged to which ewe and to put them together again. Chino often walked right in the midst of the flock, making certain to do just that.

When Cross rode up, Chino was carrying a runty-looking lamb over his shoulders. The lamb had gashes on his back and the boy explained that it had been attacked by an eagle that morning. Before he or his father could shoot the eagle, the bird had killed another lamb.

"I will try to save this one," Chino said in Spanish.

Cross examined the lamb. "There will possibly be blood poisoning from the eagle's talons."

"*Sí,*" the young man said, nodding sadly. "We can only try to do what we can."

Cross touched Chino's shoulder and smiled. "And will you carry every lamb that needs it all the way to California?"

The young man shrugged and repeated, "We can only try."

Several times the rest of that day Cross went back to check on Lilly Blackwell. He cursed himself for doing it, but he did it nevertheless. No matter what he had told her, he was as responsible for her as he was for these sheep.

Each time he would find her walking behind the rear of the last flock, leading her mule. From a distance, always where she wouldn't see him, he watched her. She walked along, hat firmly on her head, with the wind tossing her cloak out behind her. He didn't think she even attempted to get back up on the mule, and he would bet every hair on his head that she couldn't.

He considered half a dozen times going down and helping her get on the mule, but the stubbornness inside him wouldn't allow him. She'd told him to give her a chance to do it on her own; now was her chance.

But then he came upon her tugging on the mule's reins, trying to get the animal to quit eating grass. She was a sight: her beribboned bonnet shifted to the back of her head, her brown hair drooping, cloak catching in the wind, while she tugged with all her might at the stubborn mule. If that mule decided to move, the woman would fall on her little bottom and be run right over.

Cross rode across to her. She stopped and watched him come. He dismounted before Domino came to a complete stop, strode over and whipped out his knife and cut a long thin branch from a piñon, then quickly stripped it bare.

"If you want a horse or mule to go forward, get behind their shoulder, like this," he said, taking the reins from her. "Hold this stick up, like you're gonna use it." He lifted the stick. "If that doesn't work, smack his hip. One or two smacks and he'll pay attention when you hold it up at him." He extended the stick toward her.

Her face was flushed, her eyes green as the late spring grass. Slowly she took the stick.

Cross turned and left her to find out how to deal with the mule; she would have to if she wanted to go all the way to California.

He went back later to see her once again walking along, her hat and hair firmly in place, the mule obediently following at her shoulder. She had learned one thing, he thought, even if she hadn't managed to get back in the saddle. He rode away, unseen by her.

North of the flocks, he stopped on a hill and watched the sheep flowing through the grassy valley, like white clouds in a dusky sky. A familiar gray-brown color and form caught his eye—a coyote standing at the edge of a growth of sagebrush and looking at the sheep. Even as he marveled at the animal for nothing more than his wildness, Cross pulled his Sharps from its scabbard and took aim. But before he got a clear shot, the coyote slipped into the brush and disappeared. A run-of-the-mill coyote wouldn't cause him too much trouble, at least not more than once, but a bad killer would be keen enough to do a lot of damage, he thought as he replaced his rifle.

A flash—such as caused by sunlight on a rifle barrel—in the trees to the west caught his attention and sent him instinctively moving deeper into the trees. He studied the area of the flash, combing his gaze across it, but he didn't see the flash again and decided it was nothing.

He watched for several more long minutes, then turned Domino to scout the trail ahead of the sheep. He wanted to check out a stream he knew of that had a number of quiet pools along it—sheep would refuse to drink from rippling water, nor would they drink water that wasn't clear and fresh. They were fussy creatures, to say the least, that would not settle down for the night until they'd had sufficient grazing and water.

The campfire flickered brightly in the waning light. Jon and Paco Salazar, the two night herders, had retired to their bedrolls to catch a few hours of sleep before taking their late shift. Mateo Benavidez, Tomas Vargas and Uriah Plover indulged in playing three-card monte. Arrio Baca had taken first watch and was out somewhere. Chino doctored his injured lamb. He had brought it and another weak one into camp. Chino had a soft heart for sheep and indeed went hungry rather than eat sheep meat. He suffered no such compunctions for other meats.

Cross stretched the length of his bedroll and reclined against his saddle. Through no conscious attempt, he was off by himself. It hadn't been he who had pulled a ways apart but the men. Because he was the *patrón,* he supposed. Pan had come in from the herd to lie nearby, and Cross allowed it, against his better judgment. He was encouraging the dog to be more man's companion than a worker of the sheep. Cross decided it was a small weakness as he repeatedly stroked the dog's soft fur.

He enjoyed a panatela and sipped coffee that was thick with brown sugar in the Mexican way. It took one pack mule to carry all the sacks of sugar. Most of the men were also enjoying one of the panatelas Cross had passed around; as he'd thought, his bit of generosity had gone over well.

His gaze swept around the men and then settled on Lilly Blackwell. He watched her through the flickering campfire. She sat on a log that Coca Arce had placed for her near where he had unloaded the food supplies. Coca was the cook, a man of middle age, all stringy sinew, who supported at home a wife, two sisters and five daughters. When Cross had suggested Coca keep close to Señora Blackwell, Coca had said solemnly, "*Sí.* I have an un-der-stand-ing for women."

The woman looked tired and drawn in the dim firelight, with little of her former regal air. In the coolness of the night, she had pulled her cloak around her shoulders, and its dark fabric made her face sallow and plain as a mud fence. Strands of her hair had slipped from the coil at the back of her head and hung down around her face. Every now and then she pushed tiredly at it.

She'd had a rough day, Cross thought, recalling how she had come dragging into camp, leading the mule. She had barely been able to walk in those stiff little shoes. As far as Cross knew she hadn't gotten back up on the mule once she'd gotten off. It appeared she might have a long walk to California.

He found himself wondering again what her body looked like beneath all her clothes. He'd had a sense of a sturdy frame. And covered with skin the color of goat's milk, he thought with an inner smile. His curiosity was high about that.

Coarse laughter drew his attention to Uriah, Mateo and Tomas. The laugh had come from Uriah Plover. Plover would have Mateo's and Tomas's shirts before the end of the trail, Cross thought, but it would do no good to try to warn them. Mateo and Tomas were young and eager and full of themselves for being out on the trail for the first time.

However, when Cross noted Plover furtively handing something to Tomas, and Tomas passing it to Mateo, he did intervene.

"Plover..." He spoke low but loud enough to be heard across the campfire. "I believe I said there would be no drinking."

Uriah Plover looked across at him, as did the two young whelps, who had the honor to look guilty. Not Plover, though. Plover looked at Cross defiantly.

Though his muscles tightened, Cross sat up leisurely. He had made a rule and would have to make it stick. All the eyes of the men rested on him and Plover, and the only sound came from the crackling of the fire. Cross waited, his arms lying loosely across his knees, his legs ready to spring him upward.

Plover brought the bottle into plain sight, corked it and tossed it across at Coca's feet. "Hey, cookie—maybe you'll need this for medicine," he said.

The firelight glinted on his eyes as they shifted for an instant from Coca to Lilly Blackwell. Then, with a grin to Cross, he went back to his game.

Cross lay back and looked at Lilly Blackwell beneath half-closed eyes. She murmured something to Coca, then, with a bit of her customary gracefulness, she retreated to the small tent Cross had brought for her. He watched her shadowy form bend and disappear inside. He saw, too, that Plover was watching her.

Cross tamped out his cigar and rose to make a final check on everything. With Pan padding silently beside him, he went first to the rope corral for the remuda. All the horses, except for Cross's Domino, which he kept closer to him at camp, were here and unsaddled. The mules had been unloaded, and half grazed contentedly in the makeshift corral, while the rest were pastured among the sheep. Mules often proved a deterrent to coyotes, because they could kick a coyote to death.

Lorenzo had his bed stretched beneath a tree. Mules, horses, burros, all were Lorenzo's life. His wife had left him because he once brought a sick mule into their one-room jacal. On the other side of the remuda Simon Morelos was already asleep; whenever Simon sat down, he slept.

Not far away, the edge of the sheep herd began. The animals were quiet, lying down for the night. They were silvery shadows beneath a waning moon and bright stars.

Only Gaspar and Jesus remained on guard for all ten thousand head of sheep—the two men and the dogs were enough on a calm night like this. And always all the men were ready to jump into action should need be. Cross had told them of sighting coyote, though seeing one made little difference. One did not need to see the predators to know they were there; the land belonged to them, too.

Cross circled silently through the trees and came upon Arrio. "A quiet night," the young man said in Spanish, almost with disappointment.

"We're just startin'," Cross consoled him. "There will be exciting nights to come."

When he returned to the shadows outside the campfire, he saw that Coca had stretched his bedroll not far from the opening of Lilly Blackwell's tent. Cross commanded Pan to lie down at the edge of the tent, and then he brought his own bedroll and gear and stretched out on the opposite side. He thought of how he had told the woman he would not be responsible for her.

He was, though.

He slept five hours and then in the early hours of a new day, he saddled Domino by feel in the darkness, left Arrio Baca in charge of getting the flocks moving at daybreak, and rode off for Taos. If the woman was determined to make this trip, she would be safer dressed as a Mexican. In her getup, Lilly Blackwell stood out like a campfire on the Llano at night—a beacon for any renegade who came their way.

Lilly was exhausted unto death, yet she slept fitfully, drifting in and out of bad dreams. Her bed—two large woolly sheepskins spread over pilings of leaves to fashion a surprisingly dry and soft mattress—was a far cry from the featherbed she'd had back home, and in her aching state, she longed for that mattress. Each week Mammy Ethnee used to fluff it, so that it had no lumps and was like a cloud.

She squirmed deeper into the wool and pulled the blanket tighter around her. It was cold as January back home. Oh, Lord, if she could only be back home. She wondered if she should beware of a snake seeking warmth... or one of those wicked-looking scorpions... or the coarse man with the gray beard who had watched her across the campfire.

There had been a challenge between that man and Cross McCree, and with drowsy memories of the incident came further chills to her blood. Men were so savage in this land.

After a moment she realized that it was not Tyler for whom she longed for protection.

It was Cross McCree, who had looked at her across the campfire, too.

When Lilly emerged from the tent the following morning, the sun was glinting through the trees. She squinted as she looked around. The campfire was smoldering, and the men who'd sat there last night were gone—all except Coca, who was packing his mules. The grassy meadow where the sheep had been was now eerily empty.

Lilly was cold. And she was dirty and felt as if she had been run over by a herd of buffalo. The fabric against her skin, which had been soaked limp with sweat the day before, was now scratchy. Her hair hung in her eyes, her fingers were stiff and sore, and her feet pained with every step. She stood there in a daze, gazing at the empty ground where the sheep had been.

"They have gone on—hours," Coca said in his broken English, when she asked. "Sit...." He motioned to the log he'd brought up for her. "Take coffee."

He brought her a steaming cup, and Lilly gratefully wrapped her hands around it. The coffee was deliciously warm, and she even welcomed the extreme sweetness. He brought her two tortillas wrapped around meat; she didn't know what kind of meat and didn't care. It was food, and she was very hungry.

She absently watched him as he returned to packing their mules. He was a short, spare man. His skin was near the texture and color of harness leather. Lilly been frightened of him at first. His face was set in the hard lines of a savage or an outlaw, and he was dressed after the fashion of a tough vaquero. But one look into his kind eyes, and she had felt relief. She had stayed close to him when the men had begun coming into the camp.

Except for Jesus and Gaspar Perez, the herders were all young men. They had seemed polite and friendly, most even deferential, but there was one—the man with the gray beard and hair whom she'd heard called Plover. He had a face that had seen much violence. He was built like a bear, but his expression reminded Lilly of a leering wolf. The way he had looked at her had made her flesh crawl.

Cross McCree came riding up just as Lilly was finishing the tortilla. He was a spot at first, who emerged from the trees and came quickly across the grass. He was swinging down from the saddle before his horse stopped.

Lilly had nothing with which to wipe her mouth but her hand, so she used it, then touched her tangled hair. There was no help for it, nor for her rumpled, smelly clothing.

The shadow of a day's beard covered Cross McCree's cheeks, and he had one of the long dark cigars clamped between his teeth. He pulled two bundles from his horse and strode toward her. His blue eyes were on her, and she rose slowly. There was a purpose in his movements, and she had a sense of needing to fortify herself.

He stopped three feet from her. "It will be much better for you to travel as a man," he said. "As you are, you stand out too much as both a woman and an Anglo."

He knelt on the ground, slit the cords with a swift slice of his knife and folded back the canvas. Clothes spilled out. He picked up and held out a coarse woven shirt and thick duck trousers.

Slowly, mesmerized, Lilly reached out and took them from him. In amazement, she saw still lying in the canvas a second shirt and trousers, a pair of galluses and a slouch hat, which he lifted and plumped into shape. He turned to the second bundle, slit the cords and revealed a woven serape and moccasins.

"I think everything you need is here," he said, standing. "The undergarments you already have ought to do, so I didn't get any."

She stared at him, words swirling like a tornado in her mind. Then she threw down the coarse clothing.

"I am not your *employee,* Mr. McCree, whom you can order about to suit yourself." She had come a long way from society in Pasquotank County, but she had not come so far that she would stoop to wearing men's clothing. And how dare this man order her!

His gaze was steady and forceful. "This is not a civilized countryside, such as where you come from, Señora Blackwell. You would be a prize for any Comanchero to trade to the Comanches. For you, a man could get—" His gaze surveyed her boldly and intimately, causing throbbing deep in her belly and heat to flush her cheeks "—at least forty horses, perhaps more if someone takes a fancy to your silky hair. Or there just might happen along a manly Ute, or Arapaho or Cheyenne who would find you too choice a trophy to pass up. We are enough of an attraction with our sheep, horses and mules. We don't need you paradin' out here like a fresh heifer to a rutting bull."

"A fresh heifer!" Lilly clutched her hands in her skirts.

"Now you either put on these clothes...or I will do it for you."

His words were quietly spoken, with no trace of threat in his voice, but the firmness in his eyes told Lilly he was not speaking idly.

Rage, hot as fire, gripped her, but she said, "I will do as you say." She had no choice.

"Make sure you put your hair up under that hat—" he pointed "—and take off those earrings. You'll be safe among the men. They're Mexican and have respect for women. All except Uriah Plover. Keep clear of him," he said.

His eyes were upon her again for a long second, and it came between them, the flickering of desire, as vibrant and real as the flickering flames of the campfire.

He turned on his heel and strode toward his horse.

"And what about you?" Lilly asked sharply. "Who is to protect me from you, Mr. McCree?"

He stopped still, his back stiffening. Ever so slowly, with the power of a lion, Cross McCree turned to face her. His blue eyes were cool as the air blowing through the tops of the trees.

He said, "I am of English and Chickasaw blood, both a civilized peoples."

Then he touched the brim of his hat to her and swung himself easily into the saddle. He spoke tersely to Coca in Spanish and nudged his horse away at an easy canter.

Lilly watched him go, watched the power and suppleness of him.

Turning from the unsettling thoughts and feelings, she looked down at the clothes in her hand. Gripping them tightly, she turned back to her tent, took several angry strides and then stopped, her ire draining away as the pain in her feet and legs made her realize what she faced. Another day either walking or riding a mule. And after that another and another. Dirt and sweat and aches and pains.

She really wouldn't have minded dying right then and there.

But since that wasn't going to happen, and crying wasn't going to help, she had to go on.

"I must take a few minutes to bathe," she said, forcing her words past the lump in her throat and too embarrassed of the tears in her eyes to look fully at Coca. She pointed at the nearby stream.

"There is little hurry, *señora,*" he said, lazily swirling coffee in the pot over the fire. "Sheep walk slow."

Clumsy in her haste and emotion, Lilly dug fresh underclothes and a cloth from the canvas bags. She wrapped the bags back tight and took them, with limping steps, over to where her mule stood, while Coca began taking down her tent.

There were only sparse bushes near the stream to provide privacy. Determinedly she knelt at the driest spot she could find, stripped to her camisole. The air was cold and the water icy, yet she forced herself to bathe. Shivering, she sat and placed her sore feet in the water until she could no longer stand the cold.

She glanced over her shoulder to see Coca had his back to her, busying himself with the loading of the mules. Resolutely she pulled off her camisole and skirt, petticoat and pantalettes, quickly washed and then donned fresh underclothes.

The trousers and shirt Cross McCree had brought were a welcome warmth, and they fit surprisingly well, though the shirt, made for a man, or boy, stretched tight across her breasts.

She recalled how Cross McCree had looked at her—as if his eyes went straight through her clothes to her body. She fingered the fabric of the shirt. Homespun and very rough, it was far different from her fine cotton or silk dresses. She imagined Tyler's reaction to her in such clothes. He would be appalled.

But Tyler was dead, she told herself, pushing aside the heartache as she fumbled with the leather ties of the moccasins that went up her legs to just below her knees. They alone appeared to have been worn by someone else, yet they were comfortable, a relief to her aching feet. With quick, hard strokes, she brushed her hair and plaited it, then secured it with pins atop her head. She pulled on the serape, ran her hands over it. It was new and of lovely colors. It also allowed her to move more easily than had her cape. The hat, too, was easier to manage, simply placed on her head and secured beneath her chin with a horsehair chin strap.

Lastly, she remembered the earrings. She removed them, but then she felt so barren...so without courage.

She slipped the earrings back on, and with firm strides joined Coca at the waiting mules.

Her gaze swept her bundles; her straw bonnet was now crushed into one of them, and her heart ached for it. Then she saw that Coca had tied her cherrywood case on last, atop the pack mule, making the animal resemble a short, fat camel. At least she still had that.

Coca took her dirty clothes and tucked them into a bundle. Then he held, the mule for her, and she mounted with surprising ease, now that she had no skirts tangling her legs or box to block her swing. They started off, Lilly's mule this time willingly following after Coca's. Lilly supposed she would follow some mule or horse all the way to California.

They headed the sheep toward the Taos Pueblos, following the river valley and allowing one or two miles to separate the flocks, letting the animals spread and move through sparsely wooded areas as well as over the grassy meadows.

After a brief excursion ahead with Uriah Plover to scout the route, Cross rode on the fringes of the flocks, from the beginning to end, checking on things. Pan tried to follow him, but Cross commanded the dog to stay with Jesus's flock and work. There was no way the little dog could run the miles with Cross and his horse; the little critter would be footsore enough simply trying to do his herding job.

He saw Lilly Blackwell on his second ride to the rear. She and Coca came along at a steady pace, already having caught up to the last flock. Cross studied the woman and frowned when he saw the earrings remained at her ears. Still, his anxiety eased. Her shape was totally hidden, and from a distance the earrings couldn't be seen. Only face-to-face would she be recognized as an Anglo woman.

He joined them, bringing his horse beside Lilly Blackwell's mule. Her green eyes met his, and she gave him a cold, regal acknowledgment by inclining her head, as if to make certain the earrings swayed and drew his attention. That action and the fury in those green eyes brought amusement rumbling in his chest.

In Spanish he instructed Coca to take his and the woman's pack mules and ride up ahead of all the flocks and set up for the midday meal. They would not stop the bands, but the men would snatch their food as they passed. Cross would take over the care of the *señora*.

They rode side by side without speaking for half an hour. Cross pulled a piece of jerky from his shirt pocket and extended it to her. She looked at it curiously.

"Beef jerky," he said.

She shook her head, faced forward and lifted her chin slightly. A regal little queen in peon clothing.

"The trip is hard work, *señora*. You would do well to eat to keep up your strength."

"I'm not hungry," she said in her soft, haughty drawl.

Cross hid his grin; he didn't think his laughing would help matters.

Again they rode in silence. Knowing the woman's mule would follow, Cross eased his horse into the shade of the trees. Another hour, and he noticed the woman shifting uncomfortably in the saddle. She needed to rest, for she had been in the saddle for some three hours...but she would not say so.

Cross turned Domino into the timber toward the rocky bluff. "There is a spring up ahead," he said. "We can water the horses and rest ourselves."

The spring appeared some two hundred yards through the cottonwood, aspen and alder trees. The grass was tall around where the water dribbled out of a crack in the rock. Cross halted his horse and dismounted.

Lilly Blackwell gazed at him from beneath the low brim of the slouch hat, then slowly and stiffly got out of the saddle. She moved more easily unencumbered by her skirts, though he would have to admit that she was much more lovely in a dress.

Cross let Domino graze freely, and allowed the mule to do so, too, knowing that it would stick close to Domino, who wasn't likely to leave Cross.

"It's lovely here," Lilly Blackwell said in a hushed voice, almost as if she didn't realize she'd spoken.

With a cup from his saddlebags, Cross dipped water from the little spring pool. He held it out to Lilly Blackwell, who stood there in the clearing, gazing at him with those large green eyes.

Slowly she came forward. Pushing her hat off her head to hang down her back, she ruffled the wisps of hair on her forehead. She jerked off her gloves and took the cup in both her hands and drank. Her green eyes looked at him over the cup.

Cross settled himself on a rock, savored his panatela and the sight of the woman. There was a familiar sexual stirring within him, and he enjoyed it, for it brought no harm. The sunlight shone golden on the woman's brown hair. It was the first really good look he'd had of her hair in bright light. It was rich and thick and shiny. He experienced the same wash of attraction that he had all those days ago on the street in Santa Fe.

His eyes stayed on her hair as she knelt at the pool and refilled the cup, drank again, and then splashed water over her slender pale hands and wrists. She smiled, as if in memory.

All of his attention and warming blood was focused on the woman, so he failed to note the presence of an intruder. The deathly silence—the quieting of the birds and the horses quitting eating, even the stillness of the breeze—came to him too late. By the time it all registered, the man had already entered the clearing, aiming a rifle at Cross and the woman.

Rudd Puckett, the wormy little man who had vowed revenge the night his brother had been killed.

Eyes focused on the man, Cross thought of his Sharps rifle and Colt pistol attached to his saddle, some six feet away. There was no chance to get to them, nor to go for one of his knives. He allowed his hand to rest loose atop his knee, inches above the knife hidden in his boot. He could do nothing more.

Chapter Nine

Lilly slowly straightened and looked at Cross McCree. His expression was strange, his gaze going beyond her. Instinctively she turned to see what had gotten his attention. And fear skittered across her shoulders and sank to the pit of her stomach. It was a man, a *Tejano,* she thought automatically, looking from his hat to the rifle in his hands.

The man came forward, and the rancid stench of whiskey and sweat came with him. Stringy red hair fell from beneath a battered, low-crowned hat, and tobacco stained the sparse, unkempt beard. A heavy, worn gun belt circled his hips, and his thick, callused hands aimed a long rifle. He clenched the rifle so tightly his knuckles were white.

Lilly's gaze lifted back up to his eyes. They were colorless ... and half-wit mean. Fear eyes, Mammy Ethnee used to say, because she always had maintained that fear made men mean. Those colorless eyes more than the rifle in his hands terrified Lilly and held her rooted to the spot, unable to move.

"You ain't no easy man to corner, McCree," the man said. He grinned maliciously, revealing rotted teeth. "But I done it now. Yes, sirree, I kin get both of yous right chere, and be long gone afore anybody comes a-lookin' 'bout gunfire."

He wiped his sleeve across his nose and carefully stepped into a position where he had a better angle on both Lilly and Cross, who sat on a rocky outcropping in the bluff some six feet behind her. Lilly gazed at the rifle . . . the instrument of blood and death gleaming black in the sunlight.

"Reckon you know who I am, McCree." When Cross didn't answer, the little man screeched, "Rudd Puckett! You kilt my brother—or have ya forgot already?"

Lilly jumped.

Cross McCree said, "I remember who you are."

"Yeah," the little man said, cocky then. "I reckon you do." He waved the rifle at Lilly. "Pretty neat trick, dressin' her like a fella. I was more cautious comin' after ya 'cause of that." He sniffed, and gazed at Cross. "I coulda shot ya half a dozen times already. Popped ya off easy as a bird from a branch. But I wanted ya to know who sent ya to hell and why." His colorless eyes glittered with hate. "I reckon I don't need t' tell ya now. The woman don't really have nothin' in this . . . 'ceptin' it was her husband done cheated my brother, so I guess that's reason 'nough." He shifted his eyes to Lilly and licked his lips. "Pity, though, that I cain't have a sample of her first."

Lilly felt as if she was going to vomit.

His gaze went back to Cross McCree. The two men seemed to stare at each other for long seconds. Cross McCree's eyes were as bright and quiet as a candle flame. Smoke rose from the thin cigar in his mouth.

"Too bad ya don't tote a gun, *pastor.* . . ." the little man taunted. His eyes squinted. "I kin shore shoot ya afore ya kin get that knife outta yer belt." He gave a cold, hard laugh. "I ain't gonna give you no more than you did Pool. . . ." His voice broke, and he lifted the rifle slightly. Lilly saw his finger tighten on the trigger.

Oh, Lord, he was going to shoot.

The next instant there came a piercing cry, and suddenly a furry ball came shooting out from the trees—a burro, with a small, dark-haired figure atop it, who let out a bloodcurdling scream and waved a big stick.

It was Henri.

It happened as if in a bad dream. Lilly watched, unable to move or to cry out, terror pounding over her and sucking her down just as the waves of the ocean used to do back home.

The *Tejano* swung around, bringing the rifle to shoot Henri, who came on, a small figure on the small burro. Then something flew past Lilly. She saw it land in the *Tejano*'s neck—a knife, with a glossy silver handle. It sliced into the dirty little man's throat at the same instant that he pulled the trigger.

Boom! The sound split Lilly's ears and seemed somehow connected with the blood that came spurting from the man's throat, where the silver handle of the knife wobbled. Warm blood splattered on her cheek.

The man half jerked around. His colorless eyes were wide with amazement. His lips moved, as if beseeching Lilly, and still she stood rooted, watching in shocked fascination as the blood flowed from around the knife blade and ran downward, soaking the man's shirt. And then, as dusk comes across the land, death came across the colorless eyes. He crumpled to the ground, down into the verdant green grass, legs and arms all askew. His eyes were wide open and staring at the blue sky.

Cross McCree came into her line of vision; he stopped at the dead man's foot and stared downward. A thin line of smoke twirled upward from the brown cigar still clamped between his lips. His face was set in hard, cold lines.

The scream came then from inside her, swelling from the fear deep in her belly, up and out her mouth as a sound apart from her.

Startled, Cross reached out and grabbed Lilly Blackwell. She shut her mouth on the scream and stared at Puckett, her eyes wide and round as a mad woman's.

"¿Señora?" He shook her. Her eyes rose slowly to his, bright green against her skin white as fresh snow. Certain that she was about to faint, he moved to gather her up.

But instead of fainting, she jerked away from him and began hollering, her eyes gone wide with hysteria.

"Damn you! Kill...kill...that's all this land is ... death...dirt...."

With each word she hit at him, pounded on him as he tried to grab her, twisting this way and that like a windstorm, spewing out her fear and anger.

Then she broke out in sobs.

Cross took hold of her at last. She fell against him, clutching him. Slowly he lowered her to the ground, kneeling beside her and holding her, while her body trembled against him and her hands clutched him. Hardly realizing, he brought his hand up to stroke her hair. It was as silky as he had imagined it would be.

He needed to comfort her in that moment, to feel the warmth and pulsing life of her.

The woman, the blood washed from her face, stood with her arm around the boy's shoulder. Sometimes she touched his hair. The two of them watched as Cross stripped Rudd Puckett of his guns and boots and pulled a poke from the man's pocket, tucking it into his own without counting the money inside. Henri went into the trees and brought back Puckett's horse, a small sorrel. The boy hadn't said a word, though he did not appear to be in shock. During his young life on the streets of Santa Fe, surviving as he could, he had already seen violence and death many times. It was a normal part of his world. Cross reached out for the boy and lifted him onto the sorrel.

"It was a very brave thing you did," he told Henri in Spanish. "It is only right that you get the horse." He did his best to shorten the stirrups to fit, but the boy's legs were too short. The boy still had no shoes, and his callused, cracked feet hung loosely on either side of the horse's belly.

Lilly Blackwell touched the boy's foot and patted his leg. She hadn't said anything since she had quit crying.

Cross held her mule for her to mount. She trembled, and her hands fumbled with the reins when he handed them to her. He swung up on Domino, walked the horse over beside the dead *Tejano* and stared down at him. He thanked *Chihowa* for life and cursed the man to hell. It was as reverent as he got. And then he nudged his horse away. The woman and boy fell in behind him.

"Aren't we gonna bury him?" Lilly asked, finding her voice at last as she cast the dead man a fleeting glance.

"He was no good in life," Cross said. "Let him at least serve the buzzard and coyote in death." And the three of them, with the little burro trailing behind, left the peaceful glen that had been turned into a glen of death.

Lilly looked at Cross McCree's straight back and swallowed further tears. Nudging the mule, she moved up beside the man on the buckskin, and Henri rode up on her other side. She felt a sense of comfort there, between the man and the boy.

She wondered how much more violence she would experience before she was away from this barbarous land. She prayed for all their souls.

Henri had followed them, keeping far behind the rear herd in order to escape detection as long as possible, for he knew that until they were a number of days out from Santa Fe, Cross McCree would force him to return. He wanted to go to California to seek his fortune, and he would work hard to pay for his keep. He had stolen the burro from Padre

Domingo, and he was sorry for that, but the padre had three burros and a mule, so he did not think it a serious offense.

Cross McCree related the boy's tale to Lilly, in bits and pieces, as he questioned the boy. When Henri finished the telling, he looked at both of them with the hope of heaven on his face.

"He saved our lives, and he will be a help on the trip," Lilly said, looking ahead to the sheep that came into view. "And it really is too far for any of us to return."

She felt Cross McCree's gaze on her, calling her to raise her eyes to him.

"You and the boy can both return," he said tersely, around the cigar, now just a stub in his mouth. "Coca can escort you. It is only a day's ride."

She looked away again to the sheep that grew ever larger as they approached. "No," she said with a gentle shake of her head, feeling the earrings sway. "We have all come too far. There is no goin' back."

She was going ahead, to California and then to home, where people weren't always trying to kill each other and where she would live in a white clapboard house and wear fine silk dresses . . . and never again don men's clothes nor ride a mule.

The sheep were not halted. The air remained cool in the shade of the tall trees of the river valley. The herders and dogs prodded the sheep, the herders calling and waving their hats, the dogs yipping and enticing, keeping the sheep on their feet and walking slowly through the afternoon.

Cross McCree spent no more time in the noon camp than it took to munch on tortillas and spicy beans and to sketch in bare details to Coca what had taken place in the glen. Then he was back in the saddle and off to check the flocks. Two or three at a time, the men came into the camp to eat and learn of what had happened with the *patrón* and the

Americano lady. Slowly the tale spread to all the men. Several knew Henri and congratulated him as a great hero. Lilly could not understand what was said in Spanish, but she could recognize congratulations and praise. The boy was proud.

Watching him, Lilly trembled, thinking just how close he had come to death...how close they had all come to death.

The sheep continued to slowly walk past, one flock disappearing through the sparse tall trees to the north, while the next came into view from the south. Lilly helped Coca clear and pack up the camp. She knew how to do almost nothing, but she tried, needing to feel useful, needing to feel alive and perhaps make atonement for the life she was allowed. It seemed strange, going about such mundane activities, when only hours before she had been at death's door... and when a man lay dead behind them in the grass.

She thought of Tyler. It seemed as if ages had passed rather than days to be counted on one hand since she had stood at his grave. She saw herself as she had been then almost as if seeing a stranger. She looked down at herself, at the wool serape, brown trousers, worn leather moccasins. It was as if she had become a stranger.

She felt ashamed for having been so frightened as to not be able to move when the vile *Tejano* had turned his rifle on Henri. If it had not been for Cross McCree's swift action, the boy would have been killed—and Lilly would have done nothing.

Coward...coward... The word reverberated in her brain and the guilt hung heavily upon her.

Lilly and Henri stayed with Coca; Lilly and Coca walked their mules, while Henri rode the sorrel horse ahead of them, having to again and again stop the horse in order for Lilly and Coca to catch up. Lilly was just as happy to walk, for her bottom was quite sorely bruised, unaccustomed to all the riding. Her feet were sore from the previous day's walking in her high-button shoes, but they fared much better in the moccasins, except for stepping on a stray pebble here and there. Suddenly, as if through new eyes, she saw the beauty of the tall trees, of the silky grasses, the warmth of the sun. All these things seemed especially sweet and precious.

Cross McCree rode into view a number of times. He rode his horse as if born there. After catching sight of him for the third time, she knew he was keeping an eye on them. It made her feel good to know he was close at hand, that he watched over them.

He had killed, protecting her and the boy. He had done what needed doing, just as he had the night of Tyler's death.

Again and again she recalled the look in his blue eyes as he had stared at the body of Rudd Puckett, and she shivered. There had been a hardness in his eyes, an intensity that reflected no forgiveness. Killing Rudd Puckett had been no more to him than killing an animal.

And she supposed that was exactly what it had been.

Henri wanted to ride off with him, but Cross McCree would not allow it. Henri, knowing better than to push his luck, remained with Lilly and Coca.

They still did not reach the crossing place on the Rio Grande before night camp, though they had made some twelve miles that day, pushing the sheep and not allowing them to rest. Cross McCree told her not to expect to make such good time all of the trip. The sheep were fresh now, but could not be pushed this fast for many days in a row, nor when the grass grew sparse. A more normal pace would prove to be seven to eight miles a day. It was well over a thousand to Sacramento.

A thousand miles of wearing the coarse men's clothes and sleeping on the hard ground, Lilly thought. And who knew what lay up ahead.

It came to her quite starkly that it was entirely possible she would die on this trip and never see Pasquotank County again.

Cross lay on his bedroll six feet from the woman's tent and stared up at the moon. There was a faint ring around it, which could mean coming rain. He hoped to get the sheep across the Rio Grande before any rains could raise it.

It seemed months since he had bid Duffy and Marquita goodbye, rather than just two days.

He thought much of the dead man, though it wasn't regret that kept him awake. In his life he killed only what he needed to in order to live, a rule that applied to both animals and men. It was not cruelty but the law of survival by which he lived, and he wasted no pity on the man who lay back in the glen. Man could choose to live with life or against it, and life had a way of taking care of those who lived against it.

He had not killed many men in his life; Rudd Puckett had been the fourth one...that he knew of. There had been that time he and Duffy had been surrounded by Cheyenne braves intent on taking both their horses and their hair. Cross knew he had wounded a number of them, and the chances were he had killed, but he didn't know for certain.

A sound came from the woman's tent, and his eyes turned that way as he listened. It was a whimpering and mumbling, then came the whisper of thrashing.

No one had entered the tent; he'd have seen them in the dim moonlight. But perhaps a snake...

He lay there staring at the tent. The sounds grew louder. Those of nightmares, he thought and wondered what to do. Undoubtedly he was not the only one who heard; the men were those who slept lightly.

With a hand on Pan's head, Cross gave unspoken command for the dog to stay and, silent as a shadow, he moved to the tent opening. A glance showed the embers of the campfire and the dark forms lying around it. Coca lay a few feet away; his eyes were open.

With a second's hesitation, Cross slipped into the tent. It was pitch-black for several seconds, before his eyes began to adjust. The bright moonlight filtered through the tent canvas, and he could see Lilly Blackwell's dark figure in the blankets. She moved, thrashed, as if fighting someone. There was fear and suffering in her mumblings.

Crouching beside her on his heels, Cross touched her shoulder. Her eyes sprang open, and he heard the swift, fearful inhale of a scream. He put his hand over her mouth. She froze, and her silent scream was hot breath into his hand.

"It's Cross," he whispered.

Her eyes, dark orbs in the dimness, searched his face. Her hand came up and closed around his wrist.

He took his hand away; she let go of him. Following instinct, he lightly brushed his hand across her forehead and the silky hair that spread over the blanket pillowing her head. He could see the fear in her pale, shadowed face.

"You were dreamin'," he said. He felt somewhat foolish. "That's all, just dreams."

She blinked, coming to herself. "Oh...yes." Her eyes shifted, as if to avoid him, and she pushed upward. He noticed she was shaking. "I'm sorry I awakened you." Her voice sounded thick.

"You didn't."

They gazed at each other. Cross reached out and stroked her hair. It was silky, both warm and cool to his touch. She became very still, and her eyes remained on his. She did not pull away from him...her lips parted slightly.

He removed his hand and inclined his head. "Coca's bedded three feet from the front, and I'm just a few feet over yonder." He gestured. "Nothin' can get to you without comin' over one of us. You have no need to fear."

She nodded.

He gazed at her a moment longer, then shifted to leave.

"Mr. McCree . . ."

He turned.

"You saved my life today, and I haven't thanked you. I do so now. But for you, I would be lyin' back there beside the spring . . . food for the hawks and coyotes." She spoke in a bare whisper, and the words came stiffly.

"I imagine we both would, but for the boy."

Her gaze lingered on him.

"It is over and done with, *señora*. It's best forgotten."

"As easily as that?" she said, and he found the question surprising.

"Yes," he said. "What happened could not be avoided, so it was met and dealt with. It is over."

Again they gazed at each other, and he felt an inexplicable pull toward her. A part of him went, lifted her into his arms and took her to him. Desire like the breeze in the trees whispered to him. Turning a deaf ear to it, he rose to bending position and left as silently as he had come.

Lilly listened carefully. Above the pounding of her heart she heard only a soft whisper of movement. There came the sound of night bugs and birds, sounds sparse as the air here.

She lay awake a long time, her eyes kept open by remnants of the fearful nightmare and stirrings deep inside that she didn't understand. They were the same stirrings she had experienced the first time she had ever looked into the eyes of Cross McCree. She felt unsettled, and vaguely ashamed, for the stirrings were akin to pleasure.

She thought of Tyler. He was fading from her mind, and perhaps her dream of him had been his retribution. She had dreamed of the blood flowing from his middle and him asking her again and again to help him, but she couldn't stop the blood and soon she was swimming in it, and then there was the dirty little man's colorless eyes bulging out at her.

She longed to escape the nightmare and thought that if she could just get through all of this she would be back in Pasquotank County, in a featherbed, listening to the thick noise made by the crickets and frogs and cicadas all singing from the swamps.

At last, thinking of Cross McCree lying nearby, she fell asleep.

The herders and the dogs had the flocks on their feet and moving as the rays of the morning sun broke through the fluttering leaves of the tall trees. The sheep bleated and frisked in the brisk air, and the dogs yipped and ran, exercising their dominance. The extra mules and horses went out at a lope, Lorenzo Lopez and Simon Morelos riding free and easy on either side of them. For an instant Cross wished to be riding with them, away from the responsibility of the herd and the men. And the woman.

Lilly Blackwell, her hair neatly braided, came out from her tent just as Cross rode up. He'd already ridden the three miles to the river and returned.

He stopped Domino near the campfire that was only embers, dismounted and held the reins in one hand, took a mug of hot coffee from Coca with the other. "We'll cross today," he told Coca. "The river is low." Excitement skimmed across his shoulders, and Coca shared it with his eyes.

"We will be there... *poco después,*" Coca said.

Lilly Blackwell did not approach, nor even look his way. She had turned and was unpinning her tent. Cross was a little surprised at her pitching in to work.

Henri appeared at Cross's elbow. He had on a serape, socks and sandals Chino had managed to procure for him

from a *labriego* family living in a nearby jacal. He now had
a floppy hat, too, that he had to keep pushing up out of his
eyes. He had been asleep when Cross had left, and now he
gazed at Cross eagerly as he asked to accompany the *patrón*
or ride with the men.

Cross noted the boy's excitement, but still he said, "You
will stay near the *señora*." The boy's face and shoulders
sagged in disappointment. "Coca is a good man," Cross
continued in Spanish, "but he is only one man. You have
protected Señora Blackwell once, and I need you to do so
when I am too busy with the sheep. I need you to guard her
as I would myself. Can you handle so great a charge?"

A little of the excitement and pride came back into the
boy's black eyes. "*Sí...*" The boy bobbed his head. "I will
take good care of her, *patrón*."

Cross rested his hand on the boy's shoulder. "*Bueno,
compañero*."

The boy straightened to his full three and a half feet.
Cross thought how size had little to do with measuring
worth; he was glad to have the boy after all, and maybe there
would prove to be more for the *muchacho* in California.
One never could tell what fate had in store. He helped the
boy atop his horse and frowned as he saw the boy's feet
dangling near but not in the stirrups. He would have to
remedy that, or the little one was likely to fall off his horse
and break his neck.

There had already been death on this trip, and no doubt
more would come. There was no need to encourage an ac-
cident.

Cross swung atop Domino and settled himself, then
paused to look at Lilly Blackwell. She straightened and
gazed at him. The sun shone golden on her brown hair, and
her eyes were green as the leaves of the trees.

He wanted her.

"Put on your hat," he said with more harshness than he had intended. But without apology he turned and rode away.

He had no business entertaining the thoughts he was about the Americano woman. He was the leader of this grand expedition and had to keep his wits where they belonged if he was to build for all their futures. Besides, he was a mestizo—a half-breed man of the mountains, while she was a grand Anglo lady. The two did not mix.

Eager to witness the crossing, Coca led them at a trot. Lilly hung on to the mule, which she had christened Tubbs in honor of his drooping belly, and tried not to bounce off. It was quite frustrating to see the boy, without benefit of stirrups, sit atop his trotting horse as easily as he would in a rocking chair. Lilly studied him and Coca on his mule and noted that both rode quite relaxed. She tried to relax her body, but found the task rather hard when she was so frightened of falling off, and also of stopping, which Tubbs did once in order to grab bites of grass, and almost sending Lilly flying over his head.

She cursed the mule, and she cursed Cross McCree for providing him. Still, all this activity of keeping herself in the saddle and seeing all the anticipation of crossing the river lifted the heavy memory of violence that tried to cling to her.

They rode around and through the slow moving bands of sheep, and there was something about the sheep that made Lilly's heart swell. They were bright in the morning sunlight, and so fresh...adorable. She liked when her legs brushed up against them, touching her property and her future as it were. She felt a growing sense of obligation to them.

Once she spied Pan, and the little dog came rushing up to her, wagging his tail in eager greeting. She said, "Hello, Pan. How are you," even before she realized.

The little dog responded with a wagging tail, bright eyes and what would pass for a smile, before racing back to his charges.

The remuda of horses and mules was just entering the river when Lilly, Coca and Henri arrived. Before they cleared the trees, they heard the eager cries of the men. "Yeeeah! Yee-yip, yip."

The river, sheep and men came into view. Wide grins split the faces of the men driving the animals—the two wranglers and Cross McCree. The water came to the belly of the mules, just shy on the horses.

Cross McCree's trouser legs were rolled high, revealing bare feet and legs, his skin startlingly pale. Lilly was surprised; she had imagined him dark all over. Warmth rushed over her cheeks, and she looked away, but where her gaze strayed brought total, flaming embarrassment.

One of the wranglers was bare all the way to his thighs, where the edge of his shirt fell. He had removed his trousers and long johns entirely! His skin was equally dark all over, she noted, before jerking her eyes away.

Her embarrassment was not eased by Coca's amused grin. "*Mucho* better, *señora*," he said, "to remove the boots and *pantalones* than ride wet the day." He leaned on his saddle horn with one hand and pointed with the other. "See…the horses, they level the earth for the sheep when they come."

And Lilly saw how the horses' hooves cut and packed the bank into a soft slope into the water and again up on the opposite shore. In short order the remuda was across, and Cross McCree came splashing back toward Lilly, Coca and Henri.

He reined hard, and there was about him the sense of a boy having a grand time. His horse pranced and snorted, and Cross McCree handled him easily. Pushing his bare feet in the stirrups, he stretched his legs and leaned upon the saddle horn. Lilly covertly watched his movements, admiring the strength of his wiry muscles.

He spoke to Henri in Spanish, and the boy nodded eagerly. Coca dismounted and led the pack mules to a tree.

"Keep an eye from back here," Cross McCree said to her with some exultation. "We're gonna push the first band across."

Coca tossed his boots atop one of the pack mules and, with a teasing grin to Lilly, rolled up his trouser legs. "I have many women in my family," he said teasingly, then swung up atop his mule and followed Cross McCree and Henri. The three of them seemed to approach this river crossing as one grand adventure. Eagerly they pressed their horses and pulled on the reins to hold them back at the same time, seeming to encourage the horses to prance and flick their tails for no reason.

The excitement transferred to Lilly, and she found herself wishing to join in the action, too. She watched the men on horseback and those who approached on foot, all of them grinning broadly, waving their hats, as much at each other as at the sheep, who came en masse, following placidly behind the bellwether goat that strutted forward with pride.

The men did not yell at the sheep, but called occasionally a mild, "Yipp, yip, yipp." The sheep bleated, and their bodies passing through the brush and against each other made a soft shushing sound that joined with the whispering of the breeze through the treetops. The sun sparkled brightly off the water.

The sheep came to the edge of the river, and those in the front stopped, bunching up behind the bellwether goat and fanning out on either side, but not allowing their hooves to touch the water. Quietly and very slowly Cross McCree and Coca advanced on the lead goat, one man pressing on either side. Coca cut his mule back into the herd, pressing the

sheep very, very gently. Cross nudged his horse directly behind the goat, and his horse lowered his head and breathed
on the rear of the goat, who let out a bleat and jumped
ahead into the water. But there the goat stopped again.

There were cries from behind, and the sheep pressed forward. Several stumbled in the mud, and suddenly Lilly saw
two of the shepherds dashing among the herd and calling
out warning. She saw the danger: the sheep could press so
hard they would knock down those in the front and trample and drown them.

Cross McCree took his rope and dropped a loop around
the goat's neck. Coca did likewise with one of the big sheep,
and there appeared two more riders, who did the same.
Slowly, Cross McCree leading, the men tugged the sheep out
into the water. Soon the goat and sheep were swimming behind the horses.

Henri, on horseback, and the men on foot came pressing
into the herd, urging the front sheep into the water. The entire mass followed. They were an amusing sight, some
jumping from the mud into the water as if over an obstacle.
In amazement Lilly watched the sheep begin to swim when
they hit the deeper water. She had not thought of sheep as
being able to swim. They would shake like dogs, too, when
they came up out of the water—and go immediately to
chomping grass, grabbing what they could before being
urged up the bank.

On and on, like a white river themselves, the sheep flowed
across the Rio Grande. And indeed, Lilly thought, it was an
awesome sight, as were the men and dogs who guided them.

Three bands had crossed and Lilly had gotten stiff and
tired of sitting atop Tubbs, so she'd dismounted. Quite
pleased at herself for adequately tying the mule to a bush he
enjoyed eating, she sat on a fallen log and watched the activity. She wished she knew enough to take part in herding.

Once one of the herders came down to walk across and he began removing his clothes. She sat there, dumbfounded and panicky, and moved her eyes to the opposite shore. Her eyes betrayed her, however, for she glanced back and saw the man looking at her. He retied his trousers, held his shirt and rifle aloft and crossed the river. Lilly knew that her presence was the cause of many of these men having to walk the rest of the day in wet britches.

Another band crossed safely, and Cross McCree and Coca came riding toward her, splashing across the sparkling water.

"Time we got you and the pack mules across," Cross McCree told her, speaking around the thin cigar between his lips. "Coca needs to get on down the trail and set up the noon camp. You'll do best to take off those moccasins and roll up your pants legs."

She stared at him.

He said, "Leather takes a long time to dry—no doubt through this cool night and tomorrow night, too. One of the last things we need is for you to catch a fever."

Lilly leaned over and began to untie the knee-high moccasins. She glanced upward to see Cross McCree watching her every move. Her face was flaming by the time she got her moccasins and socks off. She rose and looked at Mr. McCree, at his bare, hairy legs and then at the amusement on his face. She would not roll up her pants legs and reveal her legs for all and sundry, and her expression dared him to argue.

He didn't, though his expression clearly said he thought she would have regrets.

She was forced to have him witness her fumbled mounting, as Tubbs continually and deliberately shied to the side away from her every time she lifted her foot to the stirrup. Cross McCree sat there atop his horse and waited. Glancing over her shoulder at his blank expression, she wanted to smack him.

At last Coca, having their three pack mules in tow, rode his mule against the opposite side of Tubbs and forced him to stand while Lilly lifted herself into the saddle. The stirrups pressed painfully into her tender, bruised feet.

Coca and the pack mules headed for the river, and Tubbs followed easily, just as he had for miles from Santa Fe. Coca kicked his heels into his mule's sides, and the animal plodded into the slow-moving water. The pack mules balked once and, having no choice, plodded in, too. Tubbs, however, jerked to a stop at the edge of the water; he'd finally decided he'd had enough of following.

Lilly held on as he moved first one way and then another, snorted and backed up. She squinted painfully, the bright sun reflecting from the water.

"Kick your heels into him," Cross McCree said from behind her.

Tentatively she kicked her heels as she had seen done. "Get up...go on...go..." She kicked a little harder and urged with her body and the reins. The mule stood his ground.

The next instant Cross McCree let out a "Yeeeah!" and smacked Tubbs across the rear with the end of a rope, Lilly saw out of the corner of her eyes, as she grasped the saddle horn and held on. Tubbs lit out into the water.

He did not like it at all. There in the middle he decided he was turning around and going back. He twisted, lost his balance, and suddenly Lilly found her saddle slipping sideways. It didn't matter how hard she hung on to the horn, the saddle was going, so she was, too.

Slowly, Lilly slipped into the cold water.

She went under before she managed to get her legs beneath her. The heavy wool serape was like lead weight around her, and she had to struggle to stand. Then a hoof caught her in the leg and knocked her off her feet again.

She came up for the second time, jerking the serape from her head and spitting water and curses.

"You damn devil!"

She hit out at the mule, but he was already away for the shore, dragging the saddle with him. Seeing Cross McCree riding toward her, she smacked water at him and cried, "And damn you, Cross McCree! You knew that mule was no good!"

Suddenly she saw them—the men on the shore laughing. In a huff, she turned, battled the heavy serape and trousers, and started for the opposite shore. She would get across without that damn mule. She never wanted to see that dung heap of an animal ever again!

Hearing splashing behind her, she looked over her shoulder. Cross McCree's horse was coming toward her. She tried to walk faster, but the water came to her waist, and the rocks and silt were slippery beneath her feet.

The next instant her hat, dripping wet, was dropped on top of her head. Cross McCree's horse brushed against her, and his arm came down, closed around her waist and lifted her out of the water. She came to rest with a plop right across his lap.

His face was only inches from hers. With the cigar clenched between his teeth, he grinned, splitting his thickening beard. His eyes were blue as the sky above...and laughing, too.

She felt the heat of him through her wet trousers, and heat swept her. Water trickled down her neck and between her breasts, where her heart thudded...where Cross McCree's arm pressed.

His eyes held her captive, the same as his arms. And then she saw his gaze drift downward, like a caress, to her lips. Her breath stopped in her throat, a thrilling sensation.

The next instant he heeled his horse, and the animal lunged forward. Lilly was thrown against his hard chest, and she held to his arms for dear life.

With each rocking step of the horse, Cross clearly felt the woman's little warm bottom against his crotch, through the cold, wet fabric of both of their trousers.

He deposited her beside Coca, saw her snow white feet as they set into the green grass and the outline of her breasts where the wet shirt clung. Jerking his eyes away, he gave hard rein to Domino, and rode away to retrieve the mule.

"I don't want that damn mule," Lilly Blackwell told him. Her eyes spit fire, and her pulse beat hard beneath the white skin of her neck. She held up her trouser legs and stalked away.

Nudging Domino alongside her, Cross said, "I guess you'll take him or walk."

"Well, then, I'll walk." And she set off, for all the world resembling one indignant wet hen.

Cross sat there, at a loss, watching her, his groin throbbing against his wet trousers and the mule's lead tugging on his hand.

"I am experienced with the female," Coca said, his eyes twinkling. "I will see to her." He took charge of her mule, and his expression changed to one of sarcasm. "You would be well to dip back in the cold river, no?"

Without answer, Cross again turned Domino across the river and returned to the job of getting their sheep moving—his and the woman's sheep. That's what she had hired him to do, after all.

They had a noon camp, allowing both sheep and men to rest. After an hour, camp was broken, and the men went to move the sheep out. Cross stayed behind. He fetched the woman's mule. He also brought the saddle and a dry pad. Leading the mule and carrying the saddle, the pad over his shoulder, he stopped in front of Lilly Blackwell, who sat on the trunk of an old fallen tree. She had changed into the second set of trousers and shirt and again wore her moccasins. The shirt was too small and stretched tight over her breasts. He hadn't realized how full-breasted she was. He traced the line of her neck to where her white skin disappeared into the shirt. Her hair, damp, fanned out over her back. Her hat, still wet and saggy, was drying with the serape on a nearby bush.

He said, "I bought this mule for you because he's steady. He's not gonna buck you off or run off and leave you, and he'll carry you through the mountains and the desert day in and day out without comin' up lame.

"However, it appears that some lessons are in order, for you to get along with him." He pushed the mule forward and showed the woman how to saddle him. "One of us will always lift the saddle up. It's heavy, but you need to know how to cinch it, so you can tighten the cinch yourself." He demonstrated as he spoke.

Without a word, she watched him, and when he told her to try it for herself, she did so. Allowing his arm to brush against her as he reached around her, he loosened the cinch.

"Try again."

She turned her head toward him, but stopped, not looking at him. He stood close enough to her to breathe her scent, which was all sunshine and dampness and woman.

She returned her attention to the cinch and fastened it with hard, purposeful motions. He loosened it and made her fasten it again.

Satisfied that she could do this, he showed her how to slip the bit into the mule's mouth. Only he spoke; she watched carefully but silently.

Coca moved out, Henri with him, while Cross continued the lessons. He showed Lilly Blackwell how to pull the far rein over the saddle horn, forcing the mule to bend his head and body back toward her as she mounted. When the mule stepped forward, he had the woman tighten the rein and say *"So,"* very firmly. Again and again they did this until the mule stood still for her to mount. And again and again their arms brushed, their eyes touched.

Bringing himself in line, Cross stepped away from her, refusing to come in contact with her again.

As the lesson continued he saw confidence come over the woman. She watched and listened closely and proved a quick pupil.

He attached a lunge rope to the mule and directed the animal, with the woman riding, around in a circle, until the mule moved at her direction. He instructed her how to pull the mule into a circle if he got fractious and wouldn't behave, how to direct him with her legs. For this he took hold of the woman's ankle, clothed in the moccasin, and tapped it on the mule's side. Tap and the mule would go forward; press, hold the reins tight, and he would move to the side.

The sun was far to the west when Cross finally said, "You'll do now."

He mounted Domino and was satisfied to see the woman ride the mule toward him.

Her green eyes were steady. "Thank you," she said. "I've never had occasion to ride before now. I knew nothing about it." It was the first entire sentence she had spoken since the lessons had begun.

"Could have fooled me," Cross said dryly.

And a smile played at the corners of her mouth.

Together, side by side, they trotted off to catch up with the sheep. Casting several sideways glances, Cross saw that Lilly Blackwell rode a little straighter. However, her thighs flexed stiffly, holding her bottom away from the saddle. There was no doubt that her bottom was as tender as one whopped with a stick.

He recalled the feel of her against him, wet and warm.

Forcing this from his mind, he reflected that the woman's bottom would toughen by the time they reached California.

Chapter Ten

Henri's dark eyes danced eagerly. *"Siéntese, por favor,"* he said and elaborately waved a brown hand, indicating Lilly should sit on the thick bedroll.

Lilly repeated, *"Siéntese, por favor,"* and sat as regally as if she wore her best dress rather than trail-dirty trousers. Her Spanish was getting much better.

Rising, she waved the boy to their bedroll seat and said very precisely, "Please sit down."

He repeated the English words and sat, dark hands braced on his little knees. "I am good," he said and beamed proudly.

Lilly smiled. *"We* are learning well."

Her heart tugged. So young he was, and yet he had lived enough life for a man grown. Only occasionally, such as at this moment when he was so proud, did she see the child inside reflected on his face. And on occasion he seemed to welcome her touch, a hug, a brush to his cheek. Otherwise, he wanted to be counted a man as the others, and she kept herself from embarrassing him. He deserved her respect.

"It won't be so good if we don't have camp ready before dark," she said, covering her sudden tender feelings. "Finish gettin' those mules unpacked." Her gestures toward the mules explained her words.

Mumbling studiously, "Un-packed," Henri headed away to the mules.

Lilly had already begun a small fire in a hole dug in the ground. Coca had taught her to do this—to make a pit—giving a fire that didn't blow in the breeze and that was easier to cook above. He said he had learned it from the Comanche.

She positioned the cooking grill above the fire, put water, ground coffee and brown sugar into the pot, and set the pot on the grill to "cook" as Coca had taught her. She added the few bigger pieces of wood that she had to the flames, building the fire carefully.

Coca was away hunting up wild onions and hawthorns to make a potion for Gaspar Perez's ague. Lilly intended to have the coffee brewed and water boiling when he returned. Mateo had been assigned to look out for Lilly and Henri while Coca was away—one of the men was always with them—but Lilly had asked him to go find wood for the fire. There had been very few dead limbs around the camp area, and in the mountains the nights got next to cold. The men appreciated a good fire. *She* always appreciated a fire, she thought, dreading the cool of night.

They had been traveling for well over a month now. It seemed as if she had been out in this wild land forever. She no longer had a sore bottom—or else she simply ached with fatigue so often that she didn't notice it.

Straightening, she rubbed her stiff back. She felt like a rag well used and left to dry dirty. She would have given half her profit from the sheep to be sitting in a wing-backed chair, her feet upon a footstool, and drinking a steaming cup of hot English tea.

Gazing unseeing at the tree leaves glimmering in the golden sunlight, her mind drifted back...this time of day she would be sitting in the swing on the porch of Cypress Crossing, wearing a gauzy day dress...Shandy would be feeding the stock, Mammy Ethnee preparing supper, fried chicken and greens and cornbread, fresh tomatoes...Lilly would be pushing her slippered foot against the smooth porch floor and watching the sunlight glimmer on the black water of the swamp. Peaceful it would be.

She brought herself back to the present. She was far, far away from that life she had known back home, or even her more rustic existence in Santa Fe. Looking down at herself, she saw very little resemblance to the woman who had once worn silk.

Her gaze fell to her hands; they had become quite dark, and tough. She tried to keep them covered with gloves, but so often the gloves were uncomfortable, or she simply forgot them.

Soft white hands were as far away as Pasquotank County, she thought. For an instant she recalled Tyler; he had been very careful with his hands—his true treasures, he'd always said, for he had had the gift of fingers almost sensitive enough to tell one card from another.

Thoughts of Tyler came less frequently with each day. I have not forgotten you, she thought, offering Tyler an apology. I'm just trying to survive...and to get back to Pasquotank County where I belong, and with enough money that I will never, ever have to worry about being homeless again. Tyler could certainly understand her wish to do that.

Sighing, she lifted away her sweat-dampened hat, tossed it aside for a few precious moments, and removed her serape to let her sweat-dampened shirt dry before night. Perhaps she could slip away to bathe in the creek in the dark.

She set to work unpacking the bundles of supplies: the cups, frying pan, sugar, flour and tin of grease. It was amazing what Coca could do with so little, she thought. He got much of their food from the land around them—wild onions, dandelion greens, wild yam root, rabbit and squirrel. The fare was nourishing and varied, but for her part, Lilly longed for some good buttermilk biscuits and slices of sugared ham. Coca had tried to get her to try fried frog, which he said tasted like chicken. She told him she'd about reached her limit in all things that were wild.

Coca Arce was his full name, and during their long rides together he had told Lilly some of his life in which he had been a vaquero, a soldier against the Americanos, then a bandit and trader with the Indians. It was from the Indians that he had learned to use everything the land had to offer and to make medicines. He said his daughters had settled him, and that all he had learned from the Indians helped him to deal with them.

Lilly had come to know something about each of the men. Lorenzo Lopez, the self-appointed head wrangler, would kill a man over mistreatment of a horse or mule. Burros he was not so ardent about. His helper, Simon Morelos, liked to sleep and could do so for hours in the saddle. Mateo Benavidez was a young vaquero who wanted to make a fortune in order to marry the daughter of the *patrón* he worked for—a futile dream according to Coca, for no criollo would allow his daughter to marry a mestizo.

Arrio Baca was a criollo, son of Don Antonio. Arrio was fiery and elegant and a grand vaquero, who held himself aloof from the other men, who, as mestizos and Indian peons, were far beneath his station. He was politely respectful to them, however, and appeared well thought of by all.

Jesus—no one knew his last name or even if he had one—was a lowly and devout peasant who had been a shepherd all of his life for the Baca family and considered himself blessed. After seeing the men cross themselves when in his presence, Lilly had asked Coca about it. Coca explained that Jesus's age was a matter of ripe speculation. Some said he was two hundred years old, and either a saint or a devil.

The others Lilly had little contact with and knew by name and by the set of their hats or their grins or the ammunition belts across their shoulders. Each had been scrupulously polite, as Cross McCree had said they would be. All except Uriah Plover, who spoke little and gazed at her with the raw appetite of a barbarian. Fortunately he was most often away, scouting out the trail.

Taking up two pails, Lilly walked down to the creek. She plowed through the tall grass that was partially beaten by her previous trek to the creek and refused memories of neat brick pathways.

She had tried to describe to Henri the brick pathways of her home back in Pasquotank County and how they had no fear of Indians and did not live behind plaza walls. She'd told him of the wooden buildings built up from the ground on brick pilings, with their plentiful windows and wooden floors. Of course he couldn't quite comprehend.

She had begun to think of taking Henri home with her to Pasquotank County. She had grown so fond of him and couldn't bear to think of leaving him behind. Back in Pasquotank County, when she returned as a woman of means, she would be able to give him a much better life than he would have as an orphan here in the West. There would be problems . . . his skin color, his lack of cultivation, his pure wildness. Still, these could be overcome.

The creek water trickled over pale pebbles spotted among darker ones—so different these creeks were than the ones back home, which were dark and musky from the swamps. She doubted the sheep would want to drink from the creek, because it flowed so swiftly. The men might have to form dams to make pools placid enough for the queer little animals, who demanded still waters, no matter whether they were dying of thirst or not. She had discovered that sheep were not at all practical creatures. And on mulling this, she thought men not much different.

Coming back, she saw a rider emerge from the thick trees. Involuntarily she thought of Cross McCree, and her heartbeat picked up tempo. She suddenly recalled that she wasn't wearing her hat, and she was glad, even though her braid was disheveled. At least without that floppy hat she was clearly a woman.

But then a chill swept her as she recognized Uriah Plover upon his thick buckskin horse.

She dropped the pails to the ground and reached for her hat, jamming it upon her head. She was pouring water into the small stew pot when Uriah Plover dismounted. She didn't look at him, but she heard his breathing, heavy as that of his horse. Her skin prickled with the feeling of his gaze crawling over her.

Leaving his horse, he came to the fire and around it to stand beside her—between her and the pile of supplies.

"Got us some frog weather a'comin'," he said. "Coca oughta like it, since he eats them critters." He spit a stream of tobacco into the fire, barely missing Lilly. The moist tobacco hissed.

Lilly moved aside, set down the pail and glanced toward the trees, wishing Coca or Mateo would return.

Uriah Plover said, "Saw Mateo back a-ways. He's choppin' a dead tree. Told him he didn't need to hurry—I'd keep watch on you and the boy."

Lilly's eyes swung to his.

A slow smile split his thick gray beard, showing tobacco-stained teeth. His eyes were gleaming black nuggets in his crusty face. Very slowly he turned his head and spat a brown streak into the trampled grass.

Fear squirmed over Lilly, but she told herself that Plover would not do anything and risk being thrown out of the company.

Suddenly Henri came to her side. Dropping a heavy bag of sugar to the ground, he missed Uriah Plover's feet by inches.

The big man laughed. "Big job for a little *muchacho*, eh?" and gave the boy a shove, hard enough to cause him to step backward.

Lilly stepped back, too, and put her arm on Henri's shoulder. Plover's eyes were hot with intent.

Fear tumbled with memories of blood and evil eyes. Her heart thudded in her chest, and her mind ran wild. She could scream to Henri to run...turn and run herself...off into the trees...the man would get her in two strides...and he could hurt Henri.

She stood frozen by terror.

Uriah Plover stepped toward her. Henri tugged on her trousers. Her pulse pounded in her ears...black, gleaming eyes bored into her.

"I been wonderin' if you have lily white skin to match yer name," Plover said. "Me, I don't much care, but a lot of men, they like that."

He reached out and grabbed her arm. She twisted, but he kept hold of her arm with one hand, while the other fumbled with her shirt.

"No!" Her voice came out a hoarse whisper. His fingers bit into her flesh like the teeth of a steel trap.

Henri attacked, kicking and yelling, but Uriah Plover simply gave him a hard shove, sending him reeling backward and stumbling to the ground. Then he pulled his pistol, cocked it.

"Stay back, boy, or I'll see that you do."

With the pistol still aimed at Henri, he looked at Lilly and grinned. "Now, fancy lady, you take that shirt off, or I'll shoot the boy."

Lilly couldn't move.

Uriah Plover's big hand shot out, gripped her shirt at the neckline and ripped it down the front.

"Now...that's what I call white skin." His eyes devoured her as she tried to cover herself. "Take off that fancy lace," he said. "Now!" he barked and waved the pistol at Henri.

With shaking fingers, Lilly fumbled with the buttons of her camisole. Uriah Plover's eyes filled with hot, feral lust, and his breathing came faster. Terror had Lilly in a firm grip.

"Plover!"

Cross saw the man go stiff as stone. "I imagine you can pull your trigger," Cross said, looking through the sight of his Sharps, "but I can put a neat hole behind your ear before you can move. And you've seen me shoot."

One long second Plover debated, then he pulled up his pistol, softly lowering the hammer as he turned toward Cross, with his hands in the air and a dry grin upon his crusty face.

"I found the Colorado, boss, right where it's always been," he said. "It was passable when I left it." His eyes dared Cross as he held his pistol up, his fingers far from the trigger. He knew Cross wouldn't shoot him in cold blood. "Come up on some Cheyenne sign, too—band of at least thirty. Might be they'll be interested in these sheep...or maybe the woman." He slowly turned his head and spit a stream of tobacco into the fire where it sizzled.

Cross nodded and said, "And you were just checkin' to see what she'd be worth."

"Well, I figured right off that the Cheyenne would pay me a sight more for her than they would a few strayed sheep." The big man's eyes glittered, and Cross saw that he was considering his options.

"Get on your horse, ride and don't look back," Cross said.

Slowly Plover brought his hands down, stuck his Colt
Dragoon into his holster. "Ain't ya gonna give me some
grub?"

"You got a couple of good guns and know how to use
them."

The man glared. "I guess you got that right." He walked
toward his horse, which was frothy with sweat. The man
used the animal roughly, which was as stupid a thing to do
as it was cruel. Too many times a man's life depended on the
condition of his horse.

Plover hefted his big frame into the saddle, then paused
to spit again, a gesture of defiance.

Cross lowered his rifle and said, "If I see your face anywhere between here and California, I'll consider it an invitation to kill you."

There was the tiniest jump of fire in the burly man's black
eyes. His fist clenched the reins. Another man would not
have seen it, but Cross was a man to note it.

Uriah Plover jerked his horse around and rode away at a
gallop.

Turning, Cross found Lilly, arms wrapped around herself, staring at the serape Henri brought her. The raw fear
he saw in her eyes brought a sickness to his stomach.

Slowly he went to her and crouched. He didn't know what
to say and was half afraid to touch her. She seemed so fragile that she would break should he lay a hand on her.

At last he reached out and put his arm around her.

She remained stiff, and then her eyes came to his.

"He's gone," Cross said. "You're okay."

Tears welled into her eyes, and she sank against him,
burying her face at the base of his neck.

Cross held her. After a moment he dared to stroke her
silky hair. He kept a firm hold on the stirrings deep inside
himself.

* * *

They had been pushing hard for days, and when the herd reached a hot springs, Cross ordered an early stop. They had left the headwaters of the Rio Grande far behind and were following valley after valley northwestward. The valley they had entered that morning provided abundant grazing and natural corrals in the form of rocky ridges, as well as plenty of river pools. It was a good place of rest for both men and animals—and a good place for the woman to enjoy a bath.

The men had their baths first. Tomas didn't want to, but the other men dragged him to the warm-water pool. Clothes were washed and hung around on poles and bushes, wherever the late-afternoon sun touched. Lorenzo Lopez washed his serape and hung it near the fire, causing the pungent scent of warm wet wool to mix with that of the wood smoke. The men lounged, played cards, mending equipment, or simply sleeping. Gaspar Perez's snoring could be heard quite clearly.

Cross lounged against his saddle beside Coca, who was fashioning fresh sheepskin for the inside of his moccasins. The Comanche had taught him to do it—which was what he said of just about everything. Cross sharpened a knife and kept one eye peeled on the woman's tent. He noted when the flap of the tent moved, saw Lilly Blackwell peer cautiously out. He felt her gaze, though he didn't look up. Still without looking, he knew when she slipped from the tent, a small bundle in her hand, and headed away through the tall grass and brush toward the creek.

"Keep the men in camp," Cross told Coca as he put the knife in a sheath, took up his rifle and rose.

"Who keeps you, *patrón?*" Coca asked matter-of-factly.

"I'm the *patrón* and have the responsibility of lookin' out for her," Cross answered with a grin.

He slipped off into the trees in the opposite way, but walked a wide arc to come back from the north, where rocks rose above the warm pool. The woman was half undressed.

Cross gazed at her for a long moment, at her shoulders and head bathed in the golden glow slanting over the western mountain. Then he took hold of himself and turned his back. The woman had a right to her privacy, and that was a fact he repeated to himself a number of times as he sat there.

He listened to the splashing of the water and the woman's humming. As if drawn by an unrelenting magical force, Cross's head slowly swiveled around, and he saw. For a precious moment he allowed his eyes to move slowly over her pale, tender skin from her head to her ankles in the water.

Then she moved deeper and sat. Cross turned his back once more, pulled the knife from the back of his neck, and began to whittle on a twig. All the while the sun sank beyond the mountain, he whittled the twig to nothing and listened to her humming and splashing in the warm spring.

He waited until she had dressed and rolled her things back into a bundle before showing himself.

"How was the water?" he asked, making his way down to her, rifle in hand.

Lilly whirled around. Surprise, embarrassment and delight mingled at the sight of Cross McCree. "How long have you been there?"

"I followed you from camp." There was mischief in his blue eyes.

"Oh?" she said. "And I thought you said you came from civilized people. Apparently you have your uncouth barbaric side, too."

"Would you really rather be out here all alone?"

She stared at him. He stared back at her. Embarrassment kept her silent; she hated to admit to being glad of his presence . . . and not totally for safety.

He said, "We're in Ute lands now. It's their home, and we're trespassin'. So far they haven't seemed to take offense, but we need to be ready should they decide to press

us. From now on, either Coca or myself will always be with
you. *Always.*" He pulled something from beneath his serape—a knife in a worn leather sheath. He held it out to her.
"And you'll have this."

Her eyes flew up to his. "I..." She looked back at the
knife. The horrible memory of the knife jutting from the
Tejano's neck passed across her mind. "I have my husband's derringer." She'd loaded it and kept it at hand since
Uriah Plover's attack, but she wasn't certain she could use
it.

"A derringer misfires about half the time. A knife never
does...nor are you likely to shoot yourself—or one of us—
with a knife," he said dryly. "A knife is part of your hand."

He propped his rifle against a rock outcropping and drew
the knife from its sheath. It wasn't a large knife, perhaps six
inches altogether, straight to a point, with a dark wooden
handle. He thrust it toward her, handle first. She took it
gingerly.

"Not like that...." He took her hand and formed it in a
fist around the handle and squeezed it. "Hold it tight."
With his rough hand still closed around hers, he stepped
close. "Use the force of the swing. Try for low...here...and
jab, then pull upward toward the breastbone. Use the force
of the swing."

She gazed at his serape, and her mind drew a picture of
what he was saying. Her stomach knotted.

Crouching, he tugged her down beside him. "Use the
force of a swing," he said, and he lifted her arm and
brought it down, jabbing the knife blade into the soft earth.
As he had when teaching her about the mule, he had her
practice jabbing with the knife. When she had succeeded in
sinking it to the hilt three times, he slowly straightened and
helped her up.

Meticulously he wiped the knife with his serape. "Keep it
clean and I'll sharpen it for you." He slipped the sheath

onto a strip of leather, then reached out, took her arm and
tugged her toward him. "This'll go around your waist."

She stared into his deep eyes, dark in the waning light.

His arms came around her, and he tied the sheath firmly
at her side. Then he held her hip and tugged the sheath exactly where he desired it.

"There. It's easier to cross your arm over to grab it. See?"
He took her hand and illustrated.

His gaze came up to hers. He kept hold of her hand, and
his other hand remained at her waist. Suddenly it felt very
warm, as if he were touching her bare skin. They stared long
at each other, and a strange, enormous longing stirred
within Lilly. Her gaze dropped downward over his face, over
his cheeks covered now with a thickening beard and to his
lips. She stared at his lips, and the stirring grew.

"I think it's time I got a bath, too," he said, soft amusement in his voice. "Maybe you could stand guard for me."
He raised an eyebrow, and his eyes twinkled.

He thought she would run away, she thought, but it would
serve him right for her to take him up on his taunting.

She opened her mouth for a smart retort, when suddenly
an odd sound echoed from the distance.

Cross McCree turned from her, listening. When a shot
rang out, he leaped to grab his rifle and called for Lilly to
come on. She did, running right behind him. There came the
odd echo again—a roar, she thought—and the bleating of
sheep and men yelling. Cross was far ahead of her and Lilly
out of breath, when she finally reached the edge of camp.

The camp was a melee of bleating sheep running and
hopping over things and yipping dogs trying to gather them
and men running and shouting. Lorenzo Lopez, in his long
johns and boots, came running with Cross McCree's horse.
Cross McCree waved away his horse and shouted orders in
Spanish to Paco and Jon Salazar, who were trying to saddle horses. Without pausing he ran past Coca, who threw

him his pistol, and continued out of camp, with Mateo and Tomas on his heels. Paco and Jon chased after them.

Lilly ran for Coca. He stood near the pile of stores, loading a rifle.

"What is it? What's happened? Is it Indians?"

Coca shook his head. "*Oso* . . . a bear."

Something in the way he spoke brought the icy fingers of fear across her shoulders. She strained to see through the growing twilight and trees, listening above the bleating sheep to hear the odd echo that was the bear's roar.

Henri! she thought. He had gone with Chino, out with the ewes and lambs. And she, too, began to run.

Coca caught her. "No. . .*señora*. You would only be in the way." He handed her a rifle. "It is ready."

Chapter Eleven

Cross came to the edge of the small clearing. Slowing his steps, he gasped for breath.

"*Madre Maria... oso gris,*" one of the men behind him whispered in a reverent tone.

It was a grizzly, four hundred pounds at least. The silvery tips of his fur rippled as he moved. He was growling beneath a tree, reaching up and batting at the limbs.

Cross caught a glimpse of white fabric among the green leaves of the tree the bear was assaulting. Two dogs—Pan and a companion—were barking and attacking the bear, then darting out of reach of the blows from the devil's paws.

There came a yelp as Pan's companion wasn't quick enough and was sent rolling over the ground. Immediately he was up, limping but barking again.

Evidence of the bear's destruction lay scattered across the meadow—white mounds in the green grass. There was the scent of blood and the air vibrated with menace. A bear would simply lumber into a herd and take his fill, sampling first one sheep and then another, more in evil gluttony than need.

Across the narrow meadow Arrio Baca struggled to control his horse that ran in circles in fear. Giving up, Arrio slipped from the horse and let the mount break and head away on the run.

Jesus moved through the sheep that were bunching tight. They pushed toward the rocky mountain ridge and were likely to trample and smother one another in fright.

The bear turned from the tree and his quarry and lumbered several feet away, toward sheep carcasses. The person in the tree hollered. Chino, Cross recognized by his voice. Chino shook the branch, amazingly calling the bear back again. A second later Cross realized why.

There, lying among the white lumps in the grass, was a small dark figure. And it moved. An arm came up.

Henri. Even though Cross couldn't see the boy distinctly in the grass, he knew it was him.

The bear paused and looked over his shoulder at the tree. Then he turned again to the carcasses, and the small figure. Henri was alive, and this was what drew the bear.

Cross tossed his rifle to Mateo and cried "Shoot!" And then he ran full out toward the bear, screaming at the top of his lungs.

Shots rang out, and at least one whizzed by him. The bear flinched, rose up in anger and roared. From that distance the bullets were no more than stings that got the grizzly's attention—and drew him from the boy. The shots and Cross yelling could send the beast running away...but they didn't. The crazed beast came down with a force to shake the ground and, roaring, barreled toward Cross.

When Cross was close enough to see saliva slinging from the grizzly's teeth, he stopped and shot his Colt. The bear took the first hit and fell backward, then was up and coming on again. Cross tossed away the pistol, drew the big bowie knife from the scabbard at his waist and threw himself to the ground, rolling into a ball.

The bear was on him. His ears echoed with roars and the pounding of his own pulse. Going on instinct, he jabbed the knife, felt it sink into the soft underbelly. He jerked with both hands, ripping and tearing with the knife with all his strength.

And then the bear went still, dropping every bit of his hot, dead weight upon Cross.

Lilly strained to see through the growing dimness... across the sheep that had pressed in close. Upon hearing the silence that had descended upon the valley, she had hurriedly put more wood on the fire, and it blazed brightly behind her, casting its flickering light out against the agitated herd and the trees and brush. A dog came into view, circling his charges. Coca came to stand beside her.

They heard the quiet voices, the shuffling feet, and then, like apparitions out of the shadowy sheep, walked the figures.

Cross McCree was in the front. Bareheaded, serape hanging from one shoulder... The firelight illuminated the deep lines of exhaustion and desperation on his face. He carried a figure in his arms.

Henri!

Lilly broke into a run toward them, instinctively holding out her arms, though for what she didn't know.

"He's alive," Cross McCree said.

The bear had raked the left side of Henri's head, tearing deep gashes in his scalp and leaving his ear hanging by a thin section of skin. But he was alive.

Blood. It matted Henri's hair. Cross McCree was covered with it, his shirt soaked as thoroughly as from rain.

Cross McCree tenderly laid Henri atop the bedroll that Coca quickly spread near the fire. Lilly fell to her knees and took the boy's hand, staring in horror at the gaping wounds. And the blood. Deep crimson, smeared and soaking. She couldn't stop staring. Silent screams pounded inside her brain.

Coca brought warm water and a cloth. Cross ripped off his bloodied, bear-stinking shirt, knelt and went directly to work cleaning the boy's wounds. The boy's unconscious state was a blessing, yet the small body still felt the pain, for the boy jerked and moaned.

Cross glanced at the woman, saw the madness on her face. He motioned to Coca, who lifted the woman by the shoulders. She hurried away to her tent, and Cross spared a slice of anger at her weak desertion, before returning his attention to the boy.

He'd had bears attack his sheep before, but in the past they had always been frightened away. He'd heard of such bears as this one, that did not run; now he had experienced it. He dipped the cloth into the basin, and the water ran red as pure blood. Tears came to his eyes.

He thought of how he was alive at that moment only because of the boy's bravery.

Clenching his jaw, he tenderly worked to pat the boy's flesh back into place. He was aware of the men lingering near, in the shadows, waiting, silently lending the boy their strength and prayers; these men were a faithful lot, no matter their vices.

A moment later, a shadow came forth into his line of vision.

"He needs sewin' up," Lilly Blackwell said as she fell to her knees on the other side of the boy. She plunked a box—that cherrywood box she had insisted Cross find room for on her mule—to the ground, opened it. "I need more light," she commanded, and a torch appeared at the boy's head.

Amazed, Cross watched her riffle inside the box; light glimmered on things there—thimble, colorful thread, a china pot. She came away with thread and a needle. Deftly she threaded the needle. She paused and gazed at the boy. Her face was the color of the ashes of a cold fire.

"Have you sewn up skin before?" Cross asked.

"Once," she said. "An inch on my husband's hand."

Their eyes met, and both had the same thought: an inch was a far cry from replacing an ear and patching a scalp.

"I imagine I'm the best person for the job," she said in a bare whisper.

"I imagine you are," he agreed flatly.

He saw her struggle for strength, saw the determination solidify in her green eyes as she gazed at the boy. "There has been enough death, by God," she said in the manner of a warrior meeting an enemy. She bent toward the boy. Her hands shook and perspiration shone like silver on her face, but she went about her business. Cross held the boy's head for her.

Henri twitched with the first prick of the needle...and the next...and the next. Lilly's head began to spin, and she squeezed her eyes closed, prayed, demanded that her mind clear and her stomach settle. It all did, and she proceeded. She did what she had to do.

She sewed as carefully as she would fine challis. She tried to imagine the tender skin as being just that—the fine ivory challis she had ordered from Richmond and had made into a negligee for her wedding trousseau. She had spent so many pleasant hours stitching, hours of weaving hopes and dreams into an article of clothing. Oh, Tyler had thought her lovely in it.

Dear God, I shall never forgive you if this boy dies.

When she finished, her legs and back were so cramped she could not stand. Cross stood and lifted her up.

She leaned on his arm and smiled weakly. "Oh, my...I believe I need a cup of tea." She wiped the back of her sleeve over her damp forehead.

He saw the light in her eyes fade and reached for her just as she fainted dead away. He held her there against him, felt her heart beating against his bare chest.

* * *

Lilly drifted up slowly from sleep. She heard a strange sound . . . a hard yet soft sound, like a file against a horse's shoe. Her eyes flew open, as she realized she was not watching Shandy shoeing horses back home.

She lay on soft sheepskins and was covered by blankets.

Her gaze lit upon Cross McCree. Her vision adjusted, and she saw his features. Flickering firelight reflected upon his face, illuminating a cut across his cheek just above the line of his scruffy beard. Smoke spiraled from the cigar between his lips. He was washed now, his hair neatly combed, and wearing clean shirt and trousers. Sitting cross-legged, he leaned toward the firelight. The sound she heard was the sound of him sharpening the big knife from the scabbard at his belt.

It was the knife he had used to kill the bear.

That memory brought her sitting up. It all came flooding back to her. Cross McCree carrying Henri . . . the snatched reports of the men. They said he had faced the bear and killed it with his knife.

He had killed the bear . . . just as he had killed the man. Defending them all.

Cross McCree's eyes came around to her. She brushed the hair from her face and reached out to touch Henri beside her. His skin was hot. With a jolt, she saw his head was matted with leaves.

"Coca's poultice," Cross McCree told her as he carefully put away his knife and whetstone. "It'll stem the blood flow and bring healing."

"He's so hot. He has a fever," she said.

"He should have some fever to fight the infection."

She was not so sure of that. She gazed skeptically at the matting of leaves, but she had to admit that Coca might know more than she about poultices; she knew nothing, other than that Mammy Ethnee had used some very strange concoctions for the same purpose.

Cross McCree rose, crouched in front of the fire, poured a steaming cup of liquid from a pan over the fire and brought it back to her. "Here... Coca made you some sort of tea." His voice and eyes were amazingly gentle, so much in contrast to his tough, weathered face.

She pushed away strands of her hair that slipped from her braid and accepted the cup. Feeling Cross McCree's eyes upon her, she sipped cautiously. "Why, it's sassafras!" Such an unexpected pleasure, there on a Western mountain, in the midst of wilderness.

Cross McCree gave a half smile and said, "These things can be had by trade. There's sassafras over in the Indian Nations." He propped himself against a pile of bundles— Coca's stores—and cocked one leg.

Lilly sipped again, savoring the sweet, hot brew. The scent of it wrapped her in pleasantly warm, vague memories of her childhood. The rest of the camp was silent, all sleeping. Henri murmured and twitched. Cross McCree said he had done so off and on for hours. She reached out to touch the boy's brow, hovered her hands over the matting of leaves and then smoothed the blankets covering him and smoothed them again, frustration and longing moving her hands. Her touch seemed to soothe him, for he relaxed and breathed rhythmically in sleep.

She asked about Coca, and Cross McCree told her Coca had gone along to take care of the sheep with Gaspar Perez.

Then he said, "You did well by the boy."

The approval she saw in his eyes brought tears to her own. She nodded and averted her eyes to the cup of tea.

They continued to sit there, she and Cross McCree, surrounded by the night. There were bird calls she had become familiar with these weeks upon the trail—the hoot of a distant howl, the plump cooing of a night dove. The sounds had frightened her when she'd first begun the trip, but now she found them comforting. Insects were not so noisy here as back in the South, perhaps because of the low temperatures. It was hard to remember this was now midsummer. Lilly, feeling a chill that went to the bone, pulled the blanket up around her shoulders.

She sipped from the tin cup she cradled in both hands and thought how she had spent many hours of her life sitting up in the night, hours she had waited for Tyler to come home, weeks she had waited for him to win enough to pay their bills, keep food on their table, years she had waited to be blessed with a child . . . and to go home to Pasquotank County.

She wondered now if she would ever get home. She wondered that if she did get home, if it would ever feel right. Tyler was gone...buried in foreign ground back in Santa Fe, in a grave she would never see again. All of her family were gone. And she felt almost gone from herself. Swallowed by the harshness of this land that made people fight death itself day by day.

A howl broke across the night and caused her to jump. The sound came again, crawling over her skin. She looked at Cross McCree.

"Wolves," he said. "They've been drawn by the carcasses back there in the clearin'. The men moved the bands up out of there and stretched them north. The predators will stay away from them, with other food for easy takin'."

A haunted light slipped into the woman's eyes, drew at her face. There came another howl and another, echoing against the mountains.

Cross said, "They're just callin'. And you're safe here."

She kept staring at him, and she began to tremble.

He tossed the stub of his cigar out into the fire and scooted over, reaching for her. She blinked, held herself away. He tugged on her arm. Her body remained stiff for a fraction longer. And then, like a willow bending toward the needed water, she slowly came against him, and down into the crook of his shoulder. He shifted his body, finding the comfortable spot against the sacks of flour and meal and coffee. With a deep sigh, she burrowed against his warmth.

She was cold, shivering. He thought how easily she could sicken and die. He'd seen a man take cold one night and die the next. He pulled a second blanket over her, rubbed his hand up and down her back and then kept it around her, holding her tight to him, willing his warmth into her.

And he, too, took comfort, finding it in the womanly pillow-softness and scent of her and the thrumming of her heart beating against his chest.

They lay thus, while the fire flickered low and the howls faded, the beasts filling their mouths with bounty.

"We don't have wolves back in Pasquotank County," she said softly. She still trembled some.

"Is that where you're from?" he asked.

"Yes . . . in North Carolina. That's a state back East."

"I know. My father was from the Carolina mountains."

"He was?" she said in whispered surprise.

Cross nodded. "He was a Scotsman—a Highlander. He lived some with the Cherokee and then went south, down among the Chickasaw. He took a Chickasaw wife and came west with the tribe."

Seconds passed, and she said, "Pasquotank County hasn't any Indians, except maybe Stone Reeves. I've heard he's Indian. He raises pigs and makes potions, in the swamp." She paused, and he felt her thinking. "We have roads there, and carriages, and sawmills and gins and steepled churches and white-columned houses with flower gardens. And sheep are kept in fences."

He saw in his mind, as best as he could, what she spoke of. "I've seen settlements with those things, back in the

Nation. There're Indians there, my mother's people, who have plantations."

Seconds passed again.

And then she said in a bare whisper, "And yet you are out here, with the bears and the wolves."

"Yes," he said. For an instant he smelled the bear all around him, felt its claws scraping him, and terror came to the back of his throat.

He brought his hand up and stroked her hair. It felt like warm polished silver beneath his palm. She sighed deeply and pushed her head against his hand, as if in pleasure. He dug his fingers into its fluid warmth and then stroked again. And again. Over and over, in rhythm, letting the luxurious feel of it settle inside him.

He kept his other hand lying easy at his side, kept it from moving to her. He felt the man-swelling of him and ignored it. He simply lay there, stroking her hair. And her trembling ceased as she fell asleep. Soon after, he did, too.

Sometime later he felt Pan slip up beside him. When he awoke, the dog was sleeping curled against the woman, too.

So much for a sheepdog, Cross thought.

The following morning Henri awoke. He looked up at Lilly and said in labored yet correct English, "I ... am ... thirsty."

Lilly fell upon his chest, crying. Then, still sobbing, she raced to get him cool, fresh water. Then, with a flourish, she commandeered the cook fire and made Henri some proper sweet spoonbread, which was a potion, to her mind, as strong as any Coca could come up with.

Cross instructed the men to let the sheep fan out and forage up the mountainsides and on up the valley, keeping their base camp for one more day in which the men were able to rest and get their gear in shape again.

But one day was all they could afford to keep so many sheep in a single place. There was too much danger of the animals running short of good grazing. When that happened, those that went hungry would turn to poisonous plants. They could have grazed the herds for miles ahead and returned to bed ground, but that would mean back-trailing and wasting valuable time and energy. So the second day they moved the sheep out, leaving Coca and Mateo behind with the woman and Henri, who could not yet be moving on. The boy was in too much pain to bear riding, or any type of movement. Coca brewed a potion that eased the pain but caused the boy to sleep.

They let the sheep walk slowly and forage the mountain slopes. They made no more than six miles, which was close enough for three men on horseback to ride back to the main camp and get hot grub from Coca for the night meal. The men's spirits and energies were high because of the rest and the excitement.

The men still talked about the battle with the bear, embellishing the tale with every telling. Cross had no doubt that by the time the tale circulated back to Santa Fe, the bear would have grown by three hundred pounds and Cross's knife would have shrunk to a toad-stabber.

Cross was in the saddle from first light to last, circling the herds and returning to the base camp, to keep an eye on the woman and the boy. Each time he left, he saw the nervousness enter the woman's eyes, and each time he returned, he saw the relief there. And the welcome, too.

That night Cross returned to the camp to bed down. He unsaddled Domino but left him staked nearby, on hand should there be a need to ride quickly to the herds. He was a man torn between two callings, he thought, the sheep and the men on one side and the safety of the woman and the boy on the other. Moving his bedroll far out from the light

of the campfire, he took the first watch, while Coca and
Mateo went to sleep.

The woman sat beside Henri, on the end of her bedroll.
She had her hair neatly pulled back into a braid. She didn't
have her hat on, and Cross thought that an Indian scouting
them out would shortly recognize her as a woman, especially with those earrings, though not immediately, because
a woman wouldn't be expected out here.

She looked up and smiled as Cross came into the firelight. It bothered him that she hadn't been more cautious,
more alert, in case he had been a stranger. She'd just sat
there, cross-legged, sewing; she had taken one of Coca's old
shirts and was cutting it down for the boy.

She put her finger to her lips and inclined her head, indicating the sleeping boy. "He's just gotten to good sleep.
There's coffee left in the pot," she whispered.

He crouched, poured himself a cup. "You need to be
more on guard." He blew on the hot coffee.

"I knew you were there," she said, her lips quirking into
a grin.

"I might have been someone else."

She glanced at him. "I know your step." She dropped her
sewing in her lap and gazed at him thoughtfully. "I just
knew it was you. Do you know what I mean? Sometimes a
person just knows things. And out here, there's something
that makes the knowin' stronger. I guess I can't explain,"
she added with a shrug.

He studied her face, the soft curve of her cheek, the glow
of the fire reflected on her pale skin.

"It's your spirit," he said. "The part of you that speaks
to Mother Earth. The white man might prefer to call it instinct. Your ears hear somethin' out of the ordinary, and the
instinct in you that is still linked with the earth picks it up,
whether you realize it or not...or maybe you catch a scent,

or see somethin' that isn't strong enough to get your full attention, but your instinct gets it and puts you on alert.''

"Yes . . . I suppose it's all of that," she said with a faint smile, "but my Mammy Ethnee would have simply said it was God nudgin'." She studied him. "You speak of the 'white man' as if he is a stranger to you—yet you are very much a white man, too."

He nodded slowly. "Factually, I suppose I am . . . but my father turned his back on the ways of his people, and when my mother died, he severed all ties with the Americano ways. I've more lived the life of an Indian and Mexican."

She studied him a moment, then continued with her sewing.

He settled himself down beside her and sipped on his coffee. She had the cherrywood box open beside her. He slid his eyes over to look inside. Colors shone in the firelight. The box had a thick red satin lining. Nestled there were scraps of fabric, blues and reds and yellows, spools of thread, a pincushion with the pins gleaming, a silver thimble . . . and a china teapot painted with delicate roses.

"These things are all my most precious," she said, catching him looking, and he wished she hadn't. "Good needles aren't always easy to be had, so when I come upon them, I'm careful with them. This thimble was my mama's. It came from France." She lifted the thimble on one finger. "And so was this. . . ." She touched the teapot. "With all these things, I can not only keep myself clothed, but I can busy my fingers . . . sometimes when the night is long."

Cross met her gaze. "And you can stitch up skin."

"Yes . . . yes, I can."

Their gazes held, and there was a powerful pull between them. He knew that she was thinking about the previous night, just as he was, when she had lain in his arms.

He wanted her there again. He wanted her in his arms and in his bed and without clothes between them, either.

He was the first to look away, buried his face in the cup as he finished the last of the lukewarm coffee. He set the cup aside and rose.

"Are you stayin' tonight?" she asked in a breathless whisper. She kept her eyes bent over her sewing, but her fingers stilled.

"Yep," he said and saw the relaxing of her shoulders.

He walked away into the dark shadows and brought back his saddle and bedroll, which he placed several feet away. He stretched out, propped against the saddle, and shifted his hat low, as if to doze. He needed to pull away from the woman, from the desires whispering and tugging at him like a relentless hot south wind.

The memory of holding her kept echoing in his mind, no matter that he told himself it had been the result of them both being beat-out ragged and cold and lonesome. No matter that he told himself he had enough with the work of getting them all to California alive to keep him occupied.

He found himself watching her, peering through slit eyelids. She continued to sew, there in the firelight. Often she would lean over the boy, study him, maybe adjust his blanket, which didn't need it. She appeared content as only a woman could become. For a bare instant, he built a house around her: an open fireplace, warm adobe walls, smooth-armed rocker. The best of all he would know to offer.

Her head came up, and she gazed at him. Long and steady, as if calling to him.

He didn't move.

She put her needle and thread into the cherrywood box, and gazing at it, he thought of all he'd seen there. Any house he built would not be as fine a thing as what she came from. The silk dresses she had packed in bundles upon the mule would be mighty out of place in an adobe house.

He glanced at her hands, then her face. He thought how fragile she was, how fine. And then he looked down at his own dark, work roughened hand lying upon his propped thigh. It would be rough against her skin.

Several minutes later, his ears picked up a sound. Without removing his hat from his eyes, he tensed, moved his hand near the knife at his waist. He listened and recognized the almost silent padding of feet across the night-damp ground—Pan, who came and pushed his nose at Cross's hands.

"You ain't much of a sheepdog," Cross mumbled dourly.

And as the dog settled against him, he thought that it wasn't a dog he wanted to warm him in the night.

Chapter Twelve

Cross was pushing the outfit again. They had lingered four days while waiting for Henri to be well enough to ride. The boy was ready in three, but the woman held him back for another day. They'd been on the trail again only two days when dysentery had swept the men. It laid Gaspar Perez on his back. The woman turned her energies to brewing concoctions with Coca and cooking up pans of what she called spoonbread. The sweet gruel did seem to settle stomachs. And Cross had to admit, if only to himself, that Lilly Blackwell had come in handy in nursing the boy and the men.

They had come fully into the heart of the Ute lands. In the past Cross had spent much time in the Ute lodges and at their ceremonies, while trading with them. The Ute's stamping grounds were from down into the New Mexico Territory to far up around the Salt Lake. As with all Indian tribes, there were many bands, mainly made up of families or clans. Two years ago Cross had known the various bands and their leaders. However, life and loyalties were precarious, so no doubt a number of the ones he would have counted on for friendly treatment were gone. Back in '51 the Ute, along with eight other major Indian nations, had agreed to a treaty that allowed the white man to pass unmolested through their land. But the Ute were loosely united at best, and a treaty by several bands didn't mean a treaty by all. Dick Wootton had had a skirmish with a rowdy band of southern Ute last year when he'd brought his sheep through these same mountains.

Cross had brought gifts of gunpowder and flour and corn, as well as the extravagance of three good mustangs, and he hoped these offerings would get them through without a fight.

He had found sign that the Indians were aware of the coming of the sheep: unshod pony prints and cold fires of hunting parties. After finding the pony prints on three separate occasions and noting the shape, he knew they were being watched by the same two Indians, of the Ute tribe he guessed by the shape of the few moccasin prints he found. Once he saw an Indian sitting atop a pony, watching. The rider vanished so quickly that Cross was tempted to believe he was seeing things, but his spirit knew better. He *knew* the Ute were there, watching and waiting. Why they did not show themselves could be chalked up to something as simple as they didn't feel like it. The Duff had always said that Indians were the most difficult beings to figure, and the best figuring about them was that they would never do what a white man expected. That was why Cross tried to listen to his Indian side, which told him nothing more than to be ready for the unexpected.

At the moment, however, he found more to be concerned about in the weather. It was coming upon them quickly, the air growing heavy and the skies filling with thickening clouds. Cross could not judge as well in the mountains as he could out on the Llano, but he had a feeling that what was to come was not going to be any normal daily afternoon shower from which they could take shelter beneath a tree. And, by damn, the prospect of another delay was a high irritation!

He rode around the edge of the sheep to join the woman and the boy, who were riding between the second and third bands. He tried to keep the woman in such protected positions, and always accompanied by himself or Coca. He'd decided he might as well have Pan stay with the woman, too, and now the dog, tongue lolling, followed along behind her mule, occasionally, if the opportunity presented itself, running ahead to herd straying sheep. Coca had hurried his mules around and to the front of the herds to set up the noon camp and have the food ready for the men to come and go and keep the sheep moving.

In the shadow of her wide-brimmed hat there was welcome in the woman's green eyes, though she did no more than look at him. And she didn't smile. They were skirting the fire between them, Cross thought. He often wondered how it would have been between them if they had been alone...if they hadn't had so much separating them. He would ride away and tell himself to keep his distance, and always he came back, finding some excuse to be near her.

His were no idle excuses, he thought, his gaze sweeping the tree line behind her. That she was the most vulnerable one of them all weighed heavily upon him.

He reined in beside Henri, leaned on his saddle horn and stretched his legs. *"¿Cómo te encuentras, muchacho?"*

The boy's head was bandaged with strips from what Cross believed to have been one of Lilly Blackwell's petticoats. The boy didn't wear his floppy hat because it rubbed painfully over his wounded ear. Other than the cut over his eye, most of his scars would eventually be hidden by his hair.

"I feel well, *patrón*," he said in English. "No head-ache. I am ri-ding well."

His black eyes were hopeful, and Cross gave the boy what he wanted by saying, "Good. Then you can ride back to Chino and give him a hand."

The boy cocked his head. *"¿Qué?"*

Grinning, Cross repeated his words in Spanish, adding the order that he ride through the herds, not around them. "Stay away from the trees." The boy would be safer from Indians that way.

"*Sí, patrón.*" Henri bobbed his head, then kicked his feet into the horse's belly, urging the big sorrel away. He was little, but he handled the horse well. Lorenzo had come up with stirrups made of woven leather over stout sticks and attached by rope. They helped the boy be more secure.

The woman said, "He's been waiting all mornin' for you to come and tell him he could do that."

"He is a good worker," Cross said. He rode alongside her, pulling Domino back to the slow walk of the mule.

"He likes to please you...and he thinks he's as big as any of you. It frustrates him to be stuck with me so much."

"Yet it's to you he goes every night."

"He's still a boy," she said, a tender smile upon her lips.

Cross played the ends of his reins through his hands. "It's good for him to be with you and to learn English. The Americans flow into this country like twigs flowin' down a stream. There'll come a time when their ways will dominate. The boy will need to know the Americano language and understand their ways." He cast her a sideways glance. She rocked easily in the saddle now, sometimes leaned forward and stroked the mule's neck.

Her green eyes came over to his. "I thought that perhaps I would take Henri with me...back East, after we sell the sheep. I will be able to afford it then."

Cross turned his head forward, gazed across the backs of the sheep. He watched Tomas Vargas far to the right flash his arm in order to his dog, who hopped and sped over the clumps of pale grass like a rabbit.

Cross said, "You can teach the boy English, but that's a far cry from teachin' him all he would need to know to live in your world. Even now, he removes the sandals we got for him and goes barefoot. Sometimes a tree grows with a bend one way, and when you try to change the bend, you kill the tree.''

Though she looked right at him, her eyes hid from him. "A tree, perhaps," she said, "but Henri is more a sapling."

"As the characteristics of the trees are in the seed, the traditions of hundreds of years run through the boy's blood—and his mind. You would have to bend all that.''

"Your father came out here, he brought you here. That can't be any different than Henri going back there with me.''

He breathed deeply. "It seems that the white man can come out here and adapt, even thrive. They bring their ways of life, and those ways are accepted. However, how many Indians do you know who have gone east from the West and taken their ways? If that had ever happened, there would be tepees in your Pasquotank County.''

Stubbornness glimmered in her green eyes. "Henri is not a tepee Indian.''

Cross shook his head. "No...his father was Navaho, and they don't favor tepees. But they do favor superstitions— like the piece of bear hide Henri has hanging on the leather strip around his neck. Coca put it there to ease the boy's nightmares. And it's worked.''

She looked at him, and he could see her searching for a response. "And back home we sometimes see a light in the swamp. Some say it's a light carried by my father, who's looking for my mother. When my mother died, he hung himself on a cypress tree hangin' over the water. So, you see, the Americanos aren't so different. I imagine Henri would fit right in with us.''

Thunder rolled across the sky and vibrated between the mountains. "Better get out our slickers," Cross said, halting Domino. "I've got a feelin' this is gonna be a goose-downer.''

"What about Henri?" the woman asked, casting him a worried glance as she followed suit and dug out her canvas slicker. "He can't wear his hat."

"He's got a slicker, and Chino will see he gets shelter when he needs it."

It was less than half an hour later when the skies opened and rain fell like a waterfall. It beat down like a flogging with a wet wool blanket upon the head and shoulders and ran like streams off hats. The horses and mules hung their heads and tucked their tails, and the sheep refused to move. There was no fear of the herds straying, or being stampeded by the thunder or even raiding Ute should they come. The sheep bunched tight together, edging toward the safety of their shepherd, and stuck their heads beneath the shelter of each others' bellies.

Cross headed for the trees, pulled up and alighted, and turned to getting the woman beneath the thick branches of a juniper. Pan squeezed in beside them. They waited, crouched there for nearly an hour, while the rain beat a staccato rhythm through the trees and dripped upon their hats. Beside him, the woman began to shiver.

"Let's move," Cross said, raising his voice over the sound of the rain.

"Where?" Lilly asked him bleakly.

"There's a bit of a cave up ahead." He helped her mount, then held on to her reins and led the mule. Pan, head down, followed.

He stayed within the trees and worked his way higher onto the rock line. Though it was longer and tedious, weaving around and pushing through the brush, it kept the worst of the rain off them. Whenever he looked out into the clearing he could see nothing more than a silver sheet of rain. Behind him, the woman hung on to her saddle horn and kept her hat down, her shoulders hunched.

Guided by the edge of the mountain, there was no way to get lost. He headed up the valley toward where he'd seen the cave. At last he spied an outcropping large enough to provide shelter to both them and the mule and horse. There was also enough dry timber and pine cones to start a fire. Once he had one going, he was able to add larger wet pieces. They steamed and then caught. The woman took off her slicker and soaked hat. She swung her braid forward and pulled the leather strip that bound it. Pausing, she looked at Cross.

They gazed at each other for long seconds. Cross's gaze strayed to her hair, swept the length of it to her fingers. Moisture glistened on their tips.

She retied the leather, swung the braid again to her back and turned her eyes to the fire. Her eyelashes were long and dark against her pale skin.

Cross rose and walked to the edge of the outcropping to stare out at the rain.

When the flood let up, he headed off to find Coca. Knowing another storm would follow on the heels of the first, he put his Sharps in the woman's hands and the dog at her side and left her there, sitting with her back against the back of the cave, her knees bent in soaked trousers, one hand gripping the rifle, the other holding the mule's reins to keep it from following Domino.

The storms came, one after another, with never more than a lull of a couple of hours in between. The sky cracked, and rain fell in a torrent, as if poured from a giant pitcher upon the rock and tree-covered mountains. Lilly had seen such rains; they were common back on the coast. But never had she experienced them as if being a part of them. Only the few feet of the cave and rocky overhang separated her from nature's display of power. And nothing separated her from the constant chilly dampness.

Some of the men built shelters of tree limbs draped with canvas near the cave. Those who had to stay with the sheep and the remuda draped canvas over tree branches and brush and holed up beneath it. The sheep pressed up around them.

At the front of the cave, Coca was able to keep a fire going and provide hot food and drink to the men around the clock, and the men could come there to dry off. Lilly looked continually for Henri, got tighter and tighter, until Chino brought the boy up. She hadn't meant to, but before she knew it, she wrapped her arms around him. He bore it for five seconds before wiggling away.

He'd taken the piece of bear skin he had suspended around his neck and used it to pad his ear, so he could wear his hat. He proudly showed her, and she praised his craftiness. Still and all he was soaked through; his slicker was a worn castoff. Lilly insisted he change into one of Coca's dry shirts and an extra serape. When he wanted to go back to the herd with Chino, Cross McCree allowed it. Lilly could have choked the man, though she did no more than shoot him her most furious look. He returned the look calmly and turned away from her, dug grain from the supplies and went out to feed his horse, which he kept staked in a bit of shelter at the edge of the rocky outcropping.

It was awkward for her there, surrounded so closely by males. She couldn't use her tent, for it wouldn't have held up against such heavy rain. In the small cave she stayed dry, but she also had little movement, and there was no privacy whatsoever. She couldn't wash or change clothes, and each time she had to go out into the brush to do her business it was plain to everyone.

Perhaps the most awkward thing was the numerous hours of proximity to Cross McCree. Though several times a day he would ride out to check on the herds and herders, the rest of his time he was, as she, holing up out of the rain in the cave. And each night he lay just on the other side of Coca.

She watched him in the dark hours of the night, sitting up, feeding the fire and smoking one of his cigars. She came to know his presence by the scent of that cigar.

Sometimes their eyes met. His were always unreadable, but yet, again and again Lilly would find his gaze on her. Again and again, her eyes were drawn to him.

She was drawn to him in a way she couldn't quite fathom. She'd felt something like this for Tyler, once, and yet she'd never felt anything in her life with such relentlessness. She felt herself as drawn to Cross McCree as she was to a fire on a cold winter's day or fresh water on a hot day. She couldn't stop herself.

The rain wore on, hour after hour. The gloom and dampness of it wore away at them all just as it did the rocky mountainside. Tempers flared over card games and even food. Lilly herself began to think she might go mad if she couldn't get out of the cave, couldn't ride and walk and breathe something other than wet bodies and wet sheepskin and damp smoke.

Then, during a lull between rains, like a messiah in buckskins, Lilly suddenly saw a figure riding up through the thick trees.

Cross McCree cried out, grinned and hurried to meet the visitor.

It was the very grand Duffy Campbell. He smiled at Lilly as he dismounted from the biggest horse she had ever laid eyes on.

"Well now, bless me soul," he said, "if I'm not just in time for the party." Whipping off his hat, he bowed elaborately. "Good day, madam."

His smiling good humor was like a slice of sunshine into their despair—as were the four bottles of tequila he pulled from his pack mule.

Cross McCree bent his no-drinking policy for the occasion, and he filled each man's cup as they passed in a line in front of him. Grabbing up a cup, Lilly came at the end of the line, stepped forward when it came her turn and held out the battered tin vessel.

His eyebrows rose in surprise, and he stared at her. She kept the cup extended, and after several long seconds, Cross McCree filled it as he had the others.

"I'd sip that if I were you, *señora*," he said.

"I shall, sir. I certainly shall."

"I thought ye might come to needing me while goin' through the Ute's country," Duffy said, then murmured, "and Marquita was worrying me to death. Nothin' would do for the lass but that I come up here and check on ye."

Cross observed his friend. The two sat off from the others, beneath the limbs of a thick juniper that served to keep them if not dry at least from getting soaked. Though two hours to sunset, the light was dim.

"And since when did you start kowtowin' to a woman's wheedlin'," Cross said, averting his eyes as he took a deep drink from the bottle of tequila they shared. The mention of Marquita from Duffy's lips seemed to open a black hole inside him.

Duffy didn't answer immediately, and when Cross lowered the bottle, he found the big man gazing steadily at him.

"It might be my age catchin' up, but I'll do things for Marquita that I never did for another lass, and that's about the size of it."

The Duff looked so bewildered that Cross had to laugh. "And will you marry her, too?"

The expression that passed over the Duff's face caused a tightening inside Cross.

Duffy took the bottle and drank deeply. Then he sighed. "Aye... I think it's come to that, if she'll have me."

That sat there between them. Neither looked at the other, each dealing with the idea.

At last Cross looked up to see Duffy gazing at him. His pale eyes were apologetic yet edged with brightness. "I'm gettin' along, ye know. I've had enough of cold ground and seein' the other side of the hill. And we all know how much I love comfort. I'm comfortable... even frisky with Marquita." His tone dropped. "I thought it only right I come speak to ye first."

Inside Cross sadness and jealousy swirled and then mixed with joy for his friends. Would he have chosen this, Cross thought, if he had had a choice? What did it matter? This was the way it was working out. He had no part in it, except for wishing them well.

He said, "If Marquita can make you think this way, then you shouldn't pass her up." He looked deep into the Duff's eyes. "Take care of her, Duff... and my best to you." And then he took back the bottle and drank deeply, pushing aside the pain that cut his breastbone.

They discussed the incidents that had happened along the trail since Cross had left Santa Fe. Duffy had found the body of Rudd Puckett—or rather the bones and bits of clothing. He'd wondered about it.

"Fella appeared too short to have been ye," he said confidently, "so I didn't concern myself."

He'd met with a party of Cheyenne and Uriah Plover had been with them. He hadn't spoken to the man, however. Then he'd come upon the bones of the bear and sheep and had surmised a bit of what had happened.

Cross smiled ruefully. "I can't say I haven't missed you, Duff—nor that I ain't glad to have your help. It's been wearin' me thin tryin' to keep an eye on the sheep and the woman both."

"Aye..." The Duff nodded and his gaze shifted to Lilly on the rocky outcropping above them. "It's good ye got her into trousers. Though, up close, I think it'd only fool a nearly blind man."

"The idea is not to let anyone get close."

Cross told of the Indian signs he had seen, which told him the Ute had been watching them from a distance. Duffy had seen the signs, too. He'd heard the southern Ute bands were occupied down in the canyon lands along the San Juan River, so he speculated it would be the Tabeguache band they would be dealing with.

Cross knew the Tabeguache band, had spent time in their lodges. Four or so summers ago, Duffy reminded him, one of the young Tabeguache girls had been smitten with him. Cross remembered, as he did the brave who wasn't happy about it, either.

He and Duffy speculated as to why the Ute had not appeared. "Whether in peace or spoilin' for a fight, they will come in their own time," the Duff said. "All ye can do is be ready."

Lilly's voice, singing, floated down to them, and each fell quiet to listen. "Frog-gie went a-courtin', and he did rii-de, a sword and pis-tol by his side, uh-huh . . . uh-huh . . ."

"I believe the madam may be just a little tipsy," Duffy said.

Cross crawled out from beneath the tree. Every joint in his body protested, and water dripped from strands of hair falling across his forehead. He cursed the rain as he climbed up to the rocky outcropping in the dark. The Duff slipped and slid behind him. The woman was still singing about some frog.

She sat on bundles near the flickering fire. Mateo sat back in the shadows, his back propped against the rock. Coca was rolled into his blankets.

"There's bread and cheese up-on the shelf . . . and if you wan' any more, just sing it your-self. Uh-huh . . . uh-huh!" A broad swing of her cup just about sent her tumbling off her seat. "Do you suppose I could have just a bit more of this?'' she asked and held out her cup, peering up at Cross from beneath the wilted brim of her hat.

"Sorry, *señora*... there's no more for any of us." Cross took her by the upper arm and tugged her to her feet.

Her green eyes were very near his own. Her lips were very near his own.

And then her legs crumpled. Cross caught her, hesitated a moment, then hoisted her in the air and over his shoulder, which earned him a look of astonishment from Mateo and full laughter from Duffy.

When he saw the Duff doff his hat, Cross looked over his shoulder to see the woman waving at the big man.

"I believe it's time you got some sleep," Cross said and carried her to her bedroll spread at the deepest part of the cave.

Gently he sat her on the sheepskins. She gazed at him, blinked and melted over. "Froggie went a-courtin'..." she sang softly from beneath her hat, cocked over her face.

Cross straightened her legs, then lifted the hat. The firelight reflected against the rock wall and down upon her face. She gazed up at him. Her lips parted, and her hand fluttered upward; she stroked her fingers across his beard.

He jerked back as he would from fire and hurriedly spread the blankets over her. Her eyes fluttered closed as she sighed deeply and fell silent.

When Cross came away from the woman, Duffy was lighting a cigar in the campfire. "Apparently the lady isn't used to spirits," he said, highly amused as he puffed great puffs of smoke. His eyes were speculative.

"Apparently not," Cross said, conveying by tone and expression that he didn't wish to speak of the woman.

Lilly awoke the following day with Cross McCree shaking her shoulder. His voice was thunder reverberating inside her head.

"Time to be up, *señora*."

She opened her eyes, then quickly shut them again to keep out the stabs of light. "Please . . ." She pressed her hand to her head, but that didn't stop the throbbing. Her tongue felt like a wad of cotton.

The man actually laughed. "Here . . . some coffee."

She peeked through slit eyelids.

Cross McCree crouched there, extending a steaming cup. Her eyes adjusted, and she opened them a bit wider. For an instant she wondered at his unchangeableness. He wore the same worn boots, dented and scratched spurs, striped serape and hat with the brim all bent. Neither rain nor sun could wilt him, for he seemed to move in a world of his own control.

Gingerly, trying not to bob her head, she sat up and took the cup. His eyes were warm upon her . . . and suddenly she recalled gazing into them the previous night. Recalled touching his beard, and wishing to touch more.

Quickly she averted her eyes to the cup.

"The rains have broken," he said.

The tears came before she had a chance to stop them, tears of relief, for she had thought if she had to be wrapped within the confines of these rocks many more hours she would die.

And then Cross McCree said the most amazing thing. "Would the *señora* like a hot bath?"

She stared at him through blurred vision. "A hot bath?" She didn't think such a thing something to joke about.

It wasn't a joke at all. It was a hot springs pond, and they reached it by late morning. While the men continued to push the sheep up the valley, Cross escorted Lilly to the springs.

Alighting from his horse, he pulled his rifle from its scabbard and gestured with it. "I'll sit over there."

His eyes held hers, and she saw the merriment in his. Then, leaving his horse to graze, he strode away to a grouping of rocks. Lilly looked from him to the pool that steamed slightly. She recalled the last time she'd gone for a bath and how she'd felt upon learning he'd kept watch. She looked at Cross McCree again; he had climbed up on the rocks and sat with his back to her, his rifle propped across his knees.

She wanted a bath, and it was true—she didn't want to be out here alone. Nervously she glanced over the trees and rocks that shot up the mountainside. Cross McCree had said they were in Ute lands now.

She looked again at the pool. Quickly she pulled her bathing things from the small bundle behind her saddle. Leading Tubbs to some thick grass between the hot spring and Cross McCree, she used the mule for a screen, undressed and slipped into the water.

It was wonderful, magnificent...never in her life had she experienced such ecstasy, she thought as the warmth closed around her.

Her spirits soared, leaving behind the dreary strain of the past days. The afternoon sky was deep blue, the trees glistening green, and the water pure heaven. She dunked and savored and checked the whereabouts of Cross McCree. He still sat with his back toward her. She began soaping her hair, humming...and watching him.

Mischief overcame her. "You can turn around now, Mr. McCree."

He turned slowly. She made certain to stay covered in the water.

"How's the water?" he asked gruffly.

Every part of her that was woman became attentive. "It's perfect...and I daresay, I'm not the only one who should try it."

"Is that an invitation?"

She stared at him. "It's a suggestion . . . for after I'm finished," she said primly.

He laughed, full and deep, and the sound skittered along
her spine and brought heat to her cheeks. She'd been flirt-
ing, and he knew it, and suddenly her heart was pounding.
She ducked under the water and swept through its warmth,
coming up only when she could no longer hold her breath.

Cross McCree was walking toward the pool, removing his
shirt as he came.

"Mr. McCree!"

"That pool looks awfully good, and it's plenty big
enough for two." He grinned broadly.

Lilly pushed backward in the water, and stared at him as
he came to the edge. Her mind cast about for a good, sound
protest and settled on, "If you are bathin', who will be on
guard?"

He paused and shook his head with elaborate reluctance.
"You have a point there, *señora*." Then he knelt, tossed his
hat aside and laid his rifle carefully within reach. "I suppose I'll just have to content myself with a quick rinse-off.
At least maybe I can get rid of the worst of the ripeness. Do
you suppose you'd share your soap?"

He extended his hand, and Lilly stared at it. In order to
place the soap there, she'd have to get closer to him...close
enough for viewing.

She stayed where she was. He shrugged and unbuttoned
his longhandle shirt, stripped it down to his waist. He pulled
a thong from around his neck—it held a knife. He dunked
his head, scrubbing with his hands.

Lilly threw the soap. It plunked right in front of him. He
glanced at her, fished in the water and came up with the
cake. Grinning slowly at her, he rubbed it over his bare
chest.

Lilly watched. His chest was smooth, with skin only
slightly lighter than on his hands. The lather grew and

spread. She thought of what his bare feet and legs had looked like. She thought of the power of the man.

He dunked and splashed, rinsing. His head came up, and the sun sparkled on his wet hair.

He looked at her. "I'll leave your soap here," he said. "You'd best finish up, too. We need to be gettin' back to the herd."

His manner had become curt. Wiping himself dry with his shirt, he rose and strode away.

Lilly watched him until he'd gone all the way back to the rocks and sat again with his back to her. He let his back remain bare to the sunlight.

Lilly hadn't thought she could ever be glad to be in the saddle, but she was positively joyous to be atop Tubbs and rocking along in the bright sunlight. It glittered in the trees and across the stubbly grass and the backs of the bleating sheep and upon the narrow, gurgling river. Lilly felt that if she never saw rain again, it would be too soon.

"Remember that when we get in the desert," Cross McCree told her. Ever since the previous day's bathing at the hot spring, things had been tense between them.

Cross McCree's dourness caused Lilly to pull within herself. She looked around her, at the trees and the Rocky Mountains, so well called.

A certain assurance had come over her. Perhaps it was simply feeling so much better after having a good bathing, but whatever had caused it, Lilly couldn't help but think that she had made it thus far. Thus far into this vast, harsh, unforgiving land, and she would do as well through whatever lay ahead. The reins were easy in her hands, the mule relaxed beneath her, and the knife Cross McCree had given her was tight at her waist.

Cross McCree and Duffy Campbell and the men spoke of Indians seriously now, but she wasn't frightened, at least not terrified. She could not have said why. Of course, she had heard and read the horrible stories of Indian attacks upon white people. While she had been in Santa Fe, the Comanche had raided haciendas only hours to the south; they had stolen children and raped women and then scalped them. Lilly knew that the threat from the Ute was real. But real, too, was the competence of the men in whose company she rode.

The herders, the night herders working, too, kept the sheep more closely bunched. Duffy Campbell was in the front, at the point, they called it, with Lorenzo Lopez and Simon Morelos bringing the remuda of horses and mules. Coca and Henri, with the food stores, came between the first and second bands. Cross McCree rode with Lilly between the second and third bands. Tied to his saddle was a rope that led the three mustangs, one loaded with sacks of flour, corn and gunpowder, all of which was to be a ransom to the Indians. Bringing up the rear of the herds was the young vaquero, Arrio Baca. All the men who had rifles checked them frequently, keeping them ready for firing, although Cross McCree had ordered them not to fire unless they were in danger of being killed.

Her confidence, she thought, stemmed much from the man riding beside her. In the weeks on the trail, she had come to know Cross McCree as a man who stood steady and dealt with anything that came his way.

No doubt sensing her gaze upon him, his eyes swung to her. They gazed at each other for long moments. Lilly remembered the sunlight upon his wet hair and bare back.

In that moment her unnamed emotions swirled to a crystal-clear point. She wanted this man, wanted his body, yes, but more, she wanted *him*. And she knew he knew this . . . and she knew he wanted her, too.

He turned his eyes forward and said, "Most likely the Ute are gonna come upon us with a big show. Indians like to do that. But you stick by me, no matter what happens. Don't be overcome if they come in shootin'. Your mule won't bolt—he's a good one. Just sit tight, and stay close to me."

"What do you mean by 'overcome'?" Lilly asked him.

His eyes swung back to her. They were dark in the shadow of his hat. "Well...faint, I guess." And for the first time there was a hint of uncertainty in his voice.

"I haven't fainted yet, Mr. McCree."

For a moment she saw the argument in his expression, and she thought he would bring up her falling into exhaustion after sewing up Henri. He had foresight enough not to. He simply offered her a piece of jerky, and she took it. She was coming to appreciate the taste.

Four days later the Indians came upon them with a show, just as Cross had expected. The herd had reached the scrubby, flat river plain, and the Indians came, trying to stampede the sheep with bloodcurdling yelps and the smoky boom of muskets. Those who didn't have muskets waved feathered lances. The attack served only to cause the sheep to bunch up closer to the shepherds.

Cross counted at least twenty braves, on short, barrel-chested horses that were painted with the sign of hunters, not warriors. Several of the braves pulled away, reloaded and made another pass, but they quickly made their shots and rode off, seeming to disappear into the flat, treeless ground.

"Was that it?" the woman asked, her face pasty white but her green eyes dancing excitedly.

He shook his head. "They'll be waitin' up ahead."

His eyes held hers, and he almost smiled. She'd done well, hadn't so much as let out a scream and had kept her mule under control, while Cross had struggled to keep the three mustangs from pulling off his saddle or Domino to the ground. Now she appeared more excited than scared, though he thought that she'd be better off scared.

For a moment what could happen to her brought a tightening to his chest. All the power within him shouted that he'd look out for her, and mocked him for a fool, too.

The Indians appeared up ahead, just as Cross had figured, in a line seeming to rise up out of the ground. It was the Tabeguache, led by Chief Ouray. They were not a highly adorned people, weren't that rich, but there were feathers and beads decorating their buckskins and horses. Chief Ouray wore a set of buffalo horns on his head.

Leaving Lilly Blackwell behind with Coca and the boy, Cross and Duffy rode toward the Indians, trailing the mustangs loaded with gifts.

The greeting with Chief Ouray could be termed nearly warm, as those things went. Both Duffy and Cross had spent much time in the chief's village, trading and visiting. A man coming into his prime, the chief had long black hair that hung in two braids upon his bare chest. He was short and stocky, but grand looking on a horse. He was no one's fool, either, having learned fluent Spanish and passable English. He and Cross used Spanish and spoke almost as if old friends. When he told of the gifts, Cross detected approval around the chief's eyes. On Ouray's right, however, rode a brave who apparently was a subchief of some power and who didn't look pleased at all. The instant Cross saw the brave's dark, bitter eyes, he had an inkling of trouble.

Ouray made no overture to accept the gifts. Instead he introduced the men on each side of him. The man on his left nodded stoically, but Cross judged him no problem; his eyes were bland. The man on Ouray's right, while stock-still, boiled internally like a stallion ready to explode. Ouray introduced him as Eagle Claw. Cross thought the name fit, but he doubted if it was one given to him; this man would choose such a name.

It was Eagle Claw who, using a mixture of Ute and sign language, brought up the subject of the woman.

Cross sat without expression as the Indian said they knew the small one on the mule was a white woman. They had seen her honeyed hair and her milky face. And they wanted to trade for her.

Cross stretched his legs in the stirrups, shook his head and sat back easily in his saddle. He gazed at Eagle Claw a moment and gave the expression of a man much complimented. Then he explained that the woman was not for trade, for she was his wife.

Eagle Claw surveyed Cross, his eyes testing for weakness. Cross met his gaze. The silence stretched long and thick, the brave giving no sign of relenting.

Chief Ouray spoke, inviting Cross and his wife and the Golden One, as he called Duffy, to his lodge to discuss the trading. It amounted to an order. He had still not accepted the gifts, which meant the crossing of their lands had not been settled. With guttural commands to his men, the chief turned and rode away up over the hill. Two braves remained behind to escort the *guests* to the camp.

Duffy raised his eyebrow. "Well, laddie?"

"The fella asked for the woman," Cross said, turning to gaze in the direction of Lilly Blackwell, who was only a small dot at this distance, "but I'll wager he'll settle for guns or horses."

"Oh, the lass would bring him upward of forty horses from the Comanche," Duffy said. "He might like that . . . but he might settle for yer scalp."

Cross acknowledged the truth of that with a grim nod. "And are you acceptin' the invite?" he asked his big friend.

"Oh, aye," the Duff replied casually, "unless ye'd rather I watch the sheep." He cocked a bushy eyebrow.

"I'd say you'd best come...and be a second hand in case we have to fight out of there."

"And that's why I come up to join ye, lad—so I could have to fight for my scalp." The Duff laughed as merry as ever, no worry over his life or his scalp.

With that, they spurred their horses into a lope back to the herd, where Cross had to tell the woman she'd just become his wife.

Chapter Thirteen

It took them over an hour of trotting to get to the Indian village. The swifter horses had to hold back for Lilly's mule, who went at a steady trot but never faster, though threatened mightily by one of the Indians who escorted them.

The heat of a midsummer afternoon blew around them like heat from an oven. Lilly breathed shallowly, and her skin prickled, as if she were expecting the stab of an arrow at any moment, which was silly, for she saw no bow and arrows, only long guns and knives. She rode between Cross McCree and Duffy Campbell, and one Indian man led, while the other followed, trailing the mustangs bearing gifts.

They'd come because of an Indian who wanted her. Because she was a white woman, Cross McCree had explained, and would bring at least forty horses in a trade with Comanche or Mexicans. The way he had defined it had irritated Lilly no end. He didn't put it to her that the Indian wanted *her*, as a woman. He spoke of her like a head of stock, worth at least forty horses. Never mind that he had protected her by giving her the cover of being his wife—she was piqued with him, and with these Indians who had caused her to have to ride over here. And who caused her to fear.

For what she'd been told was a temporary camp, the Indian village was much more substantial than Lilly had imagined. There were upward to fifty tepees, bearing colorful paintings, scattered over the canyon, baking in the strong afternoon sun. And here and there, like little sheds or gazebos, were shelters made of poles and juniper limbs. The heavy scent of burning sagebrush and juniper came from campfires. Hides were stretched, drying in the sun, and Lilly smelled something ... the scent of scorched hide. Her stomach turned.

Dogs came running and barking at the heels of their mounts. Tubbs kicked at one and sent it flying. Lilly thought for certain someone would shoot her dead then ... but no one did. Children, most nearly naked, came running, too, hanging back and staring curiously. People materialized from everywhere, and Lilly was assaulted with the sight of naked skin. They were a smallish people, dark skinned, almost black. What clothing the men wore was made of skins; their muscles were clearly defined, like those of carved statues. Lilly noticed, too, a number of the men dressed in the simple pants and shirt of the Mexican style and there was calico among the women.

The Indians formed a line on either side. They stared boldly but without expression. That bothered Lilly most of all—the lack of expression, neither welcoming nor threatening. Simply staring.

Cross McCree stopped in front of a line of very fierce and implacable-looking men in front of a large lodge. Lilly passed a quick glance, seeing the elaborate and colorful feathers and beads and silver, too. She wondered which one of these savage men was Eagle Claw, who had wanted to trade for her.

And then she saw him—it had to be him—a man who gazed at her with piercing black eyes. Eyes like that of a snake, coiled and ready to strike. His skin stretched tight over bones that made it seem his features had been chiseled

out of mountain rock. He had paint lines that made him
look as wild as any animal of the land.

She quickly turned away, fear swallowing her anger.

Seeing Cross McCree dismounting, Lilly did, too. Her
legs and arms shook. Then Cross McCree was there, putting his arm around her and drawing her forward. He spoke
in Spanish, introducing her to Chief Ouray. Cross McCree
had instructed her to keep her eyes downward, and she did,
hiding beneath the brim of her hat. But when the chief said,
"Welcome," she couldn't suppress one quick glance at him.
His eyes were nearly the same level as her own, and they
were shrewd, dark eyes, with a square face of dark, leathery skin surrounding them. She thought his lips quirked with
amusement for the instant their eyes touched. She felt a stab
of admiration for him.

And then again, as Cross McCree led her toward the open
flap of the tepee, her eyes met, for an instant, the black
savage eyes she had seen before.

Instinctively she reached for Cross McCree, knotted her
hand into his serape. His arm came around her, and she
sank back into the protection of him. His muscles were relaxed, and he entered the tent as if he belonged there.

The sides of the tepee were folded up about a foot all the
way around, and more light came from an opening in the
top. There was a fire going in the center, a small fire, but still
a fire, and it made the tepee quite warm. No wonder these
people wore so little clothes, she thought. The pungent,
musty scents of sweat and smoke and hides assailed her.

The men formed a semicircle, sitting cross-legged. Cross
McCree maneuvered her into sitting just behind his right
shoulder, between him and Duffy Campbell, upon buffalo
and coyote hides. Women moved among them, serving.
Cross McCree took a wooden bowl; he turned and extended it to her, and his eyes told her to take some. She did,
awkwardly with her fingers, and sniffed, then tested with her

tongue. Suddenly she saw one of the women looking at her; the woman flashed a fleeting, amused grin. Lilly stuffed whatever it was into her mouth. It occurred to her that training against being rude went very deep. Then she realized whatever she had eaten had been quite good and sweet.

Her attention returned to the men...and she saw the one she had seen outside, the man with the savage eyes, gazing at her. His gaze made her shiver, even while sweat gathered at her temples.

The men talked and smoked pipes, and Cross McCree passed out some cigars, and women brought in gourds filled with liquid. Lilly wasn't offered this liquid. She suspected it was some sort of spirits, and that as a woman she was exempt. She understood little of the Spanish and none of the Ute that was spoken. She did understand that they were receiving formal hospitality, and she thought that such hospitality was the same throughout all societies—boring.

At last the talk appeared to get back to the bargaining. Lilly tried to follow the bidding and couldn't. Once the man who wanted her spoke vehemently and looked at her. She poked Cross McCree, leaned forward, whispering, "What is it? What does he want?" He scowled at her over his shoulder, but didn't respond. The Indian was staring at her. "Just tell him he can't have me."

"Be quiet!" Cross McCree rasped.

Fuming at the command, she shut her mouth.

Duffy Campbell leaned over and whispered, "The barterin' is for the men, lass. It won't look right if Cross listens to ye."

"What is it they want?" she asked.

"Sheep...a hundred head."

"A hundred...no!" She poked Cross McCree and whispered fiercely, "Don't you give them our sheep."

Cross McCree answered quietly but forcefully, "I'll handle it."

"Well, you can give them your sheep, but not mine. I need every one of those sheep for my future."

He twisted and took hold of her chin. His eyes shot fire. He leaned close to her ear and whispered, "I'll do what I have to do get us out of here, or you're gonna end up servin' Indians and Mexes from here to Mexico City. You got it?"

She met his gaze and repeated, "Don't give up my sheep."

And he said, "Shut up, or I'll put a gag around your mouth."

She didn't think he was speaking idly. She shut up.

He threw her face from his hand and turned back to the circle of men. There was a general chuckle all around and looks of approval. Lilly scowled at them all, until her gaze came to the savage-looking one. She shrank back behind the shelter of Cross McCree.

The talking went on and on, while the sun set and darkness came. The important men, like the chief, his cohorts and Cross McCree and Duffy Campbell, had the use of backboards to lean on. Lilly did not, and her legs and back cried out in pain from the long sitting. When at last she was afraid she would embarrass herself, and Cross McCree, by falling over, the men began to stand and move out of the lodge. Lilly assumed all was settled.

"So...what do we give?" she asked as she took Cross McCree's hand to help her stand.

He said tersely, "We will be stayin' the night."

"How was the water?" Cross met the woman coming up from the creek. He caught the scent of her—that of creek water and lingering campfire smoke and some sweetness he couldn't define. Starlight provided enough of a glow for him to see her smile.

"Cool but nice." Pleasure lingered in her voice. "And they had soap...of a sort, anyway. I didn't expect them to be so nice, these women. Look—one gave me a beaded thong for my braid." She was as pleased as a child. "Do you know they don't spank their children? The chief's wife—she scolded her daughter, but she told me, we don't spank. Quite clearly in English she said it. I think she has seen white people spank a child and was much incensed."

"That was his first wife, I believe. He has a second." He chuckled at her quick turn of the head. "Still—have you discovered, *señora*, that the Indian is no more savage than the white? They are cultivated. It is simply that their cultivation differs from that of the Americans or Spanish."

He touched her arm, guiding her to the path back to the camp, then he dropped his hand.

"You are known here, Mr. McCree," she said, a certain coyness in her voice.

He nodded. "I've spent days at a time with these people."

"And there is one woman who remembers you well."

Even in the darkness, Cross felt himself blush. He didn't speak.

"She can speak some English . . . and she said you taught her. She is very pretty."

"She is not prettier than you," he said.

He felt her surprise, which was not much more than his own. In the darkness he saw her lower her head. They walked in silence for a minute.

Then she said, "I'm sorry about this afternoon . . . for intrudin' into your dealin'. It was just most frustratin' to know I was spoken of and my property was considered and not to be able to take part."

He nodded, but decided his comments on the subject were better left unsaid. The woman wouldn't understand his telling her that she needed to learn when to hold her tongue, or that he admired her spirit for guarding what was hers. He didn't understand his feelings, either, and was uncomfortable with them.

"Well...can we pass their lands?" she asked. "And what is the price—me or the sheep, or both?"

"And what if I said I traded you and sheep?" he asked, amused.

"You wouldn't."

"No...I wouldn't." He stopped near Chief Ouray's lodge. The carefully scraped hide glowed in the starlight. "Eagle Claw gave up on you, and he wanted no part of the sheep. Now he's decided he wants my horse."

"Your horse!" Despair echoed in her voice. "Oh, must you?"

"Well, I don't plan on it," he said grimly. "Eagle Claw is pushin', testin' the limits of his power. He wants to take over from Ouray, and to do that he's got to prove his strength."

It was a fight the Indian had wanted all along, but Cross didn't speak of that as he guided the woman toward the flap of the tepee. Tomorrow he would deal with it. Tonight there was the matter of bedding down with the woman.

"We'll sleep here tonight—in the chief's lodge." He gestured. He felt his throat tightening and his blood heating. "We have been given the place of honor and would insult him should we refuse."

He said in a low voice, "You and I will be bedded together...since we are man and wife."

The chief was sitting up, smoking. In the glow of the coals from the dying fire he resembled an almighty apparition out of the dark clouds. Without expression, he nodded to them and went on smoking. Lilly choked back a sneeze from the pungent tobacco. There were many people bedded around the tent, so many lumps covered in blankets and hides.

Cross McCree led her to a prepared bed of buffalo robes and blankets. "Here..." He left her and joined the chief at the fire.

Slowly Lilly lay down. She breathed lightly. It was hot in her serape. She watched the chief's and Cross McCree's faint shadows on the tepee wall. The musky scent of hides and bodies surrounded her.

She wondered when Cross McCree would come to lie beside her. She listened to his and the chief's murmuring voices. They were friends, she thought. At least, certainly not enemies.

When the fire cast only a bare glow and coolness was seeping like a mist, Cross McCree came, moving softly. She watched the bare outline of his black silhouette as he sat beside her. He took off his serape, pulled his boots, removed the knife he carried at the back of his neck. Then he stretched out beside her. His shoulder pressed hers; she could feel the even rise and fall of his chest through that shoulder.

She could feel the pulsing of his blood through his body.

He had placed her toward the outside of the tent, separating her from the others with his body. She was grateful. She wished she had removed her serape, but was too self-conscious to do so now. After a moment, Cross McCree sat up and reached to pull a blanket over them. Then he settled again, his shoulder against hers.

The darkness did not hide sound. Someone snored gently. Someone murmured. There came the sound of motion, someone turning over, someone coughing.

Lilly stared up into the darkness. Her awareness of Cross McCree beside her was a living thing, crawling over her, heating her. She thought back to when the rain had kept them confined in the shallow cave, and he had slept just on the other side of Coca. She thought of how his eyes had looked in the campfire light. She thought of how he had called her pretty. She had believed he thought her plain, which she was.

Yet, she knew well there was a pull between them. *Oh, yes, she knew this.*

The knowledge whispered through her blood.

She shifted, her muscles tensing. She thought, fleetingly, of pressing against him. Wonderings, forbidden, flitted like tender butterflies through her mind. She listened to his breathing and wondered if he were asleep.

Slowly, instinctively, she turned her head to look at him. She could not see him, but she heard the whisper of his head turning . . . felt his breath upon her face.

Anticipation . . . fear . . . longing for what she didn't know shimmered over her body.

They lay thus, for long minutes, exchanging breaths and the silent proposal. Lilly couldn't have put words to the proposal, but it was still there, as loud as if they had shouted it at one another. It was plain and clear and much repeated over the past many weeks, having first come to life that day they had met on the Santa Fe street. Each time they had sidestepped, or hidden from it . . . but it remained, echoing in their minds.

And Lilly could not turn away from it.

Then his hand came softly to her neck, and his body rolled toward her.

His thumb, rough and dear, stroked her cheek. She stilled, flashing both hot and cold . . . a most exquisite hot and cold. For a moment she was lost in the sensations.

Her heartbeat quickened, and her body tingled with expectancy . . . and fear. She braced a palm against his chest. His hand halted, but only for a moment, before moving downward, exploring, over her shoulder and into her waist and out on her hip.

There was further sound of motion beyond them.

Lilly's blood heated, ebbed and flowed within her body. She thought how they were surrounded by people. She squeezed her legs together, the image of Tyler upon her, pushing into her, filling her mind. Thoughts of him naked mingled with imaginings of Cross McCree naked. She recalled his bare legs from that day so long ago. She recalled his bare chest...and the sun on his back. The power of him.

She squeezed her legs tighter, yet leaned toward his warmth. His hand moved over her. Slowly, oh, so slowly. As if learning of her. Something inside of her waited for pain, yet savored the pleasure. Down her thigh, then back up, to her bare neck, then slipping beneath her serape. Her breath caught in her throat, and her belly yearned, and the wet pulsing ache came between her legs. His hand delved beneath her shirt. She thought to push him away.

But she didn't want to, couldn't bring herself to. She lay perfectly still, barely breathing.

His hand found her skin. It stroked lightly, then more firmly. She clamped her lips against a cry of pleasure...or pain. *Not here...not among all these people!* Would it be the same with Cross as it had been with Tyler? She remembered the pain Tyler had brought. She struggled then, pushing against his chest. But he was like solid rock. And then his hand came to her breasts...touching gently, tenderly. Caressing.

No one had ever touched her in such a manner.

Lilly held her breath, experiencing sensations she had never before experienced. She heard his breath; it came quickly. The longing grew and swelled, pounding upon her.

The woman held herself from him, but he felt the fire of her, the quivering of desire...and of fear. She pressed her arms against his chest, holding him off. Still, he couldn't stop feeling of her.

He tried to bank the fire inside. In the back of his mind he was mindful of where they were...surrounded by strangers...and that she was a lady...an Anglo lady.

And that she resisted him.

But the weeks he'd held himself away from her suddenly piled upon him, and the softness of her called to him. He recalled the way her hair gleamed warm in the sunlight, and the way her eyes could turn the color of mountain grasses, and the way her hands moved.

Gradually he felt her resistance melting like night before dawn. He hauled her against him and damned the place and the time, and the clothing separating them. He wanted to rip away the cloth.

But he did not.

He held her to him, rubbed his swollen, aching rod against her. She spread her legs and wrapped around him, pressing hard, buried her nose in his neck, and whimpered. His heart pounded near clean out of his chest. He stroked her hair and thought of taking her outside and having her in the privacy of the stars. He thought of going ahead and having her right there, as no doubt was happening on other buffalo robes. But that wasn't his way, and the woman was in his care. He was to protect her, even from himself.

He continued to hold her, to stroke her hair. Gradually he felt her body relax, her breathing settle into the evenness of sleep.

Sometime in the night he must have dozed. He awoke in the silvery light before dawn. Lilly Blackwell was still wrapped around him. He pressed against her, began to throb. She sighed and moved against him, responding naturally in her sleep. Temptation was strong as a swift-running river, and he struggled against it. And he won, because he'd learned to stay alive by having dominion even over himself.

Gently he disengaged himself, covered her against a chill, found his boots and knife and crept from the tent.

Lilly saw his silhouette when he opened the flap of the tepee. For several moments she was confused, her mind still fuzzy with sleep. She moved her hand and felt the emptiness beside her. She came awake then and lay there, heart pounding.

She yearned for him and did battle with fear and pride and the strict dictates of the only culture she'd ever known.

At last she rose, grabbed up a blanket and made her way through the bodies and out into the cool, fresh air. She had a moment of panic in which she wondered where he could have gone. Then she saw a moving shadow heading for the creek. She stood watching him go, doubts holding her.

Then she followed.

While still yards away, she stopped and watched the shadow remove his shirt and kneel, splashing water onto his face. Her heart filled as she gazed at the familiar silhouette.

With soft, hesitant steps, she approached. He heard her, for he could hear the whisper of the wind, and turned to look over his shoulder. She stopped and gazed at him. Her heart pounded in her chest. *Perhaps he wouldn't want her now.*

Slowly, fluidly, he stood. His hands hung at his sides, and he looked at her. She could not clearly see his face in the dimness, yet she felt something. Enough to propel her forward.

She was but a foot in front of him, clutching the blanket tightly at her chest. Strands of hair fell softly around her pale face. Cross felt her wanting. He knotted his hands at his sides.

"What about tomorrow?" he said, feeling he owed her the warning.

She shook her head. "What about today?" she said in a plaintive whisper. That and the way she trembled cut clear through him.

He grabbed her then and swung her up in his arms. He strode down the creek toward the shelter of young trees and brush. Setting her on her feet, he took the blanket and spread it upon the sandy soil. He spread his shirt, too, sat and pulled his boots. She sat down and began untying her tall moccasins. Her fingers shook and fumbled. He helped her, and the next instant she was slipping out of her trousers. His eyes traveled up her sleek legs, colorless in the dimness, to where the tail of the shirt hid the rest of her. She fell to her knees beside him. Her eyes were squeezed closed, and she leaned forward, as if offering herself.

He laid her back on the blanket, and still her eyes remained closed. And she just lay there, stiff and trembling, like something caught. A moment more, and her eyes popped open. He felt her fear and uncertainty.

She was as if inexperienced.... Wondering and watching her, he gently tugged her shirt and then the undergarment over her head, caressing her all the while, kissing her trembling body. And when he kissed her lips, she seemed to burst open to him, like the splitting of a wild peach in late August.

He pulled her tight against him. She quivered. Heat shimmered through his veins, swelling like a hot stream into a mighty pounding river. He savored every part of her, lost himself in the discovery of the wanton that lived inside the lady. His gentleness faded, overcome by the rabid hunger for her skin, her curves, her sweet mouth, her hot, wild passion.

He was all around her, covering her, rubbing her, entering her. She was astounded at the ways he touched her. She was astounded at the feelings that took hold of her, at the great, insatiable wanting. Wildly, with her body, which seemed to have a mind of its own, she begged for him, spreading for him, straining for him, welcoming him into her.

"Please..." she begged, frantic that he would quit, as Tyler always had.

He knew then where her fear and uncertainty came from. Holding himself on his arms, he towered over her. Slowly he covered her mouth with his and pushed deep into her, hard and swift and completely. Again and again. Letting his seed and spirit merge with hers.

For the first time in her life, Lilly experienced the throes of passion. And it was magnificent.

They exchanged no words of love, no words at all. But he held her, in the curve of his shoulder, while the sun crept up over the horizon and cast light upon their bare bodies. And he caressed her skin and her hair, tenderly. She stroked his chest and pressed her lips against him. And she cried, too, a little, overcome by the emotions stirring inside her. She felt full, complete, as never before.

She wished this time could go on forever, but of course it couldn't. There came sounds of stirring from the village; soon their idyll would be interrupted.

Gently Cross pulled from her and sat up. He reached for her clothes first, handed them to her. His hand caressed her hair before he turned his back to put on his own clothes. She sensed a proper reserve coming over him now, and she had to smile. He had not been so proper only moments before.

And neither had she, she thought with high amazement. She wanted so much to tell him how she felt, to know what he was feeling. Yet all her words were dammed up by fear of what he might say. She dressed quickly, feeling self-consciousness returning.

When he was dressed, she was still tying up her moccasins. He bent to help, doing one while she worked on the other. She recalled when he had removed them and the urgency of passion that had gripped them both. His eyes came to hers, and she saw the memory there, too.

He waited for her to replait her hair, and then he took her hand to help her stand. He held her hand as they returned to the camp. There he gave her over into the care of Duffy Campbell, then left without a word.

She stood, watching him walk away to a small, stick hut that stood outside the fringes of the tepees. "Where's he goin'?" she asked. After so long a time of silence, her voice sounded strange to her ears.

"The sweat hut," the big man said. "It'll clear his mind for the fight with Eagle Claw."

She whirled. "Fight? What fight?"

Duffy Campbell gazed at her for a moment. "Cross wouldn't trade you, and he won't trade Domino. And Eagle Claw, he wouldn't settle for sheep, so it's either have us a minor war, which we'd lose, of course, or Cross and Eagle Claw have a go at it. It's been what the young chief wanted all along, of course."

The Indians surrounding her and Duffy Campbell yelled and chanted. With clenched fists, the big Scotsman hissed encouragement beneath his breath. "Get him, lad...watch the eyes, mon...the eyes."

Lilly stood transfixed, watching in horror. She had known, for Duffy Campbell had explained. But she hadn't *truly* known, and here it was before her: the two men, the Indian bare except for a loincloth and paint, Cross stripped to his waist, both with folded cloth tied around their foreheads and with chests glistening with sweat, and their left wrists tied together with a leather thong, while their right hands slashed with glistening knives.

She wanted to run, to hide from the fearful sight, but she would not shame Cross by cowardice. And she sought to

bring him strength by her very will. So she watched the
slashing, the cuts that each inflicted, and the blood that
smeared their bodies. She watched the hot intent glitter in
the Indian's eyes and the sharp determination shine within
Cross's. They fought so little with anger, but more with the
passion for a skill. Oh, they loved it, the both of them born
of this savage land, she thought, and furiously so.

The sun bore down, and dust billowed around their feet.
Cross's foot came up out of the dust, and the Indian went
down. They rolled...Eagle Claw scrambled to his feet. He
stabbed, but Cross miraculously evaded the blade. Again
they were on their feet and circling. Blood and sweat
smeared the dirt on their bodies into mud. Cross slashed
upward, missed the Indian's torso, but caught him in the
chin—purposely, Lilly thought—and blood went spurting.
Eagle Claw grinned slightly. Quick as a rattlesnake, he
jabbed at Cross. Cross danced, avoiding the blade.

They were tired now, their chests heaving, their movements slowing, sweat pouring into their eyes.

Suddenly Cross threw himself on the ground, pulling his
opponent with him. The dust enveloped their bodies and
flailing limbs. Then Cross was straddling the Indian, pressing the Indian's arm and his own at a painful angle across
the Indian's chest. In the silence that swept the air, the tearing of sinew could be heard. Eagle Claw stared at Cross with
glittering eyes. Cross pressed the knife blade into the man's
neck until blood trickled. He pushed the arm still further,
until it appeared a thing apart from the Indian. Though his
eyes remained open, the glitter began to fade from them. His
dark, florid face grew ashen.

Then, with a great heaving breath, Cross straightened,
pushed upon his knees and lifted Eagle Claw's now limp
arm with his own. The Indian's arm wiggled at the base, as

if it had been torn from its socket, yet no sound came from him.

With a slow, clumsy motion, Cross sliced the leather thong binding their wrists. The Indian's arm fell into the dirt, as Cross heaved himself off the man and fell over into the dirt, himself.

With a muffled cry, Lilly went to her knees beside him. "Oh, God..." Her hands hovered over him, wanting to touch, not knowing how. He was cut in many places, scraped, too, by the ground. His eyes were closed, as if he had fainted. She looked up, searching for help. And she saw the movement of Eagle Claw as he struggled up, his face a mask of evil, the knife quivering in his raised fist.

"No!" she cried, and threw herself across Cross.

There was scuffling around her head, sand filled her nostrils. Then all was still. Someone touched her back. She jumped, for she'd been expecting a blade.

"Madam... Lilly, it's okay now, lass."

She raised up and saw the Indian being hauled away by his own.

A woman, the chief's wife who had given Lilly the beaded thong for her hair, brought a bowl of water and a cloth, and Lilly wiped Cross's face and wounds, or as much as he would allow. With Duffy Campbell's help he staggered to his feet.

He gazed at Lilly, put his hand to her cheek. "Now, Lilly, don't go cryin'. You still got your sheep."

"Oh, Cross." She hit his hand away, gently.

There was a deep gash angling across his side. Lilly placed the cloth the Indian woman had given her over it. Duffy Campbell helped him get his shirt over his head; the coarse fabric stuck to his wounds. Their mounts were brought around, saddled and ready. Duffy Campbell plopped Cross's hat on his head and helped him to mount Domino.

Chief Ouray came forward to speak to Cross, speaking something like a benediction.

They rode away at last, with dogs and dust stirring at the heels of their mounts, Cross bent slightly and holding on to his horn, Lilly not holding on at all as she smacked Tubbs to keep up. They rode back to the sheep, and to the friends who waited.

Henri saw them from far off and came to meet them at a gallop.

Cross lay propped against his bedroll in the sparse shade of a scrubby tree, and Lilly stitched the five-inch gash in his side. He'd drunk some of Coca's brew for pain, and his eyes showed it, but his muscles still jerked each time Lilly inserted the needle into his flesh. She did the job quickly, without feeling faint, this time thinking of when she'd sewn her brown linen gown . . . and recalling only hours before, when she had caressed this very skin.

"You'll have a good scar," Lilly said, finishing off.

"It'll go with the one on my back and the one on my arm." Then a wicked glint came into his blue eyes. "Or were you just a little too . . . preoccupied . . . to notice those this mornin', Lilly?" His speech was thick, his eyes sensuous. The way he said her name slipped over her like warm water.

"No . . . I can't say that I did," she replied honestly, her cheeks flaming, even as she was amused.

They gazed at each other.

"I would have given sheep," she said, feeling pain deep inside her, "rather than this."

"Don't matter, because that Indian didn't want sheep," Cross said. "He wanted what could give him the most power, which was you . . . or my scalp. And I never figured on givin' him either."

He reached out, grasped her wrist. Then his eyes fluttered closed, and he fell instantly asleep. Pan, who'd been waiting and watching, slunk over and wiggled close to him, rested his chin on his waist.

Lilly eased her wrist from his grasp and stroked the damp hair from his forehead. She gazed at him a long time, remembering what he had given her that morning at the creek. And wanting more.

Chapter Fourteen

The next morning Cross was in the saddle, shouting orders and waving his hat to encourage the sheep into motion.

The hat did little to stir the sheep and more to release some fury inside himself, Lilly thought, watching. Yelling at the men, spurring his horse, he was all fury and power, his body moving like a mighty he-cat coming down to the fresh territory of the foothills and making his rule known. Or perhaps he appeared so because Lilly now knew full well the strength of him, body and spirit.

He galloped to where Lilly was saddling Tubbs, pulled to a dusty stop and alighted from his horse. Only someone who knew him would notice he was favoring his side, where he'd been stitched. He didn't want to let on he'd even been hurt; he was a man to have such pride. A cut was dry and dark over his right eyebrow. That and his beard gave him a menacing look, though his blue eyes were clear as the morning sky, and without emotion.

He swung the saddle atop the mule and fastened it, all without a word and with only one long speculative look, which Lilly returned in full measure. Then he remounted, with a trace of stiffness, and rode away without a backward glance.

The days continued with clear skies blue as chicory flowers with the dew on them and fading when the sun burned hot from the west, just as chicory did. High summer, not a hint of rain. They pushed the sheep across the Colorado River, headed southwest from the mountains and then angled northwest. Lilly had never imagined there was such a land as this, and when it came to it, she had seen a lot, everything from the Atlantic Ocean to the Mississippi to the Gulf at Houston and all the way across the plains from St. Louis to Santa Fe. But this... this stretched like a kingdom.

They left the thickness of the tall mountain pines behind, and the land in places appeared swept clean as an adobe floor. It rose in peaks and grassy plateaus, swept low in valleys and split in canyons, all of it streaked with colors of a fiery sunset—orange fading into luminescent ivory and topped by crystalline blue. It gave up water in numerous creeks that cut through the earth, veins coming out of the rock mountains to the northeast to feed the land below. Grass grew in tufts and sometimes sparsely, but there was crusty brush that provided savory feed for the sheep. The nights and mornings were wonderfully cool, making bearable the afternoons that seemed to go on forever beneath a scorching sun.

Lilly and Coca, or sometimes Duffy Campbell, who often rode with her, took to riding far to the south of the herd, where the breeze would blow the dust of the herd away from them.

Nevertheless at the end of each day everyone had a fine painting of silt upon them. When Lilly's eyes watered, the tears made lines upon her face, and when she blew her nose, her handkerchief would be filled with bits of mud. Tubbs appeared to grow more gray with each passing day. She had no trouble with the mule now; he carried her securely, just as Cross had said he would. Often now she rounded up straying sheep on him; he needed no direction in doing the job. Occasionally she got down to walk, and Tubbs would follow, without benefit of lead, his nose bumping her shoulder. She'd taught him to do that by feeding him handfuls of grain she sneaked from Lorenzo's rations.

They crossed the Green where it flowed shallowly through a flat, thriving valley, and continued on their northwest course, following a small river. Here there was grass and scrubby trees, abundant wildlife, even flowers. It was a rich land, bordered on the north and east by a stretch of blue mountains. Majestic monuments to God, Duffy Campbell called them, and Lilly had to agree.

She tried to hate the untamed land, but something within her would not allow it. It spoke to her, called to a part of her that she had come to recognize in the past days, a part of her that was as wild and free as the earth itself. Where the land sapped the femininity from her flesh, it gave back to her soul by showing within herself a strength she had not known she possessed.

Day followed day, and mile followed mile, and she and Cross did not speak privately.

He came to her, once, when she was alone gathering firewood. She masked the confusion and uncertainty within herself and gave him a look that let him know she wished to be left alone. For a moment she thought he would push in upon her anyway. For a moment she wished he would. But he turned his horse and rode away.

She clamped her mouth against the urge to call him back.

Yet again and again, they gazed at each other, across the flickering flames of the fire, or squinted in the bright light of day, even over the distance of a band of sheep, when neither could see the other's eyes. They did not touch, except with their eyes... and their memories.

Lilly knew that Cross was considering, just as she was.

There had been a time when she would not have taken up with Cross McCree simply because to do so would have been shockingly improper. She had, however, passed improper a long time back. She had left it behind in the woman she had been, in the civilization she had known. Now, in this land where one's life was reduced to what it took to survive, she was guided by intuitive caution.

That morning when she'd gone to him at the river he'd asked her what about tomorrow. She hadn't cared then. Passion had ruled.

Now, however, common sense had once more taken control, as had pride and uncertainty, if the truth of it be known.

Two things dominated her mind, and those were a wanting for Cross and a fear that she was already pregnant. The fear was a crazy thing, because deep inside she had to battle the wish that she was carrying a child. A child at long last, one born of the magnificent passion she had shared with Cross, no matter the consequences.

But no! She didn't want that. Already she had her feelings for Henri dragging at her. She wanted no ties to bind her to Cross McCree, and she wouldn't allow any. She was going back to Pasquotank County.

Yet, she couldn't forget what it had been like with him. She couldn't forget the wondrous passion, the pulsing heat, the total, glorious release.

She watched him. She wanted him. And she knew he wanted her.

Cross urged the outfit onward, ever mindful of the need to cross the Sierras by early September, before the snows. In this regard, the Duff was an immense help.

"It's comin' back to me, lad," the Duff said grandly.

It was he who recalled the tributary and valley that flowed from the northwest into the Green, giving them a trail with good feed toward the inevitable desert. Cross kept the sheep moving as fast as they could go and still remain hearty. He wanted them to gain stamina while there was grass and water, before they came to the desert.

Once, five Indians were spotted, watching the herds from a distant hill. Where there were five, Cross knew there was likely to be more. Though they continued to drive the sheep, each man made ready, and Cross took position with Lilly, Coca and Henri.

Duffy rode out to speak with the Indians and reported back that they were Shoshone who were simply curious about so large a body of sheep moving into their land, but they were satisfied with Duffy's assurances that neither the sheep nor the men were staying. The Shoshone also provided the information that there were now several more settlements of Mormons south of Salt Lake City and Provo. They even drew a map in the dirt, detailing for the Duff the best trail ahead to lead them past these communities.

The Indians weren't all that happy about new settlements of whites in the land, but for the herders the report was good news. It meant an opportunity to replenish supplies before crossing the desert basin and not having to go all the way north to Salt Lake City to do it. Duffy was still for going to Salt Lake City, though, because he wanted to see where Brigham Young kept all his wives, maybe even meet a few.

During these weeks Cross spent most of his waking hours in the saddle, scouting away from the herd, but never long from the sight of the woman, always watching for her safety.

He watched her, too, for sign of her inclination.

Mostly she held herself away from him. Which made sense, he told himself. It'd been natural as the sunrise, what they had done, and he wasn't about to apologize for it. She had, after all, come to him, and he'd obliged, a term that made him laugh at himself. Still, they had no need to continue it. There was no tomorrow in it, and that was where nature made a difference between humans and animals; humans always needed to think about tomorrow. He and Lilly could ease themselves now, today, and end up with nothing but trouble when the end of the trail came.

Lilly Blackwell wasn't the sort of a woman a man could enjoy and then be on his way. She wasn't a woman a man could readily walk away from. Cross knew this. And he knew that what she would want from him, he could not give.

He could never go east with her.

Remembering how ripe they had been for each other, he thought they were lucky if she hadn't taken this time, and that was a big *if* that hung over him like a low sod ceiling that peppered him with dust every so often just as a reminder. It brought him to the fact that with each passing day she became more aloof to everyone, with the possible exception of the boy and the mule, with which she appeared to have formed a deep attachment, and that she spent long periods of time staring into the fire, or off into the distance—to the west. Always she gazed west, to the end of the trail. He wondered if her behavior sprang from her carrying his seed. Such did produce confusion in the female of the species, and she certainly was confusing. She returned his looks, called to him with her eyes and put up a no-trespassing sign at the same time.

Being an honest and thoughtful man, he figured he did about the same. It was an instinct for survival.

He was unsaddling Domino for the night when Lilly did approach him. When he looked up and saw her, she hesitated, then came on with purposeful strides. She was without her serape, and her shape was evident beneath the coarse shirt and trousers. They hung upon her body now, fit it as if the men's clothes were all she'd ever worn. There was little softness to her, except maybe, still, in her movements.

She stopped three feet from him, jutted her chin a mite and gazed out from beneath her battered hat. "I'm not pregnant," she said straight out, her green eyes opaque, clear of any emotion. "I just thought you might want to know . . . that maybe you were worried in that regard."

Her words hit him. Pregnant, she said, bold and precise, the word as much as her tone echoing of her education and life, so different from his own.

"I wasn't worried," he said, for he hadn't truly been worried. Wasn't any use worrying about something he couldn't control. He supposed he'd been uneasy about it, but he didn't think he needed to say that.

She nodded and walked away back to the fire. He watched her go, watched her small body . . . and thought of her silky skin.

He thought of the way her hands had touched him.

The night came with a splattering of bright stars and a bare, cool breath. The woman sat at the fire, on rocks she'd arranged to make a seat. Her hair, plaited as always, caught the red of the flames. The boy sat beside her. She was giving him a haircut with the small scissors from her sewing box. The two spoke low, practicing their English and Spanish; both were getting quite good.

Cross went to the fire, crouched and reached for the pot atop the grill, poured his tin full of coffee. He sipped and looked at the woman above the cup rim. Her eyes came to his. He saw the reflection of the flickering flames there in her eyes, making them near golden. She tried to hide it, tried to appear totally impassive, but he saw the raw wanting deep inside her. It brought him a strange satisfaction, but also great discomfort. A hell of a discomfort.

He rose up to walk it off.

He didn't want this. He didn't need the woman adding to it all. He'd taken on the challenge of getting this herd and company of men across a thousand miles of mountain and hills and desert. He had to do it, had to prove he could do... and all their lives were dependent on him keeping his head about him. He could not let himself be turned away from this mission.

Late the following afternoon storm clouds boiled to the north. A summer storm. Lightning could be seen forking to the ground so far away it could barely be heard. The remuda pranced and threatened to break, the horses arching their tails and crying shrilly, the mules hawing just to keep up. Lorenzo roped one lead horse and fastened him to his own mount, and Duffy came back to help, roping another, hoping the rest would follow.

The men kept the remuda and herds going. The rolling land with only scrub piñon and juniper and not much of that offered little shelter; there was nothing else to do but keep going.

It wasn't long before the storm was on them, bearing down with the force of a devil locomotive. It sent wind before it that stirred dust so thick a person could be buried alive. The spirit of the remuda was toned down some by this.

Cross, riding a loop around all the bands, pulled the bandanna he'd readied up around his nose. He finished making certain exactly where everyone was, so he could find them if need be after the storm, and then he rode back to the woman. Coca would have enough trouble handling his pack mules without having to care for Lilly.

She looked like a stuffed bunch of clothes sitting on her mule, with her hat jabbed nearly over her ears, her head ducked to the wind. The mule's head was bowed, his nose about dragging the ground, and Pan walked exactly the same at the mule's heels.

When Cross got up on them, he saw the woman was holding one of her once-white lacy handkerchiefs over her nose. Coca was having a tussle with his mules. Cross yelled to him to cut them loose, but Coca refused. He cast Cross a wave and turned with the mules to drift south, in front of the wind.

The sheep were doing the same. The men had given up trying to keep them going on the trail. There wasn't any controlling ten thousand head of frightened sheep who insisted on turning away from the face of the storm. When they couldn't escape it, they would stop and stick their heads underneath each other's bellies and cower the thing out, bunching so tightly those in the center were likely to suffocate. Cross'd had that happen with smaller herds than these. Wasn't anything to be done about it, though.

As Cross pushed Domino beside the woman's mule, raindrops as big as plates began to hit his hat with plunks nearly as hard as hail. Domino shied, but Cross jabbed him good with his spur and bumped him against the woman's mule. Snaking out his arm, Cross grabbed her around the waist and hauled her over into the saddle in front of him.

"What are . . . no!" she cried and fought him. "Tubbs . . . don't leave him!"

"He'll follow!" Cross yelled at her and settled her astraddle in front of him. Domino staggered, finding his balance with the added weight. Cross hunkered around Lilly, shielding her from the wind and the rain that poured down as if out of a water tank.

Lightning flashed so close it blinded. Instinctively Cross ducked his head against the woman, and she pressed back against him. The sound reverberated like cannon fire all around them, too damn close for comfort and making Cross's heart beat like a tom-tom. He'd once seen a man hit by lightning; it'd fried the man black as a skillet.

His eyes searched for a hill or indentation, anything to give a little protection, but he couldn't see a blessed thing other than pouring water. He left the going to Domino and trusted the storm would pass quickly.

But when lightning flashed again like a mighty power from God above his head, he was out of the saddle and dragging Lilly after him. God almighty, lightning came like bullets! Lilly started to duck underneath Domino as Cross was jerking his bedroll from the saddle.

"He's a lightnin' rod!" Cross cried to her, pulled her to him and smacked the horse away.

In ten seconds he had Lilly down with him on the lowest wallow he could hit and the bedroll a cocoon around them, as tight over their bodies as he could get it. Somehow Pan had pushed himself under with them and lay trembling against their legs.

They lay there, pressing their wet clothes between them, breathing one another's breath, feeling one another's pulse, with the storm a mighty battle above them and lightning striking all around.

It was like that for at least ten minutes. The rain kept coming in a flood, pounding on the canvas around them.

It was hot inside the bedroll. Lilly was still against him...a tensed still. She lay on her back, and Cross was half sprawled over her. Pan penned one of his legs.

Time had little meaning, seemed to stretch forever. The rain lessened from a flood to a steady downpour. Sweat mixed with the rain-wet clothing. The scent of soggy wool was strong, from his serape and the skins of his bedroll, but the scent of the woman was stronger.

Her hip pressed him, bony even through her clothes.

Tentatively he slid a hand to her abdomen. It rested atop her serape, shirt, undergarments that he knew were there. But it was her skin he thought of. He felt her quiver. Slowly her face turned toward him, her lips brushing his beard, seeking his mouth. They kissed hungrily, took a breath and kissed again, pressing their bodies together.

Each of them held back, not really intending to do any of this, not wanting to get in any deeper. It was understood between them, as if they'd spoken. Cross knew what was happening with the first kiss, told himself it would only be one…maybe another…and then another because his mind was getting fuzzy. They were there, bodies pressed together in a common seeking of shelter. In a common wanting. It was too great a temptation…and it wasn't as if there was anything else to do. Just once more…and once more.

Cross clean forgot about there being ten thousand sheep and twelve men wandering around out there—until he heard hooves pounding toward him.

His head came up, and with a breathless curse, he tossed back the canvas. The rain had stopped. Duffy came riding over the rise.

Damn! The woman had taken his mind away!

Cross looked down at Lilly, and she looked up at him. Then she shoved him, and he rolled away from her and to his feet. Pan was up and giving a mighty shake.

"I see ye made it," Duffy said in an amused tone. "When I sighted Domino and the mule wanderin' yonder, with their reins a-draggin', I was a mite worried."

"We weathered it." Cross extended his hand to Lilly, but she ignored it, got herself up. He was of a mood, too, so she could have hers. He was damn mad at himself for letting his mind be tantalized away from his duty.

Duffy stretched his feet in the saddle. "Well, the rain washed the dust from the air," he commented in the way he had of always seeing good.

Looking off in the distance, at the miles of spreading stock, Cross said, "And now we got us ten thousand sheep and a remuda headin' south."

With the rain gone, the sheep fed eagerly, spreading out over the ground like cotton bolls spread across a field by the wind. The work of gathering them was slow, tedious and ungodly uncomfortable in dripping-wet clothing. Lilly undid her braid and shook her hair loose to enable it to dry. She wrung water from her hat and then put the rumpled thing back on because she didn't have anywhere else to put it. She draped her wet serape over the back of her saddle as best she could. With her shirt and trousers stuck to her, hampering movement, she cursed rain for all time.

Lilly and Tubbs and Pan herded straying bunches of woollies toward the others that Henri and Chino were gathering with the help of Chino's dogs. It did not matter if they were ewes or yearlings or wethers; the bands would be sorted later or maybe not at all. Finding the bellwether goat, however, did matter, for wherever one of those went, plenty of the sheep followed.

Chino had a devil of a time getting the goat for his band going in the right direction. He finally resorted to looping a rope around the critter's neck and leading him for half a mile. Once started, the goat seemed happy to continue.

Lilly and Henri pushed sheep up out of little gullies and away from clumps of brush. Henri gave a cry when he found some in a thicket. It took him and Lilly getting down from the saddle and going into the thicket to flush the stupid animals out, and then the obstinate woollies went skittering off every which way. Caught by limbs and thorns that tore her shirt and scratched her face and hands, Lilly said words she hadn't known she knew. Henri grinned, though wisely remained silent as he came to help her free herself.

The sun faded from a purple sky, taking all its heat with it, and still the work went on. The full moon was both a blessing and a curse. By its light the sheep were ghostly phantoms, glowing and easy to see, but with the moonlight the sheep remained restless, refusing to bed down. No sooner would the herders get a hundred settled, than fifty would get up to wander; settle that fifty and another hundred and fifty got on their feet. And then came the call of coyotes. A healthy pack by the sound of them. Lilly shivered as their howling came closer. Tubbs pricked his ears and sniffed.

Minutes later Cross and Duffy came riding past, shadows of color in the silvery light, their rifles in their hands and bringing behind them a string of four mules. They left the mules with Chino's band to serve as some protection for the sheep. After Cross and Duffy had disappeared over a small rise, Lilly heard the echoes of two rifles firing. Silence, and then several cracks in succession—Cross firing his pistol. There came no further calls of coyotes.

Lilly began to feel they would never get the sheep rounded up. She rode back to the main camp for a dry shirt; it was easier to leave her wet and muddy moccasins and trousers on. Chilled to the bone, she exchanged her wet serape for a dry blanket tied around her. She did warm herself by the fire but she wouldn't stay there. These were her sheep; she had to work for them as hard as the men.

She had to work as hard as Cross, who didn't leave the saddle even to have coffee, but seemed to be everywhere, giving orders and seeing to all the men and animals alike.

Taking dry clothes for Henri, Lilly mounted Tubbs and headed out into the starry night. Tubbs kept going, surefooted, and she trusted herself to him.

When dawn came the bands were loosely gathered and on the trail again. According to the count they were missing fifteen.

"You stay with Coca," Cross told Lilly. "I'll go and find them."

But Lilly shook her head. "I'm not needed here. I'll go with you."

They made a wide circle, riding a quarter of a mile to a half mile apart, losing sight of each other when the land fell, finding each other again when it rose. Lilly came upon the missing sheep when Tubbs just about fell into a small wash. There, on good topsoil brought by years of storms, all fifteen fed happily on lush grasses. With a loud whoop, Lilly waved to Cross.

She was proud, and the pride made her grin broadly at Cross. He said, "Well, don't just sit there. Let's get 'em up," but he grinned just a bit when he said it.

As they rode up out of the canyon, pushing the woollies before them, Cross said, "You have them all again, *señora pastora.*"

His eyes twinkled, and she saw approval there. She held Tubbs's reins lightly, tapped her heels and rode easy beside Cross McCree.

At midday they watered the sheep at the river, which had turned into a narrow and smooth-flowing stream as it neared its headwater. The bands had to be pushed in one at a time, then pushed out again to graze on grassy hills that had begun to rise with junipers and even pine. Afterward the herders allowed the sheep to settle for a long nooning.

Cross rode from the first band to the last, checking the condition of the men and animals. None were the worse for wear, except for needing sleep, which all could do now. The sheep lay contentedly, and the men stretched their bedrolls in the shade of trees or rocky escarpments.

Coca set up a noon camp far enough from the sheep, he said, that he didn't have to see them or hear them. As he dished out plates of beans and tortillas, he professed the opinion that he was going back to being a bandit, for it was a lot easier than tending sheep.

Duffy took himself off up into the pine, Coca lay beneath a juniper and Mateo fell asleep sitting against a boulder. Henri sprawled with the carelessness of youth on a rocky ledge.

Cross found a relatively comfortable place in the shade of a juniper growing out of the rock, where he had a good view of the land and anyone or anything that might approach.

He leaned against his saddle and smoked and watched for the woman to come back from the stream, where she'd gone to wash. He'd washed, too, earlier, not a full bath but a good rinsing, and he felt a hell of a lot better. It'd been something of a luxury, not a thing he had to have in order to go on living. But for a woman it was different; Lilly needed water for bathing as much as she needed it to drink. He didn't worry, then, that she took a long time at it.

Eventually, about the time Cross was close to deciding she'd drowned, she appeared from the shelter of the brush. She had an armload of clothes that she spread on limbs in the sun. She hadn't bothered to put on her shirt, wore only that ruffled, sleeveless undergarment Americano women apparently favored and clean trousers. She probably figured modesty wasn't such a high priority at this moment. Cross was glad to see she was gaining good sense. She walked gingerly across the ground in bare feet and crawled into her bedroll hidden by the fluttering leaves and shadows of a mesquite tree.

Cross let his eyes linger on her a moment. He knew he wouldn't be staying away from her for very much longer. He stabbed out a smoked-down cigar butt and allowed himself to drift off into the luxury of a sound sleep. God would have to keep watch for the next few hours.

Lilly came awake slowly. First she heard a bird, and she thought it was outside her window that faced the river. But then she awoke enough to feel the hard ground underneath her. She sat up, brushing the hair from her face, squinting in the golden light of a falling sun.

The camp was plumb gone. As if it had never been there. She stared at the spot in front of the rocky escarpment, feeling lost.

"Have a good sleep?"

Lilly started and turned toward the sound of Cross's voice.

He sat cross-legged, his knife and whetstone in his hands, a cigar between his lips. He gazed at her, his blue eyes intent.

"Where's everyone?" she asked, though not thinking much about anyone else, not thinking much about anything but the way Cross was looking at her.

He looked down at his saddlebags near his knee and tucked the stone inside, saying, "Went on down the trail. There wasn't any need to wake you. Your mule's over there grazin'."

Lilly followed his nod and saw Tubbs and Cross's horse grazing on the other side of brush along the stream. Both were saddled. She raked her hand through her hair, brought her gaze back to Cross.

He was staring at her.

She stared back. Her breath stopped in the back of her throat.

He slowly took the cigar from his lips, rubbed it dead in the dirt. His gaze returned to her, and he got up and came toward her, stopped and crouched in front of her. All the while their gazes held.

Lilly began to pulse deep in her belly. She watched the heat slip into his blue eyes and then over his face. When his hand came out and cupped her head, she went to him, eagerly, passionately.

With purpose, she slipped her hands up beneath his shirt, caressed his hard back, and pulled him down atop her.

* * *

They had crossed a line, and there wasn't any going back from it. Both knew that. They didn't speak of it, but they knew it. They didn't speak of what they would do tomorrow, or the next day, or when the end of the trip came. Neither one of them had any answers, and right now neither of them needed them. They were absorbed in the present, in living and breathing and feeling for each other.

They rode easily beside each other in the twilight. When a covey of quail fluttered up from sagebrush on Tubbs's right, they pulled up their mounts to watch the birds, who were quickly gone, hidden again. Their eyes strayed to each other, and they smiled. Lilly smiled; Cross's smile wasn't much more than a twitch of his lips and crinkling around his eyes. But she could feel his pleasure. They had that between them ... the understanding without words.

Then his hand came out and slipped around her neck in a light caress. Only for a moment, and then they rode on.

They topped a rise and saw the sheep half a mile away, shadowy figures on the darkening land. They gazed at the sight in silent camaraderie, and then Cross nudged Domino. Lilly did likewise to Tubbs, and they rode toward the herd at a trot.

Chapter Fifteen

Some nights, when Cross returned from his checks on the herd, he found Lilly waiting for him in his bedroll. She didn't stay the entire night, only a few hours, and then she would go back to her own. She didn't sneak; neither she nor Cross made any attempt to hide that they had taken up with each other. Cross sometimes took her to ride on the saddle in front of him, and he'd even bathed with her once. But she seemed disinclined to stay the night with him, as if to keep a part of herself separated from him. He didn't ask; it was her own business, and that's how they played it.

One night, though, she fell asleep and didn't wake up until he was shaking her in the thin light before dawn. He'd already been up and out to check the herd.

"You'd better get dressed," he murmured as he kissed her neck. She smelled sweet, after all the sweat and dust. She always managed to smell sweet, and he loved to inhale her skin.

She was stark naked, and he thought she'd best dress before it got sunup. His bedroll was away from the camp and sheltered by brush, but it wasn't the same as being in a private room.

She sat up and dug down in the bedroll for her clothes. "You could help, you know," she said, when she saw him watching her and grinning at the sight.

"I am helpin'...." He held up her lacy pantaloons. She reached for them, and he jerked them away.

She pushed her hair out of her face and glared at him; Lilly really wasn't much for early mornings. "I can do without," she said in a huff and fished around for her trousers.

"Want these?" He held up her trousers, jumped up and crouched two feet away. He really had her at the disadvantage, as he was already dressed.

It wasn't often that he teased like this, and it took them both by surprise. She stared at him, and then she lunged for the trousers. But she didn't want to step off the bedroll, nor drop the covering of the hides.

"I'll give them to you...for a price," he said.

"A kiss?"

"Oh, that'll do for starters."

He crouched beside her and kissed her, though he didn't touch her. They were both breathing hard when he broke away. Her eyes were filled with wanting.

He stared at her, and she stared at him. He thought about how he needed to get back to the herd, but then his gaze fell to where her breasts showed above her camisole. Her hand came up and went around his neck, and he went down with her.

He didn't get to taking off all his clothes, not even his boots.

Lilly was a woman made for loving. He carried her scent with him all that day.

Some nights they did nothing more than lie there and stare at the stars. They talked about the land and the sheep, about the herders and their odd habits, about how far it might be to a star.

Once she told him that her mother had died giving birth. A baby girl, it had been, too early to live. Her mother had bled to death.

"My daddy couldn't stand losin' her," she said. "He hung himself."

She spoke with little emotion, kept her head cradled in her arm and eyes gazing at the sky.

"Lot of women die in childbirth," Cross said, though it really didn't need saying. He watched her features, and he saw the strain there.

"Yes," was all she said.

That was as close as she came to speaking of catching. Every morning she drank a tea that Coca claimed would keep her from getting a full belly, but there were no guarantees; they both knew that, and they continued as they were, for neither could stay away from the other. Cross didn't give much thought to what he'd do if she did fall with his child. He'd learned long ago not to consider some things until they actually came to pass.

What was he going to do after he'd sold his sheep? she wanted to know. He told her, just a little bit, because he felt self-conscious. He told her how the challenge of driving the sheep all the way to California was as much of it as making money. He talked of a place he knew that would make a good ranch, if he could make a deal with the Apache. He talked of the cattle and sheep he wanted to raise.

"Meat's gonna be needed in California for a long spell yet. People are streamin' in there like a river. And I hear tell that some ranchers trail stock to Matagorda over in Texas and ship 'em off to Cuba and the Northeast."

He looked at her, and it was on the tip of his tongue to ask her if she would be with him in his plans, but he remained silent.

She looked him straight in the eyes and said, "I'm goin' back to Pasquotank County, and I'm gonna buy back Cypress Crossin'."

It was her family place, the place where her mother had died, and her father had hanged himself. It was beside the river, with cypress trees edging the lawn that flowed like carpet. She loved cypress trees. He listened and heard the resolve in her voice.

The only time she ever mentioned her husband, the gambling man, was when she dragged Cross into a game of poker. Her husband had taught her, she said, as she deftly dealt the cards.

"Tyler was very good with cards," she said. "He couldn't pick the winner of a one-horse race, but he could play cards like a master violinist."

Cross thought he heard a warmth in her voice, but he wasn't certain. She was looking down at the cards she tossed on the bedroll. She beat him three out of the five hands they played of five-card stud. As Cross took her into his arms, and she came to him with hot, sweet fire, he figured that the gambling man's talents had been a sight more with cards than with pleasuring his wife.

Of course he didn't say any of that. There was a lot he didn't say and more he knew she didn't say, and none of it amounted to anything anyway.

So that's how it was between them. He took from her what she would give him, and he gave to her all that he could. The future, for now, was only a distant possibility, and the past was long gone, dim in memory. They were living in the here and now, the challenge and the passions overshadowing all else.

For now, this day and this minute, it was enough. It was everything.

Riding four abreast, Cross leading two pack mules, they slowly passed the sign that read Moriah. It was a tiny community. No more than six houses and four business establishments, and a church with a steeple. All were built of board lumber and whitewashed. The yards were swept clean, and one of the houses even had a picket fence, whitewashed, too, with roses planted there. Lilly pointed them out and stared at the flowers and the fence and felt oddly disoriented. It had been so long since she had seen the trappings of civilization.

Duffy had scouted the town the day before. He reported that the cost of supplies was steep. Everything was freighted in over the mountains, up north from Wyoming way. But the Mormons were a savvy people and stocked anything and everything they thought they could sell to pilgrims traveling to California. Everything but whiskey, much to his disappointment. And he still talked mournfully of going to Salt Lake City and having a look at Brigham Young's wives.

Lilly's special desire was to finally talk to a woman, hear another woman's voice—that and new, clean clothes. She'd be in heaven!

She was as excited as if she were going on a trip to Richmond. She was going to buy new pants and shirts and socks—oh, yes, socks of soft wool! And most importantly a new brush. Cross smiled and shook his head at this. Well, she explained, a comb was okay, but a woman's hair really needed a good brushing.

Henri was to get all new clothes, too, from the inside out, for he'd far outgrown his. And of course he must have boots, she said, and ruffled his hair. He took that and smiled this time; sometimes, if she forgot and did that around the men, he would frown. She tried not to forget.

Cross said that maybe in all this buying they could squeeze in a few unimportant things, like flour, coffee, beans and grain for the horses. He spoke so dryly and sarcastically, with that hint of a grin on his face. Lilly told him he could manage that on his own, she would manage the other. Duffy laughed at them all and said none of them knew what was really important, and that was whiskey. He would, however, content himself quite nicely with some crusty biscuits baked by the hand of the plump and very fair Mrs. Montgomery at her boarding house.

Two men were talking in front of the livery, a woman was sweeping her front porch, and three children were playing near the church. All stared as Lilly, Cross, Duffy and Henri rode past. Lilly took off her hat and tucked it beneath the cantle; the hat was so dusty and battered, her bare hair would look better. She'd bathed and wore the best of the two trousers and shirts she had, but that wasn't saying much.

They came to the boarding house and café, and Cross raised an eyebrow to Lilly, but she chose to go shop first. Duffy chose food and broke away, with a high smile and promise to catch them up later. He could eat twice with no problem.

Cross led the way to a building with a mercantile sign on its big square front. Slowly, her eyes on the plate glass windows and the color coming from there, Lilly dismounted and looped Tubbs's reins over the hitching rail. On the porch she stopped, gazing at a bonnet displayed. Oh, not one nearly so fine as any she had once sported, but it was a bonnet, with a spray of colorful cotton flowers, stiffened and polished, and with wide velvet ribbons, too. Longing swept her.

Henri tugged on her hand, and she went with him, following Cross into the store.

Cross, his boots scraping and spurs jingling, went straight to the counter in the rear to take care of the provisions. Henri hung back with Lilly, squeezing her hand tightly. Lilly smiled at him, and he smiled swiftly back.

The store was quite neat, amazingly so, all the barrels lined up, sacks stacked, foodstuffs on one side, dry goods on the other. Tools and kitchen utensils hung from the ceiling. Like a warehouse, she thought . . . or a fairyland chock full of glimmering sights.

She saw them then—two women at the right of the store. In cotton dresses, plain brown and blue ticking stripe, with aprons. Dust rags in hand, pencil and paper. Women, like herself. She stepped forward in eagerness, but stopped, the impulse to smile dying on her lips.

The women stared at her, the disdain on their faces the same as if they had spit at her. They dropped their gazes to Henri, as if looking at something dirty.

Suddenly Lilly realized how she and the boy must appear to these people—roughly dressed, Henri in not much more than rags, and with bare feet. And the scar that still showed above his eye.

"Were you desiring something in par-tic-u-lar?" one of the women, the one who stood behind the counter, asked, as if Lilly might not understand English. She was a skinny woman with a birdlike face and cold, birdlike eyes.

"Yes," Lilly said, her throat tight. Swallowing, she dropped her gaze to the woman's chin. "I'd like to see your shirts and trousers. For boys." She spoke precisely, yet her voice was faint.

"Right over there." The woman pointed with a bony hand. She didn't come from around the counter to help. She didn't want to get anywhere near Lilly, and that was as plain as if she'd said it right out loud.

Lilly pushed Henri before her over to where the woman had pointed. It was a small table, with not much on it. No doubt these people would make the most of their clothing.

While she looked, she felt the women's eyes upon her. It was all so strange to her, this store, these people. That she had once shopped and lived as they seemed only a dream.

She heard Cross talking to the man behind the counter, yet somehow even the language sounded strange. When Cross disappeared behind a curtain to the back of the store, Lilly felt a sudden sense of panic, as if being abandoned in a foreign land.

She riffled through the folded shirts, forcing her mind to think of what was needed. At last she found a shirt that would do for Henri, and trousers, though they were quite big. Better that than too small, for he was growing rapidly. She chose trousers for herself, and a shirt.

All the while Henri stood, patiently allowing her to hold clothes up to him, then to herself. He said not a word, simply looked around the store with big eyes. She'd found a pair of cheap galluses she thought would fit him and had turned around to measure them against him, when she found him down the aisle, staring at hats.

She stepped beside him. There were plenty of hats, stacked one on top of another, good, serviceable, brimmed hats to shelter from rain and sun.

"*Señora* really needs a hat," he told her solemnly.

"I do, huh? Brown or black?"

"Brown, I think. For your hair, its color." He touched the hats only with his eyes, left his hands hanging at his side.

Lilly found one she thought would fit, and put it on. "*Bella,*" he said softly, his black eyes glimmering like stars.

"And a black one for you," Lilly said, softly laying one on his head. "For your hair... and since you are growin'."

He grinned proudly. "Yes, I grow." Then, as if embarrassed, he averted his eyes, turned to looking around, as if not to be so taken with himself. Yet, Lilly didn't miss the cock of his head, the way he touched the brim of the hat.

She continued to peruse the stacks and boxes, looking for longhandles that would fit Henri, and socks for them both. And then she found a display case of things to delight a woman: silver and pewter hair pins, tortoiseshell and wooden combs... and brushes. A part of her heart that had been put in her pocket for months came to life. She put her hand on the glass of the case and gazed with pleasure.

Suddenly she heard a shrill scream.

"Get away from there!"

Lilly whirled to see Henri backing up, and the bird-faced woman bearing down on him.

"Don't be sticking your dirty heathen nose on the glass!"

Henri bumped into a stack of brooms and rakes propped against crates. The long wooden handles went clattering every which way.

Lilly dropped her armload of clothes and sprinted to the boy, pressing him against her, shielding his chest with both of her hands.

"What's he done?" she asked the woman, who flew around the counter toward them.

"He was after the candy." The woman gestured at Henri. "Had his dirty nose all over the glass jar." Lilly saw it clearly then, the repulsion in the woman for the boy.

Her words came out through clenched teeth, her voice rising as the fury rose, a slow thing, gathering steam as it came. "He is not dirty."

The woman's eyes met Lilly's. Lilly saw the jump within them. The woman straightened and pulled back. The base of her neck pulsed.

"And he is not a heathen," Lilly added.

The back curtain billowed out, and Cross appeared, a man right on his heels.

"What is it, Nella?" The man squeezed his head and chest around Cross. "Is there some problem?" The man was bony, like the woman, with the same nose and eyes, but there was a softness to his face that the woman didn't have.

Before the woman could speak, Lilly said, "This woman accosted my son. He was only lookin' at the candy, choosin'. We have money to pay." She employed her most cultivated tone that rang with pulpit righteousness. She intended for the man and the woman to take note, and they did. The man's eyes popped, then shifted worriedly.

The woman answered with righteousness of her own. "He was sticking his nose and hands all over the glass, and we can't have that. And if I hadn't been watching, he'd have filled his pockets. He might have done it before I saw.'' The words rolled off the woman's tongue as fast as peas off a table, and she raised a sharp, questioning eyebrow at Henri.

Cross said flatly, "The boy has no pockets." He reached out, took Henri's hand and showed them, palms empty. The look he gave the woman was the quiet blank one he used when he'd seen enough foolishness, and the woman drew back.

"Now, see, sister." The man twittered and shook. "It was a simple mistake. I'm sorry, Mr. McCree. We're getting a lot of travelers through here these days...not the best folk, you understand, some got their squaws and breeds with them, and..." His voice trailed off as his gaze moved from Cross's swarthy face to Lilly's and then dropped down to Henri. Perplexity flickered over his face, and then was covered over by good sense. "Well...ahem...a quarter pound of the candy the boy fancies would be in order, I imagine."

"An apology is also in order, sir," Lilly said.

The birdlike woman's eyebrows rose. "I don't see..." she began, but then she wet her lips and inclined her head in a coldly ungracious manner. "I apologize," she said to Lilly.

"Not to me. Apologize to my son."

The woman's eyes dueled with her, and Lilly didn't give way. The vague idea of whipping out her knife and slicing off the woman's birdlike nose played at the back of her mind.

Looking down her pointy nose, the woman said in a choked voice, "I apologize to you, little boy." Then she whirled and strode away past the counter, smacked the curtain out of her way and disappeared behind it.

Cross smiled that hint of a smile. Then he held out his hand to Henri. "Let's get that candy. A *pound*, didn't you say, Hendrick?"

"Ah, yes...yes." The skinny man bobbed and twittered.

Lilly gathered all she had chosen and, when Mr. Hendrick had finished getting Henri's candy, she had him bring boots for Henri, trying them on the boy until just the right size was found. She had her turn at choosing boots, and a hairbrush from the case, a length of calico for making bandannas, and thread. Oh, yes, and English tea, if he had it.

"We sure do, Mrs. McCree. We sure do."

Lilly started at the address, shot a look to Cross. He gazed at her with that bit of a smile and twinkling eyes. Henri peeked from beneath his hat. Lilly blushed and looked away from them both.

Now that he'd become so friendly with his customers, most especially after Cross had produced his bag of gold coin, Mr. Hendrick was quite talkative. He spoke of other sheep coming through. There'd been two herds to come through in the past month.

"Yes, sir, both herds coming all the way from Ioway," Mr. Hendrick said. "First fellow had a herd of four thousand, man by the name of Hollister. He was one determined man, I tell you. Second herd was smaller, just a little over a thousand head, belonged to a group of pilgrims bent on settling in California, like everyone was. The pilgrims had cattle, too, and wagons and oxen. Both of the companies were heading southwest, down to Los Angeles way. The year's been dry, though, and I can't see them gettin' through without trouble. It's desert country down that way. Well...most of Utah's desert, I guess, and fine the way God made it."

Mr. Hendrick shook his head. "You're pushing ten thousand head. That's a lot to have to water out on the desert."

"Heard Dick Wootton did it," Cross said.

"Oh, yes . . . yes, he did. Nine thousand I believe he had, and we'd had a good year for rain. Not every year is the same, you know."

"I know. How much do I owe you?" Cross was impatient to be on his way.

Still, Lilly asked for a place to freshen up and change into her new clothes, and she insisted Henri do likewise. "We're in a town. No need to look like heathens," she said, giving Mr. Hendrick a sweet smile.

When they left the store, Lilly was dressed in a blue shirt, brown duck trousers with black galluses, and boots, with her hair brushed until it shone, falling loose and wavy over her shoulder, and her earrings bobbing gently at her ears. Henri, too, was arrayed in his new rigging. He had trouble keeping his eyes off his boots, and almost fell down the stairs. Cross had discarded his dusty serape and had broken down and bought a new shirt, which he wore, too.

On impulse, as they walked across to the boarding house, Lilly inserted her arm into the crook of Cross's. He grinned down at her. "You are one high-headed horse," he said.

"Well, at least I no longer feel like a nag," Lilly said dryly.

And Cross said, "Oh, you never were a nag . . . a mule pretty much, but never a nag, *señora.*"

Lilly gave him a swat for that, and he came back with quoting how much money she owed him for the things she'd bought in the mercantile.

With high spirits, they entered the boarding house. For a moment, mindful that their reception might be much less than warm, Lilly and Henri hung back, crowding against Cross. But then Duffy was hailing them, and a lovely, plump woman came toward them with a wide smile upon her face.

"I'm Mrs. Montgomery, and I'm the best cook for a thousand miles. Come on in and sit." She put her arm around Henri, squeezed him and propelled him toward the table.

They all ate, food such as Lilly hadn't seen in nearly a year: ham and black-eyed peas and potatoes cooked Yankee style but, oh, so good, and cold beets and sourdough biscuits with fine maple syrup that their host said her brother sent from Indiana. Much of the food was totally new to Henri; he liked the maple syrup best.

Duffy had a piece of disturbing news.

"Uriah Plover's been here," he said, drawing all their attention. "'Bout a week ago. Riding with three other hombres now. They had supper here at Mrs. Montgomery's and gave her quite a time."

Lilly's stomach knotted, and her skin crawled as she thought of the men being in the room in which she now sat.

"They brought in liquor of their own," Mrs. Montgomery said, disapprovingly, "and they got stinking. They broke plates and glasses and dumped food on the floor before I could get the men over here to drive them out. Joe Meeker and Charlie Hall took watch that night and the three following, thinking the scoundrels might return. They didn't, thank God, and I didn't even mind not being paid. I was just glad to be shut of them."

"Did you hear which way they might have been headin'?" Cross asked. He sat back and drank leisurely of the rich coffee, as if he weren't concerned, though Lilly saw the intent in his eyes.

"Well, I certainly had no wish to speak with them at length," the plump woman said quite primly, "but I did hear them talkin' about Salt Lake City. Arguing about it, because one of them wanted to go there, but the other two didn't. They'd come from Fort Bridger, I know that, because they said it straight out. There's been trouble up there, you know. There's some that think Jim Bridger is something of a heathen. I can't say myself," she said, her gaze drifting to Duffy. "Anyway, some out of Salt Lake City went up and dispatched him out of the territory. There was good fighting up there at the Fort with the Indians, too, and the scoundrels were in it. They were probably wise not to go to Salt Lake City. When the scoundrels rode out, it was south, which I don't think really says much. It's a big country, now, isn't it?"

Mrs. Montgomery hadn't heard a word of the men since, but perhaps Joe Meeker had. He was the blacksmith at the livery, if Mr. McCree wanted to inquire.

After the meal, Cross agreed to renting two rooms from Mrs. Montgomery so they could all have naps in real beds.

Henri and Duffy had a back room, while Lilly and Cross—assumed to be Mr. and Mrs.—had the front.

Lilly stared at the room, at the chintz curtains, the braided wool rug, the enamel white bedstead, the colorful quilt. Cross sat on the bed, removed his boots and knives in their sheaths, then stretched out, arm crooked behind his head on the pillow. He gazed at her invitingly.

Slowly Lilly came to sit on the bed, ran her hand over the fine cotton. She removed her boots and belt with her knife, then stretched beside Cross. The bed was like lying upon a cloud.

"I haven't lain on a featherbed since—" she thought back, disbelieving it could have been so long "—since last fall, in St. Louis."

Memories came in flashes through her mind: Mammy Ethnee ordering the hauling of the mattresses out into the sun, the mattress curling around her on a cold night, the sinking of it beneath her body that first night Tyler took her.

"I was on one 'bout two months ago. Night before we left Santa Fe."

Lilly glanced up at him, thought about the house where he had taken her and the woman with the black hair. The woman so close to him and Duffy Campbell.

A breeze stirred through the open window. Lilly turned to Cross, and despite the heat, she pillowed her head on his shoulder, draped her arm across his stomach.

"What will happen if we come upon Uriah Plover and those men?" she asked.

"We're always ready to take on what comes," Cross said and stroked her hair, unconcerned at that moment about anything but stroking her hair.

"How long will it take us to cross the desert?"

"Maybe ten days." His hand continued to move rhythmically over her hair.

"How do we go so long without water?"

"There's always a bit of water in the desert," he said, certainty in his voice.

"I've never seen a desert. I was born in a swamp."

He didn't say anything, simply kept on stroking her hair, and Lilly let it soothe her into sleep.

When they awoke and went to get Duffy and Henri to leave, they found Henri asleep on the rag rug beside the bed.

The next morning the Duff left them to head back for Santa Fe.

Cross and Lilly rode a ways with him. On a hill where they could see dry, shrub-covered, rolling mountains behind and pine-studded rock mountains ahead, they stopped and alighted. Duffy took Lilly's hand, bowed over it.

"It has been a distinct pleasure, madam, to have met ye. I hope our paths will cross in the future."

Lilly rose up on tiptoe, kissed his cheek, and then gave in to hugging him. "I wish you safety, Duffy." Her voice was thick.

"Ah, lass, never fear for me. I walk beneath lucky stars."

Lilly looked at him a moment, then at Cross. Then she led her mule off and stood with her back to them, gazing west. She took a deep breath, forcing her tight chest to expand.

Parting from those one has come to know is always hard, she thought. And she kept her eyes on the western sky.

Duffy played his reins through his hand. "That lovely Mrs. Montgomery made me homesick for Marquita. I need to be gettin' back before the lass decides to replace me."

Cross cocked an eyebrow. "Think she'd do that?"

"She might. Marquita's got a fire of temper, if ye remember."

They gazed at each other and shared a mutual understanding of the woman one left behind and the other raced back for.

"I never was meanin' to go all the way to California with ye," Duffy said, his voice dropping with a hint of apology. "Only to get ye over the mountains in one piece and headed in the right direction." He paused. "I wouldna' leave ye, if I didn't think ye could make it, mon. Ye'll make it."

Cross quirked a smile at that, then nodded. "I've had the best teacher could be. I'm obliged for your comin' as far as you have."

Silence echoed between them, each of them dreading the final instant of goodbye.

Duffy said, "Should I tell Marquita to expect ye around November? Ye can make it easy comin' around the south, not more than a month's trail when ye are free and loose without the sheep."

Cross nodded. "I'll be comin'. If somethin' holds me back, I'll send word."

Duffy glanced off at the woman. "Think she'll be comin' with ye?" he asked, cocking a bushy eyebrow.

Cross looked at the woman, too. Her hat hung on her back by its leather thong; her brown hair glimmered in the sunlight.

He shook his head. "She's bound for back East."

"Lasses have been known to change their minds."

"Maybe... but this one hasn't so far."

"Oh, but she has," Duffy said, grinning a cat grin. "When she decided to come to yer bed."

Cross chuckled at that, both embarrassed and amused. Duffy rubbed his nose with his hand. Cross swallowed. Then Duffy reached out and hugged Cross to him.

"Keep your scalp," Cross said gruffly as Duffy mounted.

"Aye. Marquita loves it." Then he jerked his big horse into a quick turn and spurred him away at a gallop. Down the slope and back up another. He pulled up, turned and waved, then disappeared over the hill, not to be seen again.

Cross stood there, holding Domino's reins, feeling a desolation settle on him. He watched the empty land for half a minute, then he looked at the woman. She passed a quick hand across her eyes, then looked at him. He couldn't be sure, but he thought she had tears. There was something in her eyes.

Was it the same as he was thinking—that there would be a parting time for them, too?

He turned and mounted. He watched the woman mount. It came heavily on him how it was all up to him again. It was up to him to get them all to California alive and in one piece. He traced the woman's form. It was up to him to keep her alive and safe. His heart pained at the thought, and he realized then how much she had come to mean to him.

He spurred hard, sending the horse out at a gallop.

Cross set the course southwest for a bit, in order to skirt the bottom edge of the salt desert. They moved the herd through the shrub and rock hills, first along a dry riverbed, until they hit a river, running low but still with water in it that the sheep would drink. In places the sheep nearly drank it dry, which was the great hazard of passing ten thousand head of sheep across this country.

Ahead of them lay better than a hundred miles of desert. It was a daunting thought, and the men talked much of it.

Cross wasn't overly worried about crossing it. He'd prepared himself, and there was nothing else to be done, so worry wouldn't help anything. He hadn't brought wagons that could bog down in the sand or break axles in the hills, but mules and horses that were bred for hard ground. And sheep could go a ways longer without water than could cattle or other stock. The horses and mules would need it first.

They would travel in the cool of mornings and evenings as much as they could. There would be springs and pools, and possibly a little lake, too. Duffy had marked them on a map he'd drawn up from memory and from speaking with people in Moriah.

Of course they could miss the springs, and it was highly likely that the pools, maybe even the lake, could be dry, or gone poison with alkali. However, it was the same as before; the company went on, trusting they would get through.

They spent one day camped beside the little river, doctoring the stock and readying their equipment for the trek. Those sheep having sore feet had the cracks in their hooves filled with a mixture of resin and pine tree gum. For this, Arrio's and Lorenzo's expertise with the reata was employed. The two vaqueros went from band to band, roping the sheep pointed out to them as needing doctoring. Chino and Gaspar separated their sheep just as well on foot, and Cross wasn't bad in cutting out the sheep on Domino.

Lilly worked right along with the men, doing her share of getting as much of the mixture smeared on her as was put on the sheep's hooves. By the time they were getting to the last sore-footed woolly, she had learned to grab them by the horns and throw them on the ground, no small feat for a person of her size. A big one dragged her about ten feet, but she got him down, after a fashion. Another one chased her, but she ran for the safety of her mule, which dared the rowdy woolly with a drawn hoof. The woolly backed off and pranced away, having shown his stuff.

When they had finished with the sheep, Lorenzo and Cross doctored the feet of the mules and horses, too, and put dabs of pine tree gum in and around their ears to keep the pesky insects out.

When they finished that afternoon, Cross called for a party, or as much of one as they could have without tequila. Coca cooked up mule deer and partridge that Mateo and Tomas had shot, beans and tortillas and dried apples and honey that Cross had bought in Moriah.

That evening Cross spread his bedroll out of view of the camp, over a hill, where he had a view of the desert land spreading out beneath a rising half-moon. The land glowed, as if possessed of magic power. As if to entice and then catch them in a death grip, he thought.

He studied the land, and he waited for Lilly to come to him.

There was a burning inside him for her. Maybe it was knowing their trip was half done, or maybe it was what Duffy had put in his mind about her changing her mind and staying. Maybe it was that he knew the next weeks were going to be rough, and he wanted the strength and comfort she always gave him. Maybe it was just the needs of being a man. Whatever it was, he wanted her.

But he wouldn't ask her, for his manly pride wouldn't allow it. His mind recalled all too clearly her words: "I'm goin' back to Pasquotank County...."

She came, at last, when night cold was slipping over the land. She moved quietly. She'd learned to do that. She'd learned to do a lot of things, he guessed.

"You bought those boots for nothin'," he said as she sat beside him. She'd gone back to her moccasins the very next day after their shopping in Moriah. He could have told her she would.

"At least I have them now. I'll like them when it rains."

"Guess so. It'll be wetter over in California."

She had a blanket wrapped around her, and in the faint silvery light she looked almost like an Indian woman. He told her that, and she laughed a low laugh that shimmered through him.

They gazed at the desert, she, sitting there beside him, close enough for her shoulder to brush his and her sweet scent to come to him.

She pointed to the sandy hills off to the north. "They look like snowdrifts," she said.

"They'd burn your skin raw in the sun," he said.

He tossed away the stub of his burned-down panatela with impatience. He only had six left; he was rationing them, smoking them down to nothing.

The next instant he turned and grabbed her to him, kissed her hard. She kissed him back the same way. And then he was tugging down her trousers. She didn't have her moccasins tied all the way, and she'd given up wearing those pantaloons beneath her trousers, so it was a lot easier all the way around. Cross ripped off his boots and trousers, and didn't bother with his socks. Neither of them got to their shirts, simply pushed them upward as they wiggled together, grasping. With a powerful urge spurring him just as he sometimes spurred his horse, Cross covered her mouth with his and buried himself in her. He held himself there, savoring the feelings . . . and then he gave himself over to appeasing the gnawing need.

When done, he lay there atop her, inhaling the wild scents of sweat and clear desert air in her hair. The gnawing of his body was gone, but a strange aching need remained.

She pushed him away. He rolled to his back, watched her sit up and fumble around for her trousers. He felt her ire, as surely as if she shouted it. He thought that he could have slung it at her that she'd been as eager as he.

But something stronger made him sit up and kiss her neck. She pulled away from him. He kissed her neck again, and she took it. He ran his hand up her back beneath her shirt, kissed and caressed her, until he brought her back to him.

There, snuggled into the bedroll, they made love to each other, and this time it was like lying in a lazy river and letting warm water caress every part of their bodies. Their scents and sweat and flesh mingled, until neither could tell where one left off and the other began. Cross found then the filling of the empty ache inside him.

Afterward, they fell asleep holding on to each other. And when Cross awoke in the early hours of the morning, Lilly was curled against him.

He wondered again if she might change her mind and stay with him.

And then he told himself he had to see to getting the herd started across the desert. He had to keep everyone alive across one hundred scorching miles. If he didn't, wondering whether the woman would stay or go was quite useless.

She and Coca rode ahead to set up a noon camp. On a hill, Lilly looked around behind them. She saw the bands, all six of them. Sheep stretched for a mile back toward the east and spread for as much as a quarter mile wide in places. They cut a swath across the land, eating all the edible shrubs there were. The cactus they left alone, for now, Coca said. In the days to come they would start on that, too. If it had been spring, they would have feasted on desert flowers. Dogs ran at the sides of the herd, now and then nipping around sheep that wanted to dart away. Dust, beginning at the front of the herd, boiled thicker and thicker, so that the rear band was almost obliterated from sight. The remuda, herded loosely by Lorenzo and Simon, turned up their own dust cloud as they walked along, champing at each other and at clumps of grass and shrub. Above them all, the sun rose higher and hotter.

They had started hours before sunrise, with the moon gone down and only starlight to see by. In a land of no trees there was a glow to the night, a thin light that seemed to come from the land itself. The men had pushed the herd to move quickly, while the animals were fresh and before the heat sapped their strength, as it was doing now.

When the bands caught up with them, Coca and Lilly had camp set up, complete with Lilly's tent, flaps open, and three more canvas shelters supported by rough poles they had cut back in the timber. There was no shelter for the animals, nor any water. There was no shade for as far as the eye could see.

The sheep lay down easily, tired and hot. They panted with their tongues lolling out of their mouths. The horses and mules milled slowly, sniffing and grazing on what was there. Pan came into camp, and Lilly gave him water in a tin cup; the other dogs were watered by their herders, but not overly. Each person had two canteens of water, and three mules carried water barrels; this was to suffice for all the company. When it was gone, there would be only what they could find in the desert.

The humans rested in the shade of the shelters; those out minding the sheep put up tiny tents using their bedrolls or even their serapes. Jesus was content to sit in the shade of his big hat. Even his dog squeezed into that shade.

Lilly took off her serape at last. On Coca's advice she had left it on in order to hold her sweat around her. She couldn't stand it another minute, and breathed a sigh of relief as the desert air passed over her soaked shirt. She stretched on her bedroll, and flies buzzed annoyingly around her head. She had thought she'd learned to deal with the pesky things, but her patience for them quickly ran out. She plopped her hat over her face, deciding that possible suffocation was preferable to crawling flies.

She wondered where Cross was, if he'd found a nice place for bed ground. He'd ridden away earlier to scout ahead for water. Arrio was out, too, but would not range far, for he and Mateo were to keep guard.

At last, imagining an oasis, Lilly dozed.

The company headed out again when the sun was far to the west. The sheep showed little inclination to move, and the men went at them, waving hats and yelling. Slowly the animals got to their feet and began to walk, grazing on what they could find.

Gradually night fell and a moon rose, but there was no sign of Cross. Coca and Lilly went ahead to set up a camp and cook for the men, who took their food as they passed, keeping the sheep moving, faster now in the cool, using the stars as a guide.

They moved the sheep all that night. When the sun came up, they were moving at a snail's pace, but they had covered nearly twenty miles since the start from the river. They had come to land scant in foliage of any kind. Sand and rock as far as the eye could see in every direction. There hadn't been any dew that early morning to alleviate the sheep's thirst.

They made dry bed ground for the heat of the day, and the sheep were in a contrary mood and set on straying. There wasn't much rest for the men and dogs, but they caught what they could.

Lorenzo watered his remuda by hand-carried bucket, giving only scant portions to each of his precious animals, except for his favorite horse, which received half again more. Lilly took the amount of two tins for herself and gave to Tubbs what she would have used to bathe her face.

Dusting herself with a dry cloth, Lilly sat in the shade of her small tent. She had stripped down to her chemise and was too hot and sticky to be embarrassed. She worried aloud about Cross. It seemed as if he should have returned and, though she didn't speak of her morbid fears, she couldn't help but think of all that could happen to him out there all alone: snake biting him, horse throwing him, getting lost.

Coca said Cross was probably ranging far, trying to find the best water. "Or any water," he added.

"The *patrón*, he find water," Henri said with confidence.

They all looked to Cross McCree, Lilly thought. Fear fluttered in her belly when she thought of what might become of them, should anything happen to Cross.

Cross met the herd along about twilight. Lilly saw him coming and rode forward to meet him. There was eagerness in her eyes. He was glad to see her, and he laughed at himself, for he found her a beautiful sight, even though she looked like a peon boy who'd been working for a month on the range.

"We were beginnin' to worry." Her gaze moved over him anxiously.

"Had to go a ways. Ponds are dry or alkali, but I found a spring. Another ten miles, maybe twelve." Cross sighed and stretched his legs in the stirrups. He was bone tired, had only slept a few hours since riding out.

Lilly wiped the back of her hand across her eyes and turned to gaze at the sheep coming along. Her face was damp and smudged. "They won't settle down...and they seem too tired to even bleat."

Coca joined them, cursing at his mule, which refused to trot. "By heaven, you better bring good news, *patrón*."

Cross handed his canteen to the Mexican. "Try this. I found a spring. Not much more than a seep, really, but it makes a bit of a pool that we can dig bigger."

Coca sipped the water and shrugged. "It has a taste. Maybe they will like it."

They reached the spring in the morning, at dawn. The sun's coral rays washed over the small pool, with a cluster of rocks at one side. There were small shrubs here, and a trail made by wild critters that frequented the watering hole. When still two miles away, the remuda caught the scent. The horses took off, while the mules brayed and tried to keep up. The dogs yipped and nipped at the sheep to go faster.

Cross took several hands with shovels and hurried ahead. He looked back and saw Lilly kicking her legs, trying to get the mule into a trot, but the mule was having none of it. He plodded patiently.

The men went to digging, enlarging the small pool. The horses and mules drank even as the men stirred up the mud. Cross took a shovel and dug deeply at the place where the water bubbled, to encourage it to flow. It was warm as bath water.

By the time the first band of sheep arrived, there was a pool large enough for at least fifty to water at one time. Tomas and Mateo were digging a trench to form a make-shift watering trough. But when the woollies came to the edge of the water, they sniffed and tossed their heads, bleating. As thirsty as they were, they wouldn't drink.

"Let them be," Cross ordered. "Let the water clear. Maybe they'll drink then." But his hope was dim. Sheep could be the finickiest creatures on the face of the earth when it came to water.

The sheep from behind pressed up at those near the spring and had to be pushed back. The rear bands were halted. Some of the woollies lay down, while others walked around, bleating and pawing in confusion, tongues lolling and sides heaving. Thirty minutes later several made their way around where the water bubbled up, and they began to drink there. Others, frantic, pushed and shoved their way to this fresh water and soon had the hole so trampled and muddied that they all turned up their noses.

The sheep never did drink. Those at the edge were forced away and more came up in their place and did the same thing: sniffed, cried and shuffled. A few walked around to the seep, tried it, muddied everything and the process began again. Cross forced a passel of them into the muddy pool with his horse, but the stupid critters simply stood there, legs in the water, bleating.

Lilly began to cry. "They'll die," she said.

To which Cross replied, "Or I'll shoot the lot of them." He gave a wave and shouted to the men, "Move them on!"

There wasn't anything else to do but go on. Yet, then the perverse woollies tried to meander around the pool, though not a one would lower his head to drink. Not even when Chino, mad as fire, dunked several.

Cross changed horses and rode out ahead to look for water, leaving the men to again get the senseless sheep going west. He had the urge to ride all the way to Sacramento, find a whorehouse that provided a bath and forget the entire mess.

Chapter Sixteen

This hell in the desert, Lilly thought, was her retribution for not being grateful for the rains before. She wished for them now, with all her might.

They nooned the sheep there in the sun, all of them, humans and animals, caught there just as surely as if they'd been imprisoned. There were rocky hills around them now, but no respite, for the sun was directly overhead. Lilly didn't think that the sun was so hot as the desert so perfect for capturing its heat in the same manner that bricks did in an oven. In the distance were the mountains. They appeared as mirages of gray peaks shimmering above water. Far away Coca said, for he'd seen such, south in Mexico. He said Mexico had been much hotter, and Lilly said Pasquotank County could get hot, but it had water.

The sheep's sides heaved as they panted. They milled around and began sticking their heads beneath each other's bellies, crowding close to each other, where not a breath of air could get to them. Seeing the men going through the bands, forcing the woollies apart, Lilly rose up to do the same. But it was no use; the herd was too big, the animals too stubborn.

They lost ten sheep, dead from heat and suffocation.

Again they traveled by night, slowly, letting the sheep feed on what they could find. The dogs, tongues lolling, tried to keep the strays rounded, but the bands spread farther and farther. Pan's feet became so sore that Lilly bandaged them with strips torn from one of her petticoats. She lent some to Chino for the other dogs, too, and she laughed, thinking how Cross had been so angry at her bringing all her clothes.

With the sheep drifting so badly, Lilly and Coca worked right along with the others, riding on the south side and continually pushing back strays. The ground became rougher, and once Lilly almost rode right off into a wash. Only Tubbs's good sense saved her. She shivered in the cool night temperatures, but she was still thirsty. Her mouth was dry as cotton standing on the boll past picking time. Grit was in her eyes and her mouth, down her shirt, on everything she touched. They had refilled on water at the seep spring, silty as it was, but they were rationing, in case they didn't come to water soon. With each sip of her canteen, Lilly would wet her bandanna and dribble some into Tubbs's mouth. Feeling guilty because she had water and they didn't, she also did the same for several delirious sheep.

At last Cross arrived, a dark shadow coming out of the thin desert night. He and his horse were worn weary. He had taken dry canteens with him and produced them now full of fresh water, and everyone went to drinking as if it were nectar from the gods.

A stream, Cross said, cutting out of the hills ahead, spring fed, falling over rocks and gathering in small pools. Not an abundance, but fresh and relatively clear. It was nearly another full day ahead. And then he jerked his bedroll, spread it on the ground and immediately fell into a dead sleep. Lilly stayed beside him, and Henri silently joined her. Coca gave Henri a loaded rifle, and the boy held it across his lap. There, beneath the stars, the woman and the boy, mule and horse, and the dog, too, sat as sentries at Cross's side, while the sheep and herders moved slowly past, heading toward water.

The herd came to the creek late the following afternoon. While the horses and mules raced toward it, the sheep seemed to go crazy when they scented it. They bleated and stomped, but didn't seem to know where to go. The bell-wether goat to the lead flock veered, and soon the entire band was turning into a circle, drawing together in a knot.

Tomas strode into them, yelling and waving his hat, while Mateo and the dogs pushed them from behind. Finally they got them to the creek, but the poor animals were so sense-less with thirst that they ran frantically up and down the edges, bleating pitifully, but not drinking. The dogs and men shooed them, and still the sheep shied from the water.

In a fury, Lilly got down from Tubbs, stalked through the bunching sheep, screaming at them, "Get in there and drink, you woolly idiots!"

She pushed and shoved the stubborn sheep. Then she waded into one of the pools, splashing water and throwing it at the stupid creatures. Taking a ewe by the horns, she tugged furiously, while it planted its feet and fought her all the way. "Damn you!" Lilly yelled. "You're gonna drink, or you're gonna drown." She and the sheep ended up in the water together, and each time it got its head up, Lilly ducked it back.

Coca grabbed a sheep, and Cross did, too, slinging them into the water, ducking their heads under.

And at last the animals began to drink.

With her hat drooping over her head and her clothes stuck to her, Lilly sat in the water and watched the foolish ani-mals come.

For another thirteen days they crossed burning sand and wound around small rocky ranges, dry and hard as week-old biscuits. Land where it didn't seem anything could live, but some did manage to survive. Here and there were cactus and soapweed and even sagebrush, burned by the sun.

Occasionally Cross caught sight of little horny toads and
lizards, and once he saw a snake—or it saw him, for it was
the shaking of its tail that drew his attention to the reptile
curled near one of the dry pools he found. He also found
coyote tracks, though they were old, perhaps since spring
rains. Tomas shot three hens, and Coca swore he found
rabbit tracks. The presence of the little creatures meant the
existence of water, but what was enough for them to thrive
on was hardly enough to keep alive ten thousand sheep.

Again they had to go three full days without water, and
they lost six more ewes. Other times they went for two days
at a stretch on a dry trail, though thankfully no more sheep
died.

They headed west until they hit a long, craggy mountain
range, and then, guided by Duffy's map, steered a course
north along the edge of the mountains, with the salt desert
nipping at them from the east. When they looked out across
it, there was nothing but white glare with heat shimmering
up, almost like a sparkling lake above it. There was no
sound, save that of the animals and humans now walking
across the land.

Lilly seemed to withdraw into herself during all these
days. She spoke very little to anyone and often rode apart
by herself, though never out of sight of Coca or Henri.
Cross sensed that she was conserving her strength, needing
every scrap of it in order to deal with the harshness of this
land and to keep going. He understood, and yet he missed
her, as he'd never missed Marquita, or anyone. And he felt
uneasy, too, for it seemed that in her silence, the woman
grew stronger...so strong that she might not need him ever
again.

The thought made him feel strangely powerless, and he
didn't like that.

One evening he took her to ride point with him. He didn't
ask her, he just went and told her to ride with him. He

should have been pleased that she didn't protest, but the fact that she didn't appear eager, that she had no reaction at all, irritated the hell out of him.

Cross set a swift pace, until they were far ahead of the herd and alone. The red setting sun cast long shadows, but was still hot. Cross rode on the west side to give Lilly a bit of shade. He kept trying to think of something to talk about, but he was tired and couldn't seem to come up with anything. Lilly's manner didn't encourage him; she didn't say anything—until they came to the broken remnants of a wagon, and bones, too, all bleached a deathly pale.

"Those bones..." Lilly said, her voice dry and cracking.

"Oxen," Cross said tersely. The animals had died in their traces. "Lot of pilgrims come straight over the desert, and the sand's just too much for the loads they bring."

He stretched his legs in the stirrups, trying to ease his muscles and the sick feeling that had come into his stomach. He walked his horse around the scene. All of the precious, foolish things that the pilgrim hadn't been able to bring himself to leave behind were gone now, either taken by scavengers, both human and animal, or simply blown away by the wind. He caught sight of bones protruding out of the sand at the back of the wagon, and he knew they were human.

He turned Domino back to the woman, but he was too late. The woman had seen the bones. She sat atop her mule, staring.

"A grave of pilgrims' dreams," she said, her voice faint. Her eyes came around to Cross; they were large and dark in the growing long shadows. "You were wise to have us come only on horses and mules."

Looking at her, Cross felt a shiver go down his spine. She returned her gaze to the wagon and bones.

"We might as well ride on," Cross said, turning Domino.

But the woman made no move to follow. Cross nudged his horse over, took hold of the mule's headstall and turned him, starting them off again heading north. The woman looked back over her shoulder at the sandy grave.

After a little while, Cross said, "This land takes swift punishment on anyone too weak to stand up to it."

"Is that how you see it—that the weak get punished?"

He looked over at her. There was the hint of fire in her eyes.

"It isn't how I see it. It's how it is. In this world the strongest prosper, the weakest fail. It's so even back in your precious Pasquotank County...except back in civilization what is strong differs from what is strong out here. Too many times people who are strongest back there come out here, and they aren't strong at all."

The fire went out of her eyes, and she looked out at the desert beginning to gleam in dusk. "You're strong enough to survive anywhere," she said in a soft voice.

"You are, too," he said.

Their eyes met. Hers were questioning, and his were assured.

"You like this land," she said then.

He nodded. He did like it, because it was grand, wondrous in its size and untamedness, and because it was always making him prove he was equal to it. "Yep, I guess I do," he said.

He didn't quite understand it, but he saw an understanding in her eyes, and that she had such a thorough knowledge of him made him uneasy.

When they finally came upon a creek cutting out of the mountains, Cross allowed the company to rest for a full day and night. The water was scant and the feed scarce, but the sheep, after drinking what water there was, were too tired to exhibit much inclination for roaming, which was just as well, for the herders and dogs had little inclination to keep them herded up. Everyone needed rest as much as they needed water.

That night Cross went to the woman and drew her away from the campfire into the starry night. He hadn't meant to, had simply found himself doing it. He walked over beside where she sat looking into the flames and just stood there until she looked up. He knew the other men were watching him, but he didn't care, at least not a whole lot.

Side by side, but not touching, they walked far out into the desert night.

"It's a nice night," the woman said. She drew her arms inside her serape against the chill.

"Yeah, it is," Cross said. He didn't know what he wanted from her.

Eventually they sat on a hill that looked toward the salt desert. The land stretched before them, a silvery glow that dimmed to night blackness. Nothing moved, and there wasn't a sound.

Cross stretched out his arm and drew Lilly against him. She surprised him by coming easily, pressing into his side and laying her head against his shoulder. She brought the woman scent of her. He kissed her and inhaled that precious scent.

"How much farther?" she whispered, and he knew she meant until the end of the desert.

"Five, six days, no more."

She snuggled closer, and he held her tighter, felt the woman-softness of her. He considered more... but he was bone tired.

He stared at the quiet, shadowy desert, and, for those moments at least, he could forget all the struggling for survival. For those moments he experienced simply being alive, with the woman, beneath the stars.

* * *

Long before the humans could see the creek coming out of the hills the animals smelled it. The remuda took off, and Lorenzo and Simon went with them, kicking up dust and filling the air with cries of "Eeee-yahh!" The sheep picked up their pace and soon were running, too.

Cross galloped up beside Lilly, drew Domino down to match the pace of the mule, who was sufficiently stirred by the prospect of water to go into a fast trot.

Side by side, both hollering the exultant "Eeee-yahh!" they ran the horse and mule right into the creek, turned them hard and rode out again. At the edge of the creek, Tubbs drank, and Lilly tossed the reins over his head and slipped from the saddle and into the creek. The water soaked her moccasins up around her calves, good, spring water running over rock and sandstone. Bending, she splashed and looked up to see Cross at the edge, smiling at her, a full smile.

"Come in!" she cried.

"I'll keep my boots dry, thank you."

She advanced on him, splashing toward him. "You'd better get them off, because you're comin' in."

He sat in the sand, pulled at his boots, and she waited until he had them off before tugging him in with her. She plopped into the water and pulled him down with her. Laughing, she jumped on his chest and pushed his head back into the water. His arms came tight around her, and she found herself going, too, face first. She barely drew a breath when they came up, before Cross covered her lips with his in a hard, passionate kiss.

That night Lilly went to Cross's bed.

He was waiting for her, sitting there, smoking a cigar.

"Last one," he said and held it high, as if it were sacred.

She watched his hand, his fingers, as he carefully stubbed out the fire and laid the cigar safely aside. The next instant he grabbed her to him and laid her back into the warmth of the sheepskins.

His breath was hot on her neck, his hands hot upon her body, his urgency hot and pounding.

"Lilly..." he whispered, choking off.

Tears sprang into her eyes. "Cross, please... please hold me." She began to tremble uncontrollably.

He pressed her to him. "Shush. It's all right now... shush..." He held her and crooned to her and caressed her hair over and over. For long minutes they lay thus, his beard scraping her cheek, his breath caressing her ear. The man scent of him, the man strength of him was all around her, and she absorbed it with relish.

At last she turned her head, searching for his lips. And the simmering fire burst into a blaze.

Each sought comfort and release from fears neither could speak of, except with their bodies.

With a wildness born of holding themselves in check for so long, they allowed their passions to flow into one another and to wash away the tense exhaustion of the previous days the same way the creek water had washed away the sand and sweat.

They followed the creek, which was dry in places, but in others springs formed pools with enough water to keep the sheep from dying of thirst. The creek bed took them through rocky mountains and hills covered with tufts of summer-dry grasses and brush. At first it angled northwest, but soon, as Duffy's map had indicated, it took them southwest, once again pointing in the direction of Sacramento.

The sheep spread over the hills where they could, grazing eagerly on the sunburned grasses, and at times they flowed through rocky passes, like pearls rolling over the edge of a table, onto a chair and onto the floor, Lilly thought once, upon turning to look at them. The skies continued clear and the land dry, but for the spotty springs and pools, yet here was vegetation to absorb the heat and mountains to provide some shade once in a while. They seemed somehow to have risen very high; the air was clear, crisp, as if with each passing mile they were entering a fresh new world.

Lilly took to riding with Cross, who didn't need to roam so far ahead to scout for water or good camping grounds. Often they took Henri, too, and rode several miles from the herd, exploring the land and hunting for game to supplement their dwindling supplies. Lilly sometimes thought she never wanted to see beans again as long as she lived. And sometimes, too, she wished powerfully to see a tree, for she had not seen one since they had left Moriah, where small, scraggly saplings had stood in the churchyard.

Cross showed her tracks: those were coyote, those antelope . . . and those little scratches were pheasant. They even passed over Indian pony prints, Shoshone, Cross guessed; four ponies, and the tracks looked to be weeks old. The amount of crumbling around the edges of a track, the cracking inside it, was what told him the age. And from the shape and size of one of the pony prints, he could tell that one of the Indians had either been carrying double, or been twice the size of the others.

Henri and Cross scared up a covey of sage hens and shot two and later Cross got several partridges. That evening back at camp, Lilly commandeered Coca's big iron pan and tried her hand at cornbread made in the campfire. It came out quite fine and made a feast with the fresh roasted meat—all of it a definite respite from the everlasting beans and tortillas. The following night Arrio brought in a fine, big antelope, and everyone fed fat and happy, even the dogs, who got the scraps.

On their third day of traveling this direction, they struck what Cross called the California Trail, which led them down to the Humboldt River. The trail followed the river, which wasn't much of a river as rivers went, for it was slow moving and tended toward brackishness at this time of year. Still, it was water that the sheep drank, for most of the time, anyway, though Lilly wouldn't have said the sheep ever found themselves full of water, nor of grass, either, for the grasses were sparse and coarse.

This was Nevada, she was told. She thought it a land that God had burned and then left to recover on its own. Still, she found it definitely preferable to the raw desert they had crossed.

The California Trail was clearly just that, a road worn by the thousands of wagon wheels of travelers before them. Left upon the land, too, was evidence of the hardships: abandoned wagons, bones of dead oxen that had survived the desert only to be too weak to continue on, a broken wheel, half buried now in dirt, the rusty bands of barrels long broken up, splintered axles, even trunks, long ago looted for whatever they had carried. And there were graves, too, marked by whatever had been at hand.

Lilly came upon the first two graves one morning while out riding with Cross. He was at the river holding Domino and Tubbs, and she went a bit away to relieve herself. She found the graves there, covered over with dry brush that she pulled away in order to see the two ragged crosses made of rough, broken boards, likely torn from wagon sides. Someone had tried to scratch names and dates into the wood. Lilly fell on her knees to peer closely, but all she could read was one: Sara, 5 yrs.

She stared at the crooked cross and, for the first time in a month, she thought of Tyler.

His face and even his voice came to her from far, far away, indistinct, faded by all that had happened to her since she had sat holding his bloody hand. *Help me, Lilly...I won't be leavin' you penniless . . . the sheep, they'll get you home. . . .*

She had knelt on that cold dirt floor and watched him die barely three months ago. She guessed at the time, had lost track of the days weeks ago.

Forcing herself, she peered back through those months with her mind's eye, going back, as if through a tunnel. And suddenly that final time of seeing Tyler came clear and indelible in her mind. She heard his voice, saw his face, and all of it came then: the talk of California riches, Tyler telling her they could never go home . . . telling her he would make them rich in California. Oh, he'd been mad for it, mad with high talk and high hopes.

She stared at the gray crosses and shivered.

Cross's step drew her head around. "You were gone so long. . . ." He stopped, his gaze moving from her to the pitiful crosses.

She stood, brushed dirt from her knees. "I found these graves. One was a child."

He came beside her.

Lilly continued to stare at the markers, and the image of the wagon and bones they had seen in the desert floated up before her eyes.

She said, "Tyler planned to take us to California. We were to leave as soon as he got the money. We would have gone in a day or two on what he'd won that night." She swallowed. "But we wouldn't have made it. We would have died, and been nothin' more than bones in the desert, or markers out here, like these."

That was what she had known days ago, when they'd come upon the wagon and bones in the desert. She'd known the horror of it, as if those had been her bones protruding out of the wagon, but she hadn't been able to face it, much less speak of it.

"No," Cross said, his voice firm. "Your husband might have died . . . but you wouldn't have."

His belief was in his eyes, and that belief opened a hidden pocket inside herself.

"Perhaps not," she murmured, feeling somehow disloyal to Tyler.

"Does it matter?" Cross asked, almost startling her. "What might have been never matters. If it did, I'd have been dead at least a dozen times . . . Indian ambush, scalped, lost on the Llano. But that isn't what happened, and I'm here now. So are you. Though neither of us knows where we'll be tomorrow."

"No, we don't," she said at last.

Feeling a sudden need, she quickly pulled the brush clear, allowing the sun to shine on the graves, for a little while, anyway. She felt a little foolish, but Cross gave no indication that he found her actions strange. He simply stood and watched.

They rode long that day, looking at the land, and a great thankfulness as strong as the sunshine came over Lilly. She had the awareness of every moment being a gift, of being spared for one more day.

She was immensely glad to have made the trip with Cross, instead of with Tyler, which sounded so cruel, as if she were glad Tyler had died, and she wasn't. But neither was she sorry for the change in her life. She was glad to be alive, as she had never been before, and to be the woman she was now, and she knew that it was Cross McCree who had given her both of these things.

It was Cross McCree who had protected her and taught her not only what she needed to know to survive, but also to realize her own inner strengths and passions. It was Cross McCree who made her heart leap when she saw him, and who made her burn with passion when he touched her. It was Cross McCree who had taught her to cherish all she was, all she could be.

It was Cross McCree she loved, as she had never loved Tyler Blackwell.

"Whoa," she said, pulling Tubbs to a stop.

Cross stopped ahead, swung around to cast her a quizzical look. Lilly nudged Tubbs next to him, then, laughing, she flung herself over on him, toppling them both into the sharp, stiff grass. She kissed him before he could ask any questions, and then there were no questions. He wrapped an arm around her and rolled her beneath him, pinning her with his hard body, kissing her until she had no breath left and she didn't care to have.

Passion came in a rush, hard and thundering, like a summer storm, and she turned into it, accepting and savoring the power of it.

She savored the taste and smell and feel of this man she loved. She savored the sensations that came with kissing and being kissed, with touching and being touched. She savored the life of him, and of herself.

There, with the air and sun caressing their naked bodies, with birds calling and grass waving in the heated breeze, they made love. And when it came for them, it was as wild and glorious as the land around them.

They lay for long minutes, on their clothes spread in the grass, both naked to the sun. A bird called and streaked across the sky. Ten feet away the mule and horse grazed.

Lilly swung her arm over her eyes to shield them from the brightness. The sunshine was like a warm candle flowing over her body...her breasts and belly and thighs. She reached with her other hand and touched Cross's sun-warmed chest, and felt again the sensation of his hard muscles pressed against her.

It rose on her tongue. *I love you.*

But she gave those words no voice.

And then a moment later, "Would you come with me?" she asked. She had to ask, had to know if he even considered it, though of course she didn't believe he did.

She felt the stillness of him. She wished with all her might...

"No," he said.

The word cut the stillness, quietly yet thoroughly said.

She squeezed her eyes closed, and battled the swiftly rising lump in her throat.

And then, "Would you stay, at least in Santa Fe?" He spoke the question as if he already knew the answer.

"I can't," she replied, her voice coming in a bare, hoarse whisper.

And there it was between them. He would not go, and she could not expect him to, for she couldn't see him fitting into the civilized life in Pasquotank County. And she couldn't stay. She wanted to go home. She had wanted that for so long.

They continued to lie there in the sun for many more minutes, as if perhaps time would stand still, and they would never have to leave.

It was Cross who rose first. "We have a herd to see to." He didn't look at her, but turned quickly to dressing.

The days in which they followed the river went easy, as if God was giving them a chance to catch their breath, if not get a decent bath, before they had to go through hell again. They moved faster here, and both grazing and game were ample.

There were a few days of rain showers, and when they began, the woman danced in the open, waving her hat. Cross watched from the poor shelter of her tent, watched the way her clothes flattened against her body, turning her from a boy into a woman. She'd gotten skinny, and it was a lucky thing she had bought those suspenders, because her trousers might have fallen right off without them.

He watched her lift her face to the rain and hold out her hat to catch water, all the while laughing like someone who'd gotten drunk on rain.

He thought suddenly of how she had looked that day she had said she was coming with him on this trip. Mrs. Lilly Blackwell, in that dress buttoned up around the neck, all hemmed in tight, the life of her bursting at the seams.

He did not think her husband would recognize her now.

At last, thoroughly soaked to dripping, she crawled into the leaking tent and squinted upward at the sagging tent canvas.

"Might as well have stayed outside," she said, grabbing up a towel to dry her hair.

Cross didn't quite know why he was there in the tent with her. Things had been tense between them the past days.

Still, he reached out, took the towel from her and did the job on her hair. His hands strayed to her warm neck, and he bent and kissed her silky skin. She sighed, contented as a cat to be petted. She made no bones about enjoying his touch.

She enjoyed him now . . . and would not hesitate to leave him.

"Did you do much bathin' in the rain, while in your clothes, back East?" he asked.

She stilled. "I never had the need," she said.

Her eyes came up to his, and they gazed long at one another. "I didn't know you 'needed' to do it today. Seemed like you wanted to do it."

She averted her eyes to the rain outside.

"I guess you won't be gettin' a chance to do that back East. I imagine ladies don't take baths in the rain back there. And anyway, you'll probably always have a proper bathtub, when you go back," he said.

"Yes . . . and water brought right to the tub with the turn of a lever, and warmed, too," she said smartly. "Piped-in water, it's called. Many of the homes have that luxury back there." She slanted her eyes up at him. "You'd like it."

"I like rain and rivers just fine. They're always fresh." Their eyes dueled for long seconds, and then he added, "But I guess piped-in water is worth going all the way back East for."

Fury sparked in her eyes, though she didn't reply.

He tossed the towel in her lap.

"I guess we knew it all along, didn't we," he said, the inevitability of it coming over him.

She didn't look at him, and he pushed himself out of the tent.

They had made it clear between them that day along the river, he thought, as clear and naked as they had been beneath the sun. He could not go with her; she could not stay with him.

He stalked out in the rain, heading nowhere, just away from the frustration burning in his chest. He turned his face to the rain, thinking maybe it could cool him.

Oh, hell. He'd known it, had been a fool to let himself forget.

Life had taught him that all anyone ever had was what one had here and now, so the only thing to do was pay attention to today and let tomorrow take care of itself.

And because of all that, he stuffed his hurt pride away and returned to her tent. He told himself that he would take what she would give, and he'd never look back.

One afternoon, while out scouting, Cross and Lilly came to the most surprising sight of a cabin built of board lumber and canvas, sitting right out there beside the river. Off a ways from the cabin was a pole-and-rope corral holding a couple of horses, while two more horses, two oxen and a goat scattered off on the plain.

One of the horses in the corral caught Cross's attention—a big spotted horse. He headed toward it for a better look. The animal was near skin and bone, but there was no doubt in his mind.

"Is that Uriah Plover's horse?" Lilly asked, and Cross nodded. He saw her shiver.

They turned toward the cabin and saw the sign tacked above the crooked doorway: Denby's Trading Post. Then Cross saw the barrel of a buffalo rifle come snaking out the curtained doorway.

He pulled Domino up and put out a cautioning hand to Lilly. He helloed the cabin. After a number of long seconds, a man came from inside the open doorway—a tall, lean Anglo man, with a long white beard, wearing worn black trousers and suspenders. He carried the rifle, cocked to fire, propped across to his left arm, yet his weathered face was friendly.

Cross stated his and Lilly's names, and the old man said, "Howdy. If yer of a mind, come set." He offered them chairs, while keeping his rifle in place.

Cross and Lilly sat in the chairs, and the old man took a barrel. His wife brought coffee. Burl and Marthie Denby were their names. They had been bound for the goldfields, but then broke down on this very spot and decided that their fortune could be made by trading a lot easier than it could by digging gold. By the time Denby had told all that, he'd uncocked his rifle and propped it against his knee.

"How'd you come by that spotted horse?" Cross asked, and watched the old man's face.

Denby's eyes narrowed. "You knowed the feller he belonged to?"

Cross nodded. "Uriah Plover."

"That be him, wasn't it, Mama?"

The old woman snorted derisively, but she didn't speak. She hadn't said a word, though she appeared to take part in the conversation with nods and grunts.

Denby spit a stream of tobacco. "Oh...maybe two weeks ago, Plover and three others, a feller they called Red-eye and two brothers called Simpsons—whiny, skinny little fellers—come ridin' in, their horses near give out. I had half a dozen healthy mounts I'd fattened up—that's what keeps me in business. Plover, he wanted my big black gelding, but so did Red-eye, and they had a hell of a fight. Plover, he cut that Red-eye up real good afore it was over. 'Course, I knew all along they never intended to pay us—was set to rob us." He spit. "They tried to rob us, but me and Mama, we was waitin'. We put some salt in their tails, sendin' them out of here. Mama, she kilt one of them Simpson brothers while they was a-stealin' our horses. Most people don't expect Mama to be so tough."

The old woman blinked blandly, and Cross had to admit he was surprised. The woman would never see fifty again and couldn't have been over a hundred pounds, but she was a deadly shot, the old man said, and she didn't take to anyone swearing at her, which the Simpson brothers had done. "Those boys had real bad mouths," the old man said, as if that might have been worse than the stealing of his horses.

Cross had the men bed the sheep down within sight of the Denby place, and, for a dear price, the Denbys hosted a fine dinner. The old man said he didn't hold with hard liquor, but he did have some jugs of apple cider he would share, and they didn't even have to pay. It was too much to hope that he would have Cross's favored panatelas, but Denby did happen to have a little barrel of "short sixes," and Cross bought enough to fill a pocket in his saddlebag. Lilly bought dried fruits, and Coca traded some of his sassafras for dried chilies.

Before they left the next morning, the trader ended up buying five sheep. Cross let Lilly set the price, and she held out for ten dollars a head. And she got it, Denby paying in silver and gold coin.

A few more days down the river they came upon a group of emigrants, three families, twenty people in all, traveling in four ox-drawn wagons. The group was camped near the trail, and when Cross and the woman rode over to speak to them, one of the men came out and told them to halt. Peeking from the canvas of the wagon behind him were the faces of at least half a dozen children.

There was sickness, the man told them. Two of their men and three children had died—the crosses to their graves were dark silhouettes against the red afternoon sky. They needed food, if the shepherds could spare any.

"We'll leave them sheep, won't we?" Lilly asked as she and Cross rode away. "That way they can keep them growin' until they need them."

"Yep," Cross said. And he couldn't resist, "But you know that cuts into your profits."

If she could have reached him, she would have smacked him.

When the herd passed, Cross had half a dozen sheep cut out and run toward the emigrant wagons, and he had Coca separate out what could be spared of their flour, sugar, coffee, beans and grain for the oxen. When he was loading it onto a mule, the woman brought over her entire supply of dried fruit, for the children, she said. Cross left the emigrants the mule with the supplies.

Gradually the desert came upon them again. Several times Lilly experienced the insane urge to turn Tubbs and ride back the way they had come, which of course wouldn't lead anywhere but to another desert.

This one would be her last, she reminded herself.

The river ran into the hard sand and turned sour, and the sheep quit drinking it. Another day, and the horses and mules wouldn't touch it, either. Luckily Cross found a good spring pool to water the animals before their trek across the barren desert. On Denby's advice, they filled everything they could with water—all the woollen bags, the barrels, the coffeepots, even layers of canvas that they tied with a string.

It took them four nights of traveling and four days of sitting in the burning sun to get across the desert and into the blue mountains that waited.

All along the trail they found evidence of those who had come before them. Each abandoned wagon they passed stood as another monument to Cross's decision to travel only on mules and horses, and Lilly gave thanks for that. There were the bones of oxen, still in the traces, that were being covered over by drifting sand. By this point the emigrants' strength had been worn thin, and they had given up trying to haul tables and chairs. Even a cradle lay abandoned to the fierce desert.

Then, one by one a quarter of a mile apart, they came to the carcasses of three horses, picked away by scavengers, dried and burned by the sun, but not yet covered by sand. Everyone wondered if the animals could have belonged to Uriah Plover and his companions, though of course, they could have belonged to anyone, for this was a well-traveled trail. From studying the remnants of campfires and the few tracks he found, Cross said it was three men traveling together, trailing three horses now, and he guessed they were a good three weeks ahead and gaining. Be it Uriah Plover and his party or others, they appeared to be heading full out for the goldfields and would never be seen.

On the morning of the third day they came near a pond formed by a slow seep in a sink in the ground. Cross had ridden ahead and tested it and pronounced it poisoned by alkali. Perversely, where they would not drink good water before in the desert, the sheep decided they wanted the poisoned water. If there was anything Lilly had learned, it was not to be surprised by the crazy notions of a sheep.

Yet, they all were taken by surprise when the sheep began breaking and going toward the scent of the water. Frantically everyone worked to head them off. Lilly resorted to kicking and screaming herself hoarse. Somehow Jesus made and lit a torch; Chino took it, waving it at the sheep, while Jesus got another going, and then another and another, each man taking one and driving back the sheep.

When they had the woollies going in the right direction again, they were forced to keep them on the move until deep into the heat of the day, in order to distance themselves from the alkali hole.

At last Cross called a halt, and they rested, both animals and humans close to total exhaustion. The sheep, tongues hanging out the sides of their mouths and their bellies heaving, lay down, too tired to stick their heads beneath each other. The horses and mules stood, soaked with sweat, with their heads hanging near the ground.

Coca set up a cook fire only large enough to brew the indispensable thick, sweet coffee, and not much of that with the shortage of water. Shelters were struck, and everyone collapsed beneath them in patches of shade.

After half a cup of the sweet coffee, Lilly lay dozing, with her head at the door of her tent, where an occasional wisp of breeze stirred her damp hair. She could hear the murmur of voices, and the faint bleating of the sheep and yip of a dog, the occasional snort of a horse or mule, all familiar and comforting sounds. She had provided Tubbs with a bit of water in a bucket—he had, after all, worked to keep the sheep from the poisoned water—and had shared her cupful with Pan, who now lay with his nose pointed toward her. Tomorrow, she thought, there would be plenty of water for all the precious animals. Cross had promised, and he had never been wrong yet.

She had wiped her damp bandanna over her face, but she still had grit everywhere, even in her mouth. Never mind... for now she was in the shade and lying still. Every now and then she peeked at the sky straight above. It was the faded, glassy blue of bright afternoon.

They would make it, she knew then. Perhaps one more week was all, and they would have the sheep across this purgatory, over the rugged mountains, and down to Sacramento to sell. Of course she would sell them; she couldn't keep five thousand sheep, no matter how possessive she had come to feel about them.

She supposed Cross would sell Tubbs, too. Or maybe he would take the mule back to Santa Fe with him. It was plain crazy to have even the flicker of longing to take the mule with her. She couldn't. Though she really did think she would take Henri with her, no matter what Cross said.

She would say goodbye to Cross in Sacramento. Say goodbye, get on a boat and go home.

She'd buy herself and Henri some decent clothes first, of course, and a really good meal. Oh, she'd love to have some fried chicken. Then she'd say goodbye to Cross, if he was still around. And she'd go home to Pasquotank County, where the black-water swamp flowed, and where water pooled on the floor underneath windows open to the coast breeze. She wouldn't have dry skin there, and she wouldn't wear pants. Heavens, people would be scandalized if she did. She'd ride in a buggy and not on a mule, and she'd sew gowns instead of flesh.

Her life would be clean.

She could be dirty if she wanted, she thought with a suddenness. She could wear pants if she wanted. And she could ride a mule if she chose. She could if she wanted, no matter what people would say.

Of course, if she did those things, she wouldn't be invited to any afternoon teas or gala suppers or even sewing circles. She might not be talked to, though she would be talked *about,* the way they always used to talk about Sela Carpenter. It hadn't mattered that Sela Carpenter had been the daughter of one of the founding fathers; she had spent days at a time in the woods and swamps, dressed in men's clothing, watching birds and drawing them. Sela had sort of looked like a bird. Lilly had always rather admired Sela for doing what she wanted.

Suddenly footsteps hurrying past, peppering sand across her forehead, broke her from reverie. She rose up, scooted around to see. Cross was hurrying toward a mule that seemed to be teetering on his feet. *It was Tubbs!*

Lilly was on her feet and running for him.

"What is it?" She saw the mule's nose then. It was swollen big as a muskmelon.

Cross lifted the mule's head and inspected it. The animal's eyes were running, and he swayed, caught himself.

"What is it?" Lilly asked again, bending to look for herself, frantic now.

Cross stood back. "He's snake bit," he said flatly.

Lilly gaped at him, disbelieving.

"There...two marks on the end of his nose. Mules are curious. He probably sniffed at one."

Lilly looked, thought she saw the holes, but couldn't have sworn to it. "What do we do?"

"Nothin'." He turned and walked away.

Lilly came after him. "But we have to do somethin'. He's hurting...." She turned back to the mule, who had tried to follow her, but stumbled and fell to his knees. "We have to do something," she repeated, going to the mule, putting her arms around his neck. She pressed her head against him, willing her strength into him.

She couldn't hold him, and he fell over on his side, pawed the air and struggled to breathe through nostrils that swelled before her eyes. She scooted over and put her hand on his neck. "Coca!" Surely Coca could do something with his herbs. Maybe Jesus could say prayers.

She looked up, and saw Cross striding toward her, Coca right behind him. Hope flared . . . and then she saw the big pistol in Cross's hand.

The horror on the woman's face cut through him, caused his steps to falter. "Get her," he said to Coca, who was already striding around toward her.

"Don't shoot him." Tears streamed down her face. Coca reached down, lifted her up. "Give him a chance," she pleaded, her voice choked.

"Look at him," Cross said. "Look!" She did. The mule's head was near double in size, his nostrils all but closed. He was suffocating, slowly.

Coca put his arm around her and turned her. Cross aimed his pistol at the mule's swollen forehead. The shot rang out, and the mule fell still, peaceful at last. Silence swept around Cross, broken only by the sound of Lilly crying.

A few minutes later they all saw her come past with a shovel, heading toward the mule. Cross caught up with her, told her it was crazy, that she could not dig a grave big enough that scavengers wouldn't eventually dig it up.

"He served me well," she said. "At least I can do him this honor."

She jerked her arm from his grip and resolutely began to dig. Henri came with another shovel, and then Jesus came with a wooden stick that he used as a pick. With a sigh, Cross went over and took Henri's shovel and sliced it deep in the ground. They made a marker before it was all over, upon which the woman scratched: Beloved Tubbs, gallant mule.

At sunset the company prepared to move on. Cross had Lorenzo bring a mustang from the remuda, a stocky sorrel of at least five years. He put Lilly's saddle on the mustang, then brought the horse to where Lilly stood, gazing off at the mountains. She looked at the horse, then at Cross. Without expression or comment, she mounted up and rode away to the herd at an easy trot, an erect figure, moving in supple rhythm with the animal.

Cross called Henri and told the boy to ride up and join the *señora*, ride with her for the night. With an nod, the boy kicked his horse into motion. Cross noticed the boy was barefoot.

Chapter Seventeen

They got to the end of the desert before sunup, to a river with trees. Lilly hugged several of them, and when dawn got high enough for her to see, she took a bath, right out there where the water was the deepest, and dared any of the men to peek at her. By now she'd come to know how polite they all were, and they had come to look on her as a mother or sister, so she had no worries. Cross came down to the edge of the river, though, shucked off his clothes down to his longhandles and came in with her. He took her soap and washed his longhandles on his body. They ducked and splashed and had a grand time.

Two days later, everyone had bathed—even Lorenzo, when Coca refused to feed him until he did. Cleaned, well fed and refreshed, the animals and their herders started up into the Sierras. September had come, and Cross said the snows wouldn't be far behind, and everyone knew what had happened to the infamous Donner-Reed party in the snow. The tale so terrified the men that they refused to take the same pass, where there lived the ghosts of humans who had eaten humans.

The herd climbed slowly but steadily for four solid days. The trail was well traveled, wide in places, frighteningly narrow in others. Parts were rugged and rocky, causing the horses and mules to strain, but the sheep had little trouble.

Water enough for the stock was scarce, but there was adequate vegetation covered with morning dew to quench the sheep's thirst.

Once they met a party of four families in four wagons coming down.

"A den of iniquity, that's all you'll find," said the elder gentleman, who drove the first wagon and was apparently the leader. His eyes beneath thick brows burned with righteousness and doom. Lilly felt a stirring of pity for the small woman who sat beside him. She seemed to have withered within her clothes, and her eyes looked longingly at Lilly's horse.

"Even workers of iniquity need to eat," Cross said, and quite cheerfully, too.

The man's lips compressed. "Oh, that's right enough. Meat's needed. We sold our sheep for eight dollars a head, and weren't ashamed to do it." He gestured to the herd moving toward them. "What you folks got here will be white gold in Sacramento."

At that bit of news Lilly's heart leaped, and Cross cast her a wry grin.

"I wouldn't dawdle getting your herd across, though," the man said in his dooming voice. "We got a dusting of snow the other night up at the pass." He jerked the brake free and clucked to his team, abruptly starting the mules off without so much as a nod of goodbye.

Cross backed his horse out of the way and called politely, "Much obliged for the warnin'... my best to you."

He and Lilly watched the wagons move down through the sheep with such speed as to send a number of the woollies scampering for safety. Each of the men and women on the following wagons sat straight and as dour as those on the first, though in the last wagon a little boy and girl poked their heads out and waved.

Eight dollars a head. The sum reverberated in Lilly's head.

"You heard it, *señora*," Cross said, drawing her gaze. "There's a den of iniquity waiting up ahead, and we're bringin' them white gold. Hold on to your hat."

With a "yee-ah," hard spur and flick of his reins on his horse's rump, Cross bounded up the steep incline. Lilly watched him, heart hammering, and then she dared to do likewise.

Two days later the herd came to a narrow meadow with a small creek and several ponds. Just beyond was the beginning of the pass, so the sheep were halted. They were tired and weren't likely to stray off the good grass, so a single main camp was formed, with two good-sized fires for gathering around, for the nights had become very cold.

Careful to stay within sight of the men at the camp, Lilly found a spot where she could watch the light of the setting sun fade between mountain peaks. She was sitting there when Cross came up behind her. She smelled his cigar before she heard his familiar movements; the cigars he'd gotten from the trader, Denby, smelled to high heaven.

She scooted over to share her rock, though she told him to blow his stinking smoke the other way. She propped her chin on her bent knee and gazed off, thinking that the sun was still bright on the other side of the mountains.

"How many more days until we reach Sacramento?" she asked.

"Maybe four, no more than six. If we're lucky enough to find a buyer right away, you should have your profit in hand and be headin' for San Francisco within the week."

A week!

Surely in two weeks she would be heading away from this western country.

She looked at the craggy pine mountains and thought how beautiful they were with the last of the sun tipping their tops. And suddenly she wished the trail would go on and on and never end—which was as crazy a thing as she had ever thought in her life.

"I'm gonna take Henri with me," she said. The words came out before she could bite them back. She didn't look at Cross. Every cell in her body waited. She wanted a reaction, any reaction.

He was silent a long time, but his disapproval was as thick as his cigar smoke. At last she looked over her shoulder at him. He puffed on his cigar.

"Do you think it will be any different for him than it was back in Moriah?" he asked sharply.

"Yes." She nodded. "We'll be suitably attired and presentable. We'll be a part of the community." And that sounded silly.

He raised an eyebrow and took on that cocky look. "Providin' you manage to get him to wear boots."

She didn't flinch from his gaze. "He wants to go. He has said so."

He didn't look convinced.

She returned her chin to her knee. After a strained minute, she said, "What if I told you I was carryin' your child? Would you go with us then?"

She swallowed, and her throat went bone dry. From the corner of her eye she saw his puffs of smoke. She knew she was being crazy and went right on being it.

"No."

"You are a damned stubborn man, Cross McCree." She kept her chin propped on her knee.

"So I've been told."

"I'm not pregnant," she said after a minute.

He said nothing, kept on puffing. Lilly resisted the urge to jerk it out of his mouth and stomp on it. Wouldn't do any good, wouldn't change the situation, just as nothing she'd ever done had changed Tyler.

Tyler was distant in memory. At that moment she had little feeling, except despair.

They sat there, as the darkness came. A bird made a night call, and a breeze brought the pungent cigar smoke to her nose. From the campfire came the sound of the men's voices, the sounds of Spanish spoken.

"I'll miss you," she said, not allowing him a glance, embarrassed and damning him for it.

"Well, I'll miss you, too."

It was heavily said, and somehow it made her madder. Why must he be so stubborn? And why couldn't he ask her to stay? She wouldn't, but at least he could ask.

He stamped out the cigar. And then his arm came around her, bringing a blanket, she realized with surprise.

"We have now," he said low in her ear, his warm voice sending desire tingling over her shoulders.

She wanted to pull away from him, and she even did, a little bit. But his breath was warming her neck, and the door to passion cracked open. There was no closing it.

He touched her cheek, and the fire began to slip through her veins. He kissed her, drew away, kissed her again, his lips beguiling, tempting... his hands doing the same to her breasts. She simply couldn't resist, and she turned into his arms, even while she protested, "It's cold out here."

Within a minute he had them rolled in the blanket on the soft ground beneath a pine tree and was warming her with his kisses. She laughed into his neck, and squeezed her eyes against tears, yet they came anyway, streaming forth with the emotions flooding her heart.

He kissed away her tears, forced his tongue between her lips and his legs between hers.

His hands... would she ever forget his hands upon her body...the calluses so rough and sweet...the knowledge that they contained, knowing just where to touch and to probe and to stroke...knowing how to send her flying into ecstasy.

He pleasured her with all he had, and she accepted it and tried to give him her all. She savored his scent and the feel of his body hard against her and the way he made her go out of her mind with desire. And she pressed it all into memory, to carry away with her when the time came to go.

"I love you," she whispered, faintly.

If he heard, he didn't respond in kind. And she knew it didn't matter. She knew he cared for her...but that it didn't matter. They each had to follow their own road.

The crossing of the pass, which looked innocent enough, if a bit narrow in places from what Lilly could see, turned out to be one of the most tedious and nerve-racking parts of the entire trip. Perhaps it simply seemed so because they were so close to the end of the trip, so close to completing the enormous undertaking and being shut of the responsibility forever. Everyone was eager to get over these mountains and down into the excitement of seeing the goldfields. The men talked of trying their hands at panning for gold and got carried away with imaginings of impressing the ladies of Santa Fe with their wealth. But to do that they had to cross the pass.

The first thing to happen was a horse and mule fell off the side of the mountain to dash on the rocks below. Cross and Lorenzo and Simon had taken the remuda across first, and several bickering horses had caused a commotion at a place in the trail where there wasn't room for commotion. When plaintive cries were heard from the mule, Arrio shot it with his long rifle. The blast echoed in the mountains and inside Lilly, jarring her to the bone. Lorenzo stood on the trail, looking downward, and cried openly.

Cross put his hand on Lorenzo's shoulder. "We have to go on," he said after a minute.

Lorenzo looked at him, and so did the others. The woman was still staring down at the rocks below.

"There's no other pass but Donner," Cross said tersely. "Does anyone want to go back and cross over Donner Pass?"

There was murmuring then, and the men faded from the edge of the path, retreating back to the sheep.

Cross knew they were scared. He was, too, but he knew it wouldn't help for anyone to know that. The only thing to do was press over the pass, put it behind them.

It was going on midday by the time Cross, on Domino, led the first band of sheep up the narrow slope. Lilly watched from the meadow, at the back of the herd. When he paused to turn and look back, she shot up her hand and waved at him. He waved back.

Mateo and his dog walked behind Cross, leading that first band, while Tomas and his dog worked them from behind. Only a few yards behind, Paco led a second band, and Jon guided the back end. Chino and Henri and Pan had charge of the third band, and Gaspar and Jesus took the last. Lilly and Coca would come at the very rear of the herd, leading their mounts and Coca's pack mules. Arrio wasn't about to be caught doing something so humble as walking, and Cross told him to do as he wished, but he wasn't taking a chance with anyone else.

"If that horse gets spooked, you let him go," he had told Lilly. "Don't be tryin' to save him and get yourself thrown over the edge. Is that understood?"

"Who's gonna save you, if your horse gets spooked?" she asked, unable to resist the sarcasm.

"Tell you what—if I go over the edge, you're in charge of getting the herd to Sacramento, and you can have my share, too."

Now she watched him lean forward and urge Domino up the rocky path. Mateo, his rifle slung on his back, plodded after, and the sheep, filling the trail, followed their shepherd. Soon Cross disappeared around a curve, and the bellwether did, too, leading sheep flowing on and on, like an upward-moving river.

It was a good hour later when Lilly and Coca finished with their coffee, doused the fire and loaded the last bit of the camp supplies onto the pack mules. This morning Coca was extra particular with the distribution of the load on each animal. When he was satisfied, he led his riding mule and two of his pack mules across the meadow toward the dwindling herd. Lilly followed with her mustang and Coca's third mule, and Arrio came after her on his tall Arab.

The three of them waited there in the strong sun. Coca lit up one of the stinking cigars Cross had given him. Arrio got down and went to cleaning his horse's hooves. He seemed to do this about as often as he drank water. Lilly watched Henri ascend the trail and wished he would walk closer to the mountainside. At least he was wearing his boots to protect his feet against the sharp rocks. She was wearing hers now, too.

She recalled Cross removing her moccasins the previous evening, recalled the sensations his hands stroking up her calfs had brought.

She was deep in this sweet memory, Henri was nearing the curve and Gaspar had the last band well started up the hill, when gunshots rang out and bounced off the mountains like a volley of cannon fire.

All hell broke loose. The thousand head of sheep still at the base of the trail turned and took off everywhere. Lilly saw Gaspar running down the trail as her mustang jumped

sideways against the pack mule, both almost jerking her off
her feet. Her vision was a blur of horse and sheep and
mules. Then she saw three riders bearing down upon them,
saw the smoke from their pistols. Coca got his mule brought
around and was pulling the rifle from his saddle. The mule
Lilly held on to fell down dead. Coca's rifle went off with a
deafening roar. She let go of the pack mule, but held to the
reins of the mustang and turned to run for the trees near the
pass.

Then a dark mass of horse, all legs and flying hooves, was
in front of her. *Oh, Lord!* She veered, headed for the pass.
Ahead she saw Jesus in the middle of the sheep, bringing up
his ancient rifle. The dark horse and rider, his coat flying,
jumped forward and ran right over the sheep and old herder.

Screaming now, Lilly kept on running, scrambling for the
boulders at the side of the pass. She looked up and saw
Henri, in the midst of panicking sheep, fall sideways and
tumble toward the edge of the mountain.

"Henri!" she screamed.

In the blink of an eye, sheep were milling where she had
seen the boy fall. She let go of the mustang and took off
through the sheep. A horse came beside her, and she was
jerked upward like a rag doll. She kicked and screamed,
pounded the arm that bound her. Then something hit her
head, and she was flung stomach down across a man's
thighs. Through black and white dots she saw a worn army
boot tucked into a stirrup.

She recognized it as Uriah Plover's.

Lilly slipped away from the horror into a secret pocket in
her mind where there was no feeling. She was awake, yet not
so. She lay on the ground where she was dumped. Through
slit eyelids she saw sheep scattered over the meadow. She
saw Arrio lying in the grass, and a man with long black hair,
black beard and nearly black skin going through the sad-

dlebags on Arrio's horse, tossing things to the ground and pocketing others. He gave a little laugh at some of the things he found.

Where was Cross? Away . . . over the pass.

Then she saw Uriah Plover. She recognized him first by his army boots. She watched him toss Coca over his mule and tie him to the saddle. Coca's back was bloody. He moaned.

Inside Lilly screamed, but no sound came from her. It was as if someone held a hand over her voice and mind, keeping her quiet, hiding her in the secret pocket.

Uriah Plover fired his gun right behind the mule, sending the animal racing away. "That'll give McCree somethin' to think about—if'n the mule makes it over."

He turned his eyes to her. She didn't move. He came over, toed her with his boot. Instinct kept her quiet, even when he jabbed his boot heel into her stomach hard enough to bring acid to her throat. Playin' possum, Mammy Ethnee used to say when Lilly had feigned sleep to keep from having to work at her sewing.

"It's gettin' worse," came a weak, sobbing voice from someone she didn't see. "I'm dyin'...ya'all have to take me down to the valley."

Heavy footsteps in the grass. "Yep, I believe yer sinkin', boy," a deep, guttural voice said, and Lilly knew it was the dark man. There came the cocking of a hammer, and then a gun roared in Lilly's ears. She jumped involuntarily.

"He weren't much of a help, anyway," the deep voice said. The footsteps stopped near Lilly's head, and the voice came once more. "The woman didn't have nothin' on her horse, 'n none on the mule, neither. You said she'd have gold...two thousand or more. Didn't find nothin' of a woman's." His voice rang with anger, and his toe prodded Lilly's hip.

"Then it's on a mule already over the pass," Plover said. "We'll get it, after we get McCree. And then we'll have them sheep, too."

She felt the dark man lean over her, smelled his rotten breath, felt his hair brush her face. "Meybe yous hit her too hard."

"Meybe . . . but she's breathin'."

"Well, let me just see how alive she is. . . ." He cackled, and then his hands were on her, pushing up beneath her serape, tugging at her trousers. Her spirit fluttered and screamed, but her body would only lie there. *If she could just be as if dead, maybe they would leave her alone . . . maybe it would all go away.*

There came the sound of a thud, and Uriah Plover's iron voice saying, "There ain't time for that!"

The man was off her. Her eyes slits again, she saw the dark man and Uriah Plover facing each other.

Uriah Plover said, "Cross McCree's gonna be comin' over that hill any minute, and I'll let him shoot your head off, if that's what you want. If you want to stay alive, you get up in those rocks and keep a bead on him, whilst I bring him down here."

"I get her first off," the dark man said.

"She's yourn, after I have McCree."

There came the sound of feet running away, rocks rolling. She felt and smelled Uriah Plover lean over her. He jerked her up and shook her. "Time to wake up, gal." She didn't open her eyes, told her muscles they were dead.

He dragged her . . . across the grass . . . to his horse. The next instant cold water was splashed over her face. She tried not to even flutter an eyelid, kept the secret pocket closed around her. But then he was opening her mouth and stuffing the canteen into it, pouring the water.

She couldn't breathe . . . she was choking.

She coughed then, coughed and fought for air and damned herself for doing it.

She opened her eyes.

Uriah Plover's eyes gleamed. "Let's go get ready for yer fella."

He dragged her back over behind a rock at the base of the pass, held her with an arm choking her neck, and practiced sighting his pistol up the trail.

Lilly looked up the trail, saw the place where Henri had been, and felt a rent in her secret pocket through which feeling began to pour. Thoughts came with sudden clarity. *Cross…he would come for her.* She gazed up the trail, saw the curve around which he had disappeared and knew he would come back the very same way. There was no other.

She was to be the bait to draw him, and he would come to save her. And to be killed.

She closed her eyes and went limp, seeking, frantically, the safety of the secret pocket, where there was no pain, no fear, no feeling.

"Plover!" Cross's voice echoed against the mountains and down her limbs.

"It took you long enough, McCree!" Uriah hefted himself up and stepped out from behind the rock, holding Lilly in front of him like a shield. Lilly remained totally limp…a deadweight for him. "I got somethin' you want. But yer gonna have to come and get her. And if'n you don't, I'll kill her."

After the echo of Uriah Plover's voice died away, there was total silence.

Uriah Plover jerked her upward, and the cold steel of his pistol pressed sharply into her head. His arm was choking off her breath, and panic was swirling in her brain, but she didn't move, sought to hide far back in the recess of the pocket, for if Cross thought her dead, he wouldn't come down. If she were dead, there would be no reason for him to risk his life.

She willed herself to be dead.

"Did ya' hear me, McCree?" Uriah Plover sang out.

Cross sank down behind a group of rocks. Two inches to the right, and he'd step off the mountain.

He'd slowly been making his way down the trail the only way he could, which was behind boulders along the outside edge. He had no more cover from here, though.

He had brought his Walker Colt, which gave him six shots and the best range of any pistol, but it still wasn't a rifle, and he'd need to be close to hit anything besides air.

He scanned the rocks on either side of the pass; Chino had said there were three bandits. Cross saw only Plover. But there were three horses down there. Arrio lay in the middle of the meadow. No sign of Gaspar and Jesus . . . or Henri. He stared at Lilly hanging limply from Plover's arm, and his heart pounded. Was she dead? He didn't want to believe that, *couldn't* believe that, and he knew at the same time he was a fool.

Back up the trail, Mateo waited with his rifle, but there'd be no way the shepherd could get close enough to help, even if he was much of a shot.

Cross took a deep breath and called out, "I hear you, Plover . . . but how do I know she's still alive?" She sure as hell didn't look alive.

"Well," Plover called, with an evil laugh, "meybe you could sit up there behind that rock and watch what I could do with her while I'm holdin' her jes like this. If'n she screams, I guess we'll know she's alive."

Hate rose bitter and hot in Cross's throat.

He took aim, but at this distance, a bullet shot at Plover's head could drift enough to blow a hole in Lilly, which would certainly end the question as to whether she was alive or not. God, but he was in one hell of a mess this time.

He couldn't let Plover touch her, dead or alive. Provided she was alive, he couldn't let her die.

Suddenly there came a coarse laugh, and a burly black man jumped atop a rock not two hundred feet in front of Cross. "Well, I got somethin' here that's sure alive." And he jerked Henri up by the arm. Rag stuffed in his mouth, hands bound with strips of cloth, the boy struggled, legs flailing at the air. "He'd bounce real good down that mountain," the big man said with a cackling laugh.

An eerie choking cry echoed in the air, and in an instant Cross saw Lilly come to life. He jumped out into the trail, hoping to gain a few feet at least, shot a hole in the big, black fellow's forehead, found himself still standing, and whipped the gun over to Plover.

But Lilly was in the way. She stepped backward, and lifted a bloody knife in her raised fist. Plover still stood. And then Cross saw the dark stain spreading from his side and down his trousers, even as the man slowly brought his pistol up, aiming at Lilly.

"Get down, Lilly!"

She dropped, and, holding the pistol with both hands, Cross shot, not only hitting Plover's gun hand, but blowing off half the man's arm and sending him reeling backward.

As Plover hit the ground, his left hand grasped the air, as if grasping for life. His hand dropped, and Plover fell spread-eagled, in death.

Cross started to run then, grabbed up Henri as he passed, and went to the woman, pulling her into his arms, too.

"Shush...it's okay now...shush...."

He had her...*oh, God.*

It only then occurred to him to look around for someone else. But he guessed since no bullets came slicing into them, the danger was past.

* * *

Gaspar had a broken arm, and Jesus's eyesight was dim, but both old shepherds were alive and thanks was given. Coca had a bullet in his shoulder, but was far from death, too. They buried Arrio back in the meadow, on the other side from Plover and his companions. Cross hated to think of telling the noble Don Baca of the loss of his son. He covered the grave with plenty of boulders to protect the young man from predators, and he made a marker of stout poles sunk in the boulders, in case the elder Baca felt it necessary to come to retrieve his son's body.

In camp that night, on the west side of the Sierras, Lilly helped Cross set Gaspar's arm and dig the bullet out of Coca, and then she sewed the crusty Mexican up. She didn't faint, but she came close.

She wouldn't let Henri out of her sight, insisted that the boy spread his bedroll beside hers. Without comment, Cross spread his bedroll on the other side of her and held her all night long. He was there to soothe her when she cried out in her sleep.

"Shush . . . it's all right. You're just dreamin'."

Her eyes opened wide and she stared at him, but Cross wasn't certain she truly came awake. He remembered that back at the beginning of this trip he'd had to calm her from nightmares after a killing.

He stroked her silky hair and thought that he might not have been there to do that, if she hadn't turned on Plover like she had. Señora Lilly Blackwell was a hell of a woman.

The next morning he and the woman, Henri and Mateo saw to getting the rest of the herd across the pass.

"You're sure you're okay?" he asked Lilly. She still trembled.

"We've got to get over," she said logically and strode away.

Once they had all the sheep over, the four of them took Coca and Jesus and half the herd and set a brisk pace for the goldfields. The woman was determined to find a doctor for Coca, who'd begun running a high fever, and Jesus, who was still seeing only shadows. At her insistence, they kept moving from bare light to bare light. Cross didn't argue with her. He had the feeling he'd do better to argue with a bull buffalo, and it seemed they all needed to keep moving.

Two days later found them in a grassy valley, at the edge of the first settlement on the American River. It was a good thing they had reached this place, because Cross doubted any of them could have gone any farther. Lilly fell off her horse and right into his arms. It appeared the nurse had worn herself into worse shape than her patients. Coca was done with his fever, and Jesus's eyesight had begun to return, at least enough to help Cross spread a bedroll for the woman and, at Coca's direction, brew some sassafras tea for her.

As he sat there, holding the woman in his arms, Cross considered the company blessed by God. They had traveled over a thousand miles of mountains and plains and deserts, and they had lost no more than a couple of dozen sheep—those who had died of thirst and two shot on the mountain and another two that fell off the pass—and one man, all of which was no small accomplishment. And he and the woman still stood to make their fortunes. He probably should have felt better than he did about it all. At the moment he was having trouble seeing the point.

He gathered her to him and choked back tears.

Chapter Eighteen

They stopped the sheep in a big meadow north of the settlement of Elk Creek. A miner told them of a doctor farther downriver. Coca's fever had dropped, but he remained very weak, and Lilly insisted Cross go get the doctor, never mind that the men thought it all unnecessary.

"I haven't ever seen a doctor in my life," Cross said, "and I doubt Coca has, either, and he's still alive."

"You get the doctor *before* he dies," she said.

She knew he and the other men thought her addled after what had gone on at the pass. They spoke and moved softly and gently around her, as if she were a cake in the oven that would flatten if jarred. She couldn't have said they were wrong. She felt like a bag of flour split open and spilled out, needing to be swept up and put neatly back into the container again. But she felt as if she wouldn't recognize which container she belonged in. She was a stranger to herself.

"For heavensake, just go get the doctor," she said, and Cross went, and for no other reason, Lilly guessed, than to keep her calm.

While he was gone, Lilly and Coca and Jesus played poker. Lilly had to read some of Jesus's cards for him, but Coca did fine. He won five dollars from Lilly, which probably illustrated that he didn't need the doctor.

It was just as well, for had Coca or Jesus been on the verge of dying, they certainly would have done so at the hands of the doctor, who turned out to be a puny man two sheets to the wind—perpetually, Lilly suspected.

"You said bring the doctor," Cross defended himself with irritating logic and crouched by the fire, pouring himself a cup of coffee.

The "doctor" did little more than sprinkle Coca's wound with powder, which Lilly doubted was anything more than gunpowder, and say that time would tell about Jesus's eyesight. And for both he prescribed several good swallows from his pint bottle of whiskey.

"We've gotten this far, without havin' you come and kill them with that rot-gut," Lilly said hotly and gestured for the man to leave.

"I made this here brew myself," the puny man whined. "And it ain't like there's medicines to be had out here, ya know."

"Get!" Lilly said, threatening him with one of Coca's iron pans. The puny man took himself off as fast as his stumbling legs would carry him.

Lilly whirled to see Cross observing her over the rim of his coffee cup. He wisely remained quiet.

Muttering, Lilly built up the campfire and made a heaping pot of sweet spoonbread. She focused on the process, on pouring the coarse cornmeal into the water, on the way it bubbled, on the steam and plop-plop sound as she stirred the thickening mixture. Gradually these sounds seemed to overcome those of the echoing gunshots, and the smooth yellow color seemed to fade away that of fresh blood.

Everyone had a dish, and when they had eaten it, Lilly began to feel as if she might be coming together again. The following morning Coca suggested she make more, and after she'd finished she felt almost normal. Coca's solemn eyes grinned at her, and she realized he'd known she needed to make spoonbread all along.

"I am familiar with a woman," he said in the false forlorn way Lilly had come to know.

While they waited in the meadow for the rest of the sheep and herders to join them, Cross went to spread the word of their herd and locate buyers. Lilly went with him once, through several mining camps. After a number of lewd remarks, she removed her earrings, put her hair up and pulled her hat low, and stuck to Cross like glue. He told her to walk behind him, because with her looking like a boy, he wasn't about to hold her hand. And no, he wouldn't have her change into a dress, or she'd probably end up getting him into a fight.

The river area was hard and ugly, with the land scraped clean of trees and vegetation, holes dug everywhere and water wheels and sluices sucking the river dry. Men worked, digging and sluicing the rock, their faces tired and drawn. Lilly saw some women, too, working claims like men, and they looked as worn out as the land.

The most appealing place they came to was a café run by two boisterous ladies. Here she and Cross enjoyed delicious chicken and dumplings that tasted as good as any Mammy Ethnee had ever made.

The two owners had come to California looking for husbands, each said. One said she had found hers, only to leave the miserable son-of-a-gun. The ladies bought twenty sheep from Cross and Lilly, at eight dollars a head, providing the stock was delivered the following day, so the café could be the first in the area to offer mutton dinners.

Lilly observed that the real gold of the area was food, and the ladies readily agreed. One whispered that she would soon be leaving with enough to enable her to live as a rich woman back home in Ohio. And Lilly thought about how she was hoping to do the same thing back in Pasquotank County.

And her dream was almost in her hand, if the market for sheep continued this good.

That first visit to the goldfields was enough for Lilly, however, and thereafter she stayed in camp. She preferred the peaceful isolation, with the gentle sheep and the boy and men, who had become her closest friends. And, as much as she wanted to sell her sheep and reap her fortune, she found tedious discussions with Cross about offers for the herd.

"We aren't in a great hurry," she told him. "We can afford to rest awhile."

"The men need to get home to their families," Cross said. "And you will be needin' to catch your ship back East."

She averted her gaze from his. "Yes . . . that's so."

The following morning when Cross took the twenty sheep away to the café owners, she went off by herself to cry, though jingling her share of the profit in her poke bag helped some.

She needed the money to go home, she reminded herself. She wanted to go home to her house on the river, to silk gowns and afternoon teas on tall porches, with green lawns stretching out, and dinners of Virginia hams and biscuits and the scent of the swamps on sultry nights. That was what she wanted.

On the evening of the third day, the second half of the herd caught up to them and formed another camp at the north end of the small valley. Lilly was excited to see the sheep and the men. She went out, touched sheep and greeted each man eagerly, though she held back from hugging them, for it would have embarrassed them. Lilly's tent and shelters of canvas and freshly cut tree trunks were set up, and they soon had a small village made between the two large bands of sheep. That night, around the campfires, Lilly saw them all as if for the first time since the start of their trip.

They were all leaner, harder looking. Chino was sprouting a dark growth of beard, where he'd had only fuzz before. His father's hair had gone almost white. Lorenzo's clothes hung on him now, and Simon had totally lost his paunch. Coca's hard face had darkened to nearly black, had more lines, his eyes more sadness. Henri had grown taller; Lilly no longer pulled him against her, instead she would simply touch his hand. The others, too—Tomas, Jon and Paco Salazar, Mateo—had been not much more than boys when they had started, and now they were men grown. The only one who seemed not to have changed was Jesus. He'd been old and wrinkled when they started, and he was still.

When Mateo brought her a shirt he wished mended so he could wear it when he went into the camp the next day, she thought that she would miss doing this for them. She looked at Cross sitting cross-legged in the glow of the campfire, sharpening his knives, with Pan's head propped upon his leg. A pain, as sharp as the knife glistening in his hands, pierced her chest.

Those first nights after the incident on the mountain, she had lain in Cross's arms, with Henri near on the other side of her. The two of them, there where she could touch them when she awoke in the night and assure herself of their safety.

She would recall then—and did now—the terror of the evil men, and not for herself but for the two, the man and the boy. She would recall the great fury that had engulfed her and led her to plunge the knife into Uriah Plover's side, to jerk it upward with all her might, as Cross had instructed her. She would recall the hate and the desperation she had felt...and the relief when Uriah Plover and the dark man lay dead, never to threaten them again.

She ran her gaze over Cross, and he felt it, looked up at her over the flickering flames. She bent her head to Mateo's shirt, seeing the fabric and her stitching through blurred vision.

She recalled the last time she and Cross had made love, that night on the mountain. She recalled that, and knew she always would.

But she was going home.

The blurring became so much that she couldn't see her stitching. A tear fell, making a dark blotch on the pale blue fabric.

She couldn't stay...and he couldn't go with her. She knew that.

Damn it all to hell!

Cross went to Sacramento to make known the herd of sheep for sale. He returned, bringing a man who was interested in the entire herd and had money to pay, if a deal could be struck.

Conrad Springer was a portly man dressed in a suit, complete with top hat, paisley vest and gold watch. He had keen eyes and demonstrated his astuteness when he recognized Lilly as the lady she was, even dressed as she was in men's shirt and trousers.

Springer bowed elegantly over her hand. Cross was at once proud of her, of her being his, which she really wasn't, so that was foolish. And he was irritated that Springer could bring such a pleased expression to her face with nothing more than meaningless fancy words and actions.

The woman didn't continue to be so pleased, however, when, as the three of them walked out to examine the sheep, Springer addressed himself totally to Cross. The more Cross and the businessman talked, the more vexed Lilly looked. She put in little comments—about how twenty sheep had already been sold for eight dollars apiece, and how great a demand there was in the area for fresh meat, and stock, too, if more herds were ever to be raised in the area again. Springer listened politely to each comment, and then continued to talk to Cross. Lilly kept puffing up, so that Cross began to worry she was about to erupt, and her ire was sure to spill over onto him, too.

When Springer came to a firm offer of seven dollars, Cross said, "If you'll give us a few minutes, my partner and I need to talk it over." He looked at Lilly.

"Ahem . . . of course," Springer said.

Lilly thought they could get a little more than seven dollars, and Cross figured she wasn't going to be happy until she got at least a penny more, so he let her have a go at Springer.

In between telling Springer about her home in North Carolina, and arguing the points of Virginia ham versus Boston ham, she ended up getting seven dollars and twenty cents a head for the entire herd. Springer would pay them in American currency at his bank in Sacramento.

"I believe you would be quite a good gambler, Mrs. Blackwell, with your gift of knowing when to play and when to cash in," the man said when he shook hands with her and Cross. Grinning, he offered Cross a fine Cuban cigar, and as a second thought, offered Lilly one, too. Cross laughed, and Lilly frowned.

"If you gentlemen will excuse me," she said haughtily, straightening her shoulders beneath her man's shirt, "I have a great deal to get ready for leavin' tomorrow."

"Mrs. Blackwell," Springer called to her. "I would be pleased to provide a carriage for the trip down."

As graceful as a princess, Lilly inclined her head. "Thank you, sir."

That night Cross walked out to look at the sheep. They glowed beneath a full moon. He thought about how the habit was in him to check on the flock, make certain of their safety. He was going to feel lost without them.

He crouched and petted Pan and noticed the pads of the dog's feet had become thick and hard, the feet themselves almost grown outsized for the slight dog.

They had all toughened, he thought, the faces of the men coming across his mind. Each of them had changed slightly since the beginning of the trail. The woman, too, had changed from that first morning when he'd boosted her atop the mule . . . and from that morning he had first made love to her.

He straightened slowly, painfully, the pain coming from deep inside his spirit.

He'd known from the first that it had not been a permanent thing. And he had left a number of women, walked away, without a backward glance—or at least, not more than a small one.

Looking out at the sheep he had the strange, strong urge to hold on to the sheep and the men, and most of all the woman. To start out again on the trail, where they were all together, and he was in control of their world.

He saw the change inside himself, then. From the time he had begun gathering the sheep and decided to go to California, he had taken on a growing responsibility. He had taken control all these months, had been responsible for the lives of all, such as he had never been before. And now he found it difficult to let go.

Yet, it was time. He had to let the sheep and men go . . . and he had to let the woman go.

He could ask Lilly to stay, and she might. But his pride refused to ask her. He had let her know his feelings in all ways that he knew how. She had to make the choice on her own to stay. If she didn't make the choice, she'd always be looking east.

He walked back to the camp, sat and gazed at her in the flickering light. She was pressing one of her gowns, one of crimson velvet, which had been long packed in canvas, with a warmed rock. She felt his gaze, looked up at him for long thoughtful seconds. But she didn't come to him.

She disappeared into her tent sometime later. He studied the tent through the haze of cigar smoke. It was late and the moon high, when Cross walked away from camp, far away.

In the morning, when Lilly emerged from her tent, she was dressed in the crimson velvet gown and a matching jacket, her hair coiled atop her head and covered with her bonnet, a little sadly misshapen but still reflecting style, and the pewter-and-turquoise earrings dangling from her ears. She had become once more the elegant and genteel Mrs. Lilly Blackwell of Pasquotank County.

It was time to say goodbye, for down in Sacramento where Conrad Springer was to pay them, Lilly would be catching the boat for San Francisco... and home. The men stood looking at her, shyly, and maybe just a little sadly, she dared to believe.

Cross looked at her once, long and hard, and then turned away from her.

He'd shaved his beard, though he'd left his mustache. Where his thick beard had been the skin was lighter in color than the rest of his deeply tanned face. She recalled that she'd first met him with a beard, and she preferred him that way, though he was more handsome without it. He'd washed, had his hair neatly combed, shined his boots, dusted his hat. She wondered if a part of his sprucing up had been not only for going to Sacramento, but also for impressing her.

Mateo brought her cherrywood chest and set it atop her bundles of clothing. The pile of bundles looked as they had when she had left Santa Fe. Had it been only months ago? It seemed like years. "*Gracias*, Mateo," she said, and the Spanish flowed naturally off her tongue.

Henri appeared dressed in the clothes they had bought him in Moriah, worn now but clean and the best he had. "I have these things," he said to Lilly in English and handed her a small leather sack. His eyes were nervous. Reluctant, she thought, her heart constricting.

Lilly smiled at him. "We'll buy new clothes in Sacramento."

She hoped to please him, but his face remained somber. "I would see my horse," he said in Spanish, and his voice betrayed hidden tears.

Lilly told him to see the horse, and she watched him run off toward the remuda. She swallowed her tears. Then she turned to see Cross scowling at her. Grasping her arm, he dragged her aside.

"Are you thinkin' about the boy, or yourself?" His blue eyes were cool and hard.

She drew herself up straight. "You cannot imagine what I can give him back where people aren't always lookin' over their shoulder for savages that rob and kill."

"There are savages everywhere. They are simply better polished back in what is considered civilization."

They glared at each other.

"You know very little about civilization," Lilly said.

"I know what it is supposed to be and what it never is," he replied sharply. "More to the point, I know what the boy needs." He took a deep breath and spread reason over his ire. "I won't allow Henri to go back to bein' an orphan on the street. I'll keep him with me. I'll see that he has all he needs and wants, that he learns all he needs and wants to learn."

"I can give him all that and more. I can give him the world." But uncertainty burrowed like a worm, as her eyes sought the boy.

"If you take him back with you, you will take away from him who he is, because he will never be accepted as who he is back in the American states. You know that, Lilly."

She wavered, watched the boy in the distance, at the remuda reaching for his horse. She knew the truth of what Cross said, but she didn't want to know it. It angered her. She had so much to give Henri, and she wanted him with her.

She saw it quite clearly then: giving to Henri was a reason for living, just as giving to Tyler had been. But Tyler had needed what she had to give, and Henri...his needs were different.

Yes, she could give him much, but at what price?

"Let me talk to him," she said in a hoarse whisper.

Lifting her skirt, she walked out across the damp grass. When she approached, Henri glanced over his shoulder, then averted his face to his horse, wiping his face on the animal's shoulder. He was crying, and didn't want Lilly to see.

She pretended not to notice. "It is hard to leave your dear friend, isn't it? It was hard for me to lose my mule."

Henri sniffed but didn't speak.

"I need to speak to you, Henri." She drew him with her to sit on a rocky outcropping. Her gaze fell to their hands, and she saw the stark differences in their skin color. It didn't seem to matter out in this land so much, but it would back in Pasquotank County.

"Henri, I want more than anything in the world to have you with me, but perhaps coming with me isn't what is best for you. Perhaps you would be better with Mr. McCree, where you can keep your horse and the ways of your people." She sighed, at a loss for words to explain anything that the boy could understand. How could she explain about skin color and wearing shoes and the way her heart was breaking?

She settled for, "In the American states things are so different."

His solemn face came up. "Mr. McCree... he has said I could stay with him?" Excited hope flickered across his face.

"Yes, Henri... and you would rather that, wouldn't you?"

"*Sí*, to stay with the *patrón* would be a fine thing. We could ride horses together, and shoot...." He faltered. "I did not mean..." He fell into Spanish that Lilly couldn't readily follow, but she knew he was trying to spare her feelings.

She touched his knee. "It's okay, Henri. I understand," she said in Spanish.

He corrected her pronunciation, and then he regarded her curiously. "You will still go back to the American states?"

"Yes." She nodded and then dug into her purse for a handkerchief, because she couldn't stop the tears.

"But you are sad to go back."

"Yes... I am."

"Then why do you go back, if you are sad to do it?"

"Because... because it is my home."

"*Sí*," he said, though he still regarded her curiously.

She got her tears stopped, and she talked of practical things, such as to tell him that she would give Cross McCree money to buy him new clothes and for books and paper and pen to teach him to read and write. She would write him letters, she told him, and he could write her. And maybe someday, when he was grown, he would come to see her.

They heard the arrival of a carriage—Conrad Springer driving it himself. Cross and Mateo began loading Lilly's things into the small wagon bed at the back.

Henri held Lilly's hand as they returned to camp. Lilly felt the boy wasn't so much holding on to her in the manner of a child, as in the manner of a young man escorting her.

She faced Cross. "Henri says he wants to stay and return to Santa Fe with you. But he has promised to write me." Her voice cracked. Her eyes bored into Cross. "I have told him that you can teach him to read and write." She raised an eyebrow.

"I will," Cross said. "And I will see to it that he learns from a real teacher, too."

She nodded. "Well..." She rested her hand on the boy's warm, black hair and pressed the feel of it into memory. The next instant Henri threw his arms around her, and she held him, for a moment, only a precious moment.

Then she put him from her, turned to the men, looked at each of them and smiled. Lastly, she looked at Coca. His eyes solemn as ever, he doffed his big floppy hat and bowed stiffly, his arm still in a sling.

Lilly strode over and kissed his cheek. "Return to your wife and daughters where you belong," she whispered, falling into Spanish.

"Hasta la vista," he said softly. *Until we meet again,* he had said.

On the brink of sobbing, she turned and strode stiffly to the carriage. And then suddenly she saw the dog at Cross's leg. She bent, kissed her hand and pressed it to the animal's head. Goodbye... goodbye to all, she thought with a final look at the sheep.

Cross took her hand to help her up into the carriage. When she lifted her skirts, he noticed, with great surprise, that she was wearing her old moccasins, the ones he had gotten for her months ago.

She sat, and then Cross realized he was still holding on to her hand. He let go, stepped back, watched for a second as

Chapter Nineteen

Conrad Springer took them directly to his banker in Sacramento. Twenty minutes later, and a splash of good brandy all around, and Cross and Lilly, arm in arm, left the bank with their money.

"Springer said the riverboat doesn't leave for San Francisco until late afternoon," Cross said, "but I imagine you'll want to book passage now."

"Oh, there's plenty of time for that," Lilly said with a dismissing wave. "I want to help you shop for clothes for Henri. He's got to have clothes to wear for the trip back, Cross. It's almost winter." She spoke as if he'd been a fool not to think of it.

"I was goin' to get the boy some new duds, even though what he's got is fine for now. We'll be takin' the southern route back to the Territory and miss hard winter, anyway," he protested, even as she tugged him down the street to a mercantile.

Once inside he did little more than stand beside her while she loaded his arms with all and sundry, not only for Henri, but little gifts for each of the men, too. She even bought Cross a package of panatelas. The prices were double even what they would have been back in New Mexico Territory.

"You're gonna spend your entire profit before you get out of the valley," he said.

"I guess I don't need you to tell me how to spend my money."

"No, *señora,* I guess you don't."

He wondered if he should ask her to stay. But he didn't speak, instead lit up one of the panatelas.

When they emerged from the mercantile, Cross's arms were full of bundles. He was going to have to buy a damn mule to get back to the camp.

They made room around Lilly's bundles for the new ones. Then Cross suggested, "I guess we'd better get down to the docks now." He watched her face.

She shook her head. "There's plenty of time. We need to celebrate the culmination of our successful venture! I'll let you buy us dinner." She smiled, but her expression was carefully masked.

"You come back to civilization and start usin' words no one can understand," he growled, muttering *cul-min-a-tion.*

She laughed gaily and hung on his arm. She didn't have the look of a woman eager to leave him, he thought. And it did seem she was putting off booking passage to San Francisco. He began to let himself hope she would stay after all.

She would have gone into a hotel restaurant, but Cross led the way to a small cantina he had visited on his previous trip. When he spoke to the proprietress here in Spanish, he and Lilly were warmly welcomed as honored guests. He ordered a bottle of their best wine before their meal.

"I'm lettin' you pay for this," Lilly told him smartly. "It can be your goin'-away gift to me."

And that put a damper on his thin hope, he thought as he poured their glasses, then raised his in a toast. "To Lilly Blackwell, who made it with her sheep all the way from Santa Fe and is returnin' home a woman of means."

She blinked and looked away. "To Cross McCree, who made it all possible." Her voice came hoarsely. Without meeting his eyes, she sipped from her glass.

The old woman came to tell them the limited menu; she spoke in Spanish, and Lilly answered in kind. Cross watched her until her gaze came to his.

"You have learned the language," he said.

"My pronunciation can still make Henri laugh."

They had *picadillo*, which was skimpy on the meat, and frijoles and rice, with date cake for desert. Lilly ate heartily, and Cross watched her.

He leaned forward and said, "You have been away from Pasquotank County for a long time. Don't you think it might be far different than you remember?"

She paused, and confusion passed over her features. "Yes . . . of course it will be. But there are some things that never change. The house will still be there, the river."

"But you aren't the same," he said quietly, and he drew her eyes back to him. They were deep green, and certain.

"No, I'm not," she said, looking him straight in the eye. "But I still love those things that are there...the way of life that is there."

"Do you?"

She didn't respond to that.

They were quiet on the short ride to the river. Cross drew the horses to a stop in front of a gaudily painted riverboat, got down and came around to help Lilly out of the carriage. He saw again the moccasins on her feet. Her head might be in Pasquotank County, but her feet were definitely in the West.

She stood there, looking up at him, and he gazed down at her, at her iridescent green eyes, soft, smooth skin and moist lips.

"I'll see about passage," she said, and left him to find a steward to unload her things.

On impulse Lilly booked a room on the boat. She didn't allow herself to deliberate, or even understand her motives.

Her heart beat with apprehension as she strode back toward Cross, who stood leaning against the carriage. He was smoking one of the panatelas she'd bought him; he so loved those cigars. Her gaze moved over him, at the way he wore his hat low over his eyes and a little to one side, at his hair that had grown long enough to lie on his shirt at the back of his neck, at his frame she knew as solid beneath his loose serape.

Lilly suddenly felt that she had no idea of what she was doing.

She showed the steward her ticket, and he went away with her bundles. She and Cross watched him push his cart up the ramp and onto the steamboat.

"I'll have to buy a steamer trunk in San Francisco. I can't very well travel all the way home with my things in canvas bags."

She looked at Cross. He looked at her. His gaze was intense, yet strangely emotionless.

The boat whistle blew, a first call.

She lowered her gaze to his chest. All that she wished to say got choked up in her throat.

She said hoarsely, "You need to get a new serape," and touched him, lightly, her fingers aching for his bare hard chest.

"I'll wait till I get back to the Territory...or maybe south in Los Angeles."

She raised her eyes to his. His were blue as the sky above.

"I booked a room." Her mouth had gone dry. "I thought maybe you would go with me...just to San Francisco. You could return in the morning." She felt her cheeks burn, for what she was proposing.

His blue eyes narrowed, and he gazed at her a long moment. Embarrassment washed over her, and then she wished to smack him.

He said, "If I was to warm your bed again, I'd be wantin' more than just one last night to give you a memory." His voice was sharp. "You're set on leavin', so you might as well get used to a cold bed."

"And what makes you think I have to get used to a cold bed?" she replied, before she thought.

"I don't imagine you will for long."

"No, I won't."

She was amazed at her own talk. She had, after all, gotten coarse.

And then he said in a low voice, "But it won't ever be like it is with me. You can bet your entire sheep profit on that."

His blue eyes held hers, and she felt again his hand upon her skin, felt again the sweet fire he brought her.

The whistle blew, and she jumped, looked around to see the steam puffing out of the stack.

"Guess it's time you were on your way," he said.

The next instant he had taken her into his arms, crushed her against him, and was kissing her fiercely. She kissed him in return, taken away by passion and need and memories and wanting for more.

He released her so suddenly that she stumbled backward. Then he tipped his hat. "Goodbye, Mrs. Blackwell."

Aware of the stares of those around them but uncaring, she stood there as he got into the carriage. When he took up the reins, she turned, lifted her skirts and strode quickly for the boat. She heard the horses' hooves and the creaking of the carriage driving away as she stepped on the ramp. She wouldn't let herself turn to look. Blinded by tears, she asked the steward directions to her cabin. There she threw herself on the bed and sobbed.

The blowing of the whistle was like a splash of cold water over her head. It blew again, signaling for the last boarding. Into the silence that followed came Henri's voice, asking, "Why do you go back, if you are so sad to do it?"

Why was she?

Propelled by a sudden desperation, she scrambled off the bed and ran out onto the deck, looking for the steward.

"I've decided not to go," she told the man, who looked at her as if she had lost her mind. She felt as if she had lost her mind. "Please have someone get my things out of the cabin."

"Lilly!"

She whirled to see Cross striding down the blue-painted deck, coming at her with the aim and purpose of one of his knives.

"You aren't goin'," he bellowed.

The next instant she found herself scooped up and thrown over his shoulder, like so much baggage.

"Cross McCree! Put me down!" She kicked her feet and almost toppled them both.

Cross continued striding for the loading ramp and then down it.

Lilly tried to wiggle around. "Cross McCree, I do not care to be manhandled." Tears were flowing now.

And for that she got a skeptical "Huh!" which she understood very well.

He bent and slid her to her feet, caught her when she almost fell. "You're still wearin' your moccasins," he said, his eyes only inches from hers.

"Yes?" She didn't understand that at all, but her mind wasn't thinking of that. She was thinking of him coming for her.

She was thinking that he wanted her.

"You won't fit back East anymore, Lilly," he said, his voice dropping. "Don't you see that? You belong out here now. We'll start us a ranch within a day of San Francisco. I hear that's a big city. I'll build you a white clapboard ranch house, and you can get your gowns from back East, and have a carriage to ride around in, and..."

Cold struck her, and she realized she was making the same mistake she had made before, so long ago.

She put her fingers over his lips. "I don't want any of those things."

He gazed questioningly at her.

"I want you, Cross McCree. That's all. In an adobe, or a tent, or beneath the stars. I only want you."

She kissed him then, good and hard and passionate.

On their way to the stables, Lilly spied a bonnet in a small dress-shop window and cried for Cross to stop for her to get it.

"I am not gettin' married in this beat-up old bonnet, Mr. McCree," she said, yanking off the one on her head as she strode into the shop.

When they rode out of Sacramento, Cross was atop Domino and trailing two mules loaded with the woman's things and all that she had bought in the town. Beside him, on a mule she had chosen herself, she made quite a sight, riding sidesaddle, with her knee hooked over the horn, still dressed in that velvet gown and with a wide-brimmed straw bonnet swirling with puffy feathers atop her head. She turned the head of everyone they passed.

"I don't think we should settle down on a ranch outside San Francisco," she told Cross smartly, as they rode down the trail.

"Then what do you think we should do, *señora?*"

She cast him a sideways glance and a sweet little smile. "I think we should go back to New Mexico Territory and buy up some more sheep and bring them out here again, before the market dries up."

He hadn't expected that, not one bit. He stared at her.

"Well, what do you think?" she asked.

He nodded, taking to the idea as fast as a sheep to grass. "Maybe we'll get us some of those fancy merinos I've seen down in Texas and bring them out."

"Yes! I'll bet we could easily get twelve dollars apiece for breedin' stock."

Laughing, Cross rode Domino over beside her mule, put an arm around her waist and pulled her up across his lap.

"We'll have to attend to a little breeding stock of our own, woman," he said and kissed her hard.

He didn't let up until he didn't have breath left. She leaned back and looked at him, her green eyes so tender he felt an overwhelming weakness sweep his chest.

"We haven't said it." She wet her lips. "I love you, Cross."

He gazed at her. "I love you, woman."

Contentment filled her eyes. She laid herself gently against his chest, and he clucked to Domino, sending him into a quiet walk on down the trail toward the boy who would be their own and the friends who would welcome and bless them.

Cross suddenly knew he had gotten all that he had been seeking when he had left Santa Fe.

* * * * *

Author's Note

In their book *Shepherd's Empire*, first published in 1945, Charles W. Towne and Edward N. Wentworth chronicle the tales of the men who first took sheep to California from New Mexico and even from as far away as Ohio, driving herds of woollies across half a continent.

These shepherds were as brave and bold as any legendary cowboy. They could ride and shoot, braved storms and rivers, Indian and bandits, and as tough a terrain as any crossed by a cowman and his cattle. Where cattle needed quantities of water and plenty of grass, the lowly sheep could travel along for days on nothing more than morning dew, scrub brush and bark. The humble sheep could move steadily over rocky mountains and walk hundreds of miles without getting footsore.

It was these sheep that fed hungry men in the goldfields and that bred hearty new stock to build California ranches. Later the descendants of these sheep were driven north, to populate Oregon, Wyoming and Montana, and east, to the feed lots of Kansas and Omaha.

It was the hope of Charles Towne and Edward Wentworth that: *Someday a worth-while drama may be written about the flockmaster, with one of the great sheep trails for background.*

I've made a start.

Curtiss Ann Matlock
Cogar, Oklahoma

Harlequin® Historical

MORE ROMANCE, MORE PASSION, MORE ADVENTURE...MORE PAGES!

Bigger books from Harlequin Historicals. Pick one up today and see the difference a Harlequin Historical can make.

White Gold by Curtiss Ann Matlock—January 1995—A young widow partners up with a sheep rancher in this exciting Western.

Sweet Surrender by Julie Tetel—February 1995—An unlikely couple discover hidden treasure in the next *Northpoint* book.

All That Matters by Elizabeth Mayne—March 1995—A medieval about the magic between a young woman and her Highland rescuer.

The Heart's Wager by Gayle Wilson—April 1995—An ex-soldier and a member of the demi-monde unite to rescue an abducted duke.

Longer stories by some of your favorite authors. Watch for them in 1995 wherever Harlequin Historicals are sold.

HHBB95-1

Fifty red-blooded, white-hot, true-blue hunks
from every State in the Union!

Look for MEN MADE IN AMERICA! Written by some
of our most popular authors, these stories feature some
of the strongest, sexiest men, each from a different state
in the union!

Two titles available every month at your favorite
retail outlet.

In January, look for:

WITHIN REACH by Marilyn Pappano (New Mexico)
IN GOOD FAITH by Judith McWilliams (New York)

In February, look for:

THE SECURITY MAN by Dixie Browning
(North Carolina)
A CLASS ACT by Kathleen Eagle
(North Dakota)

You won't be able to resist MEN MADE IN AMERICA!

Harlequin® Historical

Why is March the best time to try Harlequin Historicals for the first time? We've got four reasons:

All That Matters by Elizabeth Mayne—A medieval woman is freed from her ivory tower by a Highlander's impetuous proposal.

Embrace the Dawn by Jackie Summers—Striking a scandalous bargain, a highwayman joins forces with a meddlesome young woman.

Fearless Hearts by Linda Castle—A grouchy deputy puts up a fight when his Eastern-bred tutor tries to teach him a lesson.

Love's Wild Wager by Taylor Ryan—A young woman becomes the talk of London when she wagers her hand on the outcome of a horse race.

It's that time of year again—that March Madness time of year—when Harlequin Historicals picks the best and brightest new stars in historical romance and brings them to you in one exciting month!

Four exciting books by four promising new authors that are certain to become your favorites. Look for them wherever Harlequin Historicals are sold.

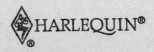

HARLEQUIN®

Deceit, betrayal, murder

Join Harlequin's intrepid heroines, India Leigh
and Mary Hadfield, as they ferret out the truth
behind the mysterious goings-on in their
neighborhood. These two women are no milk-
and-water misses. In fact, they thrive on

MISCHIEF & MAYHEM

Watch for their incredible adventures in this
special two-book collection. Available in March,
wherever Harlequin books are sold.

HARLEQUIN®

Don't miss these Harlequin favorites by some of our most distinguished authors!
And now, you can receive a discount by ordering two or more titles!

HT#25577	WILD LIKE THE WIND by Janice Kaiser	$2.99	☐
HT#25589	THE RETURN OF CAINE O'HALLORAN by JoAnn Ross	$2.99	☐
HP#11626	THE SEDUCTION STAKES by Lindsay Armstrong	$2.99	☐
HP#11647	GIVE A MAN A BAD NAME by Roberta Leigh	$2.99	☐
HR#03293	THE MAN WHO CAME FOR CHRISTMAS by Bethany Campbell	$2.89	☐
HR#03308	RELATIVE VALUES by Jessica Steele	$2.89	☐
SR#70589	CANDY KISSES by Muriel Jensen	$3.50	☐
SR#70598	WEDDING INVITATION by Marisa Carroll	$3.50 U.S. $3.99 CAN.	☐
HI#22230	CACHE POOR by Margaret St. George	$2.99	☐
HAR#16515	NO ROOM AT THE INN by Linda Randall Wisdom	$3.50	☐
HAR#16520	THE ADVENTURESS by M.J. Rodgers	$3.50	☐
HS#28795	PIECES OF SKY by Marianne Willman	$3.99	☐
HS#28824	A WARRIOR'S WAY by Margaret Moore	$3.99 U.S. $4.50 CAN.	☐

(limited quantities available on certain titles)

	AMOUNT	$
DEDUCT:	**10% DISCOUNT FOR 2+ BOOKS**	$
ADD:	**POSTAGE & HANDLING**	$
	($1.00 for one book, 50¢ for each additional)	
	APPLICABLE TAXES*	$_____
	TOTAL PAYABLE	$_____
	(check or money order—please do not send cash)	

To order, complete this form and send it, along with a check or money order for the total above, payable to Harlequin Books, to: **In the U.S.:** 3010 Walden Avenue, P.O. Box 9047, Buffalo, NY 14269-9047; **In Canada:** P.O. Box 613, Fort Erie, Ontario, L2A 5X3.

Name: _____

Address: _____ City: _____

State/Prov.: _____ Zip/Postal Code: _____

*New York residents remit applicable sales taxes.
Canadian residents remit applicable GST and provincial taxes.

HBACK-JM2